THE VAMPIRE'S PROMISE

DEADLY OFFER

EVIL RETURNS

FATAL BARGAIN

THE VAMPIRE'S PROMISE

DEADLY OFFER

EVIL RETURNS

FATAL BARGAIN

CAROLINE B. COONEY

SCHOLASTIC INC.

New York Toronto London Auckland Sydney
Mexico City New Delhi Hong Kong Buenos Aires

Deadly Offer, ISBN 0-439-55395-4,
copyright © 1991 by Caroline B. Cooney.
Originally titled *The Cheerleader*.

Evil Returns, ISBN 0-439-55396-2,
copyright © 1992 by Caroline B. Cooney.
Originally titled *Return of the Vampire*.

Fatal Bargain, ISBN 0-439-55397-0,
copyright © 1993 by Caroline B. Cooney.
Originally titled *The Vampire's Promise*.

12 11 10 9 8 7 6 5 4 3 2 1   4 5 6 7 8 9 / 0

Printed in the U.S.A.   01

This edition created exclusively for Barnes & Noble, Inc.
2004 Barnes & Noble Books

ISBN 0-7607-6132-9

First compilation printing, October 2004

Contents

DEADLY OFFER

He laughed, and this time she did not turn her head away fast enough, and she saw his laugh, like the curve of the moon. A pale crescent of evil amusement. What have I done? she thought, wanting the wind to come up, the sun to rise.

"Dawn is nearly here," he murmured. He gestured with a finger like foil toward the pink beginning of a new day. "Go to school, my dear. It will begin."

"What will?"

"Being popular, of course. Isn't that what you wanted?" His words were whispery as the wind. His skin, the color of mushrooms, faded into the dawn. His black drapery vanished among the hemlocks. The air stayed thick and swampy where he had stood.

With difficulty she drew a breath.

You did what you had to do, she told herself. And it wasn't so bad.

Chapter 1

"Suppose," it said in its voice like antique silk, faded and slightly torn, "that I could make you popular."

It did not smile, for which Althea was glad. She did not particularly want to see it smiling. She waited, but no explanations followed. Talking to it was somewhat upsetting. Althea kept her back to the wall, waiting for it to leave. Usually it left rather early, having, she supposed, appointments to keep. Tonight it stayed. Waiting. She knew it could always wait longer than she could.

Her heart snagged on that word *popular*. At last Althea asked, "How could you make me popular?"

It nodded for some time, its entire trunk pulsing slowly back and forth, as if it were on a spring. "Tell me," it said, in that slippery satin voice, "what is the most popular group in school?"

That was easy. "Cheerleaders," said Althea with yearning. The Varsity Squad was a closed unit of slim blonds and sparkly brunettes who not only never spoke to Althea, but, far worse, had never noticed her, either.

"Who," it went on like a river or a tide, "do you wish had never gotten on the squad?"

That, too, was easy. "Celeste," said Althea. Celeste had made Varsity as a freshman, which, to the sophomores, juniors, and seniors who failed to make it, seemed unfair. Celeste was quite extraordinarily beautiful. At first Celeste did not appear sufficiently energetic to cheer. She walked slowly, languidly, hands trailing. Celeste seemed more a romantic dreamer than a screaming, leaping, possibly even perspiring, member of a gymnastics-oriented squad. But cheerleading transformed her. Once in uniform, Celeste became a star.

And popular. *So popular.*

Althea longed for the popularity that cheerleading brought.

Althea was a gentle girl. She had sweet features and a demure posture. When she spoke, people quieted to hear her distinctive whispery tremor. In elementary and middle school, Althea had had a circle of giggly girlfriends, a phone that rang constantly, invitations every weekend to spend the night, or order pizza, or go to the movies. She was on the softball team, won several silver ribbons in horseback riding, and went on a wonderful group skiing trip. She had thought that at high school she would become a serious skier, and she had bought a beautiful ski outfit to shine on the snow.

But high school was horrible.

The circle of friends, like a kaleidoscope turned and refocused, had split cleanly apart, to form new groups. One group was heavily into Individuality and New Experiences; they wore trendy clothing or torn jeans, unique sweatshirts or obscene earrings. They found Althea altogether too dull to bother with. Another group had boyfriends, and Althea, without one, was unwelcome. The third group became scholarly and embarked on a soul-whipping routine of trying to beat one another out with exam grades and extra-credit reports.

Althea's throaty whisper became a liability. Nobody heard it. She had to raise her voice, and the voice felt foreign: like an intruder, like a stranger yelling.

Loneliness absorbed her life.

It was a quiet life: no phones, no laughter, no gossip, no giggles.

It was November: a month of dark and chill.

A month in which Althea saw herself, like an abandoned waif in the gutter, without hope.

"Perhaps," the voice continued, "Celeste could be taken off the squad."

She slipped down those words, as if on a water-slide at an amusement park. She noticed how the voice liked to split sentences, teasing with the first word: who . . . what . . . perhaps . . .

She did not like standing quite so close. It had given her all sorts of assurances, but did she know, for sure, that she could believe these promises? Under the circumstances?

"Would there not," it continued, in a lazy, inquiring sort of manner, as if they had all year to consider it, "be tryouts for Celeste's replacement?"

Althea nodded. The cheerleading squad was a precision team. They worked in pairs. They would have to have an even number. Althea had had years of dancing and gymnastics. Nevertheless she had not made the team.

The high school was jammed with girls who had had years of dancing and gymnastics. "There would be a lot of competition," said Althea, remembering the taste of humiliation and despair when she had been cut from the list long before the final round of tryouts.

"Perhaps . . ." the voice said, with such slowness that it seemed to be melting away, "I could arrange for the competition to be missing."

She let her mind drift over that. Skimming like a seabird on the surface of the suggestion. Not landing, no. Not part of it . . . but thinking about it. The power of it. The potential of it.

What a change it would make in her life! She would be among the lovelier, more exciting girls. The girls who partied and laughed, drove fast cars, and sat with adorable boys.

Me, Althea thought. Popular. A cheerleader.

"Perhaps someday I would even be captain," she whispered.

"Perhaps so." Its skin was the color of mushrooms.

"And date somebody on the basketball team," she breathed, imagining it. She remembered how the cheerleading squad sat on the bus with the team, how if they won the game there was laughter, and shared snacks, and a favorite CD was played while they foot-danced, because the bus driver didn't allow standing. How in the back of the bus, girls sat entwined with their boyfriends, their laughter quieter, more intimate. How couples got off the bus last, holding hands.

"Maybe even Michael," said Althea, so softly she was not sure she had let the thought out, because the thought was so precious. *Michael.*

"Maybe even Michael," the voice agreed.

Althea pulled herself together. She was envious of the popular girls, but she was kind. She didn't want anything nasty to happen. And Celeste seemed like a perfectly nice person. "What would you *do* to Celeste?" said Althea warily.

It smiled. The teeth were not quite as pointed as Althea had expected, but she shuddered anyway.

She was told, with an air of reproach, "It doesn't hurt, you know. It's just rather tiring. Celeste would simply be . . . rather . . . tuckered out."

The eyes changed their focus, leaving Althea's face. She felt as if she were released from suction cups.

It stared at the sky, at the black cloudless sky sprinkled with stars, gleaming with moonlight. It seemed to find a companion with whom smiles were exchanged. "Celeste would be back in school the next day."

"Then why wouldn't she stay on the squad?"

"I told you. She'll be tired. She'll feel a need to resign. She'll want a little time to herself. There's no cause for you to worry. Her grades won't suffer."

Althea decided not to think about the details.

She did not let herself think about being popular.

I can't condone . . . but on the other hand . . . a simple exercise that would leave Celeste . . . well . . . tired . . . and after all, Celeste is only a ninth-grader, and I'm in tenth . . . and I deserve it more. . . .

Its fingernails were gray, like foil.

"Althea," it said, stroking her name, feeding it new ideas, "think about school tomorrow. Think how you sit alone at lunch. How nobody talks to you in study hall. How nobody shares a soda with you after class."

How vivid it was. How often it had been true.

The voice was thready and sticky, like a spider's web. "But if you're a cheerleader . . ."

Althea saw herself among the slender blonds and sparkly brunettes.

"You, Althea," said the voice, softer than clouds, "you deliver Celeste."

Althea shivered.

"I," breathed the vampire, "will make you popular."

Chapter 2

But how? How was this supposed to work?

Celeste wafted down the halls of high school like a sunset of spun gold, wrapped in the possession of her friends. From a distance Althea would see that soft hair, those sparkling eyes. From around a corner Althea would hear that trembly laugh, a laugh that shivered with delight.

It was so unfair! Celeste had every beauty, every friend, every power.

You deliver Celeste. I will make you popular.

My only claim to popularity, thought Althea, is that I have the same lunch schedule as the cheerleading crowd. I get to stand in the same cafeteria line.

When Althea went to lunch, Celeste was ahead of her, shimmering like a mirage. Celeste skimmed through the line, putting almost nothing on her tray, gliding to her seat. Celeste's laugh sparkled across a crowded table, where friends jostled and squeezed.

Althea's tray was heavy, and the plates slid around, bumping one another and threatening to spill. She carried it carefully, and when she finished paying, looked around for a place to sit. A group of girls she knew fairly well filled a distant table; there was no room. A girl like Celeste could dance up and they would make room, but for a girl like Althea they did not.

Her old friends from middle school were with their new friends from other parts of town. If she joined them, she would be a river barge shoving through sailboats. They would part to let her through, but she could never join. The only thing worse than being alone was to have people tolerate you because they felt pity.

Althea's eyes swept the entire cafeteria, and in the entire cafeteria there did not seem to be an empty seat.

"Come on," said an impatient voice behind her. "Get going."

Althea lifted her heavy tray and took two steps out into the hostile lunchroom. People trotted past, their trays as full as hers, but their steps were light. They found places to sit, and people looked up and said to them, "Hey, how are ya? Sit down!"

There is no room for me, thought Althea. There never will be.

She walked past table after table, and from each chair eyes turned, inspected Althea, and turned away. Every student in the high school had a chance to say, "Sit with us." Every student in the high school said nothing. Eventually Althea was back at the counter. If she had had any appetite, it was gone. She sat her tray down, untouched.

I'll just stand outside in the courtyard till lunch is over, Althea thought. I'll pretend —

A silver shot of laughter came from the cheerleaders' table. Celeste planted a sweet kiss on the cheek of the handsome boy next to her.

I want that life, Althea thought. I want to laugh and kiss and have friends! But how do I invite her to my house? The closest I'm ever going to get is the same building.

The second day was worse than the first, for Althea could not find the courage to enter the cafeteria at all, but brought a bag lunch and sat on a bench outside, pretending she liked the outdoors, pretending she needed the fresh breezes in her hair in order to compose her thoughts.

Lies, all lies.

On the third day, she forced herself into the cafeteria again. She did not actually get in the lunch line. She drifted on the edges, trying to think of a strategy.

Cheerleaders, thought Althea, important people, jocks, the party crowd — they're always on another side of the room, sitting at a different table, laughing at a different joke. There's no way to cross that dividing line. Either you're popular or you aren't.

Her heart filled with longing to be special, the

way they were. She inched closer to hear their affectionate, silly talk.

Althea paused next to Celeste's table, pretending her attention was caught by something beyond, an interesting tableau, perhaps, of dieticians and cooks. In the cafeteria, she was camouflaged like an animal in the jungle, merely another anonymous student passing by to get extra ketchup or another dessert. They paid no attention to Althea. They just rattled on about their cars.

It seemed that Ryan's car had only one working door out of four and that to get in and out, you had to use the rear right passenger door. (Althea imagined herself in the crowd, giggling as she doubled over to squeeze in the back, crawling over boys' legs, gear stick, and parking brake to reach the front seat.)

It seemed that Kimmie-Jo had backed her new car into a tree. The car's trunk now had an interesting configuration, along with a tree print. (Althea imagined herself in the car with Kimmie-Jo when it happened, screaming, "What will your parents say? You're dead, Kimmie-Jo!", giggling, and suggesting they go to Dairy Queen and have ice cream first, and *then* deal with Kimmie-Jo's parents.)

Michael, however, had a car that was not only new to *him,* it was actually new. His father had bought it for his seventeenth birthday present last week. How like Michael, thought Althea, staring with adoration, forgetting to pretend she was neither watching nor listening.

Celeste said sadly, "I'm only fourteen. I won't be able to drive my own car forever and ever and ever."

Althea's heart hardened. I'm sixteen, and I have nothing! thought Althea.

"That's okay," said Michael, smiling at Celeste. "We'll give you a ride when you need one."

He had such a fine smile. Brotherly, welcoming — and yet sexy. He smiled like that at ninth-grader Celeste! For no reason except that Celeste was on Varsity Cheerleading!

Althea walked straight into the group.

She expected to feel the prickles of their distaste, to have Kimmie-Jo and Michael and Ryan and Celeste look at her with amazement. An intruder. A pushy unwanted nobody.

But Ryan said, "Hi, Althea. How are you?"

Ryan knew her name? She was stunned. "Fine, thank you," she said.

"You live in that huge spooky house at the bottom of the hill, don't you?" said Celeste. Celeste shuddered pleasurably. Her pretty golden hair quivered, and the boys smiled gently at her. "They say it's haunted. Have you ever seen ghosts, Althea?"

Althea did not like to lie. "I have never seen a ghost," she said carefully.

"Your house isn't haunted?" said Celeste, with evident disappointment.

"Of course not." Althea sensed the group getting ready to move. They were always in transit, these popular people, drifting like a flock of bright-feathered birds from one perch to another. She needed to hold on to them. Or, at least, on to Celeste. She made a quick offering. A dangerous offering, because it trembled on the edge of truth. But it was all Althea had. "We do have a Shuttered Room, though."

"What does that mean?" Celeste had a pretty, little giggle and a trick of biting her lower lip as she giggled, taking her breath in funny little snatches. The boys looked on adoringly.

"There's a room in the attic," Althea explained. "The circular tower. You may have seen it when you've driven by. The tower room has three windows, none of which are ever opened. There are shutters on the inside of the windows and shutters on the outside."

"What's the room for?" asked Michael.

"It's for staying away from."

"Oh, wow," said Celeste, entirely satisfied. "I knew that house was haunted."

"It is not haunted," said Althea rather sharply. "It's simply that nobody is supposed to enter the Shuttered Room."

"What happens when somebody does?" asked Michael.

She paused.

She had an answer to that now, of course. For she, a month ago, had done just that. Against all rules, against all tradition, she had touched the shutters. And now she knew what happened.

If you were to open the inside shutters, you would hear a whistling gurgle, the sound of somebody struggling for air, the sound of a living person in a locked coffin.

If you were to open the outside shutters, the wind would whirl into the tower, and the tower air would whirl out, and in the exchange of old air for new, something passed, something changed.

The vampire was set free.

She did not know where he came from: inside the tower or outside. She did not know where he stayed: inside the tower or outside. But the shutters were the key to his prison — and he was the key to hers.

The vampire could set Althea free. Free from the hostile cafeteria, free from loneliness. *You give me Celeste, and I will give you popularity.*

Althea fastened her eyes on Celeste. Althea's whispery tremor, deep in her throat, sounded frightening and mysterious. "Nobody ever has. It's a family tradition. The shutters in the Shuttered Room stay shuttered." She smiled, first at Celeste, then at Michael.

The kids laughed, repeating the rule like a tongue twister. *Susie sells seashells on the seashore. The shutters in the Shuttered Room stay shuttered.*

The bell rang, and the kids dispersed, as even popular groups must, for class or gym or art or library. Michael strode blithely alone down the hall, headed for something special, no doubt; he could not possibly take dull repetitive classes the way she had to. Ryan was bouncier; he lunged in the other direction, as if he had athletic records to set. Kimmie-Jo was sultry, stunning, the way she always was, sitting, walking, or cheering. Becky, another cheerleader, popped out of a classroom door, and Becky and Kimmie-Jo hugged with that relaxed affection popular people show each other. Unpopular people who did that would just be pathetic.

Althea caught up to Celeste and walked on with her. Think companionable thoughts, Althea told herself. Don't let Celeste see through you. Say something normal. "You know which one my house is," Althea said, "but I don't know where you live."

Celeste made a face. Even pouting, she was very pretty. "Way out of town, Althea. Miles and miles. I hate living there. I can never go anywhere unless somebody's willing to drive me. They're always willing the first time, but they make that trip once and they're not so willing a second time."

She's confiding in me, Althea thought. She's treating me like a friend.

Maybe she would not have to deliver Celeste to the vampire after all! She and Celeste would become friends, and that would be the door through which Althea entered popularity.

"Ryan came once, and after that, he's just been 'busy.'" Celeste sighed deeply, very sorry for herself. "And Becky — well, she came once, and when I asked her to drive me again, she frowned and said my parents would have to bring me to the party."

Had *she* been asked to a party of Becky's, Althea would have slogged across swamps and swum rivers. She was supposed to feel sorry for Celeste, all because Celeste had to get party transportation from relatives? "That's rough," said Althea sympathetically.

"And you heard Michael say he'd drive me, but he's dating Constance, of course, and I can hardly ask him to pick up Constance first and then come for me."

So Michael was dating Constance. Constance was one of those overwhelming people who was simply brilliant at simply everything. There was not an activity in which she did not shine, not a subject in which she was not a scholar, not a sport in which she did not excel. Constance was lovely and willowy, strong and interesting, funny and sweet.

Of course Michael was dating Constance.

Althea was exhausted by the mere thought of Constance.

Celeste gave several more examples of how unpleasant it was to live so many miles out in the country. It became increasingly difficult to grieve for somebody who had been asked to three events last weekend and could get transportation to just two of them.

"After school today," said Althea, "would you like to come over to my house?"

Celeste gave Althea a dazzling, sparkling smile. It was a smile on a par with Michael's: a world-class welcome of a smile. Althea warmed inside, forgave Celeste for whining, and thought of friendship.

"You're so sweet, Althea," said Celeste. "That's so nice of you. But I have cheerleading practice, of course."

Chapter 3

After school Althea did not go home. She drove around town in a jealous rage. Street after street passed beneath her tires, like some great black, bleak grid of life.

If only Celeste had not said *of course*!

It was that *of course* that was the knife in the back.

A light turned yellow, and in her present mood she wanted to slam down the accelerator, roar through the intersection, leave a patch on the pavement, and fill the faces of bystanders with foul exhaust.

But she drove carefully, as she had been taught. Then, like lightning filling the sky with sheets of silver, she remembered something: Celeste was too young to drive. *But Althea was not.*

I have a license. And a car. Why, I'd be happy to drive Celeste home. Or to a party. Or anywhere else that Celeste might choose. Briefly, anyway. Until . . .

. . . well . . .

And *of course*, after that, Celeste would be too tired. It wouldn't matter anyhow.

You have cheerleading practice, of course, thought Althea. Celeste, my friend, I have a car, of course. And a Shuttered Room, of course. And a vampire.

Althea turned left. Then right. She gripped the steering wheel like the compass of life. Three miles and she was back in the school parking lot.

Beyond the buildings and the tennis courts, the football team was practicing. Boys were lined up on each side of the field, hurling themselves at one another. From that distance it was impossible to tell which heavily padded body was which.

The school had many ells and additions. Althea circled the building, looking for cheerleading practice.

The grass had just been mowed, and the air smelled wonderful, like hay and countryside.

She remembered the vampire's smell. When he did whatever he did, would Celeste notice the smell first, or would she — ?

Stop! thought Althea. Don't think about the details.

Around the next brick wall was a small paved courtyard, and there they were, all twelve of them.

Mrs. Roundman, their coach, was not pleased. "Not even half trying!" she was shouting. "Not one of you! You are all so lazy! What is cheerleading — an activity for melted marshmallows? You act as if you'd run out of energy spreading peanut butter on bread! Call yourselves cheerleaders? Ha!"

Several girls were close to tears. Several seemed merely irritated, as if they had better things to do than stand around while Mrs. Roundman had a temper tantrum. And one was amused.

Mrs. Roundman did not miss this. "Celeste?" she bellowed. "You think this is a joke, perhaps?"

"No," said Celeste, trying to smother her laugh. "Of course not, Mrs. Roundman."

Althea caught Celeste's eye and giggled.

Celeste giggled back like a coconspirator.

Or a friend.

I should give her another chance, Althea thought. We could be good friends, I know we could, I can tell by the way she's sharing that giggle with me.

"One more chance," said Mrs. Roundman grimly to her squad. "I said every leg is to reach the same height on the kick, and that's what I meant."

Quite a few other people were watching practice. Two squad members' boyfriends were leaning against a brick wall, playing cards. A boy Althea did not know was doing his chemistry. His glasses had slid down his nose, and he looked sweet and childish. Three ninth-grade girls looked at their favorite cheerleaders with open adoration. A little knot of kids was sharing a single soda and monitoring one another's swallows.

She would have liked to join the card game. Help with the chemistry. Sip the soda. Even join the ninth-graders.

But after the first brief glance her way, nobody looked at Althea again.

The cheerleaders worked hard. Kimmie-Jo had the most style, and Celeste was the most beautiful, but Becky gave off an air of joyful celebration. While the other girls were breathless from exertion, Becky seemed breathless from love of cheerleading.

Finally Mrs. Roundman ended practice and stalked off. Althea did not know what she could be grumpy about. In Althea's eyes, the squad was perfect.

Celeste, out of breath and pink-cheeked, dropped to the ground next to Althea. "She's a bear," confided Celeste.

This is what friendship is, Althea thought. Somebody telling you something they wouldn't tell somebody else. "I can see. Does she always treat you that way?"

"Or worse. Honestly, I don't know where they find these coaches!"

Althea thought Mrs. Roundman was an excellent coach. Certainly the school had the best cheerleaders Althea had ever seen. But she said sympathetically, "Gosh, you must be tired, Celeste."

"I'm utterly exhausted. People don't know how difficult cheerleading is. You don't get the credit you deserve." Celeste arched her back like a cat and slowly melted down. A few golden threads of hair across her forehead annoyed her, and she stroked them into place. Rotating her long neck to relax herself, she added, "And what's more, I have to wait an hour for a ride home. A whole hour! Just sitting here! Till my parents are out of work and can come for me."

What a lovely neck she has, Althea thought. It really is swanlike, just the way they say a high-fashion model's should be. What soft white skin she has.

Since we're becoming friends, Althea thought, perhaps I'll ask her if she has ever thought about modeling. I've always wanted to be a model myself. We could go into the city together!

"I am so bored," said Celeste.

Althea looked at her uncertainly.

"*Nobody* is around," Celeste said. "Everybody has left."

Not quite everybody, thought Althea. I'm here.

Celeste ran beautifully polished fingers through her silken hair. Her nails were pale, pale pink.

But they could get paler, Althea thought. And I know somebody who would also think that's a lovely neck. "You poor thing," said Althea. "Well, I'm heading out right now. Want a ride?"

Chapter 4

His skin had darkened in patches, like fruit going bad. If she touched it, the skin would feel like a sponge. The fingernails seemed detached. She could pluck them, harvest them, fill a basket with old vampire nails.

Althea closed her eyes to block out the sight, and then quickly opened them. It was difficult to breathe evenly in his presence, but she knew that if her breathing were ragged and frightened he would enjoy it; it would give him power over her. So she regulated her breathing. She blocked out visions of Celeste being touched by the vampire's spongy skin, his foul mold against her swan-sweet neck, his smell in her hair. But she had to know. "What happened?" said Althea.

The vampire looked surprised. "You want details?" His teeth overhung his lower lip, shimmering like pearls, like Celeste's hair.

"I don't want details," said Althea hastily. "Just — well — an overall picture."

With a long bony finger, the vampire traced his lips, as if savoring something. How thin his lips were. How bloodless. Although actually he looked somewhat healthier than the last time Althea had encountered him.

Althea felt a little queasy. What could have made him healthy?

I did it, she thought. I actually gave a vampire his victim.

The air around her thickened. It crawled up her legs and crowded against her spine, and her heart, and her head. She could not see the air, but she could feel it, all woolly and damp, whispering, *That's what you did. You are bad, you are evil, Althea.*

She straightened her back and stiffened her jaw. I did what I had to, she thought. And Celeste deserved it. So there.

The dark drapery that seemed to be the vampire's clothing shifted and swirled as if it were leaving. But the vampire stood still. The hem of his black cloth blew toward Althea. She stepped back, and the black cloth reached farther, trembling eagerly. The vampire collected it back and wrapped it around himself like a container. To Althea he said, "It was only necessary for Celeste to enter the path of my control. Once you and she circled the house, she was within my light path."

"Light? You are dark. You are night."

"It is in fact a dark path," admitted the vampire. "I thought you would better understand a comparison to the rays of the sun." He smiled again, his teeth the only bright thing on earth, those notched glittering fangs that — Celeste had known.

Had it hurt? Had Celeste understood? Had Celeste talked to the vampire? Did she know who had led her into the dark path?

Althea looked off to the side. It was dark this early in the morning. Frost sparkled on the ground. The hemlocks and firs were black as night. The moon was still visible. Stars trembled. There was no wind. The world lay quietly in the shadowy circle of the house and the trees.

"I was able," said the vampire, his voice as wet and muggy as a swamp, "to migrate within Celeste's boundaries."

To migrate. It sounded like swallows and robins. It sounded rather pretty and graceful, an annual event.

She was very relieved. She had thought the word would be puncture, or stab, or even gnaw. But migration. That was peaceful. Perhaps Celeste had not even noticed.

Yesterday, Celeste had stayed on to have a Coke. Had admired Althea's bedroom. Shivered at the spookiness of the Shuttered Room. When Althea drove Celeste home, Celeste had chattered about school, about boys and clothes. Celeste had not sounded like a girl caught in a dark path.

The black cloth escaped from the vampire's twisted fingernails. Little threads from a frayed edge spun toward her, like a spider's web, hoping to snag her. The fringe wove itself into more cloth, and grew in Althea's direction.

Althea said slowly, "Am I in your dark path?"

"No. There are some people who are unreachable."

He reached me pretty well, thought Althea. I gave him Celeste. What if she knows? What if she says so in school? What if she tells people?

"You opened the shutters, Althea. You and I, we are evenly matched. We are both in control, and both of us may go only so far. But Celeste, I fear, is in a different category." He did not look as if he feared a thing. Or ever had. It was not fear that lined his lips, but hunger.

I'm not in control, Althea thought. If I were in control, I would have made myself popular the day high school began.

"So, after midnight," said the vampire, his voice wafting past like fragrance, the sound of his pleasure like perfume, "I visited Celeste."

Althea looked quickly down at the ground. It swayed. Or Althea did.

She reached out for something on which to steady herself, but the only object near her was the vampire. She yanked her arm back and shoved both hands in her jeans' pockets. Then she spread her feet for a firmer stance. She was glad to be wearing a heavy jacket. Maybe they were evenly matched, but a few extra layers of protection would not hurt. She adjusted the collar on the jacket. Tucked it under her hair. Zipped the fat silvery zipper up to her chin.

The vampire laughed, and this time she did not turn her head away fast enough, and she saw his laugh, like the curve of the moon. A pale crescent of evil amusement. What have I done? she thought, wanting the wind to come up, the sun to rise.

The black drapery flew out behind him, like bat wings. He pulled the cloth back and went on laughing.

Her breath felt stale and used. It seemed to Althea that her own breath was her soul, rising up a sad and lesser thing than it had been.

"Dawn is nearly here," murmured the vampire. He gestured with a finger like foil toward the pink beginning of a new day. "Go to school, my dear. It will begin."

"What will?"

"Being popular, of course. Isn't that what you wanted?" His words were as whispery as the wind. His skin, the color of mushrooms, faded into the dawn. His black drapery vanished among the hemlocks. The air stayed thick and swampy where he had stood.

With difficulty she drew a breath. She tasted him and spat the air out, walking backward, covering her mouth, until she was near the garden where the air was fresher.

In the house, she had little appetite for breakfast. You did what you had to do, she told herself.

And it wasn't so bad. Celeste's just going to be tired. And you — you get to be popular!

For so many months Althea had entered high school with her eyes lowered, her posture caved in, to keep from having to see that nobody saw her. Today she walked with eyes lowered and posture caved in because . . . *if they do look at me . . . will they know what I've done . . . who it is that I talk to in the dark . . . what I gave him?*

"Althea!" cried a girlish happy voice.

Althea spun around as if being attacked.

"Althea, I love your hair like that," said Becky gaily, catching up to Althea. "It's all fluffy and kind of — I don't know — sparkly."

Becky. The best cheerleader. The one Althea most wanted to be liked by, and to be like!

Althea wet her lips with nervousness. "I was out early this morning," she admitted. "The mist probably settled on my hair."

"Up early?" asked Becky. "I'm always up early, too. That's so neat to meet somebody else who does that. See, my parents always go for a prebreakfast run, down to the lake and back. Their circuit is five miles." Becky beamed joyously. "Lots of times I go with them."

How demented, Althea thought. Running five miles on purpose, when you could be lying in bed? Althea struggled to return Becky's exuberant smile.

"And why were you up early?" Becky asked.

Althea tried to think of an explanation, but nothing came to mind. "I really like the stars and the night sky," said Althea. It sounded very lame. Even more so than running five miles.

She had scarcely noticed that they had been joined by Ryan. She was dumbfounded when Ryan said, "No kidding! I took astronomy last year, Althea, and I really got into it. You know that the night sky changes continually, so that the constellation you could find in March is not the same as the one you find in November."

"You and your constellations," said Becky indulgently. She gave Ryan a friendly poke. He tugged her ponytail back. "Althea doesn't care about that, Ryan."

"I'd like to learn," said Althea. "I'm really quite ignorant. I just sort of go outdoors and stare upward. I don't know anything, really."

"Do you have a telescope?" asked Ryan seriously.

It had never crossed Althea's mind to want a telescope.

"Because that tower room in your attic would be such an excellent location," said Ryan. "I mean, you're in a really dark part of town."

If he knew how dark, he wouldn't be so eager, Althea thought.

"No streetlights," said Ryan, "no lights from all-night car dealerships, nothing to spoil your view of the stars." He smiled at her. He said, "I have a tele-scope you could learn on."

He's suggesting that he could come over! Ryan! Ryan of the football team! At my house!

Becky, bored by stars, said, "Did you get that al-gebra, Althea? I thought it was really hard."

Althea had forgotten that she and Becky were both in second-year algebra. Of course they never sat near each other. Becky sat with another cheer-leader named Dusty. Normal people could not have nicknames like Dusty. They would get teased until they actually became dust, or lint, or other under-foot objects. Only a cheerleader could say out loud, with pride, "My name's Dusty."

Ryan said, "I could bring my telescope over. We could put it in the tower room."

"The tower room," Althea repeated. Her hair prickled. No, no, no! She could not ever have any-body in the tower room. The vampire was free, his dark path lit.

"The one with all the shutters," Ryan explained, as if Althea were not familiar with it.

"Wouldn't it be neat to have a slumber party in that tower room?" Becky cried.

Althea could not think. A slumber party. Oh, how she wanted to have a slumber party! A dozen girls all at her house, all laughing and happy and glad to be there.

But the tower room?

Becky locked arms with Althea. Together they

headed for algebra. Ryan trailed after them, talking about telescopes and stars. Far down the hall Michael waved, smiling. Althea felt her popularity rising on that wave.

Becky said, "We don't have cheerleading practice today. You want to come over to my house, Althea?" Becky plopped down on the first available seat — not her usual seat near Dusty. "I mean, first we'll go to Mickie D's, of course, and meet everybody, but then we could go over to my house." She yanked Althea down next to her. Becky got a teasing, provocative look on her face. "Ryan lives next door," she said, as if making an offering. "We could play telescope together."

Ryan heaved a great sigh. He had followed them into algebra. Althea was confused. Ryan didn't have algebra. He was a year older. He had trigonometry. Why was he accompanying them here?

"My telescope, Becky," said Ryan, although he was facing Althea, "is not a toy. Although I am sure Althea and I can think of plenty of games to play." He winked at Althea.

Ryan had winked at her. Michael had waved at her. Becky had sat with her. Althea didn't care what had happened to Celeste. She would never care. She winked back at Ryan.

"You're sick, Ryan," said Becky. "Get out of here, you're annoying the algebra class. Go to your silly trig."

Ryan grinned. "I'm not sick," he told Althea.

"I'm a very interesting person. So. Are you coming to Mickie D's, Althea?"

She nodded, and he nodded back, and that was heaven. She burned with joy; she felt like a house on fire. When the algebra teacher called on her, she had the right answer; and when Becky made a joke, she had a quick laugh.

I'm here, thought Althea. I'm where I deserve to be.

Among friends.

Chapter 5

But before McDonald's came music.

Chorus was another high school group that had not turned out the way Althea had expected. She was one of sixteen altos. She had not made friends. She yearned to sit between two girls, both of whom would talk to her; instead she sat on the end of a row, sticking out into the room, next to one girl who never turned her way. Sitting on the end gave her a good view of the curved sections and the friendships other people had made.

I could sit in the middle, she thought. With a popular alto on my left and a cute baritone on my right. She steeled herself. She moved sideways over bookbags and shoes. She said to the alto, "Mind if I sit here?"

The alto beamed at Althea. "Sure! That'll be a nice change."

And Dusty, whose seat it usually was, said, "Oh,

good, I'm sick of being suffocated in the middle of the pack. Thanks, Althea."

She sat in the center. One of the crowd. The laughter and chat wrapped her up like a blanket hot from the dryer. She giggled with the boy on her right. He said, "I'm really sorry, but I don't know your name."

"Althea."

"What a neat name. I never heard it before." He smiled. "Althea," he repeated.

Before she could ask his name, the music director whacked the top of his stand with his long white stick and, in his martial-arts way, began warm-up exercises.

How special her voice sounded from the middle. Being an alto wrapped her in companionship; the boy's voice an octave lower added a dimension to singing she had never known. For the first time that year, the director met her eye, smiled, and nodded at her.

She felt like an opera star.

The director cut them off. In the silence before he gave more orders, Celeste entered the music room. Her sparkling eyes were dull. Her golden hair was limp.

There were three steps down because the room was designed for tiers of singers or instrumentalists. Celeste stood at the top. She shifted her load of books to her other side for better balance. Celeste felt her way down one step, panted slightly, and rested before taking the next step.

"You're late," said the music director sharply.

"I'm sorry." Celeste looked foggy. "I've felt sort of slow today."

"I am not interested in excuses," said the director irritably. "You are late. I do not tolerate lateness."

Celeste shuffled down another step.

The boy next to Althea muttered, "This is a cheerleader? No wonder we don't win any games." He rolled his eyes as Celeste tried to focus on the final step down. "Want a cane?" he said cruelly.

Althea no longer wanted to know the boy's name. She no longer wanted to know her own name. What have I done? she thought. Celeste was just supposed to be a little bit tired. She hardly even looks alive!

Althea tried to breathe for Celeste, to suck in rich clear oxygen that would energize her. But Celeste did not breathe deeply. Celeste stumbled and dropped her books.

The music director sighed hugely, exaggerating patience with this idiot who could not even cross a room. The girl who took attendance said dryly, "While we're waiting, Celeste, I'll make announcements. Think you can find the soprano section by then?"

If that were me, thought Althea, I'd blush scarlet. But Celeste is just shuffling on.

Then Althea herself went white as paste.

Celeste was not blushing. How could she?

To blush, you needed blood.

* * *

Becky laughed with intense excitement, as if she and Althea were going on a grand expedition, instead of just to McDonald's. Twisting and turning, Becky told every giddy detail of her day. Her black hair was pulled tightly back into a ponytail, and with every syllable, every move, seemingly every thought, both Becky and her ponytail bounced.

Althea tried to concentrate on what Becky was saying, to realize that she was going to McDonald's with the crowd, but she kept seeing Celeste's shoe inching toward the edge of the last step, trying to find bottom.

"Lighten up!" Becky commanded her.

As if it were orders from a general, Althea obeyed.

It was only two miles to McDonald's, and yet, by the time they were in the parking lot, Althea was younger, happier, and noisier. She, too, bounced out of the car. She, too, jumped up and down clapping as Ryan drove in to join them.

Ryan had been joined by a boy named Scottie, whom Althea hardly knew. It was a treat to see these two muscular young men get out of Ryan's car. First, Scottie dove over the seat back, landing like a beached whale half on the floor and half on the seat. Then, lumbering to his knees, head thrust forward, he opened the right rear door. This door, too, had its problems. Scottie emerged very carefully.

"Hey!" shouted Ryan, diving over after Scottie. "Don't close that door on my face."

"Oh," said Scottie. "Well, I guess I could wait another second or two. But I'm a fast-track kind of guy. I don't like to hang around, Ryan."

Ryan slid out. First, one long jeans-wrapped leg. Then an arm, a broad chest, a dark and handsome head of hair, and finally the other leg.

Althea had intended to daydream of Michael, but now she found herself encompassed by Ryan. Ryan was a weight lifter who talked of how many pounds he could bench press, and he knew all his muscles by name.

Everybody had a cheeseburger except Ryan, who ordered three Big Macs. He ate each in only four bites, his teeth dividing each huge burger like pie.

"Well, that's what's new in my life," Becky said, wrapping up a discussion Althea had missed while admiring Ryan's eating habits and muscles. "Althea, your turn to talk. Hold up your end of the conversation. What's new in your life?"

Ryan, Becky, and Scottie waited. They went on swallowing milk shakes. Waiting to hear what was new in her life.

What's new in my life? thought Althea. I've gotten to know a vampire quite well. His skin is the color of mushrooms. I don't know how he gets in touch with me. What do you think of Celeste, in her altered state? Do you know that I did that? This girl with whom you are having a cheeseburger — she hands people over to vampires?

Ryan and Scottie frowned slightly. Becky looked irritated.

Althea struggled to think of things to talk about. Had anything happened in class? After school? Had she gone shopping? Or even cleaned her room?

It seemed to Althea that, except for the vampire, she had no life.

Suddenly, to her horror, the vampire was standing there. Her throat closed up. Her eyes glazed.

He's not here! she thought. He can't come into a McDonald's! Certainly not in broad daylight. This is not fair. The backyard is one thing, but —

She opened her eyes.

He was not there.

Her nerves had fabricated him.

She breathed again, and realized to her shame that the solitary sigh was her only contribution to the conversation around her.

Becky giggled. "Well, that was exciting, Althea," she said. "We must chat about this again one day."

"Don't pick on her," said Ryan. "You're so mean, Becky."

"She's not mean," said Althea quickly. "I'm slow."

Ryan took this opportunity to discuss his telescope. Weight lifting was his daytime activity; stars were his nighttime activity. Scottie took this opportunity to mention several things that normal teenage boys enjoyed doing at night, as opposed to something lame and pitiful like studying satellite orbits.

"Here's what I say," said Becky. "I say we have a party at Althea's, because it's new, and we haven't partied there, and I'm sick of all the old places. Ryan can set up his telescope in that tower room, while we dance on those big old porches."

Althea's smile trembled. She had fulfilled her obligation to the vampire. She could do as she pleased. And yet . . . she had not shut the shutters. Was he still there? Where was that dark path, exactly? Could he touch other people? Would Becky . . . ?

Althea's body was rigid, as if her blood had stopped circulating — or been drained. "I don't know if that would work out, Becky. I mean, I'd love to, but —"

"All right, all right," said Becky, sulkily. "I just think it's somebody else's turn, is all. It seems to me the parties are always at my house."

"That's because your parents let you do anything all the time, Becky," Ryan said. "Most people's parents never let them do anything." He stuffed his napkins into his cup, stuffed his cup into his burger box, and squashed the whole thing into a remarkably small square. "So, what's Celeste's problem?" he said to Becky.

Althea's stomach knotted up. This was it. This was where they found out, where they understood, where they caught her!

Becky shrugged. "She didn't want to talk. Said she was tired."

"She stumbled around the school today like a zombie," said Scottie.

"She could at least have been polite," said Becky. "Here she is, a ninth-grader, everybody on the squad has been very nice to her, and she couldn't even be bothered to let us in on her problem. I asked her if I could help and she shrugged. That did it, that shrug. You can't have secrets from your teammates. They don't like it."

"Let's not talk about Celeste," said Ryan. "Let's talk about you."

He meant her. Althea. Ryan wanted to talk about Althea. An uncertain, joyous smile began on her lips. Ryan said, "Come on, more. More." He touched her lip corner with his finger and drew the corner up till Althea laughed out loud.

Celeste won't be tired long, Althea thought. She'll perk up in a few days. I'm not going to worry.

Anyway, it's worth it.

Chapter 6

How dark the yard was.

Althea had not known such darkness existed in the world. There was not a hint of light. Nothing at all that was less than black. And yet she could see where the vampire was and where he wasn't.

He was half in the hemlocks. Indeed, he seemed half hemlock. His arms were among the needled branches; his hair might have been growing straight from the trees.

"You wanted me?" he said. "How flattering. You want to give a report, perhaps? Tell me how things are going with your new popularity, perhaps? It isn't necessary, my dear. Since I created this popularity, I know exactly how it is going."

She had thought he was part of the shutters, that the tower room was his coffin, that his tomb was the house. But no. He was growing out of the trees, the thick, black, towering hemlocks. But maybe that was part of it. The trees themselves were also a tower.

I could cut the trees down, she thought. If I need to, I will cut the trees down.

She wondered why she would need to. She had finished her commitment to the vampire. It was over between them. It was just that she had a complaint to register. She said, "I didn't think Celeste would be *that* tired."

The vampire shrugged. The trees lifted and fell with his shoulders, swishing blackly. "I didn't promise degrees of tiredness," said the vampire.

Althea wet her lips, and the vampire, laughing, wet his lips.

She put a hand over her heart, and the vampire, laughing, put a hand over his heart.

He said, "All the gestures are blood symbols, did you realize that?"

"But you don't deal in symbols," she said.

"No."

Once more, the air thickened around them. The blackness of earth and sky faded to a predawn gray, and the gray was so thick that Althea thought she would suffocate, that the human body could not absorb clouds of wool. She panted, struggling for air, and stumbled away from the hemlocks toward the house.

The sun rose.

The tower of the house cast the first shadow of day. A shutter flapped where it had come unfastened. It sounded like a soul unhinged.

* * *

The school had its own broadcast studio.

The first week she attended high school, Althea had been awestruck. If you were the president of a club, or the captain of a team, you went on television and announced your meetings and games. What would it feel like to choose your outfit in the morning, knowing that you would be on television?

Kimmie-Jo had not been captain of Varsity Cheerleading when Althea was a freshman; a senior named Katya had held that honor. Katya was tall and lean and looked like an Ethiopian princess. She always wore the most awesome jewelry, and when she was on TV, Althea was overcome with admiration and amazement.

This year Kimmie-Jo made the cheerleaders' announcements. Her approach was markedly different. No exotic Cleopatra on the Nile, Kimmie-Jo was a bubblehead whose statements of when the game was, or where the practice was, or when Spirit Day would be, always sounded breathless and questioning, as if Kimmie-Jo was not entirely sure and was hoping a really kind football captain would help her out. Really kind football captains always did.

TV announcements were a time in which to say terrible things about people's hair or clothing or degree of nervousness. "It's Kimmie-Jo again! Does that girl bring her own hairdresser to school?"

"Oh, wow, look at that outfit. Kimmie-Jo could be one of those TV lifestyle reporters right now, in those same clothes."

"That would be a good career for Kimmie-Jo. Clapping and squealing. I think she has that down pretty well."

Althea never made cruel comments. If she were on the school TV, she would probably hide behind the principal rather than face the camera. She was filled with admiration for kids with nerve enough to appear live on TV. She dreamed of being the kind of girl who didn't even bother with notes, but chatted away, perfectly relaxed, as if having fun.

This afternoon, Mrs. Roundman came on. She was nicely named. Small, slightly chubby, pink-cheeked, relentlessly energetic. Althea felt that the young Mrs. Santa Claus had probably looked like that, pre-white hair and elves, so to speak.

"Good afternoon." Mrs. Roundman's smile vanished quickly, and she became fierce. "We have an unexpected vacancy on Varsity Cheerleading. Tryouts will be limited to those girls who tried out in September. Any girl who wishes to try out must commit four afternoons a week, plus the game schedule. She must have a C average or better. All girls planning to try out, sign up after school. Any girl who cannot come at the appointed hour, see me today with an appropriate excuse." Mrs. Roundman would never believe an excuse. If you were too busy to try out when Mrs. Roundman wanted tryouts held, you were worthless.

Althea's class burst into talk. "Who quit the squad?" they cried.

"Who got kicked off, more likely," said somebody.

"Who was it?" they demanded of Becky.

"Celeste," said Becky. "Isn't that weird? She telephoned Mrs. Roundman and said she just didn't have the energy for the season after all. She said it was taking too much out of her."

The boys looked doubtful that cheerleading could take that much out of you.

The girls looked doubtful that Celeste had ever wanted to be on the squad anyway, and it was her own dumb fault if she ran out of energy.

Althea tried to look ignorant of what had actually taken a lot out of Celeste. I must look sorrowful and concerned, she thought as she rejoiced.

Becky leaned toward Althea, her dark floppy ponytail quivering. "You should try out," said Becky to Althea. "You almost made it before, you know."

Even though she was thrilled at the compliment and the suggestion, Althea was a little bit shocked. Shouldn't Becky show more concern for Celeste? Hadn't they been friends? Shared practices and snacks all fall? Althea said uneasily, "Did you talk to Celeste? Maybe she'll change her mind."

Becky shrugged. "She's a quitter. Who needs a quitter? It's not that kind of squad."

The class echoed Becky. "She's a quitter. Who needs a quitter?"

But she had not quit, not really. She had been removed.

Becky said, "I'll coach you, Althea. You'll be perfect! You're exactly my height and figure, too, and

Mrs. Roundman is aiming for a better lineup. For example, although Amy's really good, Mrs. Roundman isn't going to take Amy, because Amy's too short. And she won't take Brooke, because Brooke has to be seven feet tall if she's an inch."

Althea cringed. Brooke was sitting right behind them. But of course Becky, being popular, had not bothered to look around first, because she didn't have to worry about people's feelings. They had to worry about their own.

"I'm five-eleven," said Brooke irritably. "And I'm not trying out, anyway. I have a full schedule. I'm much too busy to interrupt it for something as boring as cheerleading."

Becky and Brooke exchanged several more insults.

Then Brooke turned to Althea and smiled generously. "Good luck," she said. "You won't need it, though. You were so good at tryouts. I couldn't figure out why you didn't make it."

The smile caught Althea by surprise. It was so friendly. So honest. Maybe I will have friends who are not in cheerleading as well as friends on the squad, she thought. Maybe my life will be packed, like Brooke's. Althea smiled tentatively back at Brooke.

Becky and Althea walked down the halls, past the lockers, through the narrow passage to the coaches' offices, and into the girls' gym. Only one bleacher had been pulled out, and on that narrow bleached-gold bench sat — so few girls!

Althea couldn't get over it. Hardly anybody was trying out. *Perhaps,* the vampire had said, *I could arrange for the competition to be missing.*

"Wow," said Becky, "how come nobody's here, Mrs. Roundman?"

"Midseason replacements are problematic," said Mrs. Roundman. "The kind of girl we want is not a girl who sits around with an empty schedule. By now, such a girl has other commitments. She's a busy, active, involved person, or we wouldn't want her on our squad, anyway."

"I don't have other commitments," said Althea nervously.

Mrs. Roundman hugged her. "I think you knew a spot would open up, Althea," said the coach. "Your commitment to cheering is very strong. I can absolutely feel it, Althea!"

Mrs. Roundman took them through grueling warm-ups. Then she led them outdoors, into the same courtyard as before.

The sun was not so strong. A slight chill rose up from the grass. Althea swallowed. Becky shouted advice. Mrs. Roundman shouted orders.

A dozen kids gathered around to watch.

One of them was Celeste.

Althea tripped and steadied herself on the brick wall. The brick was slightly warm, as if it were slightly human. Like Celeste, who seemed only slightly warm and slightly human.

Celeste's face was caved in, like a sleeping child's. She did not really cry. She just stared, her mouth sagging, as if she could not understand what was happening.

"Celeste, I told you to see the school nurse," said Mrs. Roundman sharply. "What are you doing here?"

Celeste mumbled something.

She doesn't even have the strength to move her lips, thought Althea.

Mrs. Roundman said, "Celeste, you are upsetting everybody. That's very thoughtless of you. You've surrendered your place on the squad, which in my opinion was the action of a quitter. So quit. Go. Leave. Now."

Nobody went to help Celeste. Nobody spoke up on her behalf. Nobody leaned down to carry the bookbag for her. Celeste could not hoist it from the ground and instead dragged it over the pavement by a shoulder strap. Only Althea watched her go. Everybody else had better things to do.

I knew he would give me popularity, thought Althea. But I didn't know he would give me Celeste's! I didn't know she had to lose everything for me to have something! I thought — I thought —

Far across the field, the football team was practicing.

Ryan and Michael were there. Ryan, who made sure Althea was going to McDonald's. Michael, who was so perfect.

Her heart pounded fiercely, nervously, desperately. I have to get on the squad. It's my ticket to Ryan and Michael. To Becky and parties!

Out of the sun, in a cold corner, stood eight girls in Junior Varsity cheerleading uniforms. Sullenly, they watched Althea and her competition. When Mrs. Roundman allowed a brief rest for a sip of water, the JV captain walked over. Her voice was hostile. "I don't understand, Mrs. Roundman," said the JV captain. "Why didn't you bump one of us up to fill Celeste's position? It's not fair to put a beginner on Varsity when you have eight trained, seasoned JV cheerleaders available."

Mrs. Roundman frowned slightly. She looked out over the grass, and the grass trembled slightly, as if invisible feet were passing by.

"You don't have a reason, do you?" said the JV captain, trembling with anger. "You just felt like bypassing the JV squad."

Whose feet had just passed by? Who had persuaded Mrs. Roundman? What was out there on the grass?

Mrs. Roundman said, "You people are having such a fine season, with your own great coach, that I was hesitant to make any such change. There will be more squad changes when football season is over."

The JV captain brightened. "This is a temporary addition, then? Until basketball season? There'll be new tryouts then?"

"We'll see how everything works out," said Mrs. Roundman, and the JV squad went away less hostile.

Althea did not like that word *temporary*. Nor that phrase "We'll see."

Football season was half over, anyhow.

Is my popularity already half over, too? thought Althea. Is this all I get? A taste? A few weeks?

Chapter 7

But the days to come were sunny and golden.

Everything seemed bright, as if the world were made of daffodils and lilies, of springtime and sweet breezes.

How warmly the rest of the squad greeted her! Kimmie-Jo gave a charming little speech about how Althea was absolutely perfect for the team. Becky gave a little speech about how she and Althea were becoming great, great friends, and Becky knew that Althea would be a great, great friend to the whole squad.

Mrs. Roundman took pains to fit Althea's uniform perfectly. On the snowy white sweater the golden initials flared like a sunburst.

"Although Celeste was a lovely girl," said Mrs. Roundman, smoothing Althea's thick gleaming hair where the pullover had mussed it up, "with that pale coloring she simply did not shine the way you will, Althea."

Over the next several days she worked very

hard. Becky and Mrs. Roundman stayed after regular practice to help with the tougher routines. Saturday afternoon would be her first public performance, her first football game.

But either the girls were kind, or she really was good enough. Nobody yelled at her. Nobody made a face when she needed a second or third try, though once was enough for the rest. Nobody said they wished Celeste were still around.

After the hardest, longest afternoon of her life — Friday before the game — Althea staggered back to the locker room. She took a shower there, instead of waiting till she got home, something she would normally never have done. There is nothing worse than a girls' gang shower. Except maybe leaving the locker room with three hours of sweat clinging to your body.

She toweled off, blowing her hair dry, putting her earrings back on (Mrs. Roundman seemed to be morally opposed to anything that dangled), and fixing the collar beneath her pullover sweater just the way she liked it. Exhausted, she made her way to the front hall.

The high school foyer was a handsome space, with black marble floors and gray-striped marble walls. Announcements, bulletins, and the Artwork of the Week were taped everywhere. Scattered on the plant ledges and the steps were kids waiting for rides or the phone.

One was Celeste. She looked like a plant herself, drooping and in need of water. She was wearing an old dress, with too much material for her skinny body, and she was tucked into a corner of ledge and wall as if she needed several props because her bones had given way. Nobody sat with her.

Althea turned her back. It was best to accept things. Celeste had gotten too much too soon, and she would have to scrape her life back together and that was that. Althea could not get involved. Althea had enough pressure right now, what with her first game the next day.

Althea raised her chin, flipped her hair, and thought cheerleader thoughts.

Footsteps approached her. A voice said her name.

Althea cringed. She could not make herself turn around. I can't talk to Celeste, she thought, I absolutely can't, it's too much to ask. Why didn't she quit school as well as quit the squad? It isn't fair of her to keep showing up and making me remember —

A hand touched her. A hand that felt like a sponge, that seemed to have no bones and no blood.

Althea tried to run but she was rooted to the spot. She turned her head, and only her head — and it was Jennie Marsden.

Jennie had been Althea's closest friend before high school. Jennie had been the one to telephone, to sleep over, to giggle and gossip with. What friends they had been! That inseparable, essential intimacy of junior high friendship — when sleep is not possible until you share every single one of the day's thoughts on the phone.

But almost the first day of freshman year, Jennie found a whole new set of friends. She and Althea had hardly spoken since then, and when they did, Jennie was embarrassed and Althea was miserable.

"Jennie!" said Althea, relief sweeping through her with the velocity of race cars taking a turn. "Hi. Been a long time. How are you?" Althea's uniform, folded so the yellow letters could be seen and understood, lay on top of her notebooks. Swinging in her free hand were her blind-your-eyes-yellow pom-poms.

Jennie's eyes had landed on the precious sweater and the beautiful yellow letters. "You made Varsity!" said Jennie. "That is so great. I'm so happy for you!"

"Thanks," said Althea. I'm free, she thought. No more pain because Jennie got sick of me. I'm Althea, Varsity Cheerleader, and she's just Jennie, Former Friend.

"Yellow is your color," added Jennie. "It's your dark hair, I guess, and your fair skin. You look perfect."

"Thanks. I'm really excited about being on the squad."

"I'll bet," said Jennie enviously. "I never even dreamed of trying out. I could never do the routines. But you kept up your dancing and gymnastics, didn't you?"

Dancing and gymnastics we used to take together, thought Althea, and in her memory saw two little girls in matching leotards, tumbling, running around. Best friends.

Friend is a nice word, thought Althea. But *best friend* — that's beautiful.

She wondered dreamily who among all her new friends would become her best friend.

Althea made a quick and frightening decision. Becky had wanted her to have a party. She would schedule it right now, before she lost her nerve. Before she was overcome with hostess agony. "I'm having a party Sunday," she said. "Would you like to come? You'd like the rest of the cheerleaders, I'm sure."

Oh, how she loved saying that! The revenge of it! "Letting" Jennie come to a party.

"That would be so nice!" cried Jennie breathlessly. "It's so nice of you to think of me, Althea!"

Althea smiled generously. She walked carefully to the exit, keeping her eyes on Jennie, making herself forget that Celeste was on the far side of the foyer. Celeste, the only cheerleader who would not get an invitation. The only cheerleader who had been to the house before. The only one who knew.

"I love a party," said Jennie eagerly. "Want me to help?"

Althea's heart sang. Her feet danced. I'm having a party, and everybody will want to come! I did it. I'm popular! I have everything!

Chapter 8

The phone that had been so quiet for so long was busy every single minute.

Becky was delighted. "Of course I'll be there," she said impatiently, as if she and Althea had shared dozens of social events. "Call Kimmie-Jo," ordered Becky, "and have her call the rest of the squad."

"Is that polite?"

"It's the way it's done," said Becky. So Althea called Kimmie-Jo, who clapped her hands, a more frequent activity for Kimmie-Jo than for most, and said she couldn't wait and would call the others.

Althea telephoned Ryan, Scottie, and Michael. She, who had never had the courage even to look steadily into a boy's eyes, called ten boys. Everyone was delighted. Everyone said yes.

Partly it was because nobody had anything else to do on Sunday. She recognized that. Partly it was because they had never seen her house before, and it was the kind of house that everybody always wants to explore.

But partly, she thought, it's me!

With the last call completed, Althea walked slowly around the house, thinking of what she would have to do between now and then. Cleaning, shopping, food, music. The party must be perfect. It would be too cold out to dance on the porches or the lawn. Althea experimented with the furniture in the large parlor, moving it to this side or that to free up floor space.

"I'm considering," said the vampire, "who I want."

Althea's fingers closed spasmodically around the arms of a chair she had just shifted.

Where was he? How had he gotten in? From her crouching position she jerked her head back and forth to locate him. He was in the doorway, hands gripping each side. His fingernails were longer, and sharper, and seemed to be leaving dents in the woodwork. He rocked back and forth, chuckling to himself.

"So many choices!" said the vampire. The texture of his voice, usually dark, like pouring syrup, was much sunnier, as light and warm as honey.

Althea stood up. *So many choices.* He means my guests . . . he means . . .

No! This is my party! My first party! I'm popular now! He can't come back into this!

I could bash him to pieces with this chair, Althea thought. She picked it up.

"A chair?" said the vampire disdainfully. "I've avoided destruction for centuries now. A teenage girl with a chair is hardly going to slow me down."

Althea made herself set the chair down neatly and quietly to show that she was in complete control. "I'm just changing the furniture around," she said haughtily. "I am having a party this weekend, and you are *not* to be here."

His eyebrows rose. They arched like cathedral doorways, thin and pointed, vanishing under his straight black hair. With his eyebrows up, his eyes were very wide, too wide, as if they were glass balls that could fall out. "I'm quite looking forward to your party," he said. He let go of the doorway and admired his fingernails.

She thought of the people she had invited. Of the necks he could grip in those fingers.

"Get out," she whispered.

"My dear," he said.

How she hated the affection in his voice. As if they were companions of some sort! As if they had anything to do with each other! "I'm not your dear," she said. "Get out of my house."

"You forget, Althea, that I *come* with the house. I have been here longer than you, and I will be here long after you have departed."

Being addressed by name was far worse than being called "my dear." It was so much more intimate. It gave the vampire some sort of ownership over her. She wet her lips and tried to breathe evenly, but it was impossible; her lips stayed dry and her chest rose and fell like a panting dog's. "Go away," she said.

"I think not. Because I do have ownership over you, Althea."

He could read her mind? He was up inside her thoughts? Underneath her skull? Was nothing safe from him? Not heart, not veins, not even thoughts?

Althea felt the terrible cold of his presence, the wet woolliness of the air around him. "I gave you Celeste!" Her voice cracked.

"And so quickly, too," he agreed. "So craftily, carefully executed. I was grateful. But a party! Twenty guests! I am really quite eager to meet them."

She threw the chair at him.

But of course by the time the chair had crossed the room, he was elsewhere. "Try to control yourself," he warned. "There is nothing to be gained by childish impulses. You and I have been very adult with each other. We made a bargain."

"I kept it. I gave you Celeste. That's it. That's all it was, that's all it will ever be."

The vampire shook his head. She had seen him nod, many times; nod his head, nod his body, nod his cape. But she had never seen him shake his head no, and this, too, he did with his entire body, so that he rotated left, and then rotated right. She felt that he could bore a hole through the floor this way and drill himself into the cellar.

"That's not all it will ever be. There's always more. One is never satisfied with what one has, you see."

"I am satisfied! You come to my party, and I'll kill you! I will not have anything going wrong at my party! This is the first time any of them have ever been here. It has to be perfect."

"I'm afraid," said the vampire, his voice like spilled chocolate sauce, dark and spreading and impossible to clean up, "I'm afraid that you are incorrect, Althea. You cannot kill me. But in any event, nothing will go wrong at your party. It will be a wonderful party, my dear. You are a born hostess." He studied his horrid fingernails again, as if the wrinkled foil needed a touch-up. She envisioned him in some world, some room alien to her own, in front of some evil mirror, inspecting himself, admiring himself. He said, "The tower room, of course, will be left open. My dark path will intersect with —"

"No! There is to be no dark path anywhere! You don't get any more chances!" shouted Althea. "You had Celeste. That was your chance! So go away!"

"Althea, I hardly think that Celeste, and Celeste alone, is payment for what I have done for you. Cast your short little memory back over the last week. Ryan? Michael? Becky? Kimmie-Jo? Jennie?"

A terrible heat rose up in Althea, staining her cheeks red.

The vampire was amused. "Did you actually think they were paying attention to you because of the pull of your fine personality?"

Her heart turned into a furnace of rage and pain.

"How charming you look with those bloodred cheeks," said the vampire. "Blushing is a trait that's always appealed to me."

"You are sick," said Althea with loathing. Her whole body was trembling. Her skin literally crawled, as if it were coming off.

"No, Althea, I am not sick. I am a vampire. *You* made a choice, Althea. *You.*" He smiled at her, and the crescent of evil sparkled like diamonds, like the lost sparkle of Celeste's life. "You," he repeated, "you, you, you, you."

"That's true," said Althea. "But I'm not doing it again. I'm popular now, and that's what I wanted, and that's where we stop." She felt as if each muscle had detached from its bone and tendon and was fibrillating like a bad heart. How could he do this to her?

"Here's how we shall solve the problem," said the vampire.

"We shall solve it," said Althea in her hardest voice, "by you going away. Forever and ever and ever."

He tilted his head. He rested his crinkled-foil fingernails against his mushroom-colored cheek. He stroked his long earlobe. She had not noticed before how long his earlobes were. As if his victims, in the last struggle, tried to pull him off and stretched him. Very softly the vampire whispered, "And do you wish your popularity to go away, Althea? Forever? And ever? And ever?"

The shaking muscles grew still.

The pounding heart slowed.

The flushed skin went pale.

If he chose, the party that had not yet been would never be.

Nobody accepted my party invitation because of a slow day, thought Althea, or because they want to see the house, or get to know me better. The vampire made them accept. It's *his* party.

"You choose," the vampire said.

It was hard to talk or think or even exist. "Choose what?"

"Who crosses my dark path, of course. There will be twenty people you have invited, and no doubt twenty more you did not. You choose." He smiled.

She shook her head. "No. They're my guests."

"I'm your guest, too. You opened my shutters, did you not?" His voice was like tissue paper, floating slowly to the ground.

Althea decided to call his bluff. "You are depraved. You are demented. I will not do anything more that you ask. Accept that. I'm not giving in. Period. That's final," she added.

He smiled and nodded, his trunk pulsing back

and forth, as if feeling a pulse. Somebody else's pulse. Teeth hung over his narrow lips like foam on a sea wave.

"What is final," said the vampire gently, "is your popularity. Do you wish to make a fool of yourself at your first game? Do you wish people to laugh at you in public? Do you wish the squad to request Mrs. Roundman to remove you? Do you wish her, at halftime, to put in one of those oh-so-eager Junior Varsity cheerleaders instead of you?" His voice was slippery as silk and cruel as boredom. He said, "I made you. I will unmake you."

She thought, I can pretend to go along with him. That will give me Saturday's game and Sunday's party. Then I'll be safer, and I'll make it clear to him that this is over.

She turned the CD player on. Loud pulsing music, guitars and drums and keyboard, thrust its way into the room. It hammered and screamed, demanding attention. The vampire frowned and turned away. "Too loud for me," he said angrily.

She made a note of that. She would have the house shaking with noise.

"I wish to have one of your guests," said the vampire. His smile was no longer evil; it was sweet and innocent, like a child going to a picnic. "You choose the guest," said the vampire. "It's entirely up to you, Althea. I would not dream of taking a friend of yours. Surely there is somebody coming who doesn't matter. If not, simply invite a girl who doesn't matter. Lots of people don't matter."

I didn't matter a week ago, thought Althea. But I matter now. Am I going to give that up?

"At the party," he said, "make your choice clear by putting your arm around the shoulder of your choice. Then turn your choice to face those hemlocks that the sun goes down behind every night. When I see upon whose shoulder your arm rests, I will know who follows Celeste."

She picked up the chair and hurled it at him. An arm snapped off the chair, but the arms of the vampire were unharmed. She threw the chair again and again, until it was nothing but splinters.

The vampire was long gone.

Chapter 9

The tower was a black cone in a velvet sky. Black needle-tips of swaying hemlocks surrounded the tower like evil lace. Shutters banged with an oddly eager rhythm, as if something inside hoped to get out.

But no one heard.

Music screamed from every corner of the house, and the throbbing drum was the only beat the party guests heard.

The house was overflowing with teenagers.

Cars were parked everywhere.

In spite of the cold and the dark, a sizable group danced on the wide, pillared porch that circled most of the house. Some wore coats, some shivered in shirts. Several wrapped themselves and a chosen friend in a blanket and danced double.

In the kitchen, liters of soda were emptied so quickly they hardly seemed to have been swallowed — just absorbed into the party atmosphere.

In the living room, kids sat on the floor watching a DVD Becky had brought. In the family room, they lay on their backs on the rug, giggling hysterically at the jokes from a radio talk show Ryan had taped. On the stairs, kids sat in layers, like children playing school, moving up one or down one, laughing and talking about life and football victories. In the side yard, three members of the football team replayed especially precious moments of yesterday's game.

And what a game it had been! All the requirements of football had been met: It had been a beautiful day, blue-skied and chilly. The stands were packed. Beyond the stadium, autumn leaves were orange and red. The cheerleaders were brilliant, their uniforms as gaudy as circuses. The team was superb, their routines executed perfectly, their kicks as high as the goalposts.

And they won, of course.

It's true, thought Althea. Winning is everything. And I am among the winners.

It seemed to Althea that the house had been waiting for this evening. That, at last, the house could cast off doom and dark and return to the laughter for which it had surely been built. Its wide halls were meant for hand-holding couples, not ancestral portraits gathering dust. Its echoing parlor was meant for doubling the volume of music. Its huge kitchen was designed to feed dozens.

Althea circulated. She laughed here, chatted there, joined this group, and brought more chips and dip to that group. She sat briefly on the stairs finding an empty step just below Ryan, who gave her a backrub. It started off masculine and athletic, as if repairing muscles, and became softer, smoother, the harsh digs becoming affectionate strokes. She leaned back against him and held his hand in hers. He cupped her chin, tilted her head back, and they regarded each other upside down.

The house vibrated with music. Each area seemed to have been assigned to a particular sort of music: a hip-hop room, a dance-rock room, even a "Memories of Elvis" room. Everybody turned all this music up good and loud, and here in the stairwell it came together in one great chaotic throb. Speech was impossible.

The night before at Michael's had been wonderful. No kisses, but lots of friendly flirting. No best friends, but lots of loving laughter.

Being popular was temperature raising. Her cheeks glowed, her heart was full. She was hot with victory and joy. She was hoarse from cheering.

Ryan bent close over her cheek, and she held her breath, waiting for his kiss. But instead, he shouted in her ear, "I went upstairs. I hope you don't mind. I wanted to look into the tower room."

The tower room. A draft swirled down the long stairway and settled at the back of Althea's neck.

She had forgotten the vampire. Saturday — the game — the cheering — the victory — the party at Michael's afterward! There had been no room for thoughts of vampires. She had been all-teenager, all-high-school, all-pretty girl.

Ryan wanted to look in the tower room.

What shall I do? she thought. How can I stop this? Where is the vampire?

What if he appeared in front of people? What if they saw him?

"It's locked," said Ryan pleadingly. "I can't get in."

Althea smiled at him helplessly, as if locks on attic doors were the natural order of things and she could no more solve that problem than she could change the constellations in the sky. She pretended that the din of rock music made hearing and speaking impossible.

Ryan made sign-language gestures, and they went into the kitchen for something to drink.

How bright it was in there! The big double-wide fridge was open, with heads of two guests crammed in, inspecting the contents. On the counter perched a girl Althea didn't even know, crunching ice and eating potato chips. Somebody crashed my party, she thought, and she was oddly thrilled. You knew you were somebody when outsiders poured in, wanting to be part of the action.

I'm the action, Althea thought, and when Ryan spoke to her, she grinned widely and sparkled and giggled.

Ryan was only slightly taller than Althea, but much, much broader. He was wearing many layers: white cotton turtleneck under a dark blue fleece vest, with a darker leather jacket. It was a good choice; a little sober, perhaps, but oh!, so appealing. Thick as football armor, thought Althea. What would Ryan do if I hugged him? He'd probably hug back. It's that kind of party. But I've never hugged a boy. Do I start now? In my kitchen? With all these witnesses?

"You're hoarse," said Ryan worriedly. "Here. Have orange juice. Pack in that vitamin C." He pushed away the two heads at the fridge as if breaking up a huddle on the field, and one of the heads that popped up was Jennie's.

"Althea's voice is always hoarse like that," said Jennie, smiling at the memories of their shared childhood.

Ryan was disbelieving. "Come on. That's from too much cheerleading."

"You can never cheer too much," said Kimmie-Jo, taking her second Coke.

Jennie embarked on a long story of how she and Althea had once decided to be the jelly-doughnut-eating champions of the world. "It was sixth grade," said Jennie fondly, "and every single Saturday night we slept over at your house or mine, Althea. Remember? We began on jelly doughnuts on a Sunday morning. By Sunday afternoon . . ."

Althea had not thought of those sleepovers at Jennie's in a long time. What fun they had had, just the two of them!

"We had the nicest times, didn't we, Althea?" said Jennie softly.

Althea was filled with remembrance. They *had* had the nicest times. Althea's eyes grew teary. "Oh, Jennie, I've missed you!"

The girls moved toward each other, tentatively at first, and then springing across the kitchen. Althea even forgot Ryan. She thought only of that special friendship, the lovely silly years when life was golden, and doughnuts were good.

"I've missed you, too!" cried Jennie. "I don't know what happened when we hit high school. Something came between us! Let's not ever let that happen again!"

"Never!" cried Althea, full of friendship, full of love. She put her arm around Jennie's shoulder and hugged her tight.

Beyond the kitchen window, between the hemlocks, a path like a black sidewalk grew over the grass, slid across the porch, and crept through the silent windowpane. It left slime, gleaming like entrails.

Althea released Jennie and leaped back. "I didn't mean that!"

Jennie and Ryan stared at her.

Althea said, "I didn't hug you. You aren't my choice." Althea ran to the window to open it, screaming into the dark, "She isn't my choice."

But the window was already open.

The kitchen no longer smelled of potato chips and dip, of pizza and pepperoni. It smelled of mold and rot.

The kitchen was no longer bright and airy. The

atmosphere thickened. Ryan coughed and said he thought he'd go back to the other room. Jennie said dimly, "Althea?" Jennie's face was strangely blank, as if she had temporarily left her body. "I think I'll go outdoors for a while, Althea. I think I need fresh air."

"No," whispered Althea. "You don't need fresh air. Stay here, Jennie." I've got to hang on to her, thought Althea, keep her indoors. Keep her safe!

But she was too afraid. She hugged herself to keep from screaming again, and that left no hands free to reach out and hold Jennie.

Jennie's hand fumbled for the back door and could not find the knob. It did not matter. The knob turned by itself. Jennie stumbled forward and could not find the step. But it did not matter. A hand appeared to help her. A hand with long, warped fingernails. A hand the color of mushrooms.

Chapter 10

The debris of a finished party filled the house: crushed napkins and empty paper plates, ice melting at the bottom of glasses and pizza crusts on coffee tables.

"What a success it was," said the vampire. "You can be very pleased, Althea. And don't worry about the little scene in the kitchen. I will see that nobody remembers it."

Althea was screaming like a cheerleader, but throwing chairs and paintings and pieces of china instead of pom-poms.

"Jennie will not remember a thing," protested the vampire. "You saw Celeste. It takes energy to have a memory. Jennie's going to be very tired."

The smile that had stayed on Althea's face from Saturday's football game all the way through Sunday's party had exhausted her facial muscles. Now she had tics in both cheeks. Her face jumped and twitched. "That's not what I meant!" screamed

Althea. "I did not mean for you to touch Jennie! I yelled out the window. I told you to stop."

"Once things are set in motion," said the vampire, "they cannot necessarily be stopped."

"It was necessary!" she shrieked. "I told you to stop! Stopping was necessary!"

"I thought you said popularity was necessary," said the vampire. "You can't have both, you know. And you made your choice very clear."

"That's not what I meant when I hugged Jennie!"

"That's what you did, though," said the vampire. In the dark he glowed, like a phosphorescent fungus.

Althea ricocheted off the walls, pounding them, kicking them. "You know perfectly well that I was hugging Jennie because I felt affection for her!" screamed Althea.

"We agreed that when you put your arm around a girl at your party, it would be the girl who did not matter. In any event, there's no point in discussing it. It's done. It's over. There is no going back."

Althea's knees buckled. She tried to hang on to the wall, but the wall was flat and offered no support. She sank to the floor. The floor was filthy, where people had tracked in dirt and stepped on potato chips. "You — you — depraved — disgusting — horrible —" Althea could not think of enough words to fling at him. Jennie and I were going to be friends again! she thought. How dare he go ahead like that when he knew I didn't mean it!

"Kindly stop placing blame on others. It's *you*," corrected the vampire. "I told you what the arrangement would be, and you accepted. *You* chose Jennie. *You* said this one doesn't matter."

Althea crushed a dreadful thought. That girl sitting on the counter, the one who crashed the party — why hadn't Althea put her arm around *that* girl? Nobody even knew her name! *That* girl didn't matter.

Althea's hands and heart and spine turned cold and stony. I thought that, she thought. I am a terrible person. I must not have that thought again. "Everybody matters," whispered Althea.

"Why didn't you feel that way with Celeste?" asked the vampire. He seemed calm, ready to talk philosophy all night if necessary. Not that there was much night left.

She had no answer.

"Because you wanted to be popular," the vampire told her. "It's very reasonable. We all want to be popular. You made a good choice, Althea. Why, everybody at your party wanted to come again."

She thought of the good-byes. So many hugs. She had been careful not to hug back, but nobody noticed. They said what a good time they'd had, what a neat house she had, what fun it was, how they must get together here all the time.

"What interesting people you had at this party," said the vampire. His voice was full of admiration.

It glowed, like a night-light in the hall. Safe and warm. "You have so many good friends now, Althea. Better friends than Jennie. How good a friend was she to you? Wasn't she mean? Didn't she abandon you? Didn't she leave you to sit alone in the cafeteria?"

It was true. Jennie had been rotten and nasty. And Althea did have better friends now. Nobody could put Jennie in the same class with cheerleaders like Becky. Jennie hardly mattered when you compared her to Becky.

Althea felt somewhat better.

"Think what a wonderful day Monday will be," said the vampire. He was leaving. She could see him growing down, dividing away, letting himself be absorbed into the thick woolly air around him. "Friends clamoring for your attention. Friends begging to come to the next party. Friends hoping to sit with you."

He was gone, and she was smiling. Friends. Oh, what a lovely, lovely word! She would have them like a bouquet of flowers in a bride's arms: all shapes and colors and sizes of them, all beautiful and happy to be there.

Friends.

Althea straightened and looked around the house. She began cleaning. The mess extended to every corner. She swept, she mopped, she neatened. Plenty of friends had volunteered to help clean up, but she had turned everybody down. She didn't want her first party to end with scrubbing and stacking. No, her first party had to finish with laughter, and the honking of horns, and the hugging of friends.

Friends, thought Althea. Her sweeping slowed down. Her energy evaporated. Jennie had once been a friend. Celeste had thought it was the act of a new friend to offer a ride.

Althea dropped down, becoming carpet, becoming rug, flat and thin.

Jennie would be like Celeste. Vibrance gone. Energy evaporated. Jennie would trudge.

And it will be my fault, thought Althea. I did it to her. My best friend. "No," said Althea out loud, "I couldn't have done that. Not me." Her voice was all scratch and no sound, like the leftovers of a soul.

How would Althea ever sleep again, knowing what she had done?

She had destroyed Jennie, Jennie of childhood memories and childhood joy. This is how I repay her, thought Althea. I sell her to a vampire.

Althea had cleaned up to the bottom of the stairs. At the top of the stairs waited the locked entrance to the Shuttered Room.

All I have to do, thought Althea clearly, is shut the shutters. I have to close him back up. Bolt him back in.

I can't save Celeste and Jennie now. It's too late for them. But I can still stop *him*. I can prevent him from doing it again.

She lifted her chin. Took the first step up. She felt strong and full of resolution. She was the kind of woman who could conquer whole worlds.

The vampire said, from behind the door of the Shuttered Room, "Do you want the first party to be the last party?"

Althea held the broom tightly.

"Do you want to find out if Ryan will ask you on a real date? Do you want to know if Michael enjoyed himself tonight? Do you want to know if Michael was just accidentally everywhere that you were? Do you wonder why it is that Michael did not bring along the beautiful, perfect Constance?"

Althea trembled. The broom fell from her fingers and tipped against the wall.

The vampire's voice was soft as cookie dough. "Do you want to see if Kimmie-Jo and Dusty will invite you to their parties? If Becky will?"

Althea slid to the bottom step and folded over on herself, like an old sheet in a musty linen closet.

"Of course you do," he whispered. The vampire's laugh was like old leaves on dying trees. "Now, get a good night's rest, Althea. What's done is done. And nothing has happened, really. Jennie's just going to be a little tired. And you have better friends than that now, anyhow, don't you?"

Chapter 11

Monday.

Althea had dreaded Mondays for a year and a half.

The terrible building into which she was forced to walk — alone.

That horrible cafeteria in which she was forced to sit — alone.

Each room so grim.

Whether the library or the gymnasium, the English class or the chemistry laboratory, each room seemed designed as a showcase for other people's friends.

Monday.

And Jennie would not be coming to school.

Althea considered being absent herself. Staying in bed all day. Or perhaps the rest of her life.

But in the end she got up, dressed, drove to school, and parked.

Every move was heavy as lead. Putting the parking brake on left her weak and panting. Pushing down the door locks was like bench pressing. How could she move herself across the pavement? She felt as heavy as the car itself, except that she had no wheels. She had to pick up each foot, and set it down, and then pick up the next one.

Althea trudged forward. Never had the walk seemed longer, the steps higher, the doors heavier.

But the door handle was taken from her, and a larger, stronger hand pulled it open for her. "Hi there," said a boy cheerfully. "How are you, Althea?"

She did not even recognize him. She did not even *know* him.

She murmured, "Thank you," and walked into the gleaming marble foyer.

"Hi, Althea!" called a girl changing the Artwork of the Week exhibit.

"Hey, Althea, you get that math homework?" yelled a voice.

She waved. She called. She answered. She even managed a smile or two. The entire school had learned her name. The power of Varsity Cheerleading! The publicity of standing in front of the entire school for two hours, yelling! These kids knew her; they felt loyalty and affection for her; they enjoyed seeing her cheer. She was theirs.

"Hi, Althea!"

"How are ya, Althea?"

"Sit with me, Althea."

Her name was used aloud more times that Monday than in all the years of her life.

Althea. The name rang in the cafeteria.

Althea. The name bounced off the gym walls.

Althea. The name was murmured in the library.

"Althea," as a name, had always seemed both odd and stodgy. Now it sounded beloved and welcome.

Fellow cheerleaders called to her; classmates wanted to chat with her; unknown kids going down the hall actually congratulated Althea on a good game Saturday, as if her cheering had brought about the victory.

Everyone who had been at the party came up grinning and delighted to say what fun it had been, how they hoped she would have another one soon.

And everyone who had not been at the party came up shyly and hopefully, hinting that Althea might include them next time.

But Jennie was absent.

Childhood memories filled Althea like those doughnuts: heavy and lasting. Jennie and Althea going to the petting zoo; Jennie and Althea playing Chutes and Ladders; Jennie and Althea buying spring hats and being too shy to wear them; Jennie and Althea taking riding lessons and being in horse shows together; Jennie and Althea drawing up lists of cute boys, back in elementary school when there was no such thing, and giggling insanely all night long at each other's houses, daring each other to phone a boy; Jennie and Althea cutting each other's hair so badly one sleepover that

79

Jennie's mother escorted them to a mall hairdresser who was open evenings.

Jennie was absent.

Althea found herself behaving vaguely to all who spoke her name. Don't be rude, she said to herself, pay attention! People are talking to you.

But curiously enough, her distracted manner made her more desirable.

She pondered this. The popular person who doesn't have time for you becomes *more* popular! she thought.

She saved up the faces of all who spoke and laughed, thinking — did I earn this? Or did the vampire somehow migrate to each of them, and instruct them in their sleep: *Admire Althea today.*

And tomorrow? Next month? Next year?

Will they forget me as quickly as weather? Will I vanish like last Monday's sunshine, or yesterday's snow flurry?

Jennie was absent.

Her mind returned continually to that.

The vampire will ask me for another one, she thought. Not right away. But soon.

Althea changed classes, ate lunch, went to the library, got books from her locker, and wondered who it would be.

Who?

Who will I give him?

Who will he take?

Like owls fluttering through the halls, their

wings hitting her hair, the cry *who? who? who? who? who?* rang in her ears.

I cannot do that again, she said to herself. I cannot destroy another human being! I can't participate in it anymore. That's all there is to it.

"You know, Althea," said Ryan's voice, "you're more daydreamy than I realized."

She jumped, astonished to find she was sitting in a chair, and that Ryan was sitting in a chair next to her. He was smiling into her eyes, his hand resting on the chair back. "Hi, Ryan," she said, blushing. His hand shifted from the back of the chair to the back of her neck.

His fingers were callused, but his touch was gentle. He touched her skin as if exploring new worlds, lightly tugged her hair, and watched what he was doing, fascinated by his skin against hers.

Althea swallowed, thinking of somebody else who liked the backs of necks. *Jennie is absent.*

She took Ryan's hand and held it in her lap instead. He was delighted and looked at their two hands together. He separated her fingers with his and intertwined them, making a row of ten knuckles: her smooth, small, pale knuckles alternating with his large, knobby, dark ones.

"The school day," he said, managing a laugh, "has ended. Did you notice? You want to go for a drive? Maybe pizza. I can always eat pizza. I could eat yours if you're not hungry."

Michael appeared beside them. "Holding hands in public?" he teased. "I'm shocked, Ryan."

"Get lost," said Ryan cheerfully. "We're going for pizza."

Ryan pulled Althea to her feet. The library was full of kids doing research papers or homework. All were watching. She felt their eyes. The cheerleader and the football players. The popular girl and the handsome boys. The one you dream of being.

And it's me, she thought. *It's me.*

Chapter 12

The three of them made their way out of the school, bumping into one another, laughing, pushing on the steps, sheltering one another against the wind. Althea, confused about why they were a threesome, said aloud, "Michael, are you coming, too?"

Michael and Ryan roared with laughter.

"It's my car he's inviting you to use," explained Michael. "Old Ryan here is without a vehicle. If you plan to see much of the guy, keep in mind that he's going to need a chauffeur from now on."

"What about the car with three broken doors?" said Althea, who yearned to slither and slide in and out with Ryan.

Ryan sighed heavily. "The police. The cops."

She was horrified. "You were arrested?"

Ryan looked hurt while Michael grinned. "I was not arrested," Ryan said with dignity. "The police pulled me over because they could not understand how I was able to get out of such dented doors. It seems that vehicle inspection standards require that the driver and passenger should be able to get out of the car. I argued that we *are* able to get out of the car — it just takes a little while. The police said, What if I had a passenger who wasn't that agile? I said, Well, I just wouldn't take him along, would I? The police said, What about in situations where we didn't have a while to take? Like breaking down on the train tracks. I pointed out that there are no train tracks. He didn't care. He said I can't drive a one-door car until I get it fixed."

"But he's not going to get it fixed," said Michael. "It would cost a fortune."

"So yesterday," said Ryan, "I buried my servant, the car."

"It's gone to that great junkyard in the sky," said Michael.

The boys stood reverently for a moment, hands on hearts, mourning the passage of a really good vehicle.

Althea laughed helplessly, adoring them both.

She had never been able to comprehend a girl who would dangle two boys. You would think the girl would choose the better boy, get rid of the crummier one, and settle into having a great time.

Now she could see this was not such a great course of action.

Here was Ryan: sweet and funny. Cute and built and bright.

Here was Michael: all of the above, but more so.

They traveled in a pair, obviously.

She had her own car; she could drive Ryan; they could dispense with Michael. But what girl in her right mind would dispense with Michael? On the other hand, what girl in her right mind would dispense with Ryan, either?

Ryan, Michael, and Althea drove around for a while, all three in the front seat. Althea was wonderfully crushed between their thighs, and when Michael took a sharp turn, his arm on the steering wheel brushed against her, and when Ryan leaned forward to talk to Michael, his shoulder pressed on hers.

Althea thought that probably nothing, including sex or being elected president, could be as splendid as sitting in the front seat, Michael and Ryan talking to her at the same time, their wonderful masculine presence and scent and attitudes filling her with utter contentment.

Eventually, they arrived at Pizza Hut.

Of course Pizza Hut is a perfectly public restaurant, open to the world, and Althea had been there many times. And yet, if you walked in and passed the salad bar and went to the rear of the restaurant, there was a booth in the corner that was virtually a private club.

The high school club.

It was occupied continuously by one group or another, its numbers changing, diminishing, increasing, as one popular person drifted away, only to be replaced by another.

Only six could actually fit in the booth.

Usually seven or eight were crammed in, while several more sat at right angles in the adjoining, non-corner booths, which lacked the special status of the crammed corner.

In her previous life, Althea would hardly have had the nerve to lift her eyes even to look toward this corner.

In her wildest dreams, in her most desperate prayers, she had never hoped to be escorted to it by Michael and Ryan.

They had hardly been seated, hardly begun to argue over whether the pizza should have peppers and pepperoni, when Kimmie-Jo and Dusty arrived.

How interesting popularity is, thought Althea. I am with Michael and Ryan, and that is perfection, and everybody is envious, but the real stamp of approval is from the girls. Kimmie-Jo and Dusty will decide it. Boys come and go, but girlfriends stay, and judge, and count.

Kimmie-Jo shrieked, "Hi, Althea, how's your throat?" and slid into the seat.

Dusty said, "Althea, thank goodness you're here. There's so much to talk about."

Althea laughed to herself, and when Ryan tugged her backward, so that she was leaning against his chest, she cooperated fully.

Becky came into Pizza Hut.

Althea was amazed to see Becky pause by the salad bar, unsure of herself. Becky's eyes quickly scanned the booths, to see where she would be welcome. Michael, Ryan, Althea, Kimmie-Jo, and Dusty were in the corner booth. A bunch of juniors had taken the booth on one side, and some seniors the opposite booth. Becky, like Althea, was a sophomore. A cheerleader, yes, but not old enough, and with too little status to break into the Kimmie-Jo/ Dusty booth.

I've already moved ahead of Becky! thought Althea, seeing popularity suddenly as a sort of board game, where a throw of the dice, or somebody else's lost turn, had you whipping ahead, gathering points, heading for the winner's circle.

Althea waved to Becky, calling, "Come on over here, Becky, we have plenty of room."

Kimmie-Jo and Dusty frowned slightly. Becky came up breathlessly, her cheeks turning pink with excitement. Ryan and Michael acknowledged her politely.

Becky was really only a fringe member of the popular crowd. Only being on the Varsity Squad had moved her onto that fringe. Only during games and practices would she really count. Here, at Pizza Hut, Becky was minor.

Althea was overcome with a sense of power. She — who had been nobody! Nothing! Invisible! Inaudible! She could bestow popularity on Becky.

Ryan said to Althea, "So when's the next party? That one was so much fun."

Parties, thought Althea. She landed slightly, not all the way; part of her was still flying. But part of her was grounded. As Jennie had been. As

Celeste had been. She had made two choices. And now Jennie was absent; Celeste was trudging. And for what? For a slice of pizza eaten in this corner instead of that?

"I had a great time," agreed Michael.

"Me, too," said Becky quickly.

"I don't know how often I can open up the house like that," said Althea carefully.

"I know just what you mean," said Kimmie-Jo, although that seemed unlikely. "My parents get so anxiety-ridden when I even suggest a party that it's pathetic."

Talk turned to parental rules. Ryan quickly lost interest and stood up, handing money to the cashier. "Hey, Mike," he said, "you want to haul us back to the high school so we can get Althea's car?"

"Sure."

They got up. A trio. A successful popular trio. Althea was dizzy with it. "Bye, Kimmie-Jo," she said. "Bye, Dusty."

Becky shrank down into the booth. She was excess baggage now. Her hostess had left; the rulers of this booth had better people to associate with.

Althea cringed for her. "Becky?" said Althea quickly. "You want to sleep over one night this weekend? Saturday?"

"Hey," protested Ryan. "I'd like to sleep over one night this weekend."

Althea laughed, although her soul and body burned at the thought, and kept her eyes safely on Becky.

"I'd love to," said Becky, no longer shrinking. She sat tall and relaxed. Althea had spoken to her. Althea had included her.

No wonder the ancient Greeks portrayed the god Zeus with a lightning bolt. Althea could have held electric power lines and made them do her bidding. She was popular now, and the words looked and sounded alike:

Popular.

Powerful.

So Jennie was absent. So big deal. It was like any football game: You had some winners, and you had some losers.

Althea had become the winner.

Chapter 13

They had taken only one step into the parking lot — a trio of dancers getting one beat into the choreography — when a gleaming black SUV drove up. Several laughing girls rolled down their windows and called, "Hi, Michael. Hi, Ryan."

The girls were seniors — and one of them was Constance.

"Hi, Althea," the girls chorused.

Althea was awestruck. Her name was known to this set? Constance and her beautiful friends? "Hi," she whispered.

The black SUV rolled on, inch by inch; the driver had decided not to stop all the way, but to creep ever forward. Althea thought that was just right for the personality of this crowd: Nothing would stop them, and they would stop for nothing. They were the girls who would have it all.

Oh, to be one of them!

As the SUV glided past, Althea let a fantasy drift through her mind in which she mixed with this group, and laughed among them, and danced among them, and was the girl who had it all.

Ryan stepped back, pulling Althea with him, but Michael stood still, as if waiting to be run down.

Although the SUV slipped on, Constance opened the passenger door and leaned out a few inches. How lovely she was! Constance deserved to be the only model for an entire magazine. Softly, as if alone with him in a shadowy room, Constance said, "Michael. How are you? I miss you."

Michael flushed and said nothing. He seemed unprepared, like a child among adults. What had happened between these two, to make Michael stiff with nervousness and Constance soft with hope?

"May I join you?" said Constance, half out the door.

Michael smiled courteously, opened the door the rest of the way, and said, "Of course."

Now the SUV stopped.

Constance emerged. She was wearing a white wool skirt and a white silk blouse with full sleeves. A brilliant scarf lay carelessly around her throat. She looked the way every girl dreams of looking: beautiful, romantic, and mysterious.

Althea felt dumpy and dumb. No longer even felt sixteen — maybe eleven. A little kid stumbling behind a beauty queen.

The SUV moved on, circling Pizza Hut and vanishing. Michael got behind the wheel of his car with Constance beside him in the front. Althea and Ryan got in the back. It was an entirely different drive. There was no silly joking. Michael drove with great concentration, never looking at the passenger on his right. Constance sat sideways, stretching her safety belt out like a first-prize ribbon to be admired, and never took her eyes off Michael.

Constance was trying to make peace. Over what rift, Althea would have loved to know. Michael and Constance were extremely courteous to each other. Their dialogue might have been heard a hundred years ago, in more elegant times, perhaps over teacups and lace doilies. Althea was glad they had not had to talk over pizza.

She remembered Ryan and looked his way. Ryan was picking grumpily at some torn threads on his blue jeans. "Michael," he said, "you're just steering. You forgot about driving us back to get Althea's car."

Michael grinned in embarrassment. He said, "I thought I'd circumnavigate the globe. Skip high school."

"As long as you don't skip me anymore," said Constance.

For the first time Michael looked at his girlfriend and then rested his hand on her knee. She covered his hand with hers, and Althea sighed with contentment. True love had won.

Michael and Constance both laughed a little, and then were suddenly self-conscious in front of

Althea and Ryan. Constance smiled at the backseat. "I don't know if Michael's ready to be alone with me," she said cheerfully. "I think we need you two in the backseat. So how are you enjoying Varsity, Althea? I was so glad you made the squad."

"I love it," said Althea shyly. "I'm making friends already. I didn't think I would make friends so quickly."

"We're writing essays on friendship for English," said Michael. "It's a tough subject. The first essay was what friendship *gives* to you. You had to be specific and name three friends who gave you something: one from elementary school, one from a sport or an activity, and one who's not your own age."

Althea's hands were so cold. She felt as if blood had stopped circulating through her. Perhaps it had. Perhaps that was how the vampire migrated. Perhaps the vampire could dictate what they talked about, perhaps he could give out English assignments.

What if I had to set down on paper what my last two friends gave me? she thought. They gave me popularity. Jennie's the friend from elementary school, and Celeste's the friend from a sport. They gave me this. They're the reason I'm sitting here, with Ryan putting his arm around my shoulder, Constance smiling at me, and Michael talking to me.

And that third category . . . a friend not your age. Could that be what the vampire wanted next?

"Now the second essay, which I have to write tonight," said Michael, "is what *you* give to others in a friendship."

What I gave, thought Althea, is unspeakable. Unwritable. Unthinkable. But I did it anyway. I did it twice.

Ryan's large smooth hand had encircled her now and was pulling her against him, so that she was snuggled into the curve of his arm. He tilted his head against hers, and the warmth of him, the masculine presence of him, oh, it was the most wonderful thing she had ever experienced.

I wouldn't change my mind, thought Althea. I wouldn't have done it differently.

I'm sick. I'm horrible. I'm the worst person on earth. Because I'm glad it happened. I'm glad I have this ride, and these new friends, and Ryan!

Constance was still facing Michael, drinking him in almost. Her lovely profile was outlined by the setting sun, and the perfection of her gave Althea shivers.

I want to be like that, she thought. I want to be just like Constance.

She thought: I just won't think about Celeste and Jennie anymore. That's the important thing. Not to dwell on it. I have what I have. The past is past.

"It's a tough essay question," said Michael, frowning slightly. "I mean, what *do* I give to my friends?" He sent Constance a look of deep meaning, and she returned it by lifting his hand and holding it against her cheek. Althea loved the privilege of being there to see it.

"Pizza and rides are all you give your friends," teased Ryan.

"I want to get an A on that essay, you jerk," said Michael. "It has to be profound. Think of something meaningful."

"There's nothing more profound than a really good pepperoni pizza," said Ryan.

"What do you think, Althea?" Constance asked. "If you wrote about friendship, what would you say?" Constance rested her chin on the seat back and looked straight into Althea's eyes.

Every hair on Althea's head prickled.

Constance fills the requirement. She is not my age. So she must be next.

Constance? Beautiful, wonderful, lovely Constance? Getting draggy and trudgy and pitiful like Celeste? Never! That must never happen! Althea forgot to censor her speech. Right out loud she said, "I guess you don't turn a friend over to a vampire."

Michael, Constance, and Ryan burst out laughing. Michael laughed so hard he almost drove off the road. Ryan hugged Althea more tightly, as if that were a cue line for a lover; as if that statement meant they understood each other now and were actually dating, a romantic pair.

"What a great rule," said Michael, shaking his head, and getting back into the proper lane. He turned on his headlights as the sky finished darkening and the winter night closed in. He turned on the heater, and a warm wind caressed Althea's ankles.

"Next time I meet a vampire," promised Constance, "I won't turn a single friend over to him."

Laughter filled the car, as if a new form of oxygen had been created, as if a different combination of elements had invaded their little enclosure.

Michael turned up Hillside Drive.

Far away and far below, the many-angled roof of Althea's forbidding house was like a black pool in the early darkness of winter. Three chimneys, solid brick, faded red, reached up toward the night sky.

And one tower.

With three windows.

Whose shutters banged.

Michael was driving so slowly that the world seemed to have slowed down with him. Even the wind seemed to lift the bare branches slowly, while autumn leaves fluttered to the grass slowly, and people getting out of their cars closed their doors slowly and walked slowly inside.

Althea seemed to watch the shutters of her tower for a long, long time; time enough for seasons to change and friendships to end.

They were dark green shutters, shutters the color of ancient hemlocks, the color of impenetrable forests.

He's waiting for me. He'll be there when I get back. He needs somebody else. He'll want Con-

stance. But I cannot, cannot, cannot do that! Michael and Constance are so perfect together. I love them together. I love knowing that there is such perfection in the world. Such beauty.

The shutters moved in unison toward the center of each of the three windows. Gently they closed themselves. One by one, they shut out the night.

Night . . .

There had been a conversation about night . . .

What had she agreed to do at night?

Althea's hair lifted from her scalp, as if the vampire were running his horrid fingers through it, his tarnished foil nails scraping her scalp. Her spine hurt.

I invited Becky to spend the night on Saturday, she thought. I forgot Becky. I forgot her as quickly and easily as I decided to forget Celeste and Jennie. It's as if I have already given Becky away. So that I can keep Constance.

Horror filled Althea like quicksand, pulling her down the hill, hauling her body by evil gravity toward the shutters.

Toward the vampire.

Toward the end of Becky.

Chapter 14

There was so much to be afraid of!

Herself, and her capacity to do evil things.

The vampire, and his presence, the way he was changing her.

The future, and what she chose.

The friends she had, and how she would hurt them. Or hurt herself.

And this: driving Ryan home. Alone with a boy in a car.

The dark of night was a capsule around them. The interior of the car was their world. How much less relaxed they were, without Michael and Constance to dilute their emotions. They had been a group: easy laughter, easy talk. Ryan's hand rested lightly on her shoulder as she drove, and his fingers for a moment touched her hair.

The touch spooked her, and she suppressed a shudder.

She could feel the vampire behind her, thinking of her, planning for her, waiting.

Up and over yet another hill she drove.

When she came down the other side, a mass of soil and rock blocked the vampire. It was impenetrable. His dark path could not go that far; she could feel in her ribs, her spine, the flesh of her back, that they had reached some kind of safety.

She knew, as firmly as she knew her numbers and her alphabet, that the vampire could not pierce the hill.

Althea heaved a great sigh of relief. It was so huge that Ryan jumped away from her, startled, jerking his hand back and staring at her.

"Sorry," she said lamely. "I — I guess I don't drive much after dark, and I — I guess I'm kind of tired. So I sighed."

Ryan found that a difficult excuse to accept. "It's okay," he said stiffly. "Just drop me off and go straight home. You probably have lots of homework anyway."

She had a sense that she was losing him, that he was fading away from her as fast as daylight had faded on this wintry afternoon. She caught his hand to yank him back. "No, no," she protested. "I'm just really not that much of a driver."

He believed her. How amazing. If some dumb girl said that to Althea, she certainly would have some questions. What American teen ever said or believed for a single moment that he or she was a lousy driver? Nobody. Everybody on earth believes they're an excellent driver. Everybody on earth takes pride in their brilliant driving skills.

But Ryan believed her.

Did the vampire make him? she thought. How much power does the vampire really have? Can he actually invade my friends' thoughts?

Of course he can. Or he wouldn't make them my friends.

A gruesome thought invaded Althea. Had the vampire been giving Ryan instructions? Touch her. Smile at her. Take her hand.

She had to ask the vampire next time she saw him; she had to know how much of this was real. Does it count if he makes it happen? she thought. What if I find out it's not for real? Will I still be thrilled to see Constance smile, and have Ryan hug me and Michael say my name?

Ryan lived in a ranch-style house. His driveway was paved, not gravel like hers. It seemed firmer, more modern, less likely to harbor things.

"Want to come in?" said Ryan.

"I'd love to another day," she said, "but I have to get home." She kissed him. She was absolutely astounded at herself. Where had that courage come from?

Ryan, startled and pleased, kissed her back.

They laughed and kissed a second time, breathless and surprised in their sharing. Althea drove away into the night, so full of joy that she felt nothing else could ever exist in her except gladness. She liked a boy, and a boy liked her. What else is there?

She laughed all the way back to her house.

The laugh stayed on her face, like an echo in the air. The curve of her smile kept her face alight and aloft.

She was still laughing when she came in her own door, and the vampire said, "I was out tonight. Did you feel me? Did you know I was there?"

He smiled, framed by the huge, carved doorway, and his smile increased to match the door. His mouth filled more of his face than usual. His teeth were long and sharp as garden stakes.

"Get out of here!" Althea hissed. Forget the questions she had wanted to ask him! She was furious with him for existing, for making her think about what she had done. How could she find peace of mind if she was forced to remember?

"I beg your pardon," said the vampire. "I live here."

"It's my house!" she shouted. She stamped her foot. The porch shook a little from the force of her pounding foot, but the vampire was not affected.

"It's mine," said the vampire, lingering on the sentence. Then softly, he echoed himself, drooling over the words, *"It's mine."*

Althea could not get in her own door. He filled it. His swirling black cape went right up to the edges of it, like pond scum.

"And you," said the vampire, smiling cruelly, "you are mine, also."

Chapter 15

She was doing her math homework when the phone rang. Page 78. Quadratic equations lined up like little vehicles trying to cross the page. The book was very white, and the numbers printed very clearly, very thinly, like a message.

"Hi, Althea?" said an eager girl's voice. "It's Becky."

"Hi, Becky!" cried Althea.

A girlfriend was phoning. It had been years! Years since the joy of having a best friend to call up and gossip with. Althea beamed into the telephone, as if it had been invented just for her.

"I had such a good time at Pizza Hut, didn't you?" said Becky.

"It was great, wasn't it? Isn't Michael funny? Isn't Ryan terrific?"

"Oh, yes, and afterward, after you left with the boys — well, I stayed on awhile and got to know Kimmie-Jo and Dusty so much better. Kimmie-Jo told me all about this terrific place where she gets her hair done. Dusty thinks I should maybe get mine a little more layered in the back. Dusty thinks I need more volume in my hair."

Althea loved to talk about hair. She told Becky that she, personally, thought Becky's hair was extremely attractive, the way it clung to her head, and Althea loved the ponytail, which was exactly the right length, shoulder length. Becky could curl her hair for elegant occasions, but if Becky cut it layered, she would have volume, but no ponytail. And was that really what Becky was after?

Becky said she was really after a boyfriend, and hair volume kind of ran second to that.

They laughed shrilly and eagerly into the phones, and got into more comfortable positions, because this was a conversation with all-night potential. Althea was sorry she had no snack next to the phone. Althea frowned at her quadratic equations and did one.

After they were done with hair, they moved on to makeup and clothing, and then they got to the important part: what Althea had done with Michael and Ryan. Althea told Becky everything, while Becky sighed in vicarious pleasure at each description. ". . . and then he took his hand off my shoulder and touched my hair," said Althea.

"How did he touch it?" Becky said. "I mean, did he run his hand over it, or through it, or what?"

Althea did another quadratic equation. A really good equation, thought Althea, is a girlfriend on the phone asking what you did with a boyfriend in the car.

They discussed exactly what happened, Becky moaning with envy. They pondered whether Althea, too, needed more volume in her hair and should go with Becky to the new hairstylist. Then Becky was struck by the thought that perhaps Dusty and Kimmie-Jo had been trying to say that Becky looked stupid and needed professional help.

"You know them better than I do," said Althea. "Are they mean or nice? Are they thoughtful or cruel?" Althea finished up two more equations.

Becky told several interesting stories about various nice or else cruel things that Kimmie-Jo and Dusty had done. Then she said casually, and yet carefully, ". . . about sleeping over, Althea? I asked my mother about Saturday. But I thought I should check first and see if, you know, if Ryan, like, asked you out. Because I mean, I wouldn't hold you to your invitation if Ryan — well — he would come first, of course."

Althea suddenly remembered why she had stopped being friends with Jennie when they hit high school. It had been a conversation just like this one. How could she possibly have forgotten? The pain had paralyzed Althea for months! For her whole freshman year.

The conversation replayed in Althea's head like an old record: one of those big, slow records that you found boxes of at yard sales, because nobody even owned a turntable anymore.

"But you said I could stay over at your house Saturday," Althea had protested.

"I know, Althea, but grow up! Dave asked me to the movies! I mean, what counts here, Althea?"

"I'm your best friend."

"Althea!" (How irritated Jennie had sounded; as if she were looking at her wristwatch; as if she could not believe her romance was being slowed down by this dumb, dumb, dumb conversation with some worthless girl.) "Althea, this is a boy. Remember how there are two sexes? Of course, you haven't found out yet. But I have. And I'm not about to tell Dave I can't go to the movies because my friend Althea wants to come over!"

That Saturday night seemed eons ago, but it wasn't. It was only a year and a half.

A year and a half ago that the best friend of all her life, and all her joys and sorrows, had said, "Let me spell this out for you, Althea. I have a boyfriend now."

Jennie had not added — had not needed to — *I don't want you, Althea. I'm not available now. I have better things to do. Better people to be with.*

Memory was harsh and painful.

I'm not that kind of friend, she thought, proud of herself. I wouldn't write a friend off into the background like that. She said firmly, "Of course it's on, Becky. I can hardly wait. There's only one trouble. Is there any chance that I could stay at your house instead of you at mine? I mean —

well — you know how it is — I just can't have company right now."

Becky replied delicately that she understood; families could be difficult. "I'd love to have you stay here," said Becky. "Actually, that's better in a way, because even though I'm sixteen, my parents don't like me to stay overnight at anybody's house when they haven't met the family. They're really old-fashioned, Althea, you wouldn't believe it. I have so much to tell you."

Althea folded up into her chair and cuddled the phone like an infant. She was safe for another weekend, at least. Nobody would be here to cross the dark path.

"Ryan didn't ask you out for Saturday, then?" Becky asked just to be sure.

"Even if he had, I would have explained to him that I had to check with you first. I'm not that kind of friend, Becky."

She could almost see Becky smile: that wide, delighted, pixieish smile that made her such a great cheerleader. That uptilted head, that crowing laugh, that low-volume hair, and twitching ponytail!

Althea giggled into the phone. Becky's giggle matched, and they agreed to meet before school in the morning, to talk about essential things before class began.

Althea hung up. She smiled, thinking of friendship. What a beautiful thing it was. She looked down regretfully at her next quadratic equation and lifted her pencil to finish off the homework.

An oddly clear shadow crossed page 78.

A shadow like glass or mirrors.

The vampire said, "I have decided. I want Becky next."

Chapter 16

Becky's ranch house was on a hillier and rockier lot than Ryan's. The driveway was cut deeply into the earth, with high stone sides that dripped with dank climbing ivy. Hemlocks planted many years ago had grown into monsters, shouldering their way toward the windows.

Becky went in through the garage, which was dark and tumbling with boxes and shadows, leading Althea into a lower-level rec room.

Dark brown carpet and dark-paneled walls made a mockery out of the word *recreation*. Althea could not imagine bouncing, cheerful Becky inhabiting such a grim cellar of a room. She could well imagine the vampire inhabiting it, however.

Becky bounded up another set of stairs to the kitchen/living room level.

Althea frowned. On the third step she turned and looked back. A shadow clear as glass drifted behind her.

Althea shut the rec room door firmly behind

her. It was a thin door, a weak and shallow door. A door that would stop nothing.

Upstairs, mercifully, was bright and light.

The kitchen was packed with broccoli-green cabinets. The living room had been decorated to look like a garden, with white wicker furniture, and fanciful flowers danced on the drapes and cushions.

Perhaps the dark and brown things of the world would stay downstairs, and the light and bright would control the upper level.

Becky flung open the door to her own bedroom. Althea had never seen so much purple, so many hues and shades of lavender, violet, amethyst, and mauve. "I love your room," she whispered. She soaked up the joy of the room, the sheer exuberance in life that Becky's room was.

"Me, too," said Becky contentedly. "It's perfect."

Becky picked up her telephone, which was also purple, and phoned Ryan. "Come on over," she said to him. "She's here." Becky winked at Althea. "He's having supper with us," she whispered, hand covering the receiver. "He adores you."

Althea lost her breath. It was such an odd feeling, suddenly to have empty lungs and a pounding heart. *Ryan adores me.*

Becky said, "Ryan's going to tell us star stories in the backyard and teach you how to look through a telescope." Becky, laughing wickedly, said, "This whole overnight is a setup, you know."

She opened the kitchen door. A cold wind filtered into the safe warm kitchen. The yard was completely black. Althea grew cold from her feet to her eyes: a deep chill, like an early death.

Becky ran out onto the grass as if entering another, lower world.

Althea cried out. Her breath was gone again, but not from love. Fear yanked it out of her chest. "We — we can't go out there!" she said.

"You afraid of the dark?" teased Ryan, stepping from his yard into Becky's.

Althea hung on to the kitchen counter. "Come back in, Becky!" cried Althea. She smelled the foul eagerness of the vampire.

"Scaredy-cat," Becky teased.

"Make her come back in, Ryan," said Althea desperately. She had to get Becky back inside, in the bright purple bedroom, the safe green kitchen, the many-flowered living room.

Ryan wrapped his arm around Althea. It was an embrace of comfort, not desire. "I don't believe I've ever met anybody who's really and truly afraid of the dark. I'll stay with you. It'll be all right. Think of the dark as a warm and gentle friend."

Althea's laugh rasped like a chain saw.

"I heard something in the bushes," said Becky. "I'll join you two in a minute. I just have to see what it is."

"No!" screamed Althea. "No, you don't! It doesn't matter what it is! Come back in."

"Now, now," said Ryan, holding her, preventing her from saving Becky. I'm in a zoo, thought Althea. Ryan is my keeper.

She felt primitive and savage, felt as if she, like some jungle tiger, had fangs.

Or were her fangs those of a vampire?

It seemed to Althea that it took hours for Becky to return, and that when she came, she moved more slowly. Was paler.

The evening seemed to last for hundreds of years, in which they all grew old and exhausted. She could hardly wrap her mouth around the syllables required for speech. She could hardly see Ryan, could hardly remember Becky.

At last Ryan left.

She adored him, but she could not bear the length of the evening. Every quip, every move, every story consumed her, until all energy was completely sapped. She could hardly unbutton the front of her shirt. She could hardly lift her nightgown. Scarcely brush her teeth. She was actually glad that Becky had turned down the covers of the bed, because she did not know if she could summon the strength to move a blanket.

The mattress was wonderful, so soft, so welcoming, so necessary. The pillow onto which her head sank was a shelter in which she could rest forever. I'll never get up, thought Althea. I'll have to move in with Becky and take a week off from school.

A cold, cruel wind seemed to blow through her mind, filtering through her brain, blinding her eyes.

She'll just be a little . . . tired, the vampire had said.

She was too tired even to shudder.

It can't be, she told herself. I would have felt something. He can't — I mean — those teeth — it wouldn't work unless —

And yet . . . he calls it migration. A word for swallows in the sky. There's nothing in that word about feeling fangs in your flesh.

Be rational, Althea said to herself. Football games, cheering practice. Cheering, studying for exams. Of course I'm tired. I've had a very demanding week.

"Althea, hop up and change the TV channel, will you?" said Becky. "I can't seem to find my remote control."

Althea dragged herself into a sitting position and crawled to the end of the mattress. She could not quite reach the TV knobs. Like an ancient crone with arthritis, she tottered two steps, changed the channel till Becky was satisfied, leaned briefly on the shelves, and pushed herself off like a swimmer pushing off the pool wall for another lap. At last she was back in the bed, back down on the lovely good pillow. Nothing was demanded of her body. Only rest.

Rest.

It was all she wanted.

All she would ever want.

If it's him, she thought, if he was here, with me, I won't have enough energy to have friends. I won't have enough energy to be in the squad or date Ryan or sing in the chorus. Or do anything at all. I'm finished. She said, "Becky?"

"Mmm?"

"When you heard a noise in the bushes, what was the noise?"

"I was just teasing. I didn't really hear anything. I'm sorry if you took me seriously. Ryan was dying to be alone with you outdoors. He had some fantasy that you and he would stare at the stars together, and you would be overcome with uncontrollable emotion, and I would go back in while you two danced in the dark."

In the dark.

Among the hemlocks.

No, she said to herself. It can't be me. He said we were a match for each other. I'm just exhausted, that's all. I've had a hard day. In the morning, I'll be energetic and enthusiastic again.

When Becky found the remote control under a pile of fashion magazines and shouted with delight, Althea slept on, as if in something deeper than sleep.

Chapter 17

But when she awoke on Sunday morning, sun streamed in the bedroom window. It lay golden and warm upon the dark violet of the bedspread and tickled the sweet lavender of the wallpaper.

Althea bubbled with joy.

Nothing had happened. It was cheerleading, and homework, and the pressure of being interesting in front of a new boyfriend that had worn her out. Althea hopped out of bed and went into Becky's darling little bathroom, in which everything was white: white as snow. Shower, tiles, walls, everything gleamed porcelain and pure. Two tiny violet guest towels with lacy fringe hung from a white rod. Violet bath towels were stacked on a white wicker shelf. Embroidered violets peeked delicately from the folds of the shower curtain.

Althea stepped in the shower and sang under pulsing hot water.

She wrapped herself in one of the purple towels

to dry, and the towel was soft and wonderfully thick.

Life is good, thought Althea. I am in control.

She danced into the kitchen to see if she could help with or start breakfast. Becky's parents had apparently come in late, for their bedroom door was shut and the house lay quiet, as houses do on Sunday mornings while people sleep in.

Althea found cereal and milk and crunched happily. Out the kitchen window she could see the backyard, and in the sun it was such a pretty yard. The leaves were gone from the trees, but they were such graceful trees: a willow and two clumps of white birches with papery, peeling bark. The thick shrubs were covered with frost, and they glittered, half snow, half sun, utterly beautiful.

Becky walked slowly into the kitchen. Her eyes seemed to lack focus. Her body lurched slightly, and she sank into a kitchen chair as if unsure where she might be. Althea poured her a glass of orange juice that she had whipped in the blender; it was frothy and light.

Becky looked at the glass. She frowned. She said, "This is so weird, Althea. I just didn't seem to get any rest last night. I don't think I can even pick up that juice glass."

Althea became very still.

Becky said, "I think I'm coming down with something. I don't want you to catch it, Althea. Or Ryan, either. We have such important games next week. He can't get sick; the football team needs him. You can't get sick. The squad needs you."

Through uncooperative, frightened lips, Althea said, "The cheerleading squad needs you, too, Becky. Getting sick is out of the question."

Becky put her arms on the kitchen table and then rested her head on her arms. "I think it's in the question," she said, trying to laugh. "I think — I really think you'd better go on home, Althea. I think I need to go back to bed."

"NO!"

Becky focused one eye on Althea and then closed it, exhausted by the effort. "I feel as if I could sleep for a month," she said.

Althea grabbed Becky's shoulders and shook her. "Get up!" she cried. "You have to get up! You have to try. You have to stay on your feet!"

"Huh?" said Becky, falling asleep.

Becky's mother came into the kitchen. "What's the matter?" she said.

"I think Becky — um — has the flu," said Althea. "She — um —"

Becky's mother went right into action. Thermometer, aspirin, chicken soup, the works. "My poor baby," crooned Becky's mother. "You haven't been sick in years! This is not like you! I think cheerleading is responsible. It takes such time and energy and it is simply draining. I just don't think it's healthy to work so hard day after day, week after week. I've said that all season, haven't I, darling?"

"Mmmm," said Becky, leaning on her mother.

With Althea on one side and Becky's mother on the other, they walked Becky back down the hall to her bed, tucked her in, and wrapped her warmly.

"What a sweet girl you are," said Becky's mother to Althea. "So helpful and understanding. I want you to do one little thing for me."

"Anything," said Althea, who felt dead, like something evil and sick, who infected her friends, and ended their happiness. Somebody who could turn a lovely purple-and-white room of irises and violets into a purgatory of exhaustion.

"At practice on Monday, tell Mrs. Roundman that I am taking my daughter off the squad. There is simply too much being demanded of her."

"No!" whispered Althea. "I'm sure Becky will be fine by Monday. She'll be in school Monday. Send a note with Becky to say you want Becky to sit out the practice! Mrs. Roundman will agree to that. Please! Please don't take her off the squad."

Becky had fallen back asleep.

Her long, dark hair swirled on the pillow, like a winter storm cloud around the paleness of her tired face.

My friend, thought Althea. My third betrayal. I have given away Celeste, given away Jennie, and now Becky. Becky!

Her friendship with Becky played in her heart like slides in a darkened classroom: the first welcome, the encouragement at tryouts, the little speech of friendship when she made the squad. The phone calls, the laughter, the hair volume jokes.

I gave her to the vampire.

How many more will I give? When will it be over? Will it ever be over?

Becky's mother kissed her daughter's cheek. "Well," she said, adjusting the blanket hem, "I'll wait till Monday and see. But cheerleading is not worth your health."

Althea no longer knew what cheerleading was worth. She knew only one thing. She was going home. She was closing those shutters, closing them forever, and if it was the end of cheerleading, the end of friends like Becky and boys like Ryan, well, she did not deserve them, anyway.

She felt tight and strong with resolve.

Nothing the vampire could say or offer would make Althea change her mind this time.

She drove over the hills and down to the bottom of the valley.

She parked sternly, with a solid pull on the brake, as if making very, very sure that she was going to stay and see this through. She shut the door of her car not with a slam but with certainty. She strode across her yard, marched up her stairs, and climbed upward.

Chapter 18

The tower room was quiet and dusty in the sun.

It felt of nothing.

There was neither power nor evil here. It was merely an empty room.

She ran her fingers through her hair, as if strengthening herself from the top of her head to the tips of her toes.

She approached the first window. The glass pane lifted quite easily and stayed up. Leaning out of the tower, Althea took hold of one outside shutter.

It was made of wood. Paint flaked off even as she grabbed the rim. The wood felt punky and rotten under her fingers, and when she dug her nails into it, she knew she was leaving half moons of anger in the wood. The shutter whined on its hinges, as if calling out to the hemlocks.

But the sun shone on, and the shutter turned in.

Gripping the shutter with one hand, Althea

reached for its mate. It did not move as easily. She had to lean way far out of the window. She was on her tiptoes now, her center of gravity off, her stance no longer safe.

How high she was.

Below her was not grass, but stone.

Far below.

If someone gave me a push . . . thought Althea. She swallowed, wet her lips, and leaned even farther out, grabbed the opposite shutter, and pulled. It took all her strength to bring the shutters together, but they were only wood, and she was more than that.

Her fingers were cramped and raw from hauling on the splintery, paint-peeling rims, but at last she brought their edges together. She swung the heavy metal clasp on the left shutter and shoved it through the iron circle sticking out of the right shutter like a black wedding ring, and the first pair of shutters was closed.

The louvers of the shutters were fixed, slanting down, and no sun penetrated at that angle.

Now the tower room was darker by a third. The dust seemed to lie more heavily on the floor, and the echo of her footsteps seemed quieter and less important.

Althea turned to approach the middle window. The air in the room thickened and became a wall. She had to lean against it, throw her weight as if against a great invisible wind. Turning sideways Althea hurled herself like a linebacker through the air of the tower room and reached the middle window.

The window refused to lift.

She fought with it. She could jiggle it a little, but not open it.

From somewhere outdoors, through the thin old pane of glass, she heard a laugh, like the sound of dry leaves rustling on pavement.

Althea yelled at him, "Laugh all you want! I'm closing these shutters, and when I'm done with that, you are done, too! You are finished! You are history!"

Like Celeste, thought Althea. Like Jennie. Like Becky. History. They had laughed once. Had fun and friends once. Now they don't.

Well, he had freedom once, because I opened his shutters. And now he won't. So there.

But even so, she was afraid. Afraid of how high up she was. Of how height meant nothing to him. Of what would happen next.

Don't be a weakling, Althea said to herself.

She wrapped her arm in her sweater and punched the window. The glass shattered with a crystalline cry and fell to the stones below. Vicious triangles of windowpane remained in the wood. They glittered in the sun, like vampire teeth.

"You're nothing but glass," Althea whispered to the shimmering fangs. "Nothing but glass."

The window gave up its fight and let itself be lifted easily and quickly.

And the outside shutters, as if not wanting to be

destroyed, submitted to her reaching fingers and let themselves be swung inward, and allowed their clasp and ring to meet, partners forever joined.

The tower room was much darker now. The remaining window faced north. No rays of sun ever came in that window. A little daylight filtered through, but when Althea stood in front of this last window, there was not even enough light to cast her shadow.

It weakened her, as if without a shadow she were without soul as well, without courage and without hope.

After a terrible silent struggle, the third window submitted to her. She did not have to shatter it. For the third time, she thrust her body out to grab a shutter. Leaned way out over the hard stone, tilted dangerously to grasp the wooden rim. The temperature outdoors had dropped severely. She was chilled, her fingers cold to the bone.

These shutters seemed positively eager to close, almost slamming her fingers between them. These shutters want to be shut, thought Althea, and her hair crawled. *Why?* Did the shutters themselves have a scheme in mind? Had they plans? Plans for Althea?

Darkness was deep.

Only the door to the tower room let in any light, and that was from the ceiling fixture in the downstairs hall. She faced the door, trying to gain strength. But it was electric light, manufactured light; it lacked the power of the sun to nourish life; it gave Althea nothing.

That's all right, she thought. I have enough. I will finish this.

She surveyed the tower. The glass was black now, backed with the closed shutters. But there were three more sets of shutters: the inside shutters. And they were the ones that counted.

The chill and the foul-smelling damp that was the vampire swirled around the room, like invisible dervishes spinning, knowing time was up, knowing they would fall to the floor and never spin again.

"I have you now," said Althea. She was triumphant: rich and solid with victory.

She swung the first inside shutter to its closed position.

But it would not go all the way. It resisted. With muscles of its own, it pushed Althea back into the center of the empty room.

The six inside shutters regarded her with their dozens of louvered eye slits.

She threw herself at a different shutter and pushed with all her might. To her surprise it closed without a murmur. She reached for its companion shutter to bring that to the center and bolt them; they were to be coupled by long, thin, black bolts, but when she touched the second shutter, the first returned to its open position against the wall.

Althea's arms were not long enough to reach both shutters at once.

There was no way for her to slide the bolt that would hold a pair down.

The slats of the shutters curved upward into catlike smiles of contempt. *You can't close us*, said the shutters to Althea.

She threw herself at first one shutter and then another, one window and then another — but she could not close a single pair.

A laugh like broken glass spun out of the tower room, through the door, into the hall . . .

. . . and the tower room door, the door that led away from the attic and down the stairs, closed by itself.

Closed tightly and forever.

Her exit was gone.

She had planned to shut the vampire in the tower room.

It had never crossed her mind that he might shut *her* in the tower.

Chapter 19

Althea stood very still.

Nothing but stone, granite, and slate had ever been so still. There was no breath in Althea, no pulse. She was frozen in space and in time.

Is this my choice? she thought. Am I frozen in order to think more clearly? Or because I am so afraid that there is nothing left of me to move?

Her feet were part of the floor, as if nailed to the boards. Her hands hung motionless in the air, as if her bones and tendons had become oxygen and nitrogen.

Or, she thought, has the vampire frozen me? Is this his choice? Is he about to take . . . the next step?

She felt the mold and the fungus of him closing in on her.

What did it feel like?

Would she know when it began and when it was over?

She tried to remember the world. She tried to

think of sunshine and falling leaves, of laughing cheerleaders and peanut butter sandwiches.

How tired Celeste and Jennie and Becky had become. How tired they had stayed. Not just their bodies, but their souls, the exhausted skeletal remains of the girls they had been.

Not me, thought Althea. Please, not me!

She knew now that Celeste and Jennie and Becky had felt fear. That they had smelled him, and tasted him, and been sick with nerves from him. She knew now that Celeste and Jennie and Becky had tried to fight back, had put up their hands, as if ten little human fingers could fend off a vampire. She knew now that their hearts had beat with terror, that their lungs had heaved with horror.

I did that, thought Althea. When he said, "They'll just be a little tired," I let myself believe that. I guess you always want to believe that violence will really be gentle. That you aren't really doing anything wrong. That it will all come out happily in the end. Nothing to fret about, especially if you are the winner.

I am the winner, she thought, hysterical with self-loathing. This is what I have won. The chance to be alone with a vampire in a tower of black.

Her thoughts grew as dim as the tower room itself, as if her brain had softened and darkened, and she said to the vampire, *All right. Come in. I accept.*

She felt her hair lift. An odd sort of breeze cooled

the back of her neck. Spin around, she told herself. Raise your fists! Strike out and beat off the attempt.

But something had happened when she closed the shutters. She had closed off a part of herself. All that was strong in her, all that was determined, perhaps even all that was good, had been shuttered away, in some distant and unreachable compartment.

Did I ever have anything good in me? she thought. Will I ever have it again? Or has the goodness of me died inside?

Althea felt movement now, and it was herself.

She was sagging.

Leaning.

Tipping.

I feel awfully tired, she thought.

She yearned to sit. It seemed very important to sit down. Perhaps to lie down.

I need rest, she thought. What time is it? Is it nighttime? Is it bedtime? Is it tomorrow already? Who even cares?

In the tower room, there was no time. There was only dark.

She felt the foil of his fingertips on her skin.

I am letting it happen, Althea thought. I am giving in. It seems that I *have* made a choice. *I have chosen to surrender.*

She tried to see what was happening, but there was nothing to see: nothing but dark . . .

. . . darker . . .

. . . *darkest* . . .

Chapter 20

A horn honked.

A vehicle had pulled into the driveway below.

How twenty-first century! The horn's call pierced the tower room as sunshine could not. Where light cannot travel, sound can.

How beautiful is sound! The driver leaned again on his wheel, and the glorious scream of a car's horn penetrated the tower. No louvers or shutters, no dust, no vampire could stop sound.

Althea smiled into the dark, and immediately the dark was less. A smile, she thought. Happiness. Another weapon. I must remember all these. Sound and joy: They obliterate the enemy.

She straightened. She flung back her hair and opened her eyes wide. It was still dark, but now the dark was curiously friendly. Who had said to Althea that he thought of the dark as a friend?

She waited a moment, hoping her brain would sort out the voices of the week and remember.

Her feet moved; the nails that had held her to

the wooden boards had evaporated. Her hands moved; the paralysis was gone. She walked forward in the dark, encountering nothing, until she touched the wall, and it was only a wall. Plaster. Her hands scrabbled outward until she had found the first window.

Don't drive away, whoever you are, she thought. UPS, FedEx, distant relatives. Stay in the drive.

She lifted the glass without a struggle. The window squeaked slightly, as if relaxing, as if it had wanted to be open. And the iron pins that trapped the outside shutters — they slid up as if just greased. The shutters, too, yearned to swing open.

Throwing them apart, Althea leaned out the window for the second time that day . . .

. . . and it was Ryan.

He's the one to whom the dark is a friend, thought Althea. And now he has saved me from the dark.

Sunshine poured over her, like orange juice from a pitcher. She bathed in its warm yellow liquid. It was so welcome, so delightful, Althea felt as if she could get quite a tan, even though it was winter. She smiled at the sun, and then she laughed, and the vampire was driven away.

"Hey, Althea!" Ryan yelled.

Wait, she thought, don't talk to me yet; I almost understood. It crept partly into my mind. What was it? What did I half know about the vampire and about me?

"Ryan! What are you doing here? I'm so glad to see you!"

"I was just driving by, and I felt this overpowering desire to stop in. You know how it is."

No, I don't know, thought Althea. What overpowered him? What desire was it? "What car are you driving?" she yelled. "It looks like a car with four working doors."

"My father's. I'm running an errand for him. I'm supposed to be getting sandpaper from the hardware store."

"You're miles from a hardware store," she said. I've lost it, she thought. Whatever I nearly understood, I've lost.

"Yup. I'm taking advantage. When you have a car, you have to do your own errands as well. You're in the tower room! Can I come up? I'm dying to see that room."

Not a good choice of words. She shook her head. "Stay there, Ryan."

"Aw, come on, Althea. Why are you so stingy with visiting hours?" He had to shade his eyes to see her.

Stay in the sun, she thought. It's safe in the sun. "It's not night, and you don't have your telescope."

"I always have my telescope!" yelled Ryan, brandishing it. He was not wearing a jacket, although it was cold. She imagined that she could see his muscles under the dark crimson sweater that covered his arms.

Muscles, she thought. What door could stand up to Ryan? He could probably break a lock by turning the handle.

"The sun is shining too brightly, Ryan," she said. "You won't see any stars."

"But I can get oriented," he said, "and figure out what I'm going to see when I do see it."

He could close the shutters.

That was the answer. Together they would shut the vampire out forever. Or in. Whichever it was. What if I do it wrong? thought Althea. What if I accidentally lock the vampire out of doors forever? And he's free to attack forever? I don't know which side of the shutters he has to be on!

The sun vanished beneath a cloud.

The smile on her face was replaced by fear.

The temperature of the wind and the world was lower.

It's dark in this room, she thought, and I have my back to a vampire. "Ryan!" she screamed.

"Haven't gone anywhere," he said, grinning upward.

"Turn on your car radio. Dance for me."

"Do what? Come again?"

"Turn on your car radio! Hard rock! Rap! Techno! Something that hurts the ears."

Ryan was affronted. "It doesn't hurt my ears," he told her. "I love that kind of music."

"Good. Turn it up all the way."

Ryan bent over and leaned inside his father's car, turning the key halfway to get battery power, and the radio surrounded Ryan in a mist of throbbing drums and pounding rap.

Music to scare vampires by, she thought.

Ryan obeyed her. He was dancing. She loved watching him. He hardly moved his feet, but his hips swayed. "Either I get to come up, or you have to come down," screamed Ryan over the blaring music.

We've never danced together, she thought. We'll dance, Ryan and I. We'll dance tonight, and we'll dance tomorrow, and we'll dance our lives away.

"I'll come down," she yelled to Ryan, and knew that she could. The door would open easily when she touched it. She was not trapped; perhaps she never had been, except by her own fear.

She walked out of the tower room and held its door open and looked back in at the grimy shutters and the window she had left open. Wind and rain would come in now, too. But that was all right. Wind and rain were friends, like the dark.

In the hall, under the lamp, she said to the vampire, "So there." She could not see him or smell him, but she knew he was around.

His voice materialized, but not his form. "So you're going dancing?" said the vampire. "Just don't forget who gave you the chance to dance. You owe me."

"I owe you nothing. You took more than you should have."

Althea continued on out of the house, across the porch, down the stairs, and over the gravel. Ryan was still dancing. When Althea reached him, he took her hands and they danced together. Her dancing style was completely different; she flung herself forward, flung herself back, and launched toward him again. They laughed and the music screamed, and he said, "I want to see your tower room."

"No. It really is haunted, and you can't go up there."

Ryan's face split in a delighted grin. "But you can go up? The haunt doesn't bother you?"

"It bothers me on a daily basis."

"Tell you what. I'll go up there and beat it to death."

"Tell you what. We'll drive to Pizza Hut and see everybody."

"Okay. I'm an agreeable-type person."

Ryan finished his dance and slipped into the driver's seat.

Althea finished her dance, circled the car, and put her hand on the shiny chrome handle of the passenger door.

"I like this car," said the vampire conversationally. "Bloodred. It's a nice color."

"Go away," she whispered.

"You want to dance with Ryan?" the vampire whispered back. "Fine. Dance. But every dance is a debt to me."

Chapter 21

Becky was at Pizza Hut!

Althea vibrated like a guitar string. How had this happened? "Becky," cried Althea, "I thought — I mean, when I left this morning, you were — um —"

"Sick as a dog," said Becky cheerfully. "I was whipped."

Althea's head was whirling. She felt like a one-woman roller coaster.

"What do you think was wrong?" asked Kimmie-Jo.

"I don't know, but I had to get well," said Becky simply. "Next weekend is the biggest game of the season, and I'm the one that you and Dusty are throwing into the air and catching during the halftime routine. How could I ruin it by coming down with some dumb flu?"

Ryan said, "It was probably too damp and chilly last night in your yard. We shouldn't have gone outside."

Althea's whole soul felt damp and chilly.

Becky said, "Know what? I swear, when I was dancing around trying to get Althea to come out, the shadows felt like liquid moss."

Kimmie-Jo screamed. "That's so scary," Kimmie-Jo whispered. "Green, wet, shadowy stuff closing in on you?"

I foiled him! thought Althea, exulting. I got her inside before anything happened! I am a match for that vampire!

Becky said, "My mother thinks it's overwork. You wouldn't believe how she carried on. Too much homework, too many papers, too much cheerleading practice, too many hours on the telephone."

Kimmie-Jo nodded. "Probably those hours on the phone. Have some nice nutritious snacks while the other person's talking, to keep your strength up. Cookies or brownies. Then you'll be fine."

Kimmie-Jo seemed completely serious.

"In my family," said Becky, "a nutritious snack is a banana or an apple."

Kimmie-Jo was appalled. "I don't do fruit," she said. "Or vegetables, either."

"But do you do pizza?" said Ryan. "Pizza is always the final solution."

They all cheered for pizza. Althea cheered loudest and longest and she thought: I won. How intrepid I am! I got out of the tower room in spite of the vampire. I saved Becky after all. What power I have. How incredible I am!

Somebody put coins in the jukebox.

"They're playing 'Yellow Fever'" moaned Ryan, as if he had it. "It's my favorite song this week. Althea, dance with me."

"You can't dance in Pizza Hut," said Althea.

"Why not? They put music on, don't they? Do they expect us just to sit here? Of course not." Ryan stood up. Held out his hand.

Before I was popular, thought Althea, I would never have done this. I would have felt like a weirdo and a jerk. I would have been embarrassed. I would have died first.

She and Ryan began dancing between the dark glossy tables while other patrons laughed and watched. She began showing off, which was not natural to her. Ryan was a born show-off.

No, she thought, it's that he was born popular. Popularity all your life makes it possible to dance in the aisles.

Her eyes examined every patron in the restaurant. She saw that popularity, or lack of it, knew no age barrier. There was a little girl, maybe six years old, dancing next to her parents, and that little girl was blond and beautiful, and Althea knew this girl's destiny was to be popular. At another table, children stared enviously but never dreamed of leaving their seats. Two elderly women, alone with their gray hair and wrinkled hands, watched Althea with such sadness that Althea knew they were not remembering their youth when they danced with abandon; they were remembering a youth in which nobody asked them to dance.

I, thought Althea fiercely, will be the one who dances, not the one who yearns. I'm sorry about Celeste and Jennie, but I won't let that happen again, and I'm not giving up what I have.

So there, vampire!

The football team sat in the front of the bus. Every boy wore a jacket and tie and looked both distinguished and uncomfortable.

Ryan's energy overflowed. Twisting in his seat, Ryan yelled back to Althea, lustily sang verses of bus songs, and threw paper airplanes at the coach.

"Ryan," the coach kept saying tiredly, "save it for the game."

"I have more than the game needs."

"Say that when we've won," said the coach.

Althea loved watching the boys when they were apprehensive. Somehow boys never looked as if they got scared. Certainly not football players. It was rather satisfying to know that, yes, they, too, got anxious and tense and tied in knots.

Michael, the best of them, the most athletic, the most capable, was certainly the most nervous.

Since it was an away game, a whole new school's worth of girls would shortly see Michael for the first time. Althea knew well how their eyes would caress and memorize him.

I've always wanted Michael, thought Althea, but now I don't. Isn't that amazing? Michael is such perfection: Every inch of him is splendid. I have had Michael memorized for years. I'll keep him tucked in my mind, something to observe and admire. But not to have.

I like it that he and Constance are a pair.

She looked out the back of the bus. The fan bus was behind them, and she knew Constance was on it; she knew Constance would sit directly behind the cheerleaders, four bleachers up, so that the cheerleaders did not block her view of Michael playing, but so she was still in the thick of the action.

Ryan sent Althea a paper airplane and she sent it back.

How lovely popularity is, Althea thought. It give you choices. If you don't feel like talking, nobody thinks it's because you're such a loser nobody would talk to you, anyway.

You can sort through the boys and girls around you and pick exactly who you want. And with popularity, you have time to know what you want. You aren't taking the dregs or the leftovers. You have the winners, and it's a matter of choosing your own particular winner.

Ryan and two other boys began throwing a pair of sneakers around. The bus driver and the coach yelled, and momentarily the bus stopped by the side of the road while Ryan was informed that responsible young men his age did not behave like that. Ryan seemed interested, but it did not affect him particularly, and the moment the bus was back in traffic, the sneakers were back in the air.

I love him, thought Althea.

The sentence was astounding.

She felt that she must have shouted it out loud, turned it into a cheerleader's cheer, and done it to claps and jumps.

But nobody was looking at her. Not even Ryan.

I love him.

He's mine, and I love him.

O! the life that had been so dark and dreary. Only weeks later, and Althea's life sparkled and glittered like a tiara at a royal dance. She felt that she was composed of diamonds and emeralds, and that Ryan was rubies and sapphires.

Her imagination ran into the future of high school, coursing through dances and yearbooks, committees and clubs. She saw herself with Ryan, wearing jeans and prom gowns, short skirts and Halloween costumes. She saw herself in the cafeteria and the front lobby and the art rooms and at graduation.

Popular.

The boys got off the bus in a unit, sternly ordered (in fact, rudely ordered; the coach had a limited vocabulary and used it often) not to distract themselves by looking at girls. Ryan said, "I'm not going to look at *girls*. I'm just going to look at one. Althea."

He grinned at her, and she laughed back, and the entire cheerleading squad circled her, whispering and giggling and delighted and envious.

Popular.

The game was long and difficult. Once Ryan

was thrown into the mud where he lay twisted and motionless. The coach and the ref ran out to him. But he got up, limped briefly, and was fine. Althea breathed again.

Michael was brilliant.

The sky was blue, the stands packed. The fans had stadium blankets over their legs and scarves around their throats. Pom-poms rustled, and hands clap-clap-clapped. The smell of hot dogs and popcorn filled the air.

Mrs. Roundman said, "You have the right spirit for cheerleading, Althea. That smile never leaves your face. That laugh is so infectious. I would not be surprised if you become captain. You have what it takes."

Chapter 22

The vampire did not appear that night.

He did not appear the following night, nor the night after that.

I got rid of him, thought Althea. I really did it. Oh, wow! I didn't even have to shut the shutters all the way. I just had to get powerful and knock him off the planet.

Althea swaggered a little, laughed some, paraded through the house, and circled the yard, kicking autumn leaves. No laughter like broken glass shattered the peaceful night. Her breath swirled like a dragon's in the cold winter air.

She spent a night at Kimmie-Jo's and went to a party at Dusty's. She and Ryan went to a movie alone together, and another night went with Michael and Constance.

Constance was such a wonderful person. Althea decided to model herself on Constance.

Homework was easy. Quizzes a snap. Teachers admired every word Althea contributed to discussions. Younger girls chose Althea as their favorite cheerleader, and the team won the next game.

The first snow fell.

The dark bleak valley where Althea's house lay turned sparkling white — pure as true love.

She swept the porch and the steps. The snow was dry and tossed in the air like miniature blizzards. The wind blew it back in her face, and she laughed with the joy of living.

It was a night without stars or moon. It was very, very cold.

Ryan, Michael, and Constance dropped her off, and Ryan kissed her good-bye even in front of the others, and Constance said, "See you tomorrow, Althea." Michael tapped his horn good-bye.

Althea stood on the bottom step watching the red glow of their car lights disappear behind the hedge. Ryan was right, she thought. The dark is a friend. When you have friends like I do — like Constance, and Michael, and Ryan, and Becky, and all the rest — all the world is a friend, too.

Through the night came a laugh like sandpaper scraping over skin.

The vampire did not go through the crust. He walked over it, leaving no footprints. The winter wind grabbed his black cape and flung it around him one way and then another, so that he kept wrapping and unwrapping.

The only things that gleamed in the dark night were his eyes and his fingernails. She knew that when he smiled, his teeth would also shine. The crisp clean air turned foul.

The silent night filled with the creaking of shutters, as if they were craning their necks to see the action.

When she shifted position, the snow crackled beneath her boots, as if something were chewing on her ankles.

She was cold, terribly cold, right to the marrow of her bones.

But she said, "I thought you left."

"Briefly. Now I'm back."

"I don't need you," she said. "Go away and stay away."

The vampire stared at her. His jaw dropped in disbelief, and for the first time she saw his tongue. It was pointed and curled up as if rolled in a can. Then he laughed. The pitch of laughter broke the ice that lined the bare branches; the ice fell into the snow below. He said, "You don't need me, Althea? Think again."

She said, "I have thought. And I don't need you. And I won't cater to you. I'm too strong for you, anyhow. I kept Becky safe."

He took a step toward her. She stood her ground. He stank of rot and decay. She gagged. He took another step, and she could not be that close to him. She backed up, and he laughed again. He moved closer to her, she backed up again, he moved again.

"Get away from me," she said fiercely.

"No."

The single syllable was uttered softly this time, and almost regretfully, as if something were about to happen that even the vampire would not enjoy.

This time she dug her boots into the snow and did not let herself back up any more. "I will never again do anything you ask," she said.

He raised his eyebrows. He sucked in his lower lip. The long white teeth inched down toward his chin. They glittered like icicles. They dripped as if melting.

The vampire said, "All right."

To show him that she was completely in control, Althea turned her back. She walked slowly into the house. She shut the door firmly but without slamming it, leaving him in the yard.

She unlaced her boots, knocked the snow off them, and set them on the drying rack.

She unzipped her heavy jacket and hung it in the coat closet.

She took off her scarf, shook the snow away, and looped it around the hanger of her jacket.

The vampire said, "But it will not be all right with you."

Her head jerked up. He was standing on the first step of the stairs. His cape flared out by itself, as if pinned to the walls.

The vampire said, "Go to school tomorrow, Althea. Without me. And see if it is all right. See if you need me. See how strong you are. See if you need to cater to my requests."

She glared at him. "I saved Becky."

"No. The location was too far. My dark path was weak. I could not complete the migration. You had nothing to do with it. Nor did Becky. It was simply an error in navigation and planning."

"You're boring me," said Althea. She thought, I'll just learn to live with it. He'll come by and nag, I'll walk around him holding my breath. Eventually he'll get bored and go back where he came from.

"No," said the vampire. "I am rarely bored. Nor will I go back where I came from. You, Althea, are the one who will go back where she came from. Go back to being invisible. Inaudible. Unloved. Unpopular."

She shrugged.

"Even Ryan will not know your name," said the vampire.

"Get lost," said Althea.

Now he smiled. A smile of joy. The evil crescent covered the entire bottom of his face. "All right. I will get lost. And when you want me back, Althea . . . I may refuse to come."

Chapter 23

In the morning, her car did not start.

Walking was so humiliating. If you couldn't be popular, you should at least have transportation.

But I am popular, thought Althea, smiling. She telephoned Ryan to ask him to ask Michael to stop and pick her up. But Ryan had already left for school.

All right, she told herself. I can walk. One of my friends will see me and stop and pick me up. I'll get teased, but that's okay.

Althea walked to school, up the long, long hill, facing traffic. The cars of high school kids passed her, but no one stopped to give her a ride. No one waved. No one rolled down a window to yell good morning.

The temperature had risen, and the crusty snow had turned to slush. Cars flung black filth on her clothing. Althea stepped in an ice puddle and her boots must have had leaks, because her feet were soaked and painfully cold.

Althea cared deeply about her appearance. She hated people seeing her dirty and wet. I don't even have a car so I can go home and change! she thought.

I'll ask Ryan to borrow Michael's car and take me home, she decided. Or maybe Kimmie-Jo would. Nobody understands the importance of pretty clothes more than Kimmie-Jo.

But nobody noticed the mud on Althea's clothes.

Nobody noticed Althea at all.

Nobody called her name; nobody ran over; nobody registered the fact that she had walked into the school.

Althea went into the girls' room, brushed her hair, and straightened herself up as much as possible. She headed slowly to her locker to hang up her coat, mittens, and scarf.

She was overjoyed to hear her name and turned, laughing, terribly relieved, to see who was calling her.

Nobody was calling her. Two Junior Varsity cheerleaders were striding along behind her. "At least the new season is beginning," said one, giving Althea a look of loathing. "Tryouts for basketball squad will be fair. Unlike the last tryouts."

Althea lost her breath, as if someone had beaten her up. She whispered, "It was fair. I won it."

"It was given to you," said the JV girl. "What experience or background did you have? Huh? Tell me."

"Mrs. Roundman was playing favorites," said the other.

The girls had matching smirks: ugly cruel grasping faces trying to wipe her out of her cheerleading spot.

Althea's cheeks were cherry-red. "May the best one of us make the squad," she said, trying to be a sportswoman.

The girls laughed viciously. "That lets you out. You were no competition for Celeste. And you're no competition for us, either."

Althea clung to her locker, facing the thin metal closet, waiting for the JV girls to pass on. She pressed her hand against the gray door.

A gruesome chill crept up her spine.

How long her fingernails had become. The nails were scarlet and extremely pointed. They were claws. They were inhuman.

Heart pounding, Althea dropped her coat and scarf and dug through her purse to locate an emery board. What could I have been doing to let them get like that? she thought. They looked evil.

And that polish? Althea liked clear polish, or pale pink and slightly glittery. This polish was bloodred.

She could not think clearly. Far from being drained of blood, Althea felt that she had too much. Gallons of blood pounding, throbbing, racing through her veins. Her pulse snapped like drum rims.

The emery board had no effect on the scarlet weapons at the tips of her fingers.

The nails stayed sharp and pointed and . . . toothlike.

Have I become a vampire? With my hands I turned Celeste and Jennie over, and on my hands you can see the proof.

She curled her fingers into fists to hide the evil nails.

A dozen lockers away Becky chattered with Dusty. "I'm really excited about the tryouts, aren't you?" said Becky. "It's always fun to beat the competition."

"Hi, Becky," Althea called. *She's my best friend,* thought Althea.

Becky looked briefly Althea's way. "Hi," she said without enthusiasm.

Dusty said, "This time we'll get a real cheerleader. It's too bad Celeste is still feeling low. I'd like to see her back. She was fun."

"Didn't we have a great team last fall?" Becky agreed.

Althea struggled with the lock. What was the combination, anyway? She opened her English notebook to the front page where she had scribbled it down on the first day of school. She could hardly remember right from left to make the silly thing turn.

Dusty said, "People who can't even open their lockers are hardly Varsity material."

Althea quivered as if she were Jell-O and somebody had touched her with a spoon. "Becky?" she whispered. "Becky, please — I —"

"Althea," said Becky irritably, "later, okay? I'm busy."

Becky walked away.

No! cried Althea in her heart, in her soul. No! Becky is my friend!

Althea focused on hanging up her coat. She achieved it. She focused on putting her scarf and mittens on the little shelf. She chose the right books to get her through the morning. She said to herself, Becky's moody. It doesn't actually mean anything. I'm okay. It's all still okay.

She wet her lips and took a desperate breath, quieting her fears.

Down the hall came Ryan.

She expanded like a flower in the morning sun: All that was within her turned golden, and when she spoke his name, the syllables were a song of love. Smiles decorated Althea's soul. Joy trembled on her fingertips.

"Hi, Ryan," she said. "I tried to phone you this morning. But you'd already left. I needed you." She laughed a little. Just seeing him made her so happy she had to laugh.

Ryan frowned, as if unsure why she looked familiar. He said, dutifully, as one acknowledging last year's teacher, "Hey, how are you, Althea." It was not a question. It was an anonymous greeting.

He did not care how she was and did not expect her to answer.

"Not too good," she said desperately. "Ryan, I —"

"See you around," said Ryan meaninglessly.

She had turned back into the boring sophomore with the forgettable face and the blank life. Pain like bread knives with serrated edges sawed through Althea's heart.

He walked on and was gone, and the hall was empty.

Life was empty.

She had never believed that *all* her popularity was the gift of a vampire. She would have the popularity she had earned on her own.

But she had been wrong.

She had nothing because she had never been anything. She was just a creation of the vampire.

She thought of skipping class.

She thought of quitting school.

But then she would have to do something else, and what would that be? There were no other lives out there for her. She would have to stagger on through this one.

Althea walked on through the halls, which seemed to widen and lengthen, like a trick to test her commitment to staying alive. She passed the athletic department, and on the wall outside Mrs. Roundman's office was a large sheet of yellow paper with a miniature cheerleading outfit and pompoms tacked to it.

VARSITY CHEERLEADING TRYOUTS
BASKETBALL SEASON
SIGN-UP SHEET

Althea studied the names. She knew them all. There were three times as many as there were positions on the squad. This time there would be real competition. And the girls who had complained that Althea's tryout had been rigged — well, as it turned out, they were proved right, and now had a chance at a fair tryout.

She had pencils in her purse. She could add her name to the list. But why? She could never win on her own. And if she went, she would have to face Becky, and Kimmie-Jo, and Dusty, who would ignore her, or avoid her, or say vaguely, "What's your name?"

And what is my name now? thought Althea. When nobody knows and nobody cares, perhaps you don't actually have a name.

Eventually the morning passed. Eventually the clock turned and it was twelve noon, and time for lunch. Althea was silent amid the screaming hungry students. Althea was slow amid the racing feet of starving sophomores.

She reached the cafeteria last.

All the lines were long.

All the tables were packed.

Except one.

Celeste hunched over a sandwich she was not eating.

Jennie stared down into macaroni casserole she was not touching.

Celeste's eyes were cloudy like an old woman's cataracts.

Jennie's hair, faded and lusterless, fell in her face.

They were at the same table, separated by one chair, unaware of each other.

The chair beckoned to Althea.

Here's your place, whispered the chair. *Here at the table for outcasts. For nobodies.*

Althea tried to leave the cafeteria, but a group of kids came in behind her, and she was tossed forward, like a duck on an ocean wave, closer and closer to the horrible shore of that chair.

Come, said the chair, *sit. You earned this chair.*

Come.

Sit.

Be alone.

Forever.

Chapter 24

Snow has beauty. No matter how deep and troublesome, snow is a blanket of loveliness over a harsh world.

But instead of snow came sleet. Ice-laden rain that pelted down on a slippery gray world. The sky was blotted out.

Kimmie-Jo loaded her car with friends and headed for Pizza Hut. Ryan, Michael, and Constance got in Michael's car. Constance sat in front, between the two boys.

Not one of them called Althea's name.

She walked home in the sleet. Wet ice penetrated her scarf and soaked through her mittens. It was downhill. Twice she lost her balance, slipped, and fell. On the second fall, she tore the knee out of her pants, and her English notebook fell in an ice puddle. The ink ran. The notes were ruined. She sobbed, but no one glanced out of a car window to see.

The towering hemlock hedge around her house

was heavy and sagging with old snow and new ice. Tires from passing cars had flung up grime, so each branch was ugly and stained, like rust.

Althea slipped again on the porch steps. This time when she got up her ankle hurt. She had to haul herself indoors by hanging on to the railing.

I can't try out for cheerleading now, anyway, she thought. My ankle can't bear my weight.

She pulled off her wet clothes and took a long hot bath, surrounding herself with bubbles and perfumes. She wrapped herself in a satiny robe with ivory lace and tucked her feet in soft slippers.

I was going to be captain, she thought. Mrs. Roundman said so. My future is over before it began. My friends have vanished before I even memorized their phone numbers. My cheerleading uniform will be given to another girl, and nobody will remember I was ever on the squad.

She tried to comfort herself with food, but there were no snacks in the house that she could possibly have swallowed. She turned on the television but the laughter hurt her ears. The talk shows were too bright and chatty.

She stood alone in a huge house in a dark valley during a storm.

The phone did not ring.

Other people were gathering for pizza and Cokes. Other people had friends. Other people mattered.

I have algebra to do, she thought. I have to have supper and study for a history test. How can it be that I have a load of laundry waiting? How can it be that I have to open a book, turn a page, sharpen a pencil?

She cried for a long time. She did not feel better. It did not change anything. It just made her eyes red and her head ache.

She went to bed early. There was nothing else to do.

In her dreams a computer tapped out her death knell. Unseen fingers endlessly typed the closing sentences on Althea. The entire world was clicking, tapping, typing. Althea is over, Althea is over, Althea is over.

Althea woke up, cheeks wet with tears, hugging the pillows, because there were no warm bodies to hug and never would be again.

The vampire continued to tap his fingernails on the foot of her bed. The hollow iron frame vibrated with each click. His fingernails were tarnished and yellowy, like teeth that needed brushing. Althea, shivering beneath a stack of heavy wool blankets, wept again.

"You don't have to be alone," said the vampire. His voice was rich and contented, like cream soup.

Or blood.

She looked at him through her tears. He was not wearing his cape. He seemed almost not there; he was mostly voice and fingernails.

Where's the rest of him? she thought, swiveling eyes and head like an owl, afraid to turn her back, but needing to locate the enemy.

"I'm sorry you had to suffer today," said the vampire. "Sometimes lessons are painful to learn. Have you learned your lesson, Althea?" the vampire asked.

She held the pillow in the air between them.

"You may have it back now, if you're a good girl," said the vampire.

"Have what back?" said Althea weakly.

His voice whispered through the room like a cat purring. "Popularity," he breathed. The cape appeared. It leaned past the vampire's shoulders toward Althea, and this time its edges were velvet and rich.

"No," she said. The velvet cape settled on the edge of the bed and tucked its edges around her feet to warm them.

"You must keep Becky," the vampire said. "You need a friend. Becky will be your friend."

Oh, to have Becky back as a friend! To have the phone ring, laughter ring, a friend's voice ring!

Althea buried her face in the pillow.

"You give me Constance," said the vampire. His cape was as furry as a teddy bear. *Wear me,* it said silently.

Althea pulled her feet up closer to her chest and tucked herself into a little round ball, as far from the cape and the vampire as she could get.

"Constance," repeated the vampire.

Give him Constance? Who was perfect? Who was right for Michael? Who with Michael made a couple she loved?

"You'll make the basketball squad," said the vampire. "You'll be busy and happy, surrounded by friends."

Constance?

"Ryan will be waiting for you after tryouts," said the vampire. "He feels terrible that he was rude today. He cannot imagine why he acted like that."

She had no lights turned on, and yet the bedroom had a strange sheen. Pink walls, peach carpet, quilted chair — all glowed.

"A new captain will have to be elected," whispered the vampire.

She trembled.

"The most popular girl is always chosen captain," whispered the vampire. "You will be the most popular girl."

She stared at the lace edge on the pillowcase. How pretty it was. How fragile and how feminine. She touched it with her fingers. Her cruel scarlet talons nearly tore the lace. She pushed them back under the blankets. I want ordinary fingernails, she thought. Soft, rounded, pink nails.

"I would never make another request after Constance," said the vampire silkily. "You need only bring Constance into my dark path."

She would be popular again. A cheerleader again. Have friends again. Have Ryan again.

"Only Constance?" she whispered.

Their voices matched: airy and bodiless. Light

and frothy. As if they were talking of nothing. Just feathers and dust.

"Constance," he repeated. The vampire smiled. She found that she had become accustomed to his smile. There was a certain symmetry to the way his teeth lined up that other smiles did not share.

"Never anybody else?" she whispered.

"Of course not," he assured her.

She laughed bitterly. "You're lying."

He smiled. His teeth chattered. They pecked at his lip like the beaks of birds. The teeth clicked up and down; his fingernails clicked up and down; and the typing typed out, *Second chance, Althea, second chance! Just Constance, just Constance!*

"I won't be back again," said the vampire. The cape slithered off her bed. "Either you take this chance, Althea, or you do not. Either you are popular again, or you are not. It's quite simple, really." The cape tightened around the vampire like a cocoon shutting in a dying butterfly. "Now get a good night's sleep, Althea. Tomorrow is an important day for you."

She shut her eyes.

When she opened them he was gone.

She was alone.

And that was the decision, really. Not Constance. But whether she could stand to be alone for the rest of her high school life. Unloved. Unwanted. Unspoken to.

Chapter 25

Her car still would not start. But she had scarcely reached the sidewalk when Kimmie-Jo honked a horn, pulled over, and shrieked, "Althea! You can't walk in this weather! Get in! Why didn't you call me and say you needed a ride? You silly. You'll catch cold."

Althea rode to school with the captain of the cheerleading squad. Kimmie-Jo talked of boys and cheers, got the best parking space in the student lot, and danced alongside Althea as they entered the lobby. "I just love it that you're going with Ryan," she confided. "You and Ryan, and Constance and Michael, you're such adorable couples! The whole school is crazy jealous of you, Althea."

Some girl changing the Artwork of the Week shouted, "Hi, Althea!"

Some boy pushing a cart of audiovisual equipment said shyly, "Hi, Althea, how are you?"

Becky bounded over. "Althea, are you ever going to forgive me?" she said.

"For what?" said Althea, smiling. How pretty Becky was! How cute and bunny-rabbitlike she looked, her nose twitching in anxiety.

"For being nasty yesterday," said Becky, hanging her head. The ponytail fell sadly on her shoulder. "I don't know what came over me! I sat there at Pizza Hut and felt like the creep of the century. Don't be mad."

"I'm not mad," said Althea. "We're friends." *You need a friend. Becky will be your friend.* I have her for good, thought Althea. She will always be my friend.

Becky said, "Ryan won't see you till fifth period, so he asked me to give you this note." It was a sheet of notebook paper folded six times, until it was a fat cube the size of a thumb. *Yesterday was out of control. Sorry. Really, really, really sorry. Are we still friends? Love, Ryan.*

Kimmie-Jo said, "I love notes. I see Ryan next period, Althea. I'll take the answer to him. No fair folding it up so I can't read it."

They all laughed. Althea wrote with a great flourish, *Friends forever. Love, Althea.*

School flew by. Never had those fifty-minute class hours seemed so short. Never had lunch been such fun.

Ryan sat with her, of course. Settled down very close, so her wool skirt rubbed against his corduroy pants. His bright eyes were only inches from hers. He said, "I didn't know how much fun it is to be with you till yesterday when you weren't around." He blushed. He said, "I'm not letting that happen again."

Outside, the sky lightened and turned blue again, and the sun actually shone, melting the snow that had sealed the skylights. Yellow and gold filtered through. Ryan asked her to go with him to the Winter Formal.

Nobody had ever asked her to a dance before.

Michael said, "Constance and I are going, of course. Let's the four of us go together. Would you like to do that, Althea? Maybe we could have dinner out before the dance. Constance loves elegant restaurants. She'll go anywhere if she can get really dressed up."

Two tables away, Jennie sat alone, pushing macaroni around on a lunch plate until it turned cold. Celeste tried to sit with old friends, but they scorned her, elbowed her away, and Celeste, sad and limp, sat with Jennie after all.

Althea averted her eyes.

After school, at her locker, Ryan, Michael, Dusty, Kimmie-Jo, and Becky gathered. There was a heavy argument going because some people did not want pizza today, but were in hamburger moods. There was even a holdout for fried chicken.

"You decide, Althea," said Michael. "We'll follow you."

The boys stood on each side of her. Althea drank in their good looks, their smiles, their attention. My locker, she thought. My locker is where the best people meet.

Ordinary kids slipped by, pressed against the far wall, so as not to disturb the popular crowd. Some kept their heads low, to avoid notice; others were brave and stared longingly at Althea and her friends.

Celeste was in the first group.

Celeste paused to rest, leaning against the wall. She did not look as if she remembered the cheerleading crowd, and they certainly took no notice of her. Celeste fastened her eyes at the far end of the hall, planning the long journey. She picked up first one foot, and then the other, trudging on.

Constance flew toward them.

Everybody shouted, "You're late, Constance! Where've you been?"

Michael held out his right hand and still running, she clasped it, so that they both swung a few feet, till her momentum was stopped. Then they smiled secrets into each other's eyes and laughed a little.

Althea's hands turned as cold as deep water in ancient lakes.

"Hi, Althea," said Constance, smiling warmly. "We missed you yesterday."

Althea's nerves felt as if somebody were stitching needles through her skin. "Thank you," she said.

"You know what?" said Constance.

"What?" said Althea. She was out of breath. Her lungs had shrunk. She could not squeeze another molecule of air into them.

Constance put her arm around Althea's waist and gave her a slight squeeze. "You add so much when you're around, Althea."

Somehow the four of them were walking together in one straight line: Michael, Constance, Althea, Ryan. Althea felt like royalty. As the foursome passed, heads turned. People stopped talking, turning, or lockering, and feasted their eyes on the two couples.

Constance said, "Do we have to join everybody else again today? Sometimes I get so tired of the crowd. Let's go somewhere, just the four of us, and get to know one another better." She smiled, just for Althea.

It's me she wants to get to know better, thought Althea. She wants us to be friends.

"I'm still waiting to be allowed to use my telescope in your tower room, Althea," said Ryan. His hand left hers briefly to touch her hair. He seemed almost in possession, as if it were his hair now.

They reached Michael's car. Michael and Constance sat in front. Ryan and Althea sat in back.

"Well?" said Michael, turning the key in the ignition. "Where are we going? Up to you, Althea. What's your command?"

Don't do it, she said to herself. Remember Jennie and Celeste. How pitiful they are. Don't do that to Constance! She's a nice person. She wants to be your friend. Don't do it to Michael! He loves Constance. There won't be a Constance left to love if you bring her into the dark path.

But I have to, she thought. I can't have a life as lonely and worthless and dreary as last night. As the first year of high school. Nobody deserves that kind of life! I deserve friends and happiness!

"I have to make a turn at that red light," said Michael, tossing a smile back over the seat to Althea. "So you have to issue instructions before then."

If you give him Constance, you'll have betrayed a third friend!

If you don't give him Constance, you'll never have a friend again.

Althea hung tightly to Ryan's hand. She said, "Let's go over to my house. There's plenty to do there. Plenty to eat."

"And tower rooms to go in," said Ryan, delighted, squeezing her hand back.

"And tower rooms to go in," said Althea.

Constance clapped her hands. "I missed your party," she said, "and I felt so left out. Do I get to go up in the tower, too?"

"Of course," said Althea.

Chapter 26

The valley road was as low and empty as a back alley. No cars except Michael's passed through its darkness. "It's always winter on this part of the road," said Constance uneasily. She shifted position in the front seat, playing with the shoulder belt.

"What's the matter?" Michael asked her.

"It's spooky." Constance was shivering. "Aren't you ever afraid, Althea?" Constance pulled her coat around herself and buttoned the toggles.

She feels it, thought Althea. The dark path has already touched her, and somehow she knows something is wrong. She's trying to protect herself.

Constance said, "The hemlocks circle the house, don't they? Like a castle gate." Constance tried to laugh. She pointed toward the outer edge of hemlocks, which formed a dark needled tower of their own.

"Double towers," said Ryan, grinning. Nothing

had touched him. There was nothing out there but boring old trees.

"The tips of the hemlocks are waving at me," said Constance.

Michael said, "Constance, you're not usually so poetic. Next you're going to tell me you see ghosts flitting in the shadows." The boys laughed.

Constance said, "I do see something."

"It's the wind," said Ryan.

"If I lived here," said Constance, "I'd be afraid of everything always."

They were half a block from the blackness of loneliness that would enclose Constance forever once she left this bright and shining car.

Constance won't be the last one, thought Althea. The vampire was lying. He'll have to have more. I'll have to give them to him. That will be my life. Choosing his next victim. That will be who I am. The vampire's procurer.

She sank back into Ryan's arms, trying to find comfort.

But there was no hiding from the decisions she had made.

All I wanted was to be a cheerleader! To have the phone ring! To have friends! Was that so terrible? Was I so wrong?

They were only a car length away from her driveway. The cruel green hemlocks had reached down to meet them. The branches seemed to curl their tips in greeting.

It *was* terrible, she thought. I *was* wrong.

Her heart had enlarged. It was bursting with pain. She tried to hate the vampire. But the vampire was not half so important as she was. She hated herself.

I am loathsome. Human beings do not do to one another what I have done.

Even if I save Constance, that won't balance it out. Because I can never save Jennie or Celeste. They're gone. So what's the point in ruining everything? I paid so much to purchase popularity!

You can't un-pay, thought Althea. When you've done a terrible thing, it's there, forever and ever.

Since that's true, why shouldn't I keep my popularity forever and ever? What difference would it make to Jennie and Celeste?

Constance began twining a lock of hair in and around her fingers, nervously looking out into the shadows.

It would make a difference to Constance, thought Althea.

Althea thought of lonely cafeterias and silent phones.

She said calmly, "Turn around, Michael."

"Huh?" Michael kept on driving.

"I'm starving. Let's get pizza after all," explained Althea.

"I've bought you plenty of pizza," protested Ryan. "You owe me a tower."

"No," said Althea. "Don't go in my driveway, Michael."

It was too late. Michael had already turned into the driveway.

"Back up!" screamed Althea. She leaned over the seat and took hold of Michael's shoulders and shook him. "Get out of here!"

Michael stopped the car, rear wheels in the street, front wheels in the driveway. Hemlocks reached down all around them, trying to move them forward, coaxing them another few feet.

"Althea, you're so sweet," said Constance. "I'm being silly, afraid of a dumb old hedge. It's okay, Althea. I want to go to your house. Really. Don't pay any attention to me." Constance tapped the steering wheel. "Drive on in, Michael."

"No," whispered Althea. "I'm not inviting you after all."

Michael and Ryan stared at her, appalled. But Constance said, "Let's hop out here. Let's walk the rest of the way." She put her hand on her door handle.

Althea thought of Constance drained and stupid. Of Constance dulled and trudging. She thought of Constance, ignored and unloved.

"No!" screamed Althea. "Don't get out of this car!"

Now she was gripping Constance's coat as well as Michael's.

"This is a wrestling match?" said Michael politely. "Althea, what's the matter with you?"

Ryan said tightly, "She doesn't want me around,

do you, Althea? That's what this is about, isn't it?" His handsome face was marred by hurt and confusion. "You just plain don't want me at your house."

There must be a way to have it all, thought Althea. Surely, I can have friends *and* foil the vampire. There must be a way to hang on to my friends! I'll have thought up some excuse for this by the time we reach Pizza Hut.

"Fine," said Ryan. "You go to your precious tower, Althea. We'll go somewhere else." He yanked Althea's hands off Michael and Constance and leaned across Althea's lap and opened her door. He pointed to the driveway.

Althea laughed hysterically and stepped out of the car. The vampire was going to take away her popularity right now. She would not even get as far as Pizza Hut.

Ryan said to Michael, "So do what the lady says. Back up and drive away." Ryan slammed the door behind her.

Althea stood in the slush. The valley lay chilled and quiet. It was like being in a gutter, with dead leaves and torn newspaper tangling around her ankles.

Michael's car backed up. Michael's car drove away. Constance was safe.

Althea walked to her house without looking back.

The branches of the hemlocks leaned down to meet her, and the dark needles of the hemlocks closed behind her.

Hope was gone.

Chapter 27

Exhaustion unlike anything she had ever known tormented Althea. The steps up the porch were like mountains. The scale of everything had changed: She was a tiny child now, and these were the stairs of a giant.

I did the right thing! she thought, weeping. I saved Constance! Why didn't I get to keep my friends when I was good at last?

The vampire met her on the top step.

The symmetry of his teeth was hypnotic. The points of two of them were as piercing as pencil tips, fresh from the sharpener.

"An interesting choice," said the vampire, his voice as level as a lily pad on still waters. "Your cheerleaders will laugh at you. Your football player will forget you. You do have, you know, a forgettable face."

Althea opened her purse and took out her mirror. In its little square she studied this forgettable part of her body. Although the vampire stood directly behind her, when she tilted the mirror, he did not show in the glass. He has no reflection, she thought. And I, in the morning, will have no reflection, either. Nobody will know my name or face.

"As for me," said the vampire, "I, too, have made a choice."

She closed the plastic cover on the little purse mirror and put it away. There would be no need to use it again; it would never again matter how she looked.

His voice was sticky, like spiderwebs. "You are no longer a match for me, my dear."

I'm his dear, she thought. I catered to him and pandered to him. You know how low you've fallen when you are dear to a vampire.

The vampire touched her chin and lifted her face to look at him. He had never touched her before. It was as spongy as she had expected, as if he were swollen with rot beneath his skin.

"It is time, my dear," said the vampire.

"Time for what?" said Althea dully. She had no time that mattered anymore. Nobody was waiting for her or interested in her.

"For us," said the vampire. He swept his cape around her shoulders, and they walked together in its black velvet. The foul smell of him was intoxicating. She gagged, but she wanted more of it, and she breathed deeply.

He said, "Just a few steps to negotiate, my dear."

She took his hand. His fingernails, wrinkled and tarnished like old foil, glittered against her fair skin.

He said, "I do so love the view from the tower, don't you, my dear?"

She said, "Are you migrating? Is that what is happening?"

"Of course, my dear. You're just going to feel a little tired afterward."

Althea nodded. She said, "I'm not arguing with you. I thought I would argue with you. There was that time I threw chairs at you."

"You welcome my presence. You are eager. You thought you were saving Constance, but that's not really the case. You wanted to be here yourself, Althea. You wanted to be part of the migration."

Althea's mind drifted. "Like robins?" she asked. "Like swallows?"

The vampire smiled. His curly pink tongue ran wetly around his thin lips and stroked his teeth. "Not quite. There, Althea. We've reached the landing. Another few steps and we'll be at the tower door."

The vampire's face was all teeth. Sharpened at the ends like pencils.

"You said you would make me popular," Althea said.

"And you had a good time, didn't you, my dear? Being popular was quite wonderful, wasn't it?"

Althea stumbled.

The vampire said, "This is the last step, Althea."

He drooled over the words. "The very last step you ever have to take," he whispered.

The very last step, thought Althea.

But it's not the last step that matters. It's the first step.

If I had not taken the first step, I would not be here now. I brought him Celeste. It is fitting that I should surrender to him now and become like Celeste and Jennie. I deserve it. "Does our original agreement stand?" asked Althea.

"I suppose it does," said the vampire, "although that hardly matters now. Come, my dear, let's open the tower door together."

"What happens," said Althea, trying to lift her foot up that last step, trying to go with him, "after me?"

"There are others," said the vampire. "Girls who don't matter. Girls without friends. Girls who will do whatever I ask." He smiled hugely. "Girls like you, my dear."

"Who want to be popular?" said Althea.

The vampire nodded and bent over to help lift her foot over the final barrier.

Althea's voice became a whimper. She said, "I want to be popular one more time. Please? Please, please, please?"

The evil crescent of the vampire's smile covered his face.

"Because if I could be popular just one more time . . . " She begged, she groveled, she whined. "I would remember it," she sobbed. "I would frame it in my mind and keep it. I would make it last. Like an ice-cream cone. I would have it slowly. I would know how wonderful it is."

"Like an ice-cream cone," repeated the vampire, laughing. "Licking the edges, trying not to let it drip away from you." He licked his lips in a circular motion.

"Please?" she sobbed. "Please let me be popular one more time."

The vampire paused. He looked around the house, the house from which neither she nor he could ever escape. He opened the tower door. It creaked when it swung. The tower room was frigid. The window she had left open when Ryan parked in the driveway had a rim of ice on it. He looked at Althea, clinging to his hand, begging, begging, begging, for one more gift.

"Well . . . " said the vampire.

"I'll do anything," she said fervently. "I'll do anything."

The vampire laughed again. "I know, my dear. You always have."

She clasped her hands. "Then I can have my popularity one more time? I can sit with Ryan? And Becky? And Kimmie-Jo? And Michael? I can cheer in one more game?" A desperate tremor of a smile, a hideous facsimile of a smile, spurted across her face like a wound.

"Hold out your arms, Althea," said the vampire.

She held them straight out, like tree branches.

He gave her an invisible burden, spread on her

extended arms and palms as if she were carrying a freshly ironed gown. "Your popularity," he breathed. "As invisible as you will be in the morning."

The popularity was invisible, but it warmed her, the suntan of friendship. She could hear the voices of friendship: distant laughter and remote chatter. It caught her up, like traffic, rushing her down the halls, tossing her among the best crowd.

I did anything to get you, she thought. I destroyed myself to have you. I'm going to do it again, too.

A cold draft from the tower passed through the popularity, turning it as autumn winds turn leaves.

It awakened her slightly, as chilly winds do, and she looked up and into the tower.

The shutters will stay open, she thought. Long after I have sunk like Jennie and Celeste. The vampire's dark path will cross the hemlocks, and slip through the trees, and find others. Other girls who want to be popular. Who are weak.

I am going down, thought Althea. But I will *not* take another girl with me. I will take *him*. There will be nothing left of me. But instead of the popularity one last time, I will have the vampire. It will be his last time.

Resolve — warmer, hotter, sterner than popularity — filled her heart, and mind, and soul. "I reject your gift," said Althea softly. "I'm getting rid of it."

"You can't do that," said the vampire.

Althea smiled. The smile inched down her body, giving her strength, first to her face, then to her shoulders, her heart, her arms.

The vampire's teeth went back into his mouth. He looked alarmed.

"That's your source of power, isn't it?" she cried. "When weak people take what you offer, you become strong. You would have had no power if I had had the courage to ignore you." Strength from understanding crept down into her legs. Althea kicked his black cape away and stomped on it. She began laughing.

The vampire took a step backward into the tower room.

"I won't let you do it to others," said Althea. "I won't let you lay out any more dark paths."

The vampire held up his hands to stop her. She smacked them out of her way.

"No!" said the vampire. "You can't do this!"

Rhythm unbroken, feet unstoppable, Althea stomped toward the vampire. As she advanced, he backed up.

"You are nothing! And I am a match for you!" Althea cried.

The vampire kept moving back.

She leaped forward. The vampire hunched over into a ball, like a porcupine hiding its soft underbelly. Althea grabbed him. She took her popularity and pushed it against him, shoved it on him, wiped it on his face and his clothes. She mopped him with it.

"There," she said. "It's yours again."

His speech changed. He no longer sounded human. He no longer spoke English. A whimpering babble spurted from his mouth. His sharp teeth hung over the edges of his thin lips like foam.

"I'm free," Althea said.

She smiled. Not at the vampire, nor the world, nor a handsome boy, but at herself. She was free. That deserved a smile.

Efficiently she snapped the shutters together. The shutters that had rebelled when she was weak surrendered now that she was strong.

The vampire was trapped by the shutters that bound him, like lids on coffins.

She left the tower. The door locked by itself.

For a while, the vampire beat on the floor and on the door, but he had no power without a victim. Eventually the noise stopped.

I have stopped him, thought Althea. But what matters more, I stopped *myself.*

She walked down the stairs. Walked out of the house. Walked into the yard, in the sleet and the ugly dark. There were no threats. There was only weather and winter.

I have no friends. I will have to make friends the way other people do, one at a time, by being nice. I am not a cheerleader. I will have to get on the squad the way other girls do, by practicing hard.

Someday I will have it back.

But I will have earned it.

It will be mine, and I will *never* have to give it away.

I will deserve it.

The house is still there, although Althea moved away. The hemlocks are taller, thicker, and darker. When night falls, cars do not drive by and strangers keep their distance.

Two winters have damaged the tower. One of the shutters has come loose. It's banging against the tower, as if something inside hopes to get out.

The house is for sale.

It will appeal to somebody with children, somebody who needs plenty of space. One of the children might become curious about the tower. Play with the shutters.

And find a vampire.

A vampire who needs a victim.

A vampire who is used to waiting. And winning.

EVIL RETURNS

"Here's my offer," he said. "You want to be beautiful? I will give you Aryssa's beauty."

Have Aryssa's beauty! Imagine that. Imagine waking up in the morning, looking in your mirror, and seeing Aryssa there! Imagine how the boys would admire; how the girls would envy!

Aryssa's beauty.

"But what about Aryssa?"

"What about her?"

"What will she have?"

He smiled. The teeth were immense and sharp. "What she deserves," he said.

Chapter 1

"I don't think I want to sleep in the tower after all," Devnee said to her parents.

"Devnee," said her father. He was really quite annoyed. "Half the reason we bought the house was because you wanted a bedroom in a tower."

They had rejected raised ranches, Cape Cods, and bungalows and bought a dark Victorian mansion in desperate need of repair. Mr. Fountain wanted the workshop in the high dry cellar. Mrs. Fountain wanted the glassed-in room to raise flowers. Luke wanted the yard so he could play basketball, baseball, and football.

But Devnee had wanted the tower. How romantic a tower had sounded! Her own castle, her own corner of the sky. She would fling open the windows and a blue sky and a gentle sun would welcome her to a new town. She would curl up on her sleigh bed to read books, and she would brush her hair in front of a mirror with a white wicker frame, and somehow this time, in this town, this year, she would be beautiful and she would be popular and happy.

The tower jutted out of the attic, but was not part of it. It had a separate stair up from the second floor. The tower was round, and its plaster walls were cracked, its windows tightly shuttered.

Shuttered on the inside.

Devnee had never come across shutters on the inside of a house. Their new home had shutters all over the outside — louvered, broken shutters that banged in the wind and creaked in the night. But the tower had another set on the inside, strapped down with black metal, as if the tower had once held prisoners. "We'll just quick flip open these shutters," her father had said yesterday afternoon, nudging at the hasps and bolts, "and then the sunlight will stream into your new bedroom, Dev!"

But the armor of the shutters would not come free, and the moving men had been downstairs yelling where did Mr. Fountain want the leather recliner, and he had said he would get to the shutters later.

They had moved her bed into the tower. It was a romantic bed, with its sleigh back and lacy white ruffle, high mattress, and sheets with dark mysterious flowers. They had moved her chest of drawers into the tower. The chest was narrow and had seven drawers; Devnee was not tall enough to see into the top one. She also had a chair, a computer, and a sound system, but they were still sitting in the downstairs hall. There had not been enough time to move them into the tower.

The moving men left.

Her parents and her brother, Luke, were starving and insisted on going into town for something to eat.

Devnee made her first serious mistake. She told them to go without her, and bring her back a hamburger and french fries. She would stay alone in the house, and get to know her new room, and the new smell, and the new feel of life in a different state.

She did not know, last night, how different a state could be.

Luke and her mother and her father chattered steadily as they went to the car. The doors of the car slammed, and the engine of the car growled, and Devnee Fountain was alone in a house with a tower.

Devnee played the game she always played when she was alone. The beautiful game. Where the lovely funny terrific girl on the inside finally had a match on the outside; where Devnee's hair gleamed, and her smile sparkled, and her personality captivated.

She had left the kitchen. Kitchens were no place to play the beautiful game. Kitchens, like Devnee, were useful and stodgy.

She would go to the tower to be beautiful.

No one knew about the game. Devnee was so

dull and plain that people would have laughed at the mere suggestion of beauty, and then smothered the laughter in pity.

She left the kitchen and walked into the large high-ceilinged center hallway, where the wallpaper was stained from the squares of long-gone portraits. She stood on the bottom step of the wide stairs that led to the second floor.

Perhaps this time she would play bride. Or prom queen.

She pretended to fling a mass of shining hair and to widen eyes that stopped boys in their tracks.

Reality taunted Devnee Fountain. *Right,* it said. *You? Beautiful?*

I don't want beauty to be a game! she thought. I want it to be real. I want to be beautiful for real.

A sort of reverse gravity began to pull at Devnee Fountain. The backs of her eyes and the roots of her hair leaned toward the tower. Her fingers crawled up the banister and dragged her arms after them. The stairs disappeared behind her. Her hand stuck to the round glass knob of the door that opened to the tower stair. Her head went up ahead of her, but her feet argued and hung back and tried to turn around. Her eyes leaped forward.

The stairwell breathed. It filled its lungs like a runner after a race. Devnee's lungs did not fill at all. She caved in. She cried out.

And she climbed on, equal parts wind and weight.

It was darker in the tower than anyplace Devnee had ever been. The dark had textures, some velvet, some satin. The dark shifted positions.

The dark continued to breathe. The breath of the tower lifted her clothing like the flaps of a tent, and snuffled in her ears like falling snow.

It's the wind coming through the double shutters, Devnee told herself.

But how could wind come through? There were glass windows between the outside and inside shutters.

Or were there?

The windows weren't just holes in the wall, were they?

What if there was no glass? What if things crawled through those open louvers, crept into the room, blew in with the cold that fingered her hair? What creatures of the night could slither through those slats?

She had not realized how wonderful glass was, how it protected you and kept you inside.

There must be glass, Devnee thought. Something has to stand between me and — and what? What do I think is out there, except the night air?

She knew that something was out there.

She could hear it, crawling on the roof, filtering through the louvers.

Devnee put her hands out to feel the shutters.

In front of her face appeared some other hand. A hand with long fingernails of silver, wrinkled like crushed foil. Fingernails poked toward her, eager and grasping. The hand shifted the dark as if stirring ingredients, and it crossed the room toward Devnee like a growing stalk.

Her own hands rose like vapor. Devnee knew she was going to hold hands with the hand.

Devnee jerked her hands back, and tucked them under her arms for safekeeping, and staggered to the tower door. Stumbling and sick, she half fell, half flew down the tower stairs, down the second-floor stairs, throwing herself into the kitchen just as her brother came in with her bag of food.

"Hungry, huh?" said Luke, tossing it to her.

As she caught the paper bag with its red-and-gold logo it seemed to her that a second pair of hands also closed around the food: hands with fingernails so yellow and tarnished they were like old teeth in need of brushing.

Who is in this house with me? thought Devnee Fountain. Who lives between those shutters?

"If you're not going to eat that, I will," said Luke.

"She's nervous about her first day in a new school tomorrow," said their mother affectionately and soothingly. "Everybody to bed now. A good night's sleep is what we all need, and we'll worry about the rest of the furniture later on."

Devnee managed to smile. Her parents did not approve of complaining. They called it "whining" and felt that high school girls like Devnee should not whine.

So Devnee tried not to. "It's kind of creepy up there," she said, striving to sound careless and relaxed. "I don't think I want to sleep in the tower after all."

Her mother frowned. "It'll be a darling, darling little room once we have it fixed up. I see it in peach and ivory. It cries out for soft pastel colors."

It cries out for me, thought Devnee.

"The thing is, Dev, we have to do the kitchen first. That's our priority. Once we have sinks and cabinets and a new shiny vinyl floor, we can think about things like painting the bedrooms." Her mother smiled, a secret smile, her daydreaming smile. Devnee's mother daydreamed of things like remodeling. She could hardly wait to go from store to store, studying samples of vinyl floor coverings. Her mother would actually say out loud, "Doesn't it shine?" and "Do you really like this new finish?"

Devnee looked at her family: sturdy father, overgrown weed of a brother, domestic mother. Her father loved television; her brother loved sports; her mother loved cooking.

This was her life. This was the family she had drawn.

How she wished for something more special! People who did not fit into such suburban stereotypes. People with personality and pizzazz. But this was the right family for her; she was just as dull and predictable. Plain brown hair, plain pale face, plain ordinary smile, plain acceptable clothing.

Devnee crumpled the hamburger bag and dropped it in the garbage. She felt crumpled herself, exhausted from the silly beautiful game, the dumb tricks of her imagination, the nonsense of a tower that breathed.

And so Devnee went up to the tower again.

Night went on.

Sleep did not come.

Something damp and gelatinous brushed over her face.

Devnee cried out, and a hand clamped down over her mouth. Not her own hand — some other hand: cold and horny and soft like rotting fruit; as if it would burst and evil would spill out.

Devnee ripped the hand away from her mouth, whirled in the bed, and reached for the light switch on the wall. The blessed shape of the switch; the hard ivory-colored plastic. She flicked it up, and the room turned yellow and bright.

Her heart was beating as fast as a rabbit's.

Nothing was there. No thickness in the shadows. No movement by the shutters. Nothing damp and nothing rotting soft.

The only hands were her own, clutching the sheet hem as if she were a sailor for Columbus, falling off the edge of the world.

Calm down, Devnee told herself. You're just worried about the first day of school tomorrow. That's all. You gave yourself the heebie-jeebies.

For a long time she looked around the room, to see if anything came out of the cracks.

Gradually she relaxed against the pillows.

The room would be fine once the shutters were opened, pretty lacy curtains were hung, a rug put down. Once the plaster was repaired and the walls painted. Yes. She would choose cheery daytime colors and the rug would be thick and cozy-soft under her toes.

Devnee yawned, trying to entice sleep. Then she stretched, trying to get ready to lie back down. At last she folded her hands on her chest, to calm herself. I must look like a corpse laid out, thought Devnee.

She glanced down to see how she looked, and she saw something that could not be.

Her shadow had not folded its hands.

Her shadow was not attached to her.

Her shadow was on the far side of the room, exploring by itself, its black elongated fingers, like the tines of an immense fork, raking silently over door cracks and shutter louvers.

She tried to breathe, but the room itself was breathing so much it sucked up all the air. There was none left for her. She tried to think, but the ancient thoughts of all the people who had ever used the tower were swirling in the air, and she had no thoughts of her own.

Mommy, she whimpered soundlessly. *Daddy, Luke.*

Something came toward her, but it was not Mommy or Daddy or Luke.

"Come here," Devnee whispered to her shadow.

But it did not come.

If I turn off the light, thought Devnee, that would end my shadow.

But the darkness of the tower was so full of shape and texture and edge. Perhaps the shadow would stay alive even in the dark. Cruising through the room. Touching things. Touching perhaps Devnee's own cheek in the dark.

I'll close my eyes, thought Devnee, and calm myself down. This is not happening, and when I open my eyes, it will be an ordinary room with an ordinary shadow attached to my ordinary body.

But the experiment did not work, and she did not stay calm and serene.

The night was long.

A sort of dark path was lit across the room, leading to the shutters. She did not get out of the bed to follow the path. Her feet were bare, and the wood floor would be cold as pond ice in January. And the path — who knew where it led?

When Devnee awoke in the morning, the bedroom light was off.

At breakfast she said, "Did you come up and turn my light off, Mom?"

"No, darling."

"Did you, Daddy?"

"Nope."

She didn't ask Luke. Luke slept like a brick, which reflected his brainpower and personality. Even if every light in the house were on at two in the morning, Luke would never think of turning them off. Luke did not do a lot of thinking. Devnee was not sure her brother would think of mentioning fire if the house went up in flames. Luke was a big lug who played ball, and that was the limit of his mastery of the world.

In the kitchen, among the debris of remodeling and the mess of their first breakfast, she felt safe and warm. What could go wrong in a room that smelled of pancakes and maple syrup? Last night was not worth thinking about. There was too much of today to worry over.

Devnee had had difficulty deciding what to wear. Would this be a school in which girls dressed sloppily, with torn sneakers, too-big sweatshirts, old jeans? Or would they look chic? Or preppy? Or some style she had never encountered before?

Schools should send a video before you enrolled, so you could see how the kids dressed, and not get it wrong.

But then, what did it matter if Devnee Fountain got her clothes wrong?

She might be going to a new school, but she had her same old looks.

I wish . . . thought Devnee, aching to be a different person. The kind of girl who made people light up and turn to face her and call out her nickname when she walked in. A beautiful girl.

If you were beautiful, everything came with it: friends, laughter, company.

This was her chance! Her chance as the new girl to start a new life.

Oh, let it be a *better* life!

It was early; they did not have to leave for school yet.

Devnee walked outside. She did not know why. She was not an outdoor person. Certainly not in winter. Something drew her.

How cold it was in the yard. Frost during the night had whitened the grass, and water in a tilted old birdbath was frozen. The high hedge of hemlocks that encircled the mansion was more black than green, and the winter morning sky was not sunny, just less dark.

When you wish upon a star . . . Devnee sang to herself.

No wind, and no clouds. Just a faceless gray morning and a queer damp chill. She felt she should not stay outdoors too long or moss might grow on her face.

Devnee looked up at her tower and the moment her gaze landed on the circling shutters, one of them banged.

But there was no wind.

The shutter banged a second time, and the broken louvers on the shutter seemed to curve upward in a secret smile.

Devnee kicked her shoe in the dirt. She had decided on sneakers that looked like leather: black ones, quite new, but not new enough to look desperate. They would blend with any fashion.

But I don't want to blend in! thought Devnee, as filled with pain as a heart attack patient. I want to be beautiful!

I wish . . . she thought forlornly.

Devnee had not put on a coat. The chill wrapped around her, as if it had folds and fabric, like a winter coat. The chill warmed her. It was as if she had become some strange new animal and the blood in her veins would decide what was warm.

Cold was warm.

If cold can be warm, thought Devnee, perhaps plain can be beautiful. How I want to be beautiful!

Even her knuckles and fingers begged for beauty, turning white, clasping each other, beseeching the powers that be to turn Devnee Fountain into a beautiful girl.

The wish was not mild and passing.

It was sharp, intense. Every girl, every day, wishes for changes in her body, or her heart, or her life. But few wished so desperately as Devnee Fountain.

Devnee went back inside, into the warmth.

Her words lay on the air.

I wish . . .

The wish left, as her shadow had, and went on without her.

In the darkness of the hemlocks around the

mansion, against the dark shingles of the house, more darkness gathered. Thicker darkness. A darkness both velvety and satiny.

The dark path caught the wish and kept it.

Something bright glittered in the branches of the hemlocks, like a row of tiny silver bells.

Or fingernails, wrinkled like old foil.

The dark path curled around the base of a tree, and waited for the rest of the wish.

Chapter 2

Back at the breakfast table, nobody had moved.

Her mother was still pouring orange juice into the same glass.

The juice seemed to slide out of the cardboard box and into the glass forever and ever, as if her mother was just a hand holding a pitcher.

Her father was still holding a fork above his pancakes, and her brother was still lifting his napkin.

Devnee shivered.

Had she gone outside at all? What had happened to the time she had spent out there? Was it her time only, and had it not existed for the three inside the house? What was happening in this house, that time flickered differently wherever you stood, and fingernails crept out of cracks, and shadows peeled away from your body?

"I want to sleep downstairs in the guest room," Devnee said, and the family stirred slightly, as if waking up.

"Dev," said her mother, "no. We have all kinds of guests coming. You know that. Nobody in our family has ever lived in this part of the country before, and they're *dying* to visit. The little guest room is the boring room, nobody wants it full-time, and we agreed that's where we'll stuff the guests."

Luke said, "Wouldn't it be weird if the guests really did die when they came to visit? And we really did stuff them?"

Devnee could not breathe.

"Luke, try to be human," said their mother.

I wonder which of us is human, thought Devnee. I wonder if I'm human. My shadow isn't human. But then, shadows aren't human, she realized.

So why did my shadow make choices of its own? Exploring and wandering? It shouldn't be doing anything I don't do.

Devnee said, "I don't want to start school here yet."

"State laws," said her mother cheerfully. "You have to start school today. I'll drive you, since it's your first day, and you run down and check in the office and see what the nearest bus route is for tomorrow."

Her mother made "checking in the office" sound as easy as ordering a hamburger, but it wouldn't be. It would be strange halls and a thousand strange faces. Doors that were not marked clearly and people who spoke too loudly or not at all, while Devnee shuffled her feet like a broken-down ballerina.

She almost wished that she and Luke were in the same school. Then she would have company on the horrible first day in a new school.

On the other hand, who would want Luke's company for anything? It was good that he was still in ninth grade and in this town that meant junior high, while she was safely in tenth grade, and far superior to her dumb brother.

They dropped off Luke first, because the junior high was closer, and Luke bounded in as if he had always gone there, and already had friends and already knew the way to the gym and where the cafeteria line began.

What if I don't have friends here ever? thought Devnee.

What if it's a horrible hateful mean place and I'm dressed wrong? And they laugh at me?

When they arrived at the high school, Devnee's mother came in with her after all. Devnee, who adored her mother, was ashamed: Mrs. Fountain was quite heavy and needed a new, larger winter coat. Instead of taking the time to curl her hair, her mother had just tugged it back into a loose, messy ponytail.

As if taking Devnee to her first day in a new school in a new town didn't matter.

Devnee swallowed the thought and tried to stay loyal.

She glanced behind her to see if her shadow had come along and it had. It seemed curiously large for Devnee, and too dark for the thin, shivering sun of January. It seemed like somebody else's shadow.

Immediately she knew that it *was* somebody else's. It was the shadow of the fingernails, with talons like a hawk's. She forced herself to stare straight ahead. She was not going to collapse because the tower had switched shadows on her during the night. She had a first day of school to get through.

In the office, the secretary did not even look up at them. "New student?" she said in a tight, snappish voice. "What grade, please? What courses were you taking at your previous school, please? Do you have your health papers showing you are properly inoculated?" Now she looked up, scanning Devnee for disease-carrying properties. Devnee tried to look clean and healthy.

Her mother said, "Wonderful!" though what she could be referring to, Devnee could not imagine. "I'll see you after school," trilled her mother. "I'll pick you up in the front drive, darling. Have such fun!"

The secretary was wearing little half glasses, which she tilted lower on her nose to study Mrs. Fountain's exit, perfectly aware that "having such fun" was unlikely.

The secretary finished up doing important things, while Devnee leaned on the counter, wanting to die, and then at last the secretary gave her directions to the guidance office, where they would set up her schedule and take her to her first class.

The directions were so complex Devnee felt they probably led to China, not down the hall. She was close to tears, and the chilly damp of last night had come back and was penetrating her brain, making it hard to think or move.

"Oh, all right," said the secretary, "I'll take you there."

But the guidance person, a man named Fuzz (which surely could not have been the case; it was Devnee's hearing that had gotten fuzzy because she was so nervous) was quite sweet. "We have a buddy system for newcomers," said Fuzz affectionately. "We don't want anybody lost in the cracks at our school!"

The expression took on a sick reality. It seemed to Devnee that the linoleum squares parted, and huge cracks opened up, black ones filled with other people's shadows, sticky and gooey, waiting for her to step wrong.

Fuzz had a long stride, and Devnee a short one, so she was forced to gallop alongside him. Out of breath and terrified, she arrived at her first class several paces behind, as if her leash had broken. "Devnee, Devnee," he called, like a dog owner.

Devnee tried to look at the class but it was impossible. There were too many students, all staring at her, with that settled, certain-sure look of kids who had been here forever and didn't approve of newcomers.

She felt unbearably plain and dull. She could feel their eyes raking over her, losing interest immediately, because she was not beautiful, and not worth attention.

She was perilously close to tears.

"Devnee has just moved here!" said Fuzz. His voice wafted in and out of her consciousness. "Now we want Devnee to feel at home here, don't we, people?"

Nobody responded.

Fuzz read Devnee's schedule out loud, demanding that anybody with matching classes should respond and volunteer to be Devnee's buddy.

Amazingly, there were three volunteers.

Seats were shuffled so that Devnee was sitting among her "buddies."

Two girls and a boy.

She immediately forgot their names and hated herself for being a stupid worthless pitiful excuse for a human being. Probably why my shadow left, thought Devnee. Needed a better body to attach itself to.

Class ended in another quarter hour, and Devnee was not even sufficiently tuned in to figure out what subject it had been. "I'm your first buddy," said one of the girls, touching Devnee's arm and smiling at her. "I'll take you on to biology lab, and then Trey will pick you up for English and lunch."

The girl — if you could use such a boring word for this breathtaking creature — was achingly lovely.

All willowy and delicate adjectives applied to her: She was fragile, in a dark silken blouse with a long chiffon skirt swirling below. Her soft black hair was perfectly cut to fall swoopingly over her forehead and skid around her pretty ears; the back was very short, with a single wave. She seemed far older than Devnee would ever be, a sophisticated fragile creature. And yet she seemed far younger, caught in some wonderful warp of innocence and perfection, before the world touched her, before pain and loss.

"My name is Aryssa," said the girl softly, and her voice, too, was beautiful, as if she possessed a velvet throat.

Now there really were tears in Devnee's eyes. Tears of shame that she herself was so dull compared to this princess, and tears of joy that this princess had volunteered to be her buddy.

What a wonderful word — buddy.

There was hope in the world after all.

And then the boy — Trey — smiled at Devnee, too, waving good-bye, promising to be at the biology lab door, and then he would stand in the cafeteria line with her. He was not at all handsome, not the way Aryssa was beautiful. But he was what Luke would have yearned to be: utterly male and muscular and tall and slightly ferocious. His smile was vaguely threatening, as if she'd better stand in the cafeteria line the way he told her to stand or else.

The physical perfection of her two buddies overwhelmed her.

The girl buddy — whose name Devnee had already forgotten — talked about many things, giving Devnee tips for locker use, gym showers, and so forth. Devnee's brain had not gone into gear and she could not get a grip. She smiled brightly and desperately. She knew she looked like a fool.

"Hey, Aryssa," said several people, waving and beaming.

Aryssa, Devnee repeated to herself. Aryssa, Aryssa. I have to remember that. I will remember that. I have a three-syllable brain.

She and Aryssa went into biology lab together. Aryssa introduced Devnee all around. The teacher welcomed her and gave her a textbook and a lab notebook, and Devnee found herself on a stool in front of a dead frog.

While the teacher discussed dissection methods, Devnee took the opportunity to study Aryssa.

Aryssa was very preoccupied with her beauty. How could she not be? There was so much of it.

Aryssa would run the tip of her tongue over her upper lip, as if savoring her own taste and shape. She would flip her gleaming hair back with her left hand, tuck it behind her ear, and sort of kiss the air when the black locks immediately fell back where they had been. Her face was constantly in motion, it never fell into repose.

In her right hand, Aryssa held a designer pencil: tiny gold stars on silver, which she flipped between her fingers like a miniature baton.

Her hands, too, were lovely: slender and aristocratic and with perfect nails and polish that probably never chipped.

"You'll do the frog, won't you?" whispered Aryssa. Now she smiled, and the row of white teeth and the turn of red lips overwhelmed Devnee.

"Of course," said Devnee, and she did the entire lab, even doing all the notes and answers, because Aryssa clearly used her pencil only for effect, not for writing things down.

"You're a sweetie," whispered Aryssa. She actually patted Devnee's knee, and again Devnee felt like a dog on a leash. It was just that Fuzz had turned her over to a new mistress, and from now on Aryssa would lead her.

Devnee blinked back the tears. She was jealous now, too, and it was a horrible feeling, rather like the formaldehyde in which the frog was pickled; it was liquid bathing her heart, this jealousy.

Oh, to be beautiful like Aryssa!

What a pair we must make, thought Devnee sadly. Beauty and the beast.

The teacher talked for several minutes about the next step, and Devnee had time to look around. She felt safe with the high lab table in front of her, and her feet tucked around the stool, and the sharp steel scalpel in her hand. She studied the rest of the girls in the lab.

Well, she was not a beast. No, Devnee was average in this particular class; half the girls were plainer than she. Stubbier, thicker, duller.

But she remained average.

Mediocre.

Whoever set that as a goal?

Devnee forgot the dead frog and stared at Aryssa, thinking, *If only I could look just like that . . .*

I wish . . .

She tried not to complete the wish. She tried to be satisfied with her lot in life.

She failed.

I wish I were beautiful!

How satisfying it sounded. What a deep intense relief to have said the whole wish, let all her pain out, let the powers that be know what she yearned for, ached for.

I wish I were beautiful!

She felt much better for having wished; it was as cathartic as a good cry in the night. She brightened and went on with her work.

The wish — complete — entire — slid out of the schoolroom to the dark path waiting outside, where it was swallowed up, and taken home, and caressed.

Chapter 3

Aryssa sighed in relief when biology lab ended. Even her sigh was lovely, as if her soft pink lungs expired only the finest air. "This is my second time taking biology," confided Aryssa. "I just can't seem to pass a science class. I don't like thinking about any of that science stuff anyway. It makes me nervous. I don't think it's fair to have to know what's under the skin."

Devnee could identify with that.

Aryssa stroked her own hand, admiring her skin, taking pleasure in a beauty so pure it was like ice: something to skate on, something only Aryssa would ever be. The world could witness, but not have, such beauty.

But Devnee was thrilled to be addressed in that confiding voice. Even though it would cast Devnee in that always-to-be-pitied role of dull escort next to shining star, she wanted to be friends with Aryssa. "What *do* you like thinking about?" she said, to keep the conversation going.

Aryssa considered this tough question while they gathered their books and walked to the door. Devnee's second buddy was already there. Trey. Devnee gulped slightly. Two such perfect humans, and for a day, for a passing period, for lunch, they were there for her.

I wish it would last, thought Devnee.

She had a weird sense that her wishes were actually being addressed to Somebody; that Somebody was listening; that Something was happening.

Aryssa literally took Devnee's hand and stuck it in Trey's.

Trey laughed. His laughter was neither kind nor unkind, but removed, not worried about the things Devnee worried about: looks and popularity and strength and friends. "I don't think Devnee needs that much help to find the next class, Aryssa." He let go of Devnee's hand. Her hand stayed warm and tingly where he had momentarily pressed it.

Aryssa said seriously, "I didn't want anybody to get confused. This buddy system, you know — people forget who goes with who."

"You and your room temperature IQ," said Trey. "Normal people don't forget."

Aryssa's was the contented laugh of a beautiful girl who doesn't care in the least about her lack of brains — because it doesn't matter in the least.

It's not fair, thought Devnee. Aryssa doesn't need to do anything but stand there and people adore her, while I have to struggle with everything from mascara to homework just to get noticed. She wished that Trey had not let go of her hand. She wished that she could be as beautiful as Aryssa and have people speak to her so indulgently, so affectionately.

"See you tomorrow, Devnee," Aryssa said. She ran her hand lightly over Devnee's shoulders, not a hug, but sweet, passing affection.

The knife of jealousy vanished, replaced by yearning for friendship. But there would be no friendships. She knew too well the realities of high school. Her buddies would not last. They would be shepherds for a day or two and then forget her.

I am a forgettable girl, thought Devnee, and this time the jealousy sliced her heart into thin ragged strips of pain.

Aryssa looked carefully around the hallway and drifted to the right, skirt wafting, hair shining. Trey caught her arm and turned her around. Aryssa, nodding gratefully, set off in the new direction.

"She's great to look at," Trey said, eyes following Aryssa in admiration, "but as a navigational aid, you need to be careful, Devnee. Aryssa's best ability is studying the mirror."

Devnee did not want to be disloyal. "If I looked like that, I'd study the mirror, too." She dreamed that Trey answered with a shower of compliments: You do look like that, Dev! You'll give

Aryssa a run for her money! Till you moved here, Aryssa had no competition, but now! Whew!

Of course he didn't. He searched to find something about her that was interesting. "So where in town do you live, Devnee?"

Devnee told him.

He whistled without pitch. "The mansion at the bottom of the hill? Jeez. I knew the girl who used to live there. Creepy? Whew! I mean, that girl was creepy the way Aryssa is beautiful." He made a terrible face like he'd gag if he ran into that girl again.

Somebody behind them took part in the conversation. "Mega-creepy," said the person.

"Seriously creepy," added another.

"I was at that house for a party once," said Trey. He shuddered his shoulders on purpose. "Yeccchhh!"

"We're fixing up the house," said Devnee quickly. She did not want to be linked with some creepy girl who had made everybody gag. "We're going to paint it yellow to get rid of that dying mansion look."

"Take more than paint," muttered the voice from behind.

She thought of her shadow, of the cracks in the floor, and the shapes in the dark.

Yes. It would take more than paint.

"Here we are," said Trey. His face turned dark and threatening again. "English," he said regretfully. He studied Devnee for a minute. "I bet you're a real brain, huh?"

She flushed and shook her head. Trey figured someone as dumpy and dull as she was had to have something to offer. He was waiting to see it. He had a long wait.

English was her scariest subject. She was no student. She didn't mind reading homework, although it took her a long time, but she hated classroom reading. While the rest of the class flipped speedily along, page after page, she'd be slogging through the second paragraph. There were always pitying glances as the class tapped impatient fingers and waited for Devnee to catch up.

And in English, there were writing assignments. Devnee had a hard enough time putting her thoughts together inside her own head. To write them down was like being tossed in a cement mixer — upside down, head whacking against rotating walls.

If I talk out loud in English, thought Devnee, Trey will know I'm practically as dumb as Aryssa. But without the looks.

I wish I could look like that. But I wish I could be smart, too. If I were both beautiful *and* smart, what a wonderful life I would have!

This teacher was prepared to have a new student in the class; Fuzz had called ahead. Mrs. Cort had made a packet for Devnee of current readings and assignments. Mrs. Cort even said for Devnee not to worry about today or tomorrow, but just to concentrate on feeling at ease and finding her place.

What a nice, comforting smile Mrs. Cort had. And what a nice assignment: feeling at ease.

Devnee distracted herself thinking of smiles. Would she like a gorgeous, stunning smile like Aryssa? A tough, wrestling-partner smile like Trey? A kindly, neighborly smile like this teacher?

No contest.

Gorgeous and stunning. With a tough wrestling partner smiling back at her.

The class launched into a book discussion, and Devnee was surprised and delighted. Not only had her old school used the same curriculum — they'd been ahead! She had just finished reading the same book. What a gift! For several nights she would not have to do her English.

"We'll begin, please," said the teacher, "with a summary of the theories stated in the preface to the novel."

Everybody moaned. Devnee knew — because she had had this same class two weeks before in another state — that nobody ever read the preface.

A girl sitting one row ahead and one seat to the right, directly in Devnee's line of sight to the teacher, raised her hand.

"Yes, Victoria," said the teacher wearily, and Devnee knew instantly that Victoria was the kind of girl who always read, remembered, and analyzed the prefaces.

Victoria was a sort of reverse of Aryssa: a bold,

sweeping, athletic, rich beauty — a girl on a yacht, or on skis. A girl who skimmed the problems of life, laughing and full of energy. What a good name Victoria was for her.

As for her clothes, they were astonishing. Old corduroy pants, sagging socks, gaping shoes, coat-like sweater. It was clear that Victoria didn't care. Clothes were nothing to Victoria. She transcended clothing. What mattered to Victoria was exhibiting her brainpower.

She had a lot to exhibit.

Victoria more or less kept her hand up all period while the teacher looked around hopefully for somebody else to know at least one little fact, but nobody did, whereas Victoria always knew everything.

Devnee considered making a contribution. (In fact, it would be a quote from the smart kid in her last school, but who was to know?) However, Victoria also liked to argue, and Devnee was afraid she'd be in some academic argument on the first day of school, which she would certainly lose, so she said nothing.

The most surprising thing was that Victoria was interesting, even funny. It was a pleasure to listen to her comments, her unusual opinions, her scholarly jokes.

Devnee liked her immensely. She found herself smiling throughout the class, enjoying Victoria.

As Trey led the way to the cafeteria — it was

one of those interrupted classes; thirty minutes of class, twenty-five minutes of lunch, another twenty minutes of class — Devnee said, "Victoria seems like a nice person."

He grinned again. Grins seemed to come easily to him. "Hey, Vic!" he bellowed. "The new girl thinks you look like a nice person."

The class's roar of laughter filled the hall.

"Vic's smart," said one of the boys, "but nice? Ha!" But the boy was also smiling, both at Victoria and at Devnee. He, too, was handsome. Had she stumbled into a world where everybody else was a perfect physical specimen? Was she doomed to be a toad among princes and princesses?

"Nice," said Victoria, laughing, "is not a word we use very often around here. Nice is not the local specialty. But you do look like a nice person, Devnee. Have I pronounced it right? It's such an interesting name! Do you ever get called Dev?"

Victoria dropped back to link arms with Devnee. "I represent all scholarly talent in this building, Devnee. We have a very small brain pool."

Everybody was laughing.

"Now William here," she said, introducing the other perfect male specimen, "pretends to have brains. But no proof has yet emerged."

William smiled. "I'm the nice one," he promised Devnee, and this time nobody laughed, so it must have been true.

Everybody sat together for lunch; she was

jammed between Trey and Victoria. There were so many names revolving in Devnee's brain.

Trey took Devnee's tray back for her so she didn't have to clear her own place the first day. "You're too ladylike for this chore," he said to her, which prompted a fierce argument between him and Victoria on what made a lady, and whether such a creature existed, or should exist.

They went back to English at a trot; twenty-five minutes was barely enough time to stand in line, bolt down lunch, and make the return trip.

Devnee felt like taking a nap, or perhaps going back for another dessert, but Victoria, who had done extra reading, made pertinent comments about the author they were studying.

The class listened carefully. Devnee did not have the impression that anybody else was inspired to do extra reading, but they loved having Victoria around to be their brain, make great remarks, and know all the answers.

I wish I were as smart as that, thought Devnee. If I were as smart as Victoria, and as pretty as Aryssa . . .

Devnee drifted into a daydream of loveliness and intelligence.

In the dream she drew praise and applause, smiles and dates. In the dream she was the center of the room, just as Victoria was the center of this room, and Aryssa had been the center in the last one.

I'd like to be famous as well, thought Devnee. And rich, too. And very talented. Might as well have it all.

But she let go of the wishes to be famous and rich and talented. They were secondary.

Beauty was first. Then a mind. It would be so nice to have a mind that intrigued people.

Her third escort was Nina, a short-tempered girl who was obviously sorry she had volunteered. Nina kept glancing at her watch with the irritation of somebody who wants you to realize she has important things to do, and you're not one of them.

Nina never smiled. She never quite met Devnee's eyes, either, just glanced in the general direction of the new girl and set off. She didn't walk so they could walk next to each other, but she strode on ahead. She didn't glance back once to be sure Devnee was still trailing along. She waved to friends and called hello, but did not introduce Devnee.

Nina had fabulous clothes. The sweater definitely had cost more than Devnee could spend on an entire year's wardrobe.

When they reached class, Nina sat down and did not look at Devnee again. There was not an empty desk, and this teacher shared Nina's attitude; Devnee was a nuisance Mr. O'Sullivan could have done without. Devnee stood against the side wall, trying not to cry, trying to remember this was the same school where Mrs. Cort taught, and feeling at ease, and Victoria and Trey.

Finally a boy in the back row pushed his chair toward Devnee. It didn't reach her, so he kicked it again. It scraped on the floor, unwilling to travel toward Devnee. The class snickered. The boy kicked it a third time, and this time it sped over the floor and hit her in the kneecaps.

The boy lounged on top of his desk, legs swinging, expression cruel. Mr. O'Sullivan seemed amused. Devnee sat exposed on the chair, no desk in front to protect her, hands folded on her lap, as if she were praying, which she was.

When class finally ended, the boy launched himself off the desk like a rocket and vanished, while Nina took off with her friends. Devnee tagged after them, afraid of this huge school, these many floors and wings and courtyards. "Nina?" Devnee said nervously. "Can you show me how to get out?"

Nina stared at her, repelled, as if finding a raw clam on her peanut butter sandwich. "How to get out?" repeated Nina, arching her eyebrows. "I suggest a door." Nina and her friends laughed and walked on.

Devnee forced herself to laugh, also. "I mean, the school is so big and I don't exactly know where the front entrance is. Where my mother is picking me up."

"Your mother is picking you up?" said Nina, as if normal people stopped having mothers when they left elementary school. "You don't have your own car?" Nina's eyebrows went up again. Her friends imitated her.

Their scorn filled the halls.

Devnee hated them.

Nina sniffed, making a big deal of Devnee being in her way. "Trey!" Nina yelled down the hall. "Hey, Trey! Show the new girl where the front hall is, will you? *I'm* not taking that much of a detour."

Trey had a bookbag on his back and an athletic bag in each hand. He was with William, who was similarly burdened, clearly heading for the gym and some sport or other. "Sure, be glad to," said Trey.

"Come with us, Dev," added William.

"You don't have to take me," Devnee said quickly. "It's out of your way. Just point me in the right direction."

"The right direction includes several turns and two different stairs. Don't worry about it. And don't worry about Nina, either. She doesn't exactly have the greatest personality in the world." William's smile was like Mrs. Cort's, as easy and kind as a backyard swing.

"She does have the greatest car, though," said Trey.

"Does she ever," agreed William. "What I wouldn't give to be as rich as she is."

"How rich is she, Bill?" asked Devnee.

William stopped dead, sneakers squeaking. He dropped his gym bag. "I'm William. No nicknames. Let's get this relationship started out right. William, okay?"

I can't even talk right, she thought. She wanted to start crying right then, but tears would drive them off forever. Her father was right; no one could stand a whiner. "William. Okay."

They shook on it. Her hand was sweaty and damp, and his was strong and smooth.

"Nina," said William, answering the question, "could probably buy and sell the town."

Devnee would settle for the sweater. And palms that did not sweat.

Trey and William not only took her to the door, but right on out to the car, where her mother sat with the engine idling.

"See you tomorrow, Devnee," said Trey.

"Thanks so much, Trey," she said, turning to wave good-bye. "Nice to meet you, William."

Behind the two boys, the school loomed large and solid, red bricks glowing in the afternoon sun. As the boys charged back into the building to get to practice on time, Devnee's shadow slipped out the school door, rushing to catch up.

Nobody else saw it.

A slip of black, coasting on a sidewalk.

Quivers of sickness climbed up her throat like a scream. *Why weren't you with me? I can't be a person without a shadow!*

"So how was school?" said her mother happily. "My day was wonderful. Wait till you see all I've accomplished!"

Devnee held the door open, and her shadow got in the car and disappeared against the upholstery.

Chapter 4

That night, the tower was ordinary.

The hours of darkness passed serenely.

She slept well.

In the morning, the sun smiled, the snow glittered, and the sky was pure. School was perfect. It was too soon to have friends, but everybody was friendly. Trey and Aryssa, William and Victoria and all the rest — what a fine school this was! What a fine life she was entering!

Only that last period, with Mr. O'Sullivan's sneer and Nina's contempt, was difficult. He did not order another desk, and Devnee remained exposed on the chair, taking notes on her lap. But now she knew the school well enough to run down the hall alone when class ended, catch Trey and William, and be escorted to her car by two laughing handsome boys.

Over the weekend she went shopping with her mother, looking for clothes similar to what Aryssa wore. (Nobody would want to dress like Victoria, and nobody could afford to dress like Nina.) It was one of those wonderful shopping expeditions when everything fit, every price was right, every style was flattering. Devnee spun home, twirling in delight.

Her father and brother had been at work in the tower.

The interior shutters had been opened and fastened by the strangely heavy, prisonlike clasps. "One window was broken, Devnee," said her father. "I just reglazed it, and your brother and I washed the windows inside and out. I hung on to Luke's knees while he sat on the sill to do the outside. He also fixed the banging shutter on the outside."

"Hey, great," said Devnee. How airy, how bright the room was! A special room for a special person. A room for giggling friends and silly slumber parties. Devnee danced. Her father went downstairs with the tools.

Luke stayed in the tower, a strange expression on his face. He started to laugh but it turned into a croak. Started to shrug, but twitched instead. Started to talk, but mumbled incoherently.

"Luke, you're so worthless," said Devnee with a sisterly laugh.

"I think you should take the downstairs bedroom after all," he said.

"What? You bum! You want the tower now, huh? You think just because you washed a window you get the tower? Forget it."

"No! I want —" He broke off. He looked around

him, as if thinking they would be overheard and punished. He whispered, "I want you to be all right."

For a moment her heart crashed, her hands iced. She remembered her shadow, the slimy touch in the night, the breathing room in the dark. What had Luke felt up here, touching those shutter slats where her shadow's long black fingers had explored? What did Luke know, from this creepy room that knew all the secrets of night?

"Place is spooky," muttered Luke. He headed for the stairs. His movement broke the spell.

My own stairs, thought Devnee, laughing again. Wait'll I have Aryssa over. Will she ever be impressed! "Honestly, Luke," she said. "I have a chance to be happy and you try to make things up to scare me."

"I'm not making anything up. And the least you could do is thank me for fixing your stupid window. I hate having a sister."

"Well, I hate having a brother. Get out of here."

"Not till you say thank you!"

"Thank you. Now get out. I want to try on my new clothes."

He was almost down the stairs when he turned to look at her. His body was no longer visible, only his head. Decapitated, the lips moved anyway. Devnee shuddered, and a hand ran gently over her back, and stroked her neck under her hair. She whirled to face it, but of course there was nobody there.

"You deserve whatever you get," said Luke. "So there."

The next Thursday, Devnee was late to school. She had to spend a few minutes in the office getting yelled at and being marked Present after all. The secretary seemed to feel that if you were going to be late, you should just be absent, and save everybody the trouble of reentering you in the day's computer list. Devnee didn't mind. She loved this school now, and could even love a sulky, short-tempered secretary.

She was happy within these walls.

As for nights in the tower and shadows at her feet, she could only assume that the first day in a new town had scared her so badly she'd given herself bad dreams.

Devnee gathered her things and went slowly down the hall.

Was she lucky that her new down jacket was so slippery it slid from her grasp? Was she lucky that she had to kneel and scoop it up with her two free fingers, then try to stagger to her feet without also dropping six books, homework, and chorus folder? Was she lucky that everything slid onto the floor a second time, so she remained bent like a clumsy acolyte kneeling in front of a school altar?

Kneeling like a beggar or a slave, Devnee heard two voices.

Just around the corner, laughing and low, each

voice had a rich texture. Talking between classes — telling secrets — had thickened the voices. But they were not so thick that Devnee failed to recognize them.

"She's absent today!" said the first voice. Aryssa's voice. From the throat of velvet and the lips of red. "What a relief."

"I know," said the second voice. Trey's voice. "If I have to waste time with her much longer, I'm going to puke."

Devnee's knees crunched on the floor. Her new clothes did not seem so pretty, nor her jacket so trendy.

"The trouble with the buddy system," said the first voice, "is that they really think you're their buddy." It was Aryssa.

Dread clamped down on Devnee's joy. I don't want to hear this, she thought. Go away. Don't say it out loud. I can guess now. Don't make me know the truth. Please. Let me pretend I'm pretty and nice.

"That's the trouble with being friendly," Aryssa went on. "You can't just be friendly. You end up with this person who thinks she's really your friend." Aryssa laughed.

Trey clucked sympathetically. "There's nothing really wrong with Devnee," he said. "We'll let her tag along for a while. Eventually she'll make real friends and drift off."

"No," said Aryssa, "I know that kind. She never catches on. She never picks up a clue. She'll be there forever. You'd have to run over her with a truck to convince her you don't want her around."

Trey laughed. "Why did you volunteer to be her buddy anyway?" he asked.

"Because I'm failing biology again," said Aryssa. "She looked smart and I figured she could do my labs for me and during tests I could crib off her. But she turned out to be just as dumb as I am. You should see us in bio lab, Trey. We're pathetic."

Trey laughed. "*She's* pathetic," he said. "You're beautiful."

Aryssa laughed. "Thank you, darling." There was a smoochy sound.

Devnee was gripping her books so hard she broke a fingernail.

"Why did *you* volunteer?" asked Aryssa.

"You know why. I wanted to make time with Victoria, and Victoria approves of being decent to the pitiful ones. Victoria's very big on charity. Look how Victoria is sitting with Devnee at lunch." There was another smoochy sound. "But Victoria doesn't matter now, either, does she?" said Trey, and he and Aryssa laughed together.

Devnee was still crouched over her belongings. One of the pitiful ones to whom Victoria felt people should be charitable.

If Trey and Aryssa came this way, they would find her, like a dog outside its kennel, waiting to be kicked.

But they walked in the other direction. Trey's

heavy shoes and Aryssa's delicate heels played a duet on the hard cold tiles. And Devnee Fountain remained a solo, as she had always been, without friends, without beauty, without hope.

The strange thing was that Devnee did not hate them.

Instead she felt guilty for being a burden. They were beautiful people, interesting people, and they were right: She had attached herself like a poison ivy vine to a tree. Of course they didn't want her there. She was giving them a rash.

I was born plain, she thought, and Luke is right. I deserve whatever I get. I had daydreams too big. I wanted to be happy, and pretty, and popular. Instead I was a nuisance and made Trey want to puke.

So after biology lab, Devnee said to Aryssa, "You've been a great buddy, Aryssa. But I'm pretty well oriented now. I'll be okay."

Aryssa gave the incredibly sweet smile that had so impressed Devnee the first day. This was the gift Aryssa wanted, not friendship, not company, not a slumber party in a tower — but freedom from the burden of Devnee. "You're so darling, Dev," Aryssa said.

Devnee could not speak another syllable. Her voice would break. She nodded. Aryssa smiled again, like an archangel, like a star in the heavens, and danced over to her real friends.

How final the passage was.

How complete the end of Devnee's plans for a new life in a new school.

Devnee knew that her heart had still been hoping. Her heart had beaten on, telling itself that Aryssa would answer, "Nonsense, Devnee, we're *real* buddies, you and I; I'm so glad you moved here!"

Her heart was a fool.

Devnee stood alone, without a buddy, in the door of biology lab, and saw that Aryssa was not the only beautiful girl. She was part of a crowd of beautiful girls; a page full of magazine models, haughty and perfect.

Now she knew they had been laughing at her all along.

"Hey, buddy," said Trey cheerfully.

Her heart dissolved this time; she had an acid bath in her chest. She said bravely, "Thanks for being my buddy, Trey. I'll be fine on my own now."

"Hey, great," said Trey. He knotted his big hand into a friendly fist and gave her a friendly tap on the shoulder.

I want a kiss and a hug, she thought, and I'm getting a clenched-fist good-bye.

"You're a very well-adjusted person, you know that?" said Trey. "I mean, you settled in really well, Devnee." He, too, left to be with his real friends, with handsome William and the others. "You take care of yourself now, Devnee," he called back, as if he would never see her again.

And he did not.

In the days that followed, Trey, who was in two classes with her, plus lunch, never saw her again. He moved in his crowd, the beautiful crowd, and Devnee blended into the ordinary group, the ones on whom Trey's eyes would never focus and with whom Aryssa would never laugh.

The only person who continued to be a friend was Victoria. Victoria, who told her potential boyfriends they had to be nice to losers, or Victoria wouldn't be nice to them.

I'm a loser! thought Devnee. She perfected the art of tilting her head back to keep the tears from rolling down her cheeks.

If only I were beautiful! Oh, how I wish I could be beautiful!

Chapter 5

The school bus drove down the long slow hill. Even the road seemed reluctant to get to the bottom where Devnee's mansion lay among the dark and angry evergreens. The road was filled with little rises, as if trying to escape arriving in the valley.

From the school bus window, she could see the many-angled roof, the tall chimneys and the tower.

There was no sun, of course; it was not a day for sun. And yet the windows of the tower gleamed, and spoke to her, and called her name.

The bus stopped.

Only Devnee got off.

Nobody said good-bye.

Nobody watched her go.

Nobody saw that her shadow went first.

The shadow waited for Devnee to catch up, and Devnee knew that they were going to the tower together. She knew that the tower was waiting for them both. The tower knew things she did not. Could not. Should not.

She was oddly excited.

Her scalp prickled but she did not shrink from it.

She felt that perhaps her personality had split, just as her shadow and body had split. She was going to be two people in this town: a tower person and a school person.

"How was school?" her mother asked gaily. Her mother was so involved in kitchen remodeling, so happy choosing faucet styles and cabinet knobs that she thought everybody was just as happy.

"Pretty good." Devnee could not even remember the happiness of last week.

"Oh, darling, I know we made the right decision moving to this town and buying this house!"

Devnee had difficulty getting warm. The winter dampness had entered her bones, her lungs, even her heart. She put a kettle on the stove, heating water over the gas burner instead of sticking a mug in the microwave, just to get heat from the tiny blue flames. The flames curled away from her, as if even they found her too dull and plain to even heat water for.

The house creaked and groaned. During supper, her father got up twice to see where the draft was coming from, to shut a door here and check a window there.

Devnee's dreams from the first night crept up her back and lodged against her neck. Something dark and cold, something of ink and something of fungus crawled over her skin.

"I'm rotting," she said out loud. "I have nothing to offer, and my body knows it, and it's rotting."

Her father gave her his most irritated look.

Luke gave her his "why is this my sister?" look.

Her mother of course ignored the statement. Her mother hated being reminded of how dull, how ordinary her daughter was. Instead her mother said, "Now don't let this old house worry you, sweet pea. The house does make eerie noises, but it's just an old-fashioned heating system warming up and cooling off. Why, soon it'll feel as if you always lived here."

Perhaps I always have, thought Devnee. My shadow already knows every room; my shadow has been here before. My shadow will stay here after I am gone.

She went to bed early.

The tower was even colder than the rest of the house.

She was not surprised when her shadow peeled away, when it crossed the tower room. Cautiously, as if testing the waters.

When Devnee turned out the light, her shadow did not evaporate. It became a darker dark than the rest of the room.

Her soul darkened with it, and all her hatreds and jealousies filled the spaces of the tower, crowding against the walls, against the windows. Through the crowded anger, the packed despair, came a voice, as liquid as oozing mud.

The voice sounded trapped, condensed, underwater. It sounded heavy and drowning.

Devnee could not understand the words. Perhaps they were not words, but rumblings from ancient history.

Devnee Fountain got out of bed, holding her hands in front of her to feel her way through the dark, trying to find the voice.

Her shadow wrapped itself around her legs, hanging on to her. Pushing her back toward the bed. She kicked the air to free herself from the clinging shadow. This is how Aryssa felt toward me, she thought. I was nothing but dark air to her, to be kicked off at the end of the week.

Devnee was wearing a long flannel nightgown, because it was cold in the old house. Icy drafts crept between every crack. The nightgown caught between her feet, and tripped her. As she tumbled to the floor, the cracks in the wood widened as if the tower were having an earthquake. She cried out and clutched the wall to keep herself from falling into a crack. It opened as wide as a crevasse in Antarctica, to swallow a dog team or a downed plane, and she found a handle on the wall and held it.

She was suffocating.

She was hot and her head was throbbing from tower thoughts. Her shadow — her shadow was coming off — but not by choice — it —

— was being torn off.

There was no pain, but a severing. She had been amputated.

The shadow had not chosen to go.

The shadow had been taken.

I have to have air, thought Devnee, and flung open the window.

Wind screamed into the tower as if it had been bottled for years. The pressure of its arrival knocked her back into the center of the room, and the room felt huge, as if she could run backward for days and not hit the other wall.

She might have opened her heart as well as the window. Body and soul were exposed, more painfully than even in Mr. O'Sullivan's room. With every breath, her lungs ached in the bitter wind.

A piece of darkness became solid, and she caught it, thinking it was her shadow. It wrapped around her.

Velvet, lined with slime.

Not her shadow.

It was the answer to her wish.

Devnee could not quite see the answer.

It — he — floated in and out of focus like a distant mirage far down a highway.

He came from the cracks in the shutters, and he remained attached to them, legless. His cloak drifted toward her and shifted back, the way sea anemones did in the aquarium, tentacles rising and falling with the tide. His cloak rose and fell with her breathing, as if she had become his lungs.

Together they breathed in the tower air.

Together they studied each other.

She could not see his body, although she was aware of it, glowing and phosphorescent behind the desk. His face was visible only when the cloak was not weaving in front of it.

His eyes glittered like ice cubes. His teeth were like frozen, sharpened milk. His lips were stretched like pale rubber bands.

She wanted to run, but she wanted to be part of him and know him.

Her shadow embroidered the dark, stitching itself in the corners and darting past the shutters.

The dark drapery of his garments shifted and swirled and the hem blew toward Devnee's fingers. In a voice as sticky as spiderwebs, he said, "Touch it."

She shook her head.

How could it be so dark, so black and midnight, and yet she continued to see? Dark had become light, and the darkness of him made a path.

"Yes," he said. His voice purred. "A path. It will take us both where we want to go. I think I heard you make a wish, my dear. A wish. I came for your wish."

A wish? She could not remember wishing for anything. Except the impossible. Beauty. Friends. Fun.

The cloak stroked her hand.

She whimpered and yanked the hand back, but

the cloak arranged itself into fingers and tightened its grip. Chill surrounded her ankles like a damp moldy blanket. She could not move or think.

"Wish on it," he breathed.

She wanted to put her other hand down and peel away the cloak. But what if it caught both her hands? Where would she go then? How would she get free?

"You wished, I think," came the voice, as rich and comforting as melted chocolate, "for Beauty."

Aryssa entered her mind, as clear and devastatingly beautiful as a portrait in a gallery.

If you possessed Beauty, the rest came of its own accord. Beautiful girls stayed gracefully in one place, while along came Fame, and Riches, and Friends. If you had Beauty, people loved to look at you; and the longer they looked at you, the more they fell in love with you. If you had Beauty, there was nothing you could not do: no problem you could not conquer, no pain you could not assuage.

For a dark moment she tasted Beauty, and all that it could mean. Then her shadow swept down around her and touched her feet. For a moment she felt normal.

The shadow pressed closer, and she knew this was what her shadow wanted. She took a step back, and the cloak fell from her hand, the wind lessened, and the chill evaporated. Devnee took another step back and felt for the wall switch. The shadow clung to her arm, coaxing her back to bed.

"If, my dear," he said, "if you were beautiful . . ."

He covered his mouth and smiled behind his hands. His fingers were all bone and no flesh.

She was shocked. "You must be starving," she said.

"Yes." The *ssss* of the word lasted a long time, singing in her ears, deafening her. "I am starving," he agreed. "That is *my* wish, Devnee Fountain. Something to feed upon. Perhaps, my dear, we could trade wishes. I will give you mine, and you will give me yours."

She tried to think about this, but the *ssss* of his *yessssss* curled around her and seeped into her ears and her eyes and her thoughts, and confused her.

"What is your wissssshhhh?" he whispered.

The *ssssshhhh* floated through her brain, and she said firmly, "I want it all."

Now he laughed. It was the sound of breaking glass. "Nobody has it all, my dear."

"But they do. On TV all the time you see somebody who has it all. And in school, lots of girls have it all."

"Name one."

"Aryssa."

"She has only beauty."

"It's enough," said Devnee. "She has everything because she has beauty. If I had beauty . . ." I would have buddies who really love me, she thought. I would link arms and make phone calls and have fun. All it takes is to be beautiful, but I was born plain and I will never have a chance to be anything else. "Still," she said, "I want it all."

"That is a thousand wishes. You must start with one. Gradually you will collect it all, my dear. I promise you that in exchange. But you must choose the place to start."

Wishes were important to Devnee. Whether she wished on a birthday candle, or a wishbone, or the first star of the evening, she really pondered her wish, to be sure she wished right, that there were no hitches, that it really was her first choice.

"Aryssa," he repeated. "Such a lovely name. Such a lovely girl."

Yes, thought Devnee. Such a lovely girl. That dark hair, such a perfect cut. That fair face, such a lovely form. Those sweet soft eyes so deep beneath her brow. Her walk, like a dancer lingering with her partner.

His cape flew back and tightened around him, celebrating something. "What a wonderful description!" he breathed. "Yes, definitely the right choice."

Devnee looked at him uneasily. "I didn't say anything out loud."

"You don't need to," he said. "I am in your mind."

She shuddered. Her shadow trembled. "Give me back that thought," she said. "It's mine."

"No. You are in my tower. And I am in your head and heart." How brittle the laugh was. How desperate. What was it that he wanted? And how could she, Devnee Fountain, give it to him?

"Aryssa is not a very nice person, is she?" he

went on. "Should a mean, small-minded person like her be allowed to have such beauty?"

Devnee stood very still.

"While a gentle, kind, hardworking person like you, is . . . well . . . perhaps . . . a little less beautiful?"

"I'm plain," she said. She found herself holding Aryssa responsible for this. How dare Aryssa be born so perfect?

"Plain. A dreadful word," he sympathized. "Nobody wants to be plain. I know how you wish you were beautiful."

She nodded.

"I love wishes," he said. "I have one myself."

She was bending toward him. Her shadow was bending away.

Make a wish," he breathed.

Devnee caught the edge of the cape. For one sick, dizzy moment she felt as if she were holding the edge of a swamp, a pond full of poison. A queer stench rose up and she tried to turn away, tried to catch a breath of fresh air. The tower seemed close and fetid, as if something there were rotting in those terrible cracks that opened by night.

"Make a wish!" He drooled over the words. His trunk pulsed back and forth, as if he were on a spring. He isn't a ghost, she thought. He has too much form. And he is too dark.

She wanted to run downstairs to the kitchen full of sawdust and paper plates and family laughter.

He said, "Here's my offer."

I have to get out of here, thought Devnee. She managed to focus her eyes, managed to find her shadow, managed with her eyes to draw it back to herself. Its thin presence snuggled weakly against her.

"You want to be beautiful?" he said. "I will give you Aryssa's beauty."

Have Aryssa's beauty! Imagine that. Imagine waking up in the morning, looking in your mirror, and seeing Aryssa there! Imagine how the boys would admire; how the girls would envy!

Aryssa's beauty.

"But what about Aryssa?"

"What about her?"

"What will she have?"

He smiled. The teeth were immense and sharp and dripping with slime. "What she deserves," he said.

Oh, what a wonderful thought — that people got what they deserved! Yes! Aryssa should get what she deserved. Aryssa and Trey, saying that being buddies with Devnee made them puke! She would show them! They wouldn't say that again in a hurry!

"I wish I were beautiful," cried Devnee Fountain. "I wish I looked like Aryssa."

The cape jerked free, rasping over her skin, as painful as a handful of paper cuts. The cape wrapped itself around him like a container. Just before he vanished, she saw how his teeth overhung his lower lip, sharp as a row of garden stakes.

He was a vampire.

In that dark and terrible moment, Devnee Fountain knew what would happen to Aryssa.

But she did nothing. She did not take back her wish. Hot revenge filled her mind, ugly as a hundred vampires.

Aryssa would get what she deserved.

Devnee smiled, and the smile was sharp, and cruel.

Her shadow did not come back.

Chapter 6

In school they liked you to think. Thinking carefully and logically was a reason for school. You got graded on your thinking and Devnee tended to think more inside the building than out of it.

Today, however, Devnee Fountain sat, carefully *not* thinking.

Not thinking took a lot of energy. It required concentration far beyond mere thinking. *Not* thinking meant taking complete control of her mind and eyes and daydreams.

Not thinking required Devnee to split her personality and allot some to the teacher, some to the paper, some to the human beings around her, and none whatsoever, not a whisper, not a glimmer, to last night.

Last night.

It crept into her mind even as she fought its memory.

She saw it, smelled it, tasted it, felt it, and most of all . . . heard it.

244

"You see," he had whispered, "I cannot get anything for myself. It must be given to me. And so I offer you, my dear, a fair exchange."

His voice echoed. It did not stay where it belonged, twelve hours before. It spread like spilled oil on a pond, its dark sticky slime rimming the edges of her soul.

Her wish.

It was there. She could have it. She could take it.

It required only Aryssa.

In biology lab they were still partners. Aryssa still did not want to touch anything, and especially not today, when they had progressed to an eyeball. It came from a cow, said the teacher, and today they would —

Aryssa covered her ears and squinted her eyes shut. "You do it, Devnee," ordered Aryssa.

Devnee did not look at Aryssa. She looked at the rest of the biology lab class. Nobody wanted to look down at the metal dissection tray, and several people had chosen to look at Aryssa instead. Girls looked at Aryssa with a sort of distant longing. Boys looked at Aryssa in admiration mixed with a much closer longing, a longing called desire.

The girls wanted to look like Aryssa, but the boys wanted to have her.

If I looked like Aryssa . . . thought Devnee.

And *last night* he said, *"But you can! So easily!"*

Devnee, too, shut her eyes and winced, but it was not because of the eyeball. It was because of a certain darkness out in the school yard, a long straight glimmering path of . . . *him*.

Aryssa was too curious and eventually had to look down. She literally gagged, put her hand over her mouth, and swallowed hard. Then she went white, panting and acting faint.

"Are you all right, Aryssa?" said the boys solicitously. "Devnee, do it for her."

"Are you all right, Aryssa?" said the teacher gently. "Take a deep breath and that will help you pull together."

"Are you all right, Aryssa?" said the girls. "Devnee, she can't do that kind of thing. You're her buddy. You do it."

Aryssa managed not to throw up or pass out. She patted Devnee's knee. "I'm glad I have you, Devnee. It's so nice to have a buddy."

The eyeball before them was immense, as if it were several eyes rolled together. Its texture was both jellylike and rocklike. The rest of the class gripped and dug in. The room was noisy with the squeals of horrified girls and the grunts of sickened boys. The room was definitely on an equal opportunity basis when it came to being squeamish.

Devnee looked at Aryssa's lovely fragile face, her gentle mouth, her sweet eyes, her hair flowing like a dark and shining river.

"If I dissect it for you," said Devnee, her voice and her resolve faltering, "what will you do for me?" She was horrified to hear her voice break, hear herself begging. She might as well be on her knees.

She might as well be weeping. *Be my buddy. Like me. Sit with me because you enjoy my company. Say something nice to me! Please!*

Aryssa was amazed. Me, do something for you? her eyebrows said.

Surely Devnee was joking. The equation did not go both ways.

I want friendship even more than beauty, Devnee realized suddenly, and she almost decided against beauty; she almost waited for the next night, to explain to him that —

But then she thought: None of these people really like Aryssa anyway. It's her beauty they like. They don't want her to faint or throw up because she wouldn't be beautiful anymore. She wouldn't be something for them to adore.

She tried to sort out what was beauty and what was friendship but they were running out of time.

"Girls," said the teacher sharply.

Devnee looked up guiltily.

Aryssa opened her eyes to see that Devnee was not dissecting, either. "Come on, Devnee," she said impatiently. "Do it."

A queer sick thrill ran through Devnee.

Aryssa had just chosen her future. Aryssa had just given permission.

Aryssa had just made a very serious mistake.

"All right," said Devnee. The thrill ripped through her, like some weird electrical charge that did not kill, but energized. Devnee's eyes were very wide, they felt as large as the cows' eyes; they felt as if they would burst. How clearly she could see the dark path now.

She got up off her high lab stool.

She did not even blink. She felt less human, as if no bodily functions were going on, no blinking, no digesting, no breathing, no pumping.

She was all desire.

She was all choice.

She knew where she was going, and she did not care.

She was going to be beautiful.

For a moment she stumbled, as something was wrenched away, and she looked around in surprise, and almost in anger, but nobody had touched her and nobody had seen anything.

Only her shadow. It had pulled loose again.

Her shadow would attach itself only to a human, and what Devnee was going to do was not human.

For a moment she let herself think. For a moment the thoughts — terrible, shameful, evil thoughts — circulated in her brain.

But nobody was paying any attention to her. Even the teacher did not care that Devnee was walking to the back of the room instead of working. Even Aryssa had lost interest. Devnee Fountain was not worth the effort of tracking.

In the rear of the classroom, Devnee opened a window.

A shaft came through. Not light. Not as if the sun had suddenly come out. But as if the dark had suddenly come in.

It lay vibrating, that path.

Devnee went back to her stool. She picked up her scalpel. "If you want, Aryssa, you can stand over there at the back of the room till I've finished up."

The eyeball looked right through Devnee, into her heart. It saw what she was doing, and how.

She carefully did not think. If she thought, she would know. If she knew, she would stop. So it was best neither to think nor to know.

Aryssa slipped off her high stool and drifted to the back of the room.

The teacher said with a frown, "Aryssa?"

"I have to get a sip of water," explained Aryssa, giving the teacher her meltingly beautiful smile, and getting the usual melting response.

The eyeball stared on.

Devnee put a scalpel through it.

The tower was dark, and she did not bother to turn on the light. He was more likely to come in the dark anyhow. It was a matter of waiting. She waited a long time.

She wondered what he was doing all that time.

All night long.

When he came, it was almost dawn. At first he was quite hard to see: He was all oozing cape and wrinkled foil fingernails.

And then he smiled.

She had never seen him smile before.

His teeth were immense as posters on walls, dripping blades.

Dripping blood.

Devnee gasped. "What —" she whispered.

"What did you think?" the vampire said.

"I thought —"

"You knew," said the vampire calmly.

"I —" Devnee staggered backward. "I thought you were — like — a visitor — or — a — night creature — or — like — a dark ghost."

The vampire laughed. He sounded rich and contented, like cream soup.

She cried, "I thought you would — like — haunt her!"

"Now, Devnee. You knew what I would do. You saw the tools of my trade. You counted the hours of night in which I was busy."

This night — this night in which she had done her homework, and written up her lab experiment, and argued with her brother, and had an extra snack — this night he had . . . the vampire had . . . Aryssa had . . .

She could not think about it.

It was not decent to think about things like that.

"It was a good trade," he told her. "You got Aryssa's beauty, and I got —" He smiled again. He dried his teeth on his cape, and once more they gleamed white, shimmering like sharpened pearls.

Now she knew why the cape was dark and crusted, and why it stank of swamps and rot.

Devnee licked her lips and wished she hadn't. She clung to the shutters for strength and wished she hadn't. At last she said, "But what happened?"

"What do you think, my dear?"

"I'm trying not to think," said Devnee.

"Ah yes. You humans are very good at that. It's probably for the best, Devnee, my dear. And of course, a beautiful girl does not need to think. And now you are beautiful." His eyebrows arched like cathedral doorways, thin and pointing, vanishing beneath his straight black hair. With his eyebrows up, his eyes seemed much wider. Too wide. As if they were from biology lab. As if they were half dissected.

"Is Aryssa — is she — I mean — will she — that is —"

"She'll be fine," said the vampire. "She's just rather tired right now. She won't be in school much for the next few weeks. And of course when she does come back, she'll be plain. Nobody will notice her. The way it was for you. But that's all right, isn't it, Devnee Fountain? You thought it quite a reasonable exchange, didn't you, Devnee Fountain?"

"Don't call me by both my names," she said to him.

"Why? Does it make everything too real?" He laughed drowsily. He rocked back and forth contentedly.

Devnee tried not to think about that.

Actually, he did look healthier. His skin, usually the color of mushrooms, had a pinkish tinge. As if for the first time blood circulated in his body.

"What about my shadow?" said Devnee.

The vampire blinked. Frowned. The eyebrows

landed and sat heavily over his eyes, as if keeping them from falling out as he rocked. "Your shadow?"

"It keeps on separating from me."

The vampire's smile was slow and pleased; his lips spread like drapery over a dark window. Teeth hung over the narrow lips like foam on a sea wave. "It does, doesn't it?" he said dreamily. "Shadows," said the vampire, separating the words in a cruel, bored way, "shadows . . . prefer not . . . to be present . . . when the . . ." He smiled again. ". . . when the event . . . occurs."

"Event?" said Devnee. She was very cold. Her skin felt slick, as if she were growing mold. Or as if the vampire's mold was migrating and attaching itself to her flesh. She wrapped the quilt more tightly around herself, pulling its hem up around her neck, until she was hooded in a comforter. It did not comfort her.

Especially when the vampire touched her cheek. She flinched and jumped backward.

"Shadows love the dark. I am the dark. Your shadow needed, as you say in this century, to make contact."

She heard a noise outside the tower. The wind increased and came through the closed windows as it had before, and the chill was greater and the mold colder.

"Morning," said the vampire.

He sifted back through the slits of the shutters, into the vanishing night.

"What are you made of?" said Devnee.

"Shadows," he said. "Victims of many centuries. Collected in one cape. Under one set of teeth, as it were. I am thick with the shadows of the dead."

"Aryssa?" cried Devnee. "I thought — *she isn't dead, is she?* I thought you — I thought I —"

"She's not beautiful anymore," said the vampire. "She might as well be dead. Isn't that what *you* told me?"

He was all gone except his fingernails, wrapped around the final slat.

But his voice continued on. A separate funnel of sound and horror.

"Sweet dreams, Devnee," his voice said.

And his laughter curled into the dawn, his dark path retreated and, after a long time, Devnee Fountain turned around and went to find a mirror.

Chapter 7

She paused without looking in front of her own mirror in the tower. Anything in the tower was suspect, could be corrupted. She kept her eyes lowered. She needed a real mirror, one that would not lie.

How strange, thought Devnee. My lashes feel longer. I can feel them against my cheeks.

She went down the tower stairs to the second floor. There was no need to turn on the light. The dark path lit a way for her. It caressed her ankles and spread a velvet carpet to escort her down.

But the bathroom she shared with Luke was also uncertain. It knew her. She needed a pure, untouched mirror.

Down the final flight of stairs she went. Into the wide hallway with its wallpaper half stripped off. Back toward the kitchen, past the debris of remodeling, the tiles torn off, the lights dangling by wires. She could see as clearly as if it were noon. Through the pantry she went, to the powder room door.

The heavy dark wood of the bathroom door was not flat, like her tower door or the bedroom doors. It had panels of wood, making a raised T. Or a cross. She smiled at the cross. The vampire had not entered this bathroom. This mirror was of the world.

Devnee took a deep breath. She turned the handle. There was no need to step in. The mirror faced the door.

She lifted her lashes and looked at her reflection.

A beautiful girl looked back.

A girl whose dark hair was not lank and dull, but clouds of curling wisps.

A girl whose complexion was not pale and worn, but as fair as springtime, tinged with bright pink energy.

A girl whose eyes were not tired as dishwater, but whose eyes laughed and sparkled, and whose lashes swept mysteries before them.

Devnee laughed, and the new face laughed with her, teasing and coaxing and adorable.

Devnee raised her eyebrows and the new eyebrows were both comic and inviting.

Devnee thought deeply, and the face turned sober and gentle and full of compassion.

I am beautiful.

I have it. I have beauty.

I am not Aryssa. I do not look like her. And yet I have what she has: I have beauty. I have what makes people stop and stare. I have what makes people yearn and love.

I am Devnee Fountain.

I am beautiful.

She stood for a long time facing the mirror; stood, in fact, until dawn had come, and alarm clocks had gone off, and the rest of her family was stumbling into wakefulness.

Devnee, too, awoke.

But there was no stumbling now. No early morning heaviness. No dull resignation about yet another difficult school day ahead.

Tingling with excitement, she danced to the bathroom she shared with Luke, and wonder of wonders, he was still asleep. The floor was not covered with wet towels, and the soap was not lying in a disgusting soppy puddle at the bottom of the tub.

She felt thinner and more graceful.

The water showered down on her as if it were a privilege.

When she stepped out and wrapped herself in a towel, she tugged the pale blue plastic shower cap off and let her hair fall around her shoulders. In the foggy mirror of the hot bathroom, she looked at her reflection.

Clouds of hair, curly with humidity, wafted around her face like a bridal veil.

That's what I am, she thought. A bride. Today I go to school for the first time with the veil lifted. I used to be covered by a plain dull boring face and body, but now I am what I deserve to be.

Beautiful.

Even my brother wished this for me, she thought, laughing with wild delight. I hope you get what you deserve, he had said, and I have! Her exuberance rose up in her like a storm of fireworks, celebrating from the inside out. She wanted to scream and shout and drive through town honking a horn. Look at me! I am beautiful!

She corralled her exuberance. It would not do. She must look as if she had always looked this way.

The girl in the mirror was still Devnee, but both sharpened and softened. Nature had not quite come through for Devnee at birth, but the essential elements of Devnee's features had been good, and now because of last night she had been brought into perfection.

Devnee stroked the reflection in the mirror, and even with the fog wiped off the glass, she remained beautiful. She was not a cloud. Not a mirage. She was real, and she was beautiful.

Luke began pounding on the door. "Get outta there, Dev!" her brother bellowed. "You think you're the only one living here?"

For a moment the insides of her — the person who had not changed — the person who was still the old Devnee — was thrown.

Who *was* living here?

She stared at the mirror and instead of being thrilled, she was terrified and confused. *Who is that?* Pieces of Aryssa, pasted together? Leftover

257

victims of the vampire, summoned from the grave to be reflected in a mirror?

Where did the old Devnee go? Who is Aryssa now? Where is Aryssa now? Is Aryssa all right? What *did* happen last night?

Is this beauty only in my mind? What if the vampire just convinced me there was a trade?

Devnee opened the door before Luke smashed his way in.

Her yucky worthless brother paused in the doorway. A glare remained suspended on his face. The face itself became confused. Her brother was staring at her with awe.

"Gosh, Sis," he said. "You look great. I like your hair like that."

Luke, saying something nice?

Devnee walked out of the bathroom and her brother moved out of her way. Didn't block the door, tweak her hair, call her names or anything. In fact, when she turned to look back, he was still staring at her. "Yes?" said Devnee, curving her lips in a teasing sisterly smile.

Luke shook his head. "Dunno," was all he could manage. Then a grin, then a shrug, then once again, "You look great."

She flew up the stairs.

Lying on the little armchair was the outfit she had laid out early last night: jeans, sweatshirt, and sneakers. She could hardly believe it. Had she actually meant to show up in public in that?

I'm feminine now, thought Devnee, and graceful, and beautiful. I will never dress like that again.

She settled on a long black skirt with a filmy brown-and-gold overskirt and, on top, a thin black sweater, very baggy. A gold necklace picked up the glints in the skirt. She debated for some time between gold curlicue earrings and long gold bangles with crystals. When she flicked her hair back so her ears would show, tendrils of dark hair curled against her cheek the way she had always wished her straight plain hair would curl.

Devnee gathered her makeup. She arranged it in a row in front of the lighted mirror and prepared to get to work.

But this Devnee needed no help. She had lashes so dark and lovely that mascara would have been comic. She had cheeks so high and bright that rouge would have been clownish. She had hair so full that a curling iron would be overkill.

She went downstairs for breakfast.

Her parents blinked. "Darling!" said her mother. "You look so lovely!" A funny excitement spread over her mother's face, the same excitement Devnee had felt and corralled: celebration; the ugly duckling is a swan after all; I can relax, my plain baby girl is finally blossoming into a lovely woman.

Her father was just confused. "Did you darken your hair, Dev?"

"Daddy," she said, scolding him gently.

"You don't have to fiddle with what nature gave

you," said her father. "You look beautiful just as you are."

Devnee smiled at him. He smiled back. He said, "You look great, honey. I'm so proud of you these days."

Her mother said, "This year let's get a family portrait done. We've been talking about it for years but we've just never gotten to it. You wear your hair just like that, Dev. You look so lighthearted and happy and" — her mother laughed with surprise — "well, beautiful."

Devnee didn't even want a sip of orange juice; anything might upset the chemical balance that had caused this.

Her father said, "Why don't I drive you to school, sweetheart? I hate for you to put those shoes into the snow."

Devnee smiled graciously at her parents.

The high school lobby was impressive. Sheets of marble, hard and glittering and black, were separated by tiny strips of gold. It looked like a state legislature building, where brilliant — or stupid — decisions were made. Not like a school, where brilliant — or stupid — kids hung out.

Long wide marble steps were topped by large planters, filled with greenery that kids either admired or threw crumpled tissues into, depending on their attitude toward life.

Art exhibits filled the long blank wall.

Students were everywhere. This was the room

in which to meet, to plan, to wave, to talk, and most of all, to be seen.

Devnee entered the lobby.

And she was seen as she had never been seen before.

Girls turned to look at her. Girls whispered to each other about how Devnee wore her hair. Boys tilted their heads the way boys do when they were thinking about what you'd be like.

Devnee stood on display, turning slightly, bestowing on them a side view, and then a slight smile, and finally a slight wave.

Slight, thought Devnee (her insides wildly excited, her outsides calm and perhaps even bored), because I'm used to this, and I hardly think about it anymore.

Nina came running over. Buddy number three. Mean old Nina with her fabulous car and her magnificent sweaters. "Hi, Devnee!" cried Nina. "I love your hair. You look great, Devnee. What a skirt. Where'd you get that? I wanna skirt like that."

Devnee had never had a chance to snub anybody. "I forget," she said, and walked on. Snubbing Nina felt wonderful. She would have to do it often. It was so powerful, so rewarding, to snub somebody.

Devnee's stride, usually halting and unsure, changed. Now she was a dancer, smooth and easy. She could feel how her hair rested on her shoulders, and how her smile decorated her face.

I didn't know you could feel being beautiful

from the inside! she thought. What an extra treat. You don't even have to be in front of a mirror. You can see yourself mirrored in other people.

And I thought the vampire was kidding. I owe him. This is fabulous. This is unbelievable! This is life the way it should be lived!

Everybody commented.

Even the teachers commented.

"I love your hair like that," everybody said to her.

"Gosh, you look great today, Devnee!"

And at lunch, both Trey and William commented. Trey said, "Wow, Dev! Way to go! You look great. Really great."

William nodded, a smile never leaving his face. "This is your year, huh, Devnee? You look great."

Nothing about Devnee Fountain had ever been "great" before. Now it was great to see her, and she looked great, and it was great to be in school.

People kept saying, "What did you do?" as if expecting an answer like "Changed lipstick" or "Used a blow-dryer."

Never in her life had the world come to her.

Never in her life had there been such confidence, such pleasure, in just being alive.

She was not self-conscious. Not worried. Not timid.

She was beautiful.

She ate differently. A beautiful girl did not stuff her face and snatch extras and lean across to grab more, she thought. A beautiful girl spent the entire lunch period nibbling delicately on the rim of a single cracker.

When lunch ended, they all rose, making the usual passes around the cafeteria to dispose of trash, return trays, say hello to people they hadn't spotted before.

Devnee stood very still, accepting homage. Thinking — this is so fabulous. Having people look at you — not because you're new, or you're stupid, or you look funny, or your clothes are weird — but because you are beautiful.

A girl separated herself from the rest and strolled over to Devnee. Devnee knew her. Eleanor. A leader of the senior class. Eleanor was almost regal. She did not seem seventeen, but ageless: like a medieval princess who deserved a stone parapet. "Hello, Devnee," said Eleanor seriously. "I wanted to talk to you about something."

"Of course," said Devnee.

"As you know, the Valentine's Day Dance is coming up," said Eleanor.

Devnee had not known this; in fact, she had not thought of Valentine's Day at all. Now she remembered the holiday: the candy hearts that said BE MINE and KISS ME; the silly cards you addressed to everybody in your class; the red roses your father gave your mother, and the heart-shaped cake she frosted white and sprinkled with coconut.

"Nominations for Valentine Sweetheart must be made this week, and the Sweetheart will be crowned at the dance," said Eleanor.

"How quaint," said Devnee.

Eleanor laughed. "I know. It's rather embarrassing that we still do that kind of thing. But the peasants like it, you know." Eleanor cast a meaningful look at the crowd of the plain and dull that filled most of the cafeteria. She and Devnee laughed together.

Eleanor said, "I'd like to nominate you, Devnee, but of course I want your permission first because so many girls just don't want to be bothered with this beauty queen stuff."

Eleanor, although lovely, was too stern to be nominated for anything as frivolous as Valentine Sweetheart. If Devnee were to name any girl sufficiently frilly, fragile, and lace-edged for such a title, it would be Aryssa.

But I'm Aryssa, thought Devnee.

The pasted-together pieces of her — the old person, the new face, the old memories, the new admiration — they clattered together, and seemed almost to fall apart and hit the ground. Like Cinderella's glass slipper.

She felt broken and afraid.

Where is Aryssa? Is she me? Is she half me? Am I half her? Is she in school today? Does she even exist to come to school? Has her shadow joined the vampire's body? Where is my shadow?

Who is Eleanor nominating — the me who is me, or the Aryssa who is me, or the Aryssa who is not anybody now?

Behind her, William said, "I second the nomination, Devnee."

She turned, trembling, the ice of fear blowing cold between her broken pieces, to see both Trey and William, like a matched pair of horses being readied for a race, steaming and snorting and pawing the ground.

Neither of them wanted Eleanor.

They wanted her.

Devnee stroked the new thick cloud of dark hair on her head as if accepting a different crown. She ducked her head modestly. She smiled her gentlest smile. She said, "That's so sweet of you."

She thought, *Valentine Sweetheart*. The most beautiful girl. The most loved. The most photographed.

I'll need a really special dress. Something in pale pink, something with ribbons.

I'll need a date. Which boy should I take? Trey or William?

She smiled. The joys of being beautiful were like a great basket overflowing with goodies. A nomination here, a handsome boy there, a mirror on this side, a camera soon to go off on that.

They were emerging from the cafeteria into the hallway. The fluorescent lights went strangely dim, and a dark path centered itself on the floor. People shivered slightly in the sudden chilly draft.

The filmy gold-and-black overlay of Devnee's skirt lifted, and swirled, and settled. *He's here.*

He's in school with me. He's in my mind, even now, he's reading it, knowing it.

Eleanor said, "Then you accept the nomination?"

"Of course," said Devnee graciously.

The vampire's laughter, like a maniac with a knife, rose up out of the floor. The rest also heard, and momentarily froze, but then they shrugged, thinking it was nothing, perhaps distant breaking glass.

But it was not nothing.

It was him, and he was here.

A tiny foolish sentence flew back from her memory: a tiny foolish wrong sentence she had allowed herself to think, and now it banged inside her head like metal striking metal, clashed and shouted up inside the thoughts where the vampire could live anytime he chose: I owe him.

She had thought it, and it counted.

I owe him, she had said.

And already he had come to collect the debt.

Chapter 8

Mrs. Cort smiled at the English class. Her smile lingered on Devnee. Even when Victoria said something of great brilliance, Mrs. Cort was hardly distracted. There were only a few minutes left in the period when she said, "Please pass your reports forward. As you know, this counts for one quarter of your grade this marking period."

The usual moans and groans mixed with the shuffling and slapping of papers being passed down the rows.

Devnee's heart missed a beat. She had forgotten to finish her English paper. She had had the rough draft done several days ago, but last night . . . what with everything she had to think about . . . well . . .

"Devnee?" said Mrs. Cort. "I don't seem to have a paper from you."

Devnee opened her new eyes very wide. She bit her lip in the desperate sweet way that worked so well for Aryssa. Of course, Aryssa didn't have Mrs.

Cort. And Mrs. Cort was so solid and sensible. But it was worth a try. Devnee said anxiously, "Oh — I'm so sorry — I — do you think I could pass it in tomorrow? Please?"

"Well . . ." said the teacher.

"I have my rough draft done," said Devnee. "I tried so hard, Mrs. Cort. But my computer crashed and I didn't get it printed out."

"You should have e-mailed me," said William. "I would have printed it for you, Devnee."

"She hasn't really been in town that long," said Victoria. "I mean, it hasn't been easy for Devnee, Mrs. Cort, getting into the rhythm of things."

"It's all right, Devnee," said the teacher understandingly. "These things happen."

The class divided, into those who thought it very fair that a beautiful girl should be allowed an extra day, and those who thought it very cruel that rules were bent for beauty.

They will never bend the rules for Aryssa again, thought Devnee suddenly. Aryssa will have to get her papers in on time and pass her tests and do her lab sheets. Nobody will make excuses for her and nobody will forgive her.

She felt afraid for Aryssa. How would Aryssa stand up to it — she who had always been protected by her looks?

Devnee's heart hardened. Her arteries and veins changed, too, becoming metallic and sterile.

She remembered Aryssa that day. Telling Trey she'd been nice only to get a lab partner to do the scut work for her. Telling Trey the trouble with being nice was that people expected you to go on being nice, even when you were bored to death with it and them. She remembered Trey and Aryssa laughing.

The hardness in her did not quite feel human, it was so steely.

But then, I'm not quite human, she thought. I'm a makeover from a vampire.

The room whirled and spun, as if gravity were letting go of her, as her shadow had let go of her. She would go into some sick horrible orbit occupied by vampires and dark paths, she would —

How silly, she said to herself. Silly, silly dreams. I'm beautiful because I'm growing up at last. Blossoming. New shampoo. Vampires, indeed. What nonsense.

She tossed her hair and felt the beautiful thick curls of it settle on her lovely slim shoulders, felt the eyes of her class turning toward her. She gripped the desk to steady herself, and returned the steady gazes of her classmates. They were surveying her. Admiring. Enjoying. Feasting their eyes on her beauty.

Feasting, thought Devnee, and she gagged.

How did it happen? What did he do, exactly? Is Aryssa all right?

How much red there suddenly seemed to be in the room. Red fingernails, red jewelry, red skirts, and somewhere, red blood.

I want to be beautiful, but I don't want —

Well, it probably wasn't *really* like that. He probably didn't *really* —

English ended.

Her silly twisted daydream and dark fantasies ended.

Victoria and William smiled at her. She basked in it. She had never had a day in which the world came to her rescue and smiled back. Never a day in which there was such pleasure just to be alive.

She stood up gracefully, smoothing her pretty skirt, readying herself to join them.

Victoria and William leaned against each other, laughed together, wrapped arms around each other, and headed in tandem for their next class. She had not seen them as a pair, was certainly not expecting the jolt of jealousy that ran through her.

She gritted her teeth but stopped that immediately, knowing it could not be a beautiful expression. She whirled to find Trey. Trey would be alone now that there was no Aryssa here.

But Trey had caught up to Victoria and William. He bounced alongside them, a jock puppy tagging along.

Devnee never forced herself on people, but she knew her beauty did no good unless people were looking at it. She rushed after them, speeding past, and then slowing herself, lingering like the end of a dance. And sure enough, their haste ended, the twosome softened, self-interest dwindled. They feasted their eyes on Devnee.

"What's everybody doing after school?" said William.

"Guess I'd better check on Aryssa," said Trey, running up the wall to leave his shoe prints.

"Is she sick, do you think?" said Victoria worriedly.

Trey admired his shoe prints. "Nah. She had an English paper, too, you know. She's always sick the day a paper is due." Trey laughed. William and Victoria laughed.

They still think Aryssa is beautiful, thought Devnee, so they still forgive her for being dumb. What will happen when Trey goes over there?

She imagined Trey, staring in confusion, perhaps in horror, at the thing Aryssa would be now. She imagined him reaching out to touch her, heal her, and then shrinking back because of the change in her. She imagined him seeing something on her throat, frowning, leaning forward, saying, *Aryssa, what happened to you?*

And Aryssa.

Would she know what had happened? Would she say, *A vampire came in the night. Devnee sent him. Remember the creepy girl who used to live in the mansion? Well, another creepy one lives there now. Devnee chose me, Devnee picked me out and ruined me and took all I had, Trey!*

And Trey. What would he do next? Would he run away from her? Would he turn on Devnee? Would he tell the rest of the world? Would he shout: *Do you know how she got that beauty? Do you know the trade she made?*

Devnee faltered, touching the wall for support.

Terror infected her lungs like a parasite.

It can't be real. There is no vampire. There is no such thing as a vampire. I don't believe in vampires. Nothing happened to Aryssa; she just didn't get her paper written.

Time had changed character for Devnee. It had the capacity to absorb her, like the center of a cyclone. While she had been in the cyclone, evil thoughts whirling, William and Victoria had moved on, and Trey left for his car. She was alone in the hall with Nina. Nasty Nina with nothing but money and sweaters. I must not fall into my thoughts like that again, Devnee told herself. I must keep my thoughts on beauty and on myself.

Nina and Devnee had to turn a corner, enter a stairwell, head down another wing. When they passed a girls' room, Devnee ducked inside. She had to check the mirror. See if she was still beautiful.

Yes.

The beauty had not gone anywhere.

Nina said, "You're exactly like Aryssa, you know."

Devnee flinched.

"Always going to the girls' room to look in a mirror. Isn't it enough to be beautiful, Devnee? Do you have to have proof ten times a day? What do girls like you see in that mirror? Why don't you feel safe? It's going to last, you know. Either you're beautiful or you aren't."

Devnee laughed nervously.

She went to the frosted glass window of the girls' room and tilted it inward and open for fresh air.

It was snowing lightly. New-fallen snow blanketed the old ugly crust blackened by car exhaust.

Like me, thought Devnee Fountain. I, too, am new-fallen.

I sold Aryssa.

Was it worth it?

The very second she questioned whether the beauty was worth it, her beauty began to slide off. Like a mud mask. It peeled away from her skin and slid toward the window.

No! she thought, putting her hands up to hold her cheeks, hold on to her beauty. You gave it to me, you can't take it back!

If it isn't worth it to you, I'll give it to somebody else, the vampire said from right inside her mind. She had forgotten that he shared it with her now. That he could live there if he chose.

If I'm not real, said the vampire, *you aren't beautiful anyway, are you?*

She turned frantically toward the window, where outside the world lay dim and wintry.

You've insulted me, said the vampire. *Insulted my gift.*

She could see his dark path well — a shadow cast where there was nothing to cast it.

It's real, you're real! she said to the dark path. *I take it back, it was all real!*

Her face was half on, half off. She could not turn back to Nina or look around toward the row of mirrors above the sinks.

You are a vampire, she said to him. *You are real.*

Inside her head the vampire raised his eyebrows.

Her beauty trembled, unsure, not quite leaving, not quite staying.

And I really gave you Aryssa, she admitted. *And it was worth it.*

Her beauty returned. It returned with a permanency that was solid and sure. It would never slide off again. She had Aryssa's beauty and the vampire had Aryssa.

And it was worth it, she said to herself firmly.

Chapter 9

Devnee walked slowly to her locker and then slowly to the lobby.

People smiled at her. They continued to remark on how nice she looked today — was it her birthday or something?

Devnee had never been the center of anything. Even at her own birthday parties, it always felt as if the little girls she had invited were being polite.

Today she was the center of it all.

She had not known that beauty was literally pivotal: that heads would turn, bodies would turn, eyes would turn — all to look at Devnee Fountain.

She had not known how differently she would stand and pose; how her chin would lift, and her head would tilt, and her eyes would tease.

Usually she could leave school — any school, the last one, this one — in a few seconds.

Today, what with talking and waving and smiling and flirting, it took a long time. There was so much to do, so much to say.

This is how perfect people live, thought Devnee, stunned.

They're busy. Busy being beautiful.

She laughed with the sheer joy of it and, listening to the sound of her laugh, realized that it, too, was different; not just an ordinary everyday garden-variety laugh — it was a beautiful cascade of joy. Everybody laughed with her, and the afternoon was free and soft and lovely.

And the real Devnee — her soul, her personality — was at last where it belonged: in a perfect, matching body.

She knew now why they had bought the house with the tower. It was because she, Devnee, was destined for beauty. The vampire had simply straightened out an error of birth. It was only right and just.

Finally the crush of students in the lobby dwindled, as people went on to sports events, or orthodontist appointments, or the pizza place.

And Trey came back to school.

She saw his car coming to the front drive. Such an ordinary car for such a fabulous boy. A dull four-door sedan. Matronly. Middle-aged. And yet it didn't matter, because with Trey on the inside it was incredibly exciting and wonderful.

He parked right in front of the front door.

Not allowed.

Students had a student parking lot. Even disabled students had to park down below and come in the bottom entry.

She wondered if handsome boys, like beautiful girls, could get away with things. Was Trey parking there because he knew nobody would tow his car?

Trey came up the stairs, opened the lobby door, and looked around.

He looked wrong.

He looked off balance.

He looked — well — spooked.

"Trey?" said Devnee.

He seemed to see her with difficulty. As if focusing his eyes were hard. As if she were coming and going from his sight. He walked over unsteadily and said, "Devnee. I'm so glad somebody's still here. I just went to see Aryssa. She's — she's —"

He couldn't finish.

Devnee's hair prickled. Her skin stood out from her bones. Her soul stiffened. She said, "She's what, Trey?"

He shook his head. "I don't know how to describe it." Trey shuddered.

Devnee said softly, "Let's go to the Doughnut House and talk about it."

"How did you know I love the Doughnut House?" said Trey, half laughing and half still upset.

How *did* I know? thought Devnee, and now half of Devnee, too, was upset. She could feel the vampire tickling the edges of her mind and she hated it — that he could live there like that, that he was part of her and she was part of him.

In Trey's car they went to the Doughnut House. They could not find a space right in front and parked down a block. They had to walk slowly, picking their way around slush and ice piles.

A guy in a mason's dump truck honked at Devnee and grinned.

A city bus driver tapped his horn and gave her a thumbs-up.

Two men on a rooftop repairing shingles whistled.

A woman in a store window changing the display gazed at her with the complex admiration of a plain woman for a beautiful one.

Once inside, snuggled up to the counter and each other, they ordered hot chocolate, which she loved to stir more than to drink. Although she loved jelly doughnuts, they were messy, and beautiful girls did not risk eating messy foods, so she had a plain sugar doughnut instead.

"See, she's all kind of — well — lumpy," said Trey. He ate his first jelly doughnut in precisely two bites. Two huge raspberry-running bites. The raspberry filling dotted the corners of his mouth like blood.

Devnee swallowed, although she had nothing in her mouth but panic.

"Aryssa is always dumb," said Trey. "I mean, that goes with the territory." He half laughed, half shrugged. "But this time — I don't know what's wrong with her. She's kind of heavy and thick and — well" — Trey looked as if he could not figure the next word out — "ugly," he said at last. "She's really ugly, Devnee."

Ugly? thought Devnee. She looks like I used to? I wasn't ugly! I was just ordinary. Wasn't I?

Trey said, "I mean, I didn't want to spend time with her. The kind of girl that guys puke if they get stuck with. You know. A real dog."

Devnee was chilled. Trey could not have been with Aryssa ten minutes. Did he really judge completely, entirely on looks?

Devnee could not help herself. She said, "Maybe Aryssa is just coming down with something. You know. A bug. A virus. Maybe in a few days she'll feel better and all that."

Trey shook his head. "Nah. I could tell. This is for good."

"Was there" — Devnee paused, feeling her way — "anything else different?"

"Like what?" said Trey, eating a second doughnut. Another two bites and it vanished. She wondered if the vampire's appetite was that great. If the vampire had —

For a terrible cruel moment, it seemed to her that Trey was also a vampire. She gripped the hard edges of the yellow counter in both hands, until the rims dented her palms, and then she looked back at Trey. No, he was still handsome, sexy, impressive.

He said, "So, Dev." He grinned, putting Aryssa on the discard pile with his raspberry-stained napkins. "There's a dance coming up."

Her heart pounded. No boy had ever even hinted that he might like to take Devnee Fountain to a dance.

"A Valentine's dance," said Trey.

They smiled at each other; small knowing smiles.

He said, "I hear Eleanor nominated you for Sweetheart."

She ducked her head modestly.

"Come on," said Trey. "You know how gorgeous you are."

She laughed.

He said, "It's funny. I misjudged you. I guess with new kids, it's kind of easy. They're nervous and you get thrown off and don't really realize who they are. I mean — I was thinking you were —" Trey shrugged again. It was a frequent habit with him. It was, Devnee suddenly thought, almost girlish. He used his broad shoulders to escape the ends of sentences the way Aryssa had used her beauty.

He said, "So."

She raised her eyebrows.

They both laughed.

"Want to come with me to the Valentine's dance?" said Trey. He knew she would. They both knew she would. Beautiful people, she realized, always understood what other beautiful people were thinking.

She was in no rush to answer.

It had also come to her that beautiful people were not desperate.

They were not threatened. They were in no hurry. They could say yes if they felt like it . . . or no.

She said to Trey, "I think that would be lovely, Trey."

"Like you," he said, and he preened, and this time it did not seem girlish, but more like a peacock flaring its feathers, and it came to Devnee that there was nothing to Trey but his exterior.

He was a boy who could dump a girl in, literally, a heartbeat.

All because that girl had a bad day.

Inside her head, the vampire corrected her. Bad night, actually, said the vampire, and the vampire laughed and laughed and laughed, and the laugh came out of Devnee's mouth, and Trey was startled at the length of her laughter, but he joined in, because life amused him, and beauty amused him, and as long as Devnee remained beautiful, he would remain with Devnee.

Chapter 10

Luke's basketball game began at 6:15. They all had to go and cheer him on.

She was furious at this waste of time until she arrived.

People actually turned to look at her, flinging hoods off their heads, tucking scarves down, adjusting glasses. "Who's that?" they whispered to each other.

"New girl," came the answer. "Lives in the mansion at the bottom of the hill."

"She's beautiful!"

It worked everywhere, this beauty, with everyone. With adults and teenagers, with teachers and toddlers.

A crowd of kids from the high school decorated the top two bleachers on the right. In her old school Devnee would not even have tried to join the crowd. She would have known she was unwanted and a pest. In this new school Devnee would not have tried to join. She knew how people like Aryssa and

Trey saw her: as the kind of girl who never understood that you didn't really want her there.

But this was now, this was beauty; she climbed easily up the bleachers and people who saw her coming smiled and moved apart, knowing that she of course was going to the top.

She hardly even knew the kids at the top, but she joined them without a flicker of concern, and sure enough, they were delighted to have her. Devnee basked in their attention, and went with them at halftime to buy candy from the fund-raiser in the lobby, and when her brother made baskets everybody in her row cheered extra hard. Not because she was related to Luke — but because Luke was related to her.

She was the one who mattered now.

There was only one bad moment.

She was introduced to Aryssa's parents.

"Where is Aryssa?" said everybody else.

"She doesn't feel well," said her parents uncertainly. "She's under the weather." They looked at each other, deeply upset, confused, disoriented. Perhaps they did not even know the teenage girl who had gotten up that morning.

They were nice people.

They reminded Devnee of her own parents. Solid, dull, uninteresting, ordinary people. How did they have a daughter like Aryssa? she wondered.

But they don't now.

Aryssa isn't, now.

How hot the gym was. How loudly the sneakers squealed, how cruelly the cameras flashed.

"Do you feel faint, Devnee?" said one of the girls solicitously. "Want me to help you? Somebody buy Devnee a soda."

Two boys bounced down the bleachers to buy Devnee a soda.

At last, at last, she was alone in the tower. Her family had wasted so much of her time, fawning over her, complimenting her. Suffocating her. Really, couldn't they tell she had better things to do than fuss with them?

She was strangely angry at them. Why did they have such a light in their eyes? Where had that light been for the first fifteen years? Why did it have to take beauty to make them proud of her?

What if they find out? she thought. What if they learned what I did to get this beauty?

There were questions to ask. Futures to decide. Facts to learn.

She did not bother turning on the light.

He was more likely to come in the dark anyhow.

She waited.

He came by mouth, teeth first, like green shoots in the spring, moss covered. He wiped them on his black cloak and the fungus was gone, leaving stains on the cloak, leaving his teeth white and gleaming and ready.

Her blood seemed to cease circulating, as if it

knew what those fangs were for, what those teeth had been doing, what could happen next.

All the things she had meant to say evaporated.

Her head was as empty as her soul.

Devnee sat absolutely still in her bed, watching the smile drip, and advance. To her surprise, her shadow joined her. In the dark her shadow was soft and fuzzy, like a friend. Like somebody on her team.

The vampire smiled, and something phosphorescent oozed from his fangs. His mouth was a cave, and stalactites were forming even as she watched.

She knew better than to let her terror show. She said to her shadow, "You stay here! You hear me?"

The shadow said nothing.

The vampire said, "A nice girl, Devnee . . ."

But I'm not nice, she thought. Trey isn't, either. He goes only by looks. But that's what I go by of course, and I'm not nice, either; we have proof of that now, don't we?

"Say what you have to say," said Devnee sharply, "and get out. I have to get some sleep."

"Beauty sleep," said the vampire, "isn't that what they call it?"

She closed her eyes, although it was difficult in his presence. She felt as if she needed several more sets of eyes, so some would always be open, always be a sentry to protect her in the night.

"Yes," breathed the vampire, "beauty sleep. A

different kind of sleep than you have ever had before, isn't it, Devnee? A sleep in which you are beautiful! What a wonderful feeling. To be beautiful at last."

His voice was soft and rumbly as a purring cat's.

Her shadow lay back on the bed with her. She felt sleep coming, and he was right — it was different.

"You are glad you made that wish, aren't you?" he whispered.

She nodded against the pillow. She was glad. How could she not be glad? Some things have a price, she thought. I just have to accept that. Aryssa has to accept that. I accepted being plain for fifteen years, now it's her turn, so there.

"Of course, a nice girl would give it back," said the vampire briskly.

Give it back?

She opened her eyes.

"I mean, is this really kind to Aryssa?" said the vampire.

Of course it wasn't kind. It was horrible.

But —

A hundred *buts* came into her head. But I like being beautiful. But it isn't my fault. But I didn't go out and get this beauty. You're the bad guy! "You gave it to me," she said finally. "It's up to you what happens to it."

The vampire laughed. "No, my dear. It's up to *you*. Isn't that a wonderful thought? Aren't you thrilled? You have the power to go back to being plain again. You have the power to decide to be dull and boring. Just wallpaper. Just another sample in the book. Just another faceless member of the crowd." He had retracted his teeth like turtle legs; his smile was sweet and kind. "You can make Aryssa happy and beautiful again, Devnee. What a wonderful feeling! You can be kind."

She was holding hands with her shadow.

Or was it an extension of the vampire's cloak? Both were thick and cloudy and velvety. But this had a taste. It tasted of vapor and mold. She gagged slightly. She tried to remember why she had actually wanted the vampire to come tonight. She had had questions. What were they?

"Of course," said the vampire, "everyone has a streak of selfishness in her. Some of us more than others. But it's inevitably present in a human being. It's simply a matter of tapping the selfishness." He studied his horrid fingernails in a girlish way, as if his wrinkled foil needed a touch-up.

She envisioned him in some world alien to her own, in front of some evil mirror, inspecting himself, admiring himself.

The vampire raised his eyebrows. "But my dear, that's exactly what you do. I saw you today, in front of the mirror, inspecting and admiring."

"You followed me?" She was outraged.

"I *am* you."

"Don't be disgusting!" she shouted.

The vampire smiled and this time held his

hand neatly over his mouth, keeping his weapons delicately hidden.

She said in a low voice, "Aryssa isn't actually hurt, is she?"

"Of course not, my dear. How could you think that of me? It doesn't hurt. Aryssa is simply . . . rather . . . tuckered out."

Devnee was feeling rather tuckered out herself. But she doubted if it was the same thing.

The vampire said, "Sleep well, my dear."

Right, she thought.

"Tomorrow in school . . ." He laughed gaily, like a child going to a picnic. "You will cross paths with Aryssa. My path will be there, too, of course. Just another shadow, you will think. But of course there is nothing ordinary about my path." The vampire smiled proudly at his dark path.

He said, "It will happen in the lobby, my dear. Such a pretty room. All that glittering marble in which you — the beautiful stunning you — will be reflected. And as the paths intersect . . . yours, Aryssa's, mine . . . you will have the choice, dear girl, of whether to stay beautiful . . . or . . . be kind."

He blinked several times, as if slamming doors with his eyes.

He slid away toward the shutters and she felt her shadow being suctioned off her, and she clung to the shadow, holding it in her fingers, and this contest she won; the shadow was hers.

But the choice was still to come.

She could be nice. Or she could be beautiful.

                    *   *   *

"Oh, what a beautiful morning!"

It was an old, old song. Devnee did not know where it came from.

Her mother was singing in the kitchen. "Oh, what a beautiful morning!" She could hear the shuffling slide of dancing feet. For her mother, the day, her life, her daughter — it was all so beautiful it had to be sung about and danced to.

Sun was everywhere.

Snow had fallen during the night, and the sun glittered on the pristine white world, and gleamed through every window and sparkled on every surface.

Devnee went downstairs to find her family in wonderful moods, her mother trilling, her father bouncing, her brother leaping.

Her mother kissed her on each cheek. "Isn't this a beautiful day?" she cried.

Her father hugged her. "I *do* have a beautiful daughter," he said proudly, holding her off for a better view and then hugging her again.

Even her brother grinned and saluted.

Always before she had seen *them* as worthless and *herself* as worthy. But was this true? She who worked with vampires? Just who was worth anything around here?

"Last night at the game?" said Luke to his sister.

"Yeah?"

"One of my friends wanted to know who you were," Luke said. He was pleased. He was proud.

Luke — who used to be sickened that he had a blood relationship with Devnee.

Blood. I must not think of blood.

Her father spread strawberry jam on a toasted bagel and for a minute seemed to be sticking his knife into a jar of congealed blood.

Devnee held on to herself, and for one queer horrifying moment her self seemed to detach as the shadow had, leaving her with nothing but the beautiful shell.

"Which friend?" she asked Luke. She picked up her orange juice. It was crimson. She nearly spilled it.

"Cranberry juice," said her mother, chirping like a canary. "I thought it would make such a pretty change."

They sat together, eating hastily. Mornings were never leisurely. Too many people rushing too many places. And yet she had time to look at her family, and see them anew.

"Jesse," said her brother. "Too young for you. But among your admirers, Dev."

No sarcasm.

Their father said, "I've been thinking about that family portrait. I do want to do it. I've got such a nice family, and we're at such a nice stage in our lives. We've fit into this town so well. We all love our jobs and school and house. Don't we?"

"A beautiful family," agreed her mother.

Devnee's hair prickled. Her mother was much prettier than usual. Her mother was glowing and —

No.

No, the vampire had not also corrupted her mother.

No, these things could not be. It was Devnee who lived in the tower, and Devnee who had made the bargain. Her mother was innocent. Had to be. That's what mothers were.

Devnee thought of the test to come. The meeting in the lobby. The crossing of the paths of Aryssa, Devnee, and the vampire.

I can be kind or I can be beautiful. I cannot be both. That's so unfair! He has no right to put me in that kind of situation.

This is all his fault, for being hungry and greedy. None of this is my fault.

Devnee gathered her school things, put on her coat, remembered her scarf and mittens, but did not put them on; carried them as colorful accessories instead. They went out the door, Devnee to her bus and Luke to his.

Luke ran on ahead, because Luke ran everywhere, pumping muscles wherever he could, getting his daily pleasure from the mere throbbing of his own legs.

She walked sedately after him, aware of her beauty; aware that she, too, sparkled like snow.

Her shadow kept its distance.

It came . . . but it was not attached.

It was judging her. Waiting to see what happened in the lobby.

Chapter 11

In the lobby Eleanor, queenly and elegant, flourished a decorated cardboard box in which Sweetheart nominations had been dropped. It was a shoebox, the kind that in grade school you decorated with red construction paper and lace doilies and cutouts from women's magazines, and cut a slit in the top of. Then on Valentine's Day you collected those silly little cards from everybody in class.

In grade school, the teachers made everybody be nice.

If you weren't going to give a card to everybody, you couldn't give cards at all.

And yet you could still tell who was loved and who was not.

Perhaps the cards for the popular girls were larger. Or lacier.

Perhaps the party given on Saturday included only a few.

Perhaps the cupcake handed to you by the

number one kid in the class had less icing on it than the one he gave to his real friend.

But in elementary school, on Valentine's Day, you had to be nice.

"Hi, Devnee," said Eleanor. "How are you today?"

"Fine, thanks, how are you?"

"Couldn't be better. You look lovely. You must tell me how to put on makeup like that."

Devnee was wearing none.

Eleanor opened the cardboard vote box, which was surely not proper democratic procedure, but then, as Eleanor pointed out, what is democratic about a princess?

A pile of paper squares lay on the bottom of the box.

Her name was written again and again: DEVNEE FOUNTAIN, DEVNEE FOUNTAIN, DEVNEE FOUNTAIN FOR VALENTINE SWEETHEART.

"Of course, these are only nominations," said Eleanor. "We don't know till the Sweetheart Dance who has actually been voted Sweetheart." She laughed a knowing, superior laugh. "I'm not worried, though. Are you, Devnee?"

Devnee laughed, also, equally knowing, equally superior.

A boy she did not know smiled nicely at her. "Guess you're going to be the Sweetheart, huh?"

She gave him her flirtiest smile. "Are you voting for me?"

He blushed. He shuffled a little, embarrassed

by attention from somebody as important and special as Devnee. "Well, actually . . . I guess I'm voting for my own girl," he said. And put his arm around a plain and ordinary girl at his side, and smiled at her. Smiled with love.

Devnee's heart hurt.

For one incredible moment she actually yearned to be his girl — to get his vote no matter who was prettier.

But she set that thought aside.

William came into the lobby. What a hunk he was!

She waited for William to come to her and say something sweet.

But his eyes were elsewhere. His eyes were on Victoria. Devnee was amazed. Impressive as Victoria was, interesting, intriguing, smart, all that — still, William could do so much better. William could have Devnee.

But William's eyes lingered on Victoria, and eventually he grew courageous and let his hand linger on her, too. Just barely. Just the back of her waist. But Victoria seemed oblivious to William's intentions. That was an act of course; nobody on earth could be oblivious to William.

Aryssa walked in.

Perhaps it was an exaggeration to say "walked."

She slumped in, dragging her feet. She moved as if she were a dead weight on the end of a tow rope.

Hardly anybody looked at her.

Only Victoria seemed to recognize Aryssa. "Aryssa," said Victoria, going over instantly, not even noticing as William's hand fell from her waist, leaving him behind without a thought. "Aryssa, what's wrong? You really look down and out!"

Aryssa's smile did not quite appear. It was just a feeble slow lip twitch. "I think I — I think I'm tired," she said.

"You should have stayed home another day," said Victoria. "You don't look well enough to be in school."

"It's the last day for nominations for Sweetheart," said Aryssa. "I wanted to be here."

Several people looked at her with disgusted laughter and pity. They whispered softly to each other. Devnee knew what they were saying — that lump? A dance queen? Please.

Eleanor said softly to Devnee, "Aryssa's let herself go so badly. I don't know how she could possibly be anybody's Sweetheart. She looks more like anybody's candy wrapper. Ready for the trash."

Eleanor's group laughed meanly.

Be kind to her, thought Devnee, a little shocked.

A dark path oozed out from a crack in the marble. The crack was filled with a strip of gold, and the purity of the gold remained intact, even though the dark path tried to compromise it.

I could be gold, thought Devnee. I could give up my beauty. Right now. Aryssa could go back to who she is, and people would still admire her, and she would have Trey.

And I would be kind.

And plain.

Dull.

Unloved.

The dark path unrolled, like a stained and moth-eaten carpet.

She stared at it, wondering where it was going, where it would stop, who would trip on it and fall in.

"Hi, Devnee," said another boy. "Going to be Sweetheart soon, huh?"

She smiled back as sweetly as she knew how, to show that her heart was a match for her beauty.

William caught up to Victoria and said, "Aryssa, you want me to drive you back home? You really look wiped out."

Victoria gave him a look.

William did not know how to interpret it and looked nervously back.

Victoria said to Aryssa, "William and I are nominating you for Sweetheart, Aryssa." She gave Aryssa a hug.

Devnee thought of the last person to give Aryssa a hug and quivered.

Person? said the vampire in her head. *Really, my dear. I am not a person.*

Get out of my mind! said Devnee silently.

Why? I like it in here. It's so similar to my own.

Devnee flinched, and Eleanor, next to her, said in that snippy successful voice, "Problem?"

"Of course not," said Devnee, laughing.

Kindness brightened the receiver. Aryssa was

recovering slightly because Victoria was being nice. Because William was there. She didn't look beautiful again, of course, but at least she didn't look like a dead body.

Devnee was relieved. She didn't have to do anything after all. Aryssa was going to be fine. Devnee did not have to get involved or sacrifice anything. Victoria would take care of it.

She had answered Eleanor correctly. There was no problem.

The dark path rolled on.

The shadow of Aryssa, the shadow of Devnee, and the shadow of the vampire intersected on the gleaming marble, and for one moment they could not be distinguished. They had, as shadows do, blended.

Interesting, said the vampire in her head.

Go away, said Devnee.

I actually thought you would be kind, said the vampire. *You come from a kind family. I attempted to enter your mother's mind, you know. She could not quite communicate with me. That happens with nice people. Honor required that I give her daughter a second chance.*

Go away! screamed Devnee.

He did not answer. His dark path stayed in the lobby.

I didn't have to be kind, Devnee told him. Victoria was kind for me.

He laughed.

They could almost hear it, the students in the

lobby, and they looked around vaguely, as if wondering whose CD player that was.

Nobody can be kind for you, my dear, said the vampire. *But I don't mind, of course. I have you now. There's no escape, my dear. You and I, Devnee Fountain, are a team.*

"Now you go home, drink a gallon of orange juice, take tons of vitamins, and sleep all weekend." Victoria beamed at Aryssa. William got out his car keys. "Then you'll be fine."

She won't be fine, thought Devnee. I stole her fineness. You can nominate her for all the Valentine's Day Dances in the world and she still won't be fine. Because I decided against it. I chose beauty over kindness.

Trey entered the lobby from the opposite end. He did not see Aryssa, or Victoria, or William. How could he? The glitter and glitz of Devnee took up all his attention. He galloped across the room toward her.

He was tough, and half violent, stunning without being handsome.

And I was right, thought Devnee, getting ready for Trey.

Beauty over kindness any day.

But "any day" no longer existed for Devnee Fountain.

The old Devnee — her days had been any old

day, one blending seamlessly into another, dull, fogged, pointless days.

Now the days spun and sparkled.

The exciting crowd burbled around her, and she within it. Aryssa did not come back for a week, and when she did, even Victoria and William seemed only to half know her. Aryssa was a half person.

Devnee was relieved.

Now she need only half worry.

Aryssa probably couldn't even tell what had happened. Aryssa was just a thing now. A half event. To whom people gave half their attention.

Or none.

Chapter 12

A Valentine's Day Dance.

Thanks to a generous parent in the restaurant business, it was not held in any gym or cafeteria, but at the Silver Cloud. This sounded to Devnee like a Montana ranch or an America's Cup sailing ship.

It was a perfectly named restaurant. Silver walls — yes, silver! They reflected a thousand times more than the dark marble of the school lobby. Crystal prisms hung from a thousand ceiling lamps, and tiny hidden lights, like miniature Christmas tree lights, rimmed unexpected ledges. Rainbows flitted from one crystal to another, and colored shadows danced on the silver walls.

The high ceilings were hidden by something gauzy that Devnee could not quite see; truly cloudlike.

She felt airborne. Felt ethereal. Felt beautiful.

She floated, because silver clouds floated.

Trey was a wonderful dancer, and the dance was a wonderful dance.

And Devnee Fountain had no competition in the beauty department. She had never been worshiped. She had never even been noticed. And at this dance, she reigned.

Something had changed inside her as well.

She could feel things happening in the room, happening in other people, that she had never felt before.

She knew, absolutely knew, that every girl in the room wished she could look like Devnee Fountain. She could *feel* their wishes. The room was full of wishes. Quivery, like gelatin, the wishes cluttered the room, and she felt as if she were swimming among them.

Wishes for beauty, for grace, for love, for boys, for more, and more, and more, and more.

She was glad they were so far away from the tower, and the shutters, and the hemlocks of the vampire.

Too many wishes here for him.

A hundred girls in a hundred pretty dresses swirled by, and their wishes throbbed in her ears and pulsed against her heart.

How easily his fangs . . .

"Why are you doing that?" said Trey.

"What?"

"Putting your hand over your mouth like that."

She had not been aware of doing that.

"Every time you laugh, you cover your mouth," said Trey. "I mean, what for? Something wrong with your teeth?"

Her laugh was tinged with fear. Did her hand know, as the shadow had known, that Devnee was no longer right? Was the hand trying to cover her up, as the shadow was trying to escape? If she looked in a mirror right now, along with the beauty, would she see long, pointed, dripping —

She laughed. She said, "Silly habit. Now I'll break it." She kissed Trey on the cheek.

Trey kissed her back. On the lips. "Keep breaking it," he said.

They were doing this when William and Victoria waltzed up. They didn't really waltz, of course; Devnee had never actually seen anybody waltz. But they were so graceful together the only possible dance word was *waltz*.

Victoria said, "I was just wondering, Trey. Not to be rude or anything." She smiled gently at both of them, and then especially at Devnee. "But I phoned Aryssa and couldn't get much out of her. What exactly is wrong? Why isn't she coming back to school?"

Trey frowned a confused little-boy frown, as one bewildered by global events beyond control. "I dunno," he said. Very little boy. Carefully not associating himself with a former girlfriend gone weird.

"Well," said Victoria, "her spirits are so low these days that the rest of us have done a lot of thinking, and we think that in order to make her feel better, maybe coax her back, get her laughing again, all that —"

What was coming here? Devnee felt terribly threatened. She tried to keep a sweet kindly smile on her face, but she was trembling all over. What had Victoria done?

"— we should elect her Sweetheart even though she's not at the dance," said Victoria. "I've got enough votes, I think." Victoria repeated her kindly smile, and Devnee wanted to swat it.

Where did Victoria come off, snatching the Sweetheart crown away from Devnee minutes before she won it? *I am the most beautiful here!* thought Devnee. *And those are the rules.*

"That's a great idea," said Trey, who clearly could not care less.

"Isn't it?" said William, who clearly cared a lot. "Victoria thought of it herself." He stared adoringly at Victoria. Then he turned to Devnee. "Do we have your vote, too, Dev?"

The blackmail of it.

What could she say, here in the middle of the room, with admirers listening? *No, you can't have my vote! I want me!*

"Of course," said Devnee warmly. "That's a lovely, lovely idea, Victoria. I can't believe I didn't think of it myself."

Victoria gave Devnee a thorough look. Victoria definitely knew that Devnee would never have thought of it, and if it had been suggested, would have vetoed it with all her power.

And so Aryssa was elected Sweetheart. It was unanimous.

And the night, which had been Devnee's, became Victoria's.

Victoria had not even been nominated, and yet she became the dance's real sweetheart. Because she had one: a truly sweet heart.

Devnee had to stop using the electric blanket because the wiring in the house was so old and faulty it kept failing, and she'd wake up freezing under this paper-thin nothing. Now she had two wool blankets and a thick puff of a comforter. Devnee wrapped up mummy-style.

"Really," said the vampire mildly, "this is not necessary."

Devnee simply looked at him. "It's necessary," she said.

His cape fluttered around him like pond scum.

"Get out of my room," said Devnee. "I want to be alone."

He was amused. "You are never alone now, my dear."

It was true. She had not been alone in many, many days. He had infected her, and she carried him like a virus in her soul. I wish he would disappear, she thought. Just leave my beauty and disappear. I wish I were as smart as Victoria. I'd think of a way to outwit him.

The vampire's laugh rattled like hard candy falling on a bare floor. "You have a most interesting mind, my dear. Filled with wishes. You are never satisfied. I like that in a girl. Opens many doors."

"Get out of my mind!" said Devnee.

The vampire shook his head. His neck did not rotate as human necks did, so that when he shook the head the entire trunk of his body shook with it, giving him a sickening Jell-O effect.

"You let me in," said the vampire. "You didn't have to, you know. You had a choice. You could have been satisfied with what you were."

"I'm satisfied now," said Devnee sharply. "So leave me alone."

"Are you really satisfied?" said the vampire. "Odd. That's not the wish path I see emanating from your heart. I see you wanting William now. Because you know the real Trey, and the real Trey is something of a disappointment. The skin-deep variety always is. And William really loves Victoria, whereas Trey loves only a beautiful escort. Victoria, you know, is brilliant. William is one of those rare young men attracted to brains." The vampire smiled and it lit his eyes, incandescent lights inside his skull.

"Aryssa's going to be all right now," said Devnee. "The dance voted her Sweetheart to make her feel better."

The vampire glowed. "It worked wonderfully, too, my dear. She felt much better." He studied his fingernails. The flesh on his long thin fingers was pink. Not the darkened patches of fruit going bad.

Not spongy as if swollen with rot beneath the skin. But nice, healthy —

"I have just had another excellent meal," said the vampire.

Devnee's heart almost stopped. "Another one?"

"Once the path is open, it's open," he said. "Naturally I will use all of Aryssa that is available." He giggled like a little kid who had just TP'd the teacher's car. Not a vampire. He said, "Of course, there isn't much left of Aryssa. Still . . ."

Oh, Aryssa! Devnee was sick with the knowing of it. That he had gone back!

Those fangs — did they?

That cape — did it?

That laugh — that smell — those glittering evil eyes?

"Now, now, we can't hide from what we've done," said the vampire. "In part, we cannot hide because . . ."

She forced herself to look at him.

". . . because . . . we're going to do it again."

"What are you talking about? I wanted to be beautiful and I am!"

"I thought you wanted it all," said the vampire. His speech was slippery as silk and cruel as boredom.

All.

Oh, yes.

Oh, how she wanted it all.

She wanted riches, too. And brains. And fame. And talent.

She was weak with all the things she wanted; they turned her knees to jelly and made her heart pound.

She studied her own fingernails, so long and lovely and polished and perfect. I'm beautiful now, she said to herself; that's enough.

"Enough?" said the vampire. "Is it really enough, my dear?"

She caught her breath.

He said, "Envision, if you will, English class. Envision yourself, if you will, as the sort of person who simply gets A's, without effort or design."

There were people like that. Victoria was one.

When asked "Did you study?" Victoria would laughingly reply, "I never study." It was true. Devnee would sit consumed with envy. Even if she studied for a month, she could not get the grade Victoria got without effort.

"Ah, yes," said the vampire, "just so."

She threw a pillow at him but he was not there by the time it passed through the air. In fact, when she turned to look, she could not quite find him. She could sense his darkness and smell his mold, but he was as out of focus as a bad photograph.

Did Aryssa smell that? she thought. When he — when it — when —

She said, "I'm beautiful. That's enough. Go away."

"Enough," whispered the vampire. "Enough. I doubt it, Devnee, my dear."

She was very still.

"Perhaps . . ." said the vampire, his voice as

level as a lily pad on still water. "Perhaps . . . you could have Victoria's brains."

Victoria, who was nice. Victoria, who was generous. Victoria, who was thoughtful. Victoria, who was loved by William.

She would like to have Victoria's brains . . . but the vampire would then have Victoria. And would go to her again and again, as he was going to Aryssa. Victoria would be over.

No, I won't take Victoria's brains.

But wouldn't it be glorious to be brilliant? And witty? And have people stop talking and lean forward to hear what I have to say?

No, I'm beautiful. That was my wish. And that's fine.

But, oh! To have it all!

The vampire sank, as if he were snorkeling. He slid, and he slithered. He was underwater in some other world. Devnee hung on to the wall, lest he pull her along and drown her.

He said, "You and I, Devnee . . ."

The air was thick and swampy where he stood.

"We do what is necessary, do we not, Devnee?"

William was an honor student and did things like Model United Nations, and High School Bowl, and French Club, and Chess. He was not an athlete but loved sports, and was the announcer for the basketball season, the manager for the baseball season. In music he was the saxophone player who led the Jazz Band and Pit Band.

Devnee struggled to breathe in the mossy air, the wet drowning air.

Her wish glittered in her head, brilliant and bright and full of knowledge. She tried to grab the wish and break it on the floor, like a piece of glass, but instead it shone like a mirror, and she saw herself reflected in it: brilliant and bright and full of knowledge.

And the wish came out of her mouth, and trembled in the room, and became the possession of the vampire.

"I wish I were smart," said Devnee.

But the room was empty.

The vampire had left.

To fulfill the wish.

Chapter 13

Devnee never did paint the tower room. She never did put a carpet on the floor, nor bright curtains over the shutters.

Her mother stayed in the kitchen, happily designing shelves into which the coffeepot and the blender would fit perfectly; her father stayed in the workshop, busily making the little nooks and crannies for the kitchen; her brother stayed at school, playing every conceivable ball game and proving that it does not matter how many state lines you cross — the star athlete can still skip homework.

As for Devnee, she, too, could skip homework.

And get an A-plus doing it.

How delightful it was to sit in class, always having the answer, always getting the point, always catching the teacher's eye and sharing a rueful smile when the other kids were too thick to get the joke.

How strange it was to fill in the blanks without thinking. To write an essay without pondering. To know that your spelling and punctuation were correct. To glance down at the multiple choices and be amused; to spot a little joke on the teacher's part, a joke observed only by the really bright members of the class. To finish the one-hour test in eighteen minutes and spend the rest of the time looking around.

At first Devnee was careful not to look at Victoria.

Victoria had walked in with long demanding strides, daring you to keep up, and despising you if you fell behind. Victoria no longer had the walk. She was just a female thing who slouched from one desk to another, confused and mumbling.

During quizzes Victoria bent over her desk in that hunched desperate way of people who can't think of any solution except to get closer to the paper. Victoria clung to her pencil as if the lead itself might know the answers. She had the tense, frightened look of a little kid on a strange doorstep, wondering if a boogeyman will answer the door.

Well, one had.

Devnee was asked to substitute for Victoria on the High School Bowl team.

This was a group she had heard about, but certainly had never seen in action. Devnee had had difficulty following the strategy of a volleyball game, never mind a sort of young person's *Jeopardy*.

Trey and William were on High School Bowl.

She knew William was brilliant, but had never assessed Trey that way. His rough, hard looks and his swaggering possession of the ground almost hid his brains.

Devnee, Trey, and William sat behind one long table while the opposition sat behind another. A nasal-voiced vice principal from a third school — for objectivity — read aloud questions taken moments before from a sealed envelope.

"What are the basic structural units of proteins?" said the vice principal sternly, as if interrogating enemy troops.

"Amino acids," said Devnee, pushing her buzzer first, and answering instantly.

"Name two types of arthropods."

Easy, thought Devnee. "Arachnids and crustaceans," she said, laughing. She poised her finger over the buzzer for the next question.

Of course they slaughtered the other team.

Devnee scored more than twice as high as anybody else, answering things she had no idea that she knew. It was eerie, not to be acquainted with the interior of her own mind.

Because it's not my mind, thought Devnee. It doesn't even belong to me. I stole it.

Quickly she thought of it in another light.

It's Victoria's own fault. I deserved to be Sweetheart at the dance, and if she'd let me be elected, instead of campaigning for Aryssa, who hardly even exists anymore, let alone deserves to be a dance queen, well, I would have let Victoria keep her brains.

She felt almost generous because, after all, Victoria had had a chance to stay brilliant and blown it.

"In what year and in what city was the second Continental Congress?" said the vice principal.

Devnee had to laugh out loud. Baby questions. "1775, Philadelphia," she said.

How impressed Trey was. "What a dark horse you are, Devnee. I never realized you had such a great background."

A week ago she would not have known what "dark horse" meant; she would have had to ask or else never known, or even — in her dull moments — never wondered. But tonight she knew, of course, that a dark horse was an unexpected, unknown winner in a race.

How right Trey is, thought Devnee. I am a dark horse.

Following a dark path.

They went out afterward to celebrate, of course. The teacher who supervised High School Bowl was Mrs. Cort. "Oh, Devnee, I'm so excited that you moved to town," she said. "We need minds like yours."

Devnee cringed. There was no mind on earth like hers. A stolen mind. What was Victoria's mind now? Dim? Unlit? Confused? Did Devnee have the entire contents of Victoria's mind? Or just the academic facts? Would she one day slide into Victoria's life as well, with Victoria's family and history?

Trey smooched Devnee. The kiss she would have given her soul to get a month ago was nothing. Damp lips bunched up and tapping her cheek. Trey had no idea what he was kissing and didn't care. He wanted only looks.

But so did I, thought Devnee. I wanted only looks. So this is fair.

"And what does your brilliant mind want on its ice-cream sundae?" asked Trey.

Victoria's brains, thought Devnee.

She bit her lip to keep from saying that out loud, covered her mouth with her hand, wondering if the fangs in her mouth . . .

No.

I don't have the fangs. The vampire has the fangs. I must keep my story straight.

"Chocolate, of course, like you," said Devnee. And then, because she could not help herself, "How's Victoria?"

William looked confused, as if when Victoria's mind was emptied, the minds and memories of her friends were also sapped. "She's fine," he said dubiously. "She just . . . I don't know . . . I guess . . . I guess I don't know." He stirred his chocolate sauce into his melting vanilla ice cream. He shrugged. "I'm not really sure what's going on," he said.

"Women," said Trey, dismissing half the race. "They can really be a pain." He grinned at Devnee. "I go by looks, and that spares me the trouble of ever worrying about their problems."

Lovely, thought Devnee. Just the kind of boyfriend we all want.

"I guess Victoria's just in kind of a slump," said William.

"We miss her on the team, of course," said Mrs. Cort briskly. "But life goes on. Now, tomorrow we'll have practice."

The boys moaned.

"You practice for High School Bowl just the way you practice for any other team," said Mrs. Cort firmly.

"Dev doesn't need to practice," said Trey. "She knows it all already."

In the English class where once Mrs. Cort had only had Victoria to call on, Devnee had all the answers, while Victoria was simply dense.

Mrs. Cort loved test questions in which you must know the facts in order to answer, but you don't write the facts down. You write down an independent conclusion. Devnee had always failed these questions.

It was Victoria who did not have to think; Victoria's questing mind would have already probed at the difficulty this aspect of literature presented.

Whereas Devnee would certainly never have thought of it before and would be completely flummoxed having to think of it now.

But things were different.

Now it was Victoria whose mind didn't lead anywhere. Just sat at the desk, thick and uncertain. It was Victoria who nervously bit a lock of hair and nervously drummed a pencil eraser, and nervously stared at the wall clock and then her wristwatch.

Is that how I used to look? thought Devnee. Pathetic? Hopeless?

She could not bear the sight of Victoria. You could actually see Victoria's mind scrabbling for facts, like a falling mountain climber scrabbling for a crack in the rock.

A dreadful taste coated Devnee's mouth.

A queer moldy glaze coated her eyes.

Victoria ran out of energy. She lay down her pencil, turned her test over, and put her head on the desk, eyes not closed, but soul not looking out, either. Just dim staring.

What have I done? thought Devnee Fountain.

Her mind skipped on without her: Victoria's mind, actually; a mind redolent of intriguing observation and complete knowledge. Thoughts so amusing they begged to be shared with the class. Intelligence so excellent it demanded a pencil, so she could write down her conclusions.

Inside the new body, isolated from the new mind, Devnee herself sat very still. I never knew the real Devnee, she thought, and now I'm not going to. I'm going to be pieces of other girls instead.

Sunlight poured in the side windows and the

shadows, as clear as drawings, of the students were outlined against the walls: silhouettes of pencils poised and heads bowed in thought.

Only Devnee cast no shadow.

She stared at the blank wall.

My shadow hates me, thought Devnee. The vampire lied. It isn't that my shadow doesn't like to be around when the event occurs. It's that my shadow doesn't want to be around somebody like me.

Somebody whose wishes destroy other people.

Devnee had a hideously clear view of herself, as if she had turned to ice, and all the inessentials were chipped away.

She was bad.

Event. What a ridiculous word. Those were not "events" — those moments that destroyed Aryssa and Victoria. Those were betrayals: the selling of friends to evil.

But it is not possible to look at oneself for long. The sight is too dreadful. So Devnee quickly looked away.

At the end of class, to remind herself of why she had done it, she stopped in at the girls' room, where a row of six mirrors awaited the desperate reflections of desperate girls.

It was delightful to stand at a distance. Smiling. Knowing her hair was perfect, knowing she was perfect. Pitying the stubby, faded girls who leaned up close to the mirrors, repairing or changing faces and hair, in a futile effort to have what Devnee had.

One of the girls was Aryssa.

What happened to Aryssa is not my fault, Devnee reminded herself. How was I to know he was a vampire? It was just a wish. A plain old wish. Lots of girls wish to be beautiful. How could I know it would really come true?

Stolen beauty is not like stolen jewelry. There's no prison sentence, no time in jail. The police can't catch me.

Aryssa was looking at Devnee. Her lusterless eyes were seeking answers. Large eyes, those of a waif in the gutter, hoping for handouts. The eyes of Aryssa came to rest on Devnee.

She knows I did it, Devnee thought. Her heart went into spasms.

But Aryssa said, "Hi, Devnee. Are we still buddies? I kind of forget. I've been having a bad time lately. I'm sorry I haven't kept in touch."

Devnee flinched and drew away. Bumped into Victoria. Not a leader now, but merely somebody in the line.

It was remarkable how her personality had been sapped. She was even more of a husk than Aryssa; when Victoria's demanding presence collapsed, there was not much left.

"I love how you do your hair," said an unknown girl to Devnee. "I mean, you look so perfect all the time. I wish I looked like you."

Two other girls turned away from the mirror, also, and smiled at Devnee. "You should go into modeling," said one of them. "My sister is a model. But you'd be even better."

"You have the bones for it," agreed the first girl.

Devnee turned her back on the remains of Aryssa and Victoria.

Chapter 14

Devnee was not a particular fan of television, being too attached to her radio to turn on the TV. Devnee had three stations from which she continually switched. One was soft old-fashioned rock, beginner rock, so to speak. The next station was current rock, but not the kind that got parents up in arms. The final station was country, where the lyrics told sad stories and the rhymes were like greeting cards.

She loved them equally. She could not bear talk shows, or advertising, or news.

Her mother, however, loved a local station full of friendly local weather idiots, and giggling local celebrities, and dim local thinkers.

Devnee came home from another day of triumph and beauty to find her mother swaying in the kitchen to the beat of a local department store jingle. Really, how pathetic, thought Devnee. This is the best I can do for a mother? A mother whose radio station plays bingo and describes spaghetti suppers at the firehouse? Please.

I deserve better than this.

"Hello, darling," said her mother, kissing her swiftly. "Tell me what you think of this wallpaper for the breakfast room."

"It's perfect," said Devnee, not looking.

"Here are two possibilities, Devnee. Help me choose."

"Mom, you have a great eye for color. Whatever you choose is perfect."

"Come on, Devvy," said her mother, pulling out the old baby name.

"Ma."

"Dance with me," said her mother, pulling out the old baby after-school activity.

"Ma!"

Her mother deflated. She stepped away and looked sadly at the wallpaper samples, as if she had expected great things to come from them; as if she had expected to transform both the wall and her life and perhaps also her relationship with her daughter.

Her mother stared out the kitchen window. The backyard was grim and wintry, and the hemlocks were like a dark green prison wall. No sky, no town, no neighbor was visible.

"I don't know, Devvy," said her mother sadly. "You are a different person since we moved here."

Devnee had decided several days ago to stop

thinking about the differences. It just gave her an upset stomach. The point of life was to be beautiful and have fun. She was not going to think of the techniques used to arrive there.

"I can feel you full of wishes," said her mother. "Wishing to be somebody else. To be somewhere else. Wishing you had a different family."

The truth stung. Devnee must not let her mother see any more of it. She rallied. "I like the wallpaper with the ribbon effect, Mom. I think your water-colors would look terrific against it."

Her mother continued to study the hemlocks. She frowned slightly, tilted her head, and looked more intently.

"I don't even feel as if I recognize you these days," said her mother with infinite sadness.

"I'm just wearing my hair differently," said Devnee casually.

Her mother nodded. "I love it like that. You're beautiful, sweetheart. I love looking at you. But — Devvy, you don't even talk the way you used to! What's going on? Tell me. Please."

"I'm just learning to manage my study time better, Mother. Aren't you proud of me?"

A shadow crossed her mother's face. She fiddled with the wallpaper samples. She tilted her body, looking out the window again, toward the hemlocks. Devnee followed her gaze.

Caught in the hemlocks like an immense moth was the vampire's cloak.

"There's something . . ." Her mother's voice

trailed off. "I can't quite focus on it. My perspective is off. There's — I don't know — it looks like — I think it's dirty laundry stuck on the tree."

Only her mother would look at a vampire's cloak and see laundry. Her mother was probably even now thinking of bleach and detergent; probably even now making the kind of pitiful plans that filled her day: *I'll just go out there and get that; run a load of laundry and have it all nice and sparkly clean and freshly white.*

Pathetic, thought Devnee. I wish I had a different mother.

The wish went right out the window, fluttering toward the hemlocks.

A different mother, thought Devnee.

Her heart stopped. Her tongued thickened.

She looked with horror at the woman standing in her kitchen: a happy woman, who liked her life and her family. Who loved her daughter.

"No," said Devnee. "No!" And then much louder, *"No! I didn't mean it!"*

Her mother did not seem to have heard. She moved toward the back door. Put her hand on the knob.

"No," said Devnee, "don't go out there, Mom. You stay inside. You — listen, I love this wallpaper. I'll go out there and get that thing off the hemlocks and you — um — well, let's go to the wallpaper store together! Huh? Won't that be fun?"

"Really? Would you like to?" said her mother. "Maybe while we're there we can look at paper for the tower. I know you love it the way it is, Devvy, but somehow when I'm up there alone, it feels dark to me."

Devnee's laugh was hysterical. "Don't go there alone, Mom, okay? I keep my room clean. You don't need to go there."

Her mother was still frowning, still confused. "I don't know, Devvy, there's so much about this house. . . . Sometimes in the day I feel as if I'm not alone. . . . Sometimes I even seem to hear someone laughing."

It was Devnee who was laughing now. Horrible little bursts of insane hysterical laughter spurted out of her.

Her mother shuddered. "Just like that, Devvy. Don't laugh like that. It makes me so nervous."

Devnee stopped laughing, as if she'd sliced off her laugh with a machete. "I'll be right back, Mom," she said. "You stay here where it's warm. Promise?"

Her mother was getting her jacket. Getting her gloves.

"Mom," said Devnee, "let's have a cup of tea. You put the water on to boil. I'll have apple mint, okay? We haven't had a cup of tea together in weeks." She put her mother's jacket back. Stuck the tea kettle in her mother's hand.

Wild distant laughter pealed. Mother and daughter swung toward the kitchen window and saw hemlocks shaking, as if the heavy green branches were crackling with fire.

How dare that sick, twisted, perverted vampire try to get near her mother! Devnee would kill him!

"Wait here," she said sternly to her mother, and she stormed out the back door, strode over the dead grass of winter, marched to the hemlocks, and grabbed hold of the cloak.

"Don't you dare go near my mother," said Devnee Fountain.

The vampire's teeth appeared, loose in the trees, a fang here, a fang there. "I believe you made a wish."

"I take it back. I wasn't thinking."

"Pity," said the vampire. "I'm afraid it's still a wish."

"You scum!" spat Devnee. "How dare you!"

"I'm afraid," said the vampire, "I cannot quite follow your distinctions. Why was it fine to wish for Aryssa's beauty and Victoria's brains, but not fine to wish for a different mother? I think you deserve a better mother, too."

"This is the one I have!" said Devnee.

"That was the body you had," pointed out the vampire, "and the mind. You wouldn't settle for them. Why settle for a pathetic excuse of a mother? Other girls have mothers who are successful attorneys, or brilliant novelists, or creative designers."

"I'm keeping my own mother."

"Mmmmm. The wish, however, my dear. The wish is here, you know. I possess it. It was a very complete wish. I was in your mind at the time, and

I saw quite clearly the kind of mother you would prefer."

"You did not! I prefer my mother!" Devnee yanked at the cape and sure enough, a piece of it came off in her hands. But it was not cloth. It was some sort of moss, and in the heat of her hands it melted into algae, into scum, and stained her hand green. She wiped her hands on her jeans and stained the jeans. "Get off me!" she shouted.

"I'm *in* you," he said.

"I don't want this! You can't have her! I take it back! Go away! Take your cloak and go!"

He shook his head. His trunk, his cape, and his trees shook with him, swaying back and forth like some encapsulated inland gale. "You opened my shutters. You let me in. You sent me wishes. You presented me with your shadow."

"No."

"What do you mean — no? You can't change your mind in the middle of your transformation, Devnee. You wanted it all, and you're getting it all. You will be perfect. You will have beauty and brains and money and talent . . . and an interesting mother worthy of such a daughter."

"I will blot you off the landscape if you touch my mother."

He vanished.

Ha! thought Devnee, triumphant.

But instead, the voice of the vampire came through the bottoms of her feet. She cried out and lifted first one foot and then the other, but she could not lift them both at the same time, and the vampire oozed through her soles and into her body and up, up, up into her mind.

Blot away your beauty, too?

Blot away your brains?

I doubt that, Devnee. There will be no blotting. Because your real wish, your real first wish, Devnee, your real wish was to have it all.

Have it all.

That means more, my dear.

More, and more, and more.

"I don't want it now," she said. She was very, very cold. The stain on her hand hurt like a burn, and the stain on her jeans stank like a swamp.

"Please?" she said. She was crying now, and the tears hurt even more than the stains; they seemed to be cutting trenches in her face; she would have scars from her eyes to her chin; where the tears hit the ground there would be pits eaten away from the acid that was Devnee.

"Please don't hurt my mother," she said brokenly.

"Well . . ." said the vampire. "I am willing to postpone your mother."

"Fine," said Devnee. "Anything."

His smile was immense. His fangs were all around her now, like some gruesome winter wreath: icicles closing in on her neck.

"I have certainly enjoyed Aryssa and Victoria," said the vampire. "But there is a girl my eye keeps going to. Her name is Karen."

"I don't remember a Karen," said Devnee dully.

"No? She's in your gym class. She's the one who's so excellent in sports."

Now Devnee remembered. She didn't much care for athletes. Karen was sweaty and musclebound. She was always dribbling a basketball or doing backbends. Devnee herself loathed games. Gang showers. Sweat. Coaches. And most of all basketball. Devnee could never remember which end of the court was her basket. In gym, people despised her.

Perhaps only gym is where I'm still real, she thought. In gym, I show.

His teeth came out again: long and thin and very slick, for puncturing without slowing down.

His laugh was the sound of a car that will not start on a winter morning: grinding, dead, batteryless.

"Karen," he said.

She closed her eyes.

What had Karen done to deserve this? Karen had never even spoken to Devnee!

"No, I can't," said Devnee. "I've done this enough. I —"

"Fine. I accept your mother."

Devnee's tears rolled to the edges of her mouth and there they tasted not of salt but of blood.

"I'm a little out of control," said the vampire. "I'm so hungry, you see. All this chatter has whetted my appetite. I want more. Just like you, Devnee, darling."

"All right," she whispered. "Karen."

"Tomorrow," he said.

"Tomorrow," she said.

The vampire vanished.

Devnee staggered back to the house. The tea was steeped and waiting. Her mother had heated a cinnamon coffee cake she had made that morning. The kitchen smelled of love.

"What was it?" asked her mother.

"Nothing. Some old piece of plastic that blew into the yard. I threw it in the trash."

"Thank you, darling." Her mother set the cup of tea before her. Steam rose up from the tea cup and Devnee thought of evil genies rising out of Egyptian urns. What had risen in this house?

What had she, Devnee Fountain, given permission to?

From across the table, her mother blew Devnee a kiss.

The kiss was visible: as clear on the air as a leaf falling. And fall it did. The kiss did not reach Devnee. It fell in the middle of the table, between the sugar and the lemons.

She tried to pick it up, but it broke in her hand.

She was no longer human. Even kisses could not touch her now.

Chapter 15

After school, Victoria burst into tears. "My parents are really on my case!" she said. "My grades have fallen and I don't have any energy and they're so mad at me."

Devnee could hardly bear to look at Victoria. But she forced herself to examine the girl. Lost was Victoria's athlete-breaking-the-ribbon look. Now, she more closely resembled the torn and frayed ribbon itself.

My mother could be next, thought Devnee. *My mother.*

"That's rough, Victoria," said one of the other girls.

How unnoticing they were. Victoria's problems hardly skimmed the surface of their day. How absorbed each girl was by her own existence, how selfish about others.

Selfish! thought Devnee. I am actually annoyed with the rest for being selfish? I — who caused this collapse?

"I don't know what to do," wept Victoria. She was wilted, like a flower that had once been a proud tulip and was now just a broken stem.

I never thought of Victoria as a real person, thought Devnee. I never thought of Victoria as having parents and problems, or even *life*. I pretended she was just an object, and I could have part of her.

William gave Victoria a hug. "You'll feel better in a few days," he promised, as if he could control it.

Devnee knew otherwise. It was, after all, her own wish, but she could not control it, either.

Or can I?

Can I gain control?

Devnee straightened, firmed, drew herself in.

He wants Karen. But what he actually said was: He would postpone having my mother. But he does not seem to be able to go out and get victims on his own. He has to have a conduit. He needs to have somebody like me to open his dark path.

I can't give him another girl. I can't give him Karen.

But if I don't give him Karen, my mother is right in the house with him! The path is surely already open. What if my mother went into my room to straighten up? What if my mother decided suddenly to wash windows in the tower?

That sounded like her mother.

What then? Where would the dark path go?

Victoria dried her tears, but she did not look

done with crying. "I feel as if somebody scooped me out."

Devnee almost screamed. She had a vision of the vampire with an ice-cream scoop, taking this and that out of Victoria's head, and leaving her with pits and holes instead.

"You probably have mono," diagnosed William.

"No. I'm brain-dead."

No, no, no, no, thought Devnee. No, I didn't wish for that! I wished for brains, but surely, surely, I didn't really wish to destroy Victoria to get them. Did I? Please, please, tell me I didn't wish to hurt anybody like this.

"How can you tell?" said William gently.

"I'm failing every class," cried Victoria. "Good clue, huh?"

William's hug turned to comfort. "I love you anyway," he said.

How nice William was. How rare the quality of niceness had turned out to be. Plenty of people had beauty, plenty of people had brains, plenty of people had money — but who in this immense school, with its huge student body, had turned out to be just plain nice? Certainly not Devnee Fountain.

I should have wished for that. To be nice.

The wish teased along the edges of her mind and thoughts. If she were nice, as well as beautiful and brilliant . . . why, she would —

There was a softening of her skull. A weakening

of her brain. A feeling of wind through her ears. The vampire was within a step of her thoughts.

He comes in when I let him! thought Devnee. I thought he could come of his own accord, but he can't. I actually open the door myself: I wish for anything — and he comes in.

She drew her thoughts and her soul together and removed any wishes, stalled any yearning. Even for being nice. For anything at all. She grew hard and solid, like concrete bunkers.

The vampire was gone before he had quite gotten in. He was not able to converse with her on the inside of her head, the way he had in the past. She had kicked him out.

Pulses of triumph rocked her body; she throbbed with power.

"I can't stand girls who whine," said Trey, muttering about Victoria. He frowned at the way William was holding her, as if to offer comfort were to break the rules. "Jeez," he added. He sighed heavily, burdened by the mere presence of a girl who whined.

I sold out for him? Devnee thought.

No, I sold out for beauty. But I needed the beauty to attract a Trey. To make friends. I love my beauty. I don't want to give it up. It's absolutely wonderful being beautiful.

But it doesn't make a selfish hunk into a nice boy.

I wish —

Across the lobby the shadows shifted and became a single line and oozed slowly over the glittering marble toward Devnee.

I don't wish!

She had caught it in time, slashing off the edge of the wish before the dark path could gather speed.

But if I foil him . . . If I don't surrender again and give him Karen . . . what position will that place my own mother in? And we're not moving! That's our house! We're stuck! We're all stuck. My mother, my father, my brother, me . . . and the vampire.

There is no way out.

And the vampire knows it.

"Hi, Devnee," said an unfamiliar voice.

Devnee looked up. She felt as if a plate of translucent glass had been dropped between herself and the world: She could see the shapes, but not the people. Because I don't want them to be people, she thought with horror. I want them to be body parts that I steal.

"Karen," said the unfamiliar voice, reminding Devnee.

A gurgle of sickness rose up in Devnee's throat and she fought it down. Weakness could no longer be allowed. "Hi, Karen," she said brightly. "How are you? What's happening? Did you just come from practice?"

Karen was damp from a gym shower. Not a pretty girl, Karen had personality — armloads of it: She seemed to vibrate behind that sheet of un-clear glass with friendship and other good things.

Good things waiting to be destroyed, thought Devnee. What could be worse for a dedicated ath-lete than a vampire's visit?

Visit.

Who am I kidding here?

Let's say it plainly, Devnee Fountain, and make yourself realize what is actually going on. Admit the truth. You turned Aryssa and Victoria over to a subhuman beast who sucked their blood for his lunch. A beast whose next victims will be innocent Karen and your very own mother.

Devnee looked down, hugging herself, trying to pull herself together, to think of a way out of this mess. She was wearing a very short skirt and a shirt with the sleeves partly rolled up. Her ivory satin skin glowed.

Aryssa's skin, really.

Devnee gagged and swallowed hard. She had the feeling she could unzip herself and step out. Leave Aryssa's skin lying on the lobby floor, while the real Devnee — the plain, dull Devnee — would go on as she had before: unnoticed, unloved, un-wanted.

Give up my beauty? thought Devnee.

Brilliant thoughts swirled in her head; quota-tions from Shakespeare and the Bible and Lincoln were complete and meaningful behind her eyes.

Victoria's thoughts and quotations.

Give up my brain? thought Devnee.

If I give up my beauty, my father won't be proud of me anymore. My brother won't brag about me to his friends. I won't have any friends. Looking in a mirror and putting on clothes will be just as depressing as it used to be. If I give up my brains, I won't be with William and Trey on High School Bowl. Mrs. Cort won't fawn over me. I'll be that ordinary girl nobody notices, nobody cares about, nobody wants.

She had begun to cry, but she could not feel the tears on her cheeks.

Because it's Aryssa's skin, thought Devnee. Perhaps Aryssa feels the tears, because she's inside *my* skin.

"Dev?" said a gentle voice. "What's wrong? Tell me."

Devnee opened her eyes. It was Victoria.

"You seem so down," said Victoria. "What's wrong?"

Devnee laughed hysterically.

Victoria said, "Believe me, I know how it feels to have a bad day. About all I seem to be able to do this week is get out of bed. I have dried leaves for a brain. Lots of rustling around when the wind goes through my head."

Dried leaves rustling in her head did not have to come from emptiness. It could come from the presence of the vampire. Sometimes his very laughter sounded like the cruel rasping of branches in winter.

"Maybe you'll feel better next week," said Devnee. But she did not know if the victims got better in the end, or if they stayed tired and worn and too exhausted to function. Even if Victoria isn't tired next week, thought Devnee, she'll still be dumb. Even if Aryssa isn't tired next week, she'll still be plain.

"I hope so," agreed Victoria. "Maybe it's just a stage. But what's happening with you, Dev? To make you so sad?" Victoria was truly concerned. She had left William's side and come over to ask.

I had three assigned buddies, thought Devnee. Aryssa, whom I gave to a vampire; Trey, who is a hunk but conceited and shallow; Nina, who is nothing more than a checkbook.

But Victoria really is a buddy.

If she knew . . .

If anybody knew . . .

"I'm not a very nice person," said Devnee Fountain. That was the wish she should have made: to be nice.

The very word *wish,* even when she was not making a wish, was terribly dangerous. Across the lobby the dark path began again to ooze forward, so it could arrive at the intersection of his victims.

No! thought Devnee. I cannot let this happen! "I have to go to my locker. Come on and talk to me while we go." Swiftly she linked one arm with Karen and the other with Victoria and trotted them out of the lobby.

School had ended some time ago.

Even the late buses were long gone. Sports

practice was over. Tutoring had ended. The custodians had turned off most of the hall lights.

Light came only from behind, from the lobby.

Long black shadows, much much taller than the girls, trotted on ahead, as if scouting out the territory. *Three shadows. For three girls.*

My shadow is back! thought Devnee. My shadow forgave me. My shadow thinks there's a chance that maybe I can be human after all.

"Gosh, Devnee," said Karen, "thanks for including me."

"Sure," said Devnee, rushing them on, turning the corner, leaving the dark path behind.

Devnee was the kind of nonathlete whose stumbling stupidity caused any team she might be on to lose any game it might play. Victoria was fairly good at sports that required time and money, but not teamwork, like horseback riding and skiing. Karen, however, was a superstar among athletes and, in a year or two, would be recruited by college coaches with big plans. Devnee, Victoria, and Karen were not a likely trio.

But Karen did not appear to notice.

"Let's — um — go get a doughnut," said Devnee. "Want to go to the Hole and have doughnuts?"

None of them had a car.

"We'll have to catch the boys if we're going to go," mumbled Victoria. "I wish I had some strength. I can hardly make my feet shuffle. You'll have to order my doughnut for me."

"This is so nice of you," Karen said. "I'm new in town, too. I feel so special that you're asking me to go with you."

Devnee had had no idea that Karen was new in town. Karen seemed so established.

"I hardly have any friends yet," confided Karen. "I got on all the teams without any trouble, and we're buddies, and I have a good time, and yet I don't really have friends. You know what I mean?"

"I know what you mean," said Devnee.

Karen beamed at Devnee. Happiness transformed her. She was suddenly beautiful.

Beauty, thought Devnee. I don't even know what it is anymore.

Karen's smile demanded a smile in return. When Devnee's beautiful borrowed face broke into a real smile, some of her inhumanity dissolved. Some of the real Devnee surfaced.

And thinking occurred.

Real thinking.

Not the stolen thoughts out of Victoria's brain, not quotes, not formulas and facts.

Genuine shrewd planning and strategies.

I won't give him Karen. I didn't make a wish anyway, so he can't have Karen, no matter how much he wants her. He can't have anybody if I don't turn them over, can he? They have to be part of my wish, don't they? Karen isn't. So he can't have Karen.

I did make a terrible wish about my family,

back at the beginning of all this. Even my mother felt the truth about that wish. He half possesses that wish.

I am calling it back.

He cannot have that wish.

Somehow — some way — using what weapon I don't know — paying what price I don't know — I have to stop him.

Stop him forever.

And return what I stole to the rightful owners.

She looked behind.

The corner, dim and distant, blackened.

The dark path crawled around the lockers.

Laughter like a million breaking souls crept along the floor.

She could see the edge of the cape now, and smell the rising swamp gas of his shadow.

"Quick," said Devnee Fountain, pushing Victoria and Karen ahead of her. "Outside. We'll meet the boys there."

They ran because she made them.

Behind her, the dark path oozed on.

But ahead of her, equally dark, attached to her feet the way it ought to be, spread her own shadow, huge and threatening in the setting sun.

Chapter 16

In High School Bowl practice Devnee asked the only question that really mattered. "How do you kill a vampire?" she said.

Nobody blinked an eye. They were used to an assortment of study topics from chemistry to famous dancers, so the subject of how to off a vampire seemed normal.

"I am not sure," said Mrs. Cort, with a frown of uncertainty. "I believe it's necessary to put a stake through its heart."

Trey said, "You carry a cross when you do it."

"And chew garlic," added William.

Devnee had not expected any of these answers. "Have you had experience with this?" she said.

"No," said Trey, "but that's why houses lots of times have wooden doors with crosses on them."

Devnee wasn't certain if she had ever seen a door with a cross on it.

"Wood molding," explained William, "in the

shape of a big T. Or cross. That way, the vampire can't get in the door."

Devnee's mouth fell open. Trey laughed at her.

Mrs. Cort stuck to the ever-essential subject of High School Bowl questions. "Every now and then they do ask questions on superstition and myth. Where is Transylvania, what is voodoo, which mummies escaped their tombs, who wrote *Dr. Jekyll and Mr. Hyde*."

Superstition and myth, thought Devnee. I should be so lucky that he is nothing more than superstition and myth.

She felt the vampire tapping at her skull and did not let him in. Force of mind could keep him out of her thoughts. It was only when she weakened, lowered her guard, or had wishes and yearnings and aches for things to be different — only then could the vampire come in.

There was nothing now that Devnee wanted except to be free of him, and have her mother be safe.

Not much, she thought, oh, no, not much.

Just life and breath and family.

Well, she did not think much of the suggestions of the High School Bowl team. Chew garlic? Please. The vampire stank of swamps and putrid gas already. He wouldn't even notice garlic. Wear a cross? That was possible. But Devnee felt she should not stand behind the symbol of a god she had not trusted. She had not asked God for beauty and brains. She had asked the vampire. It would be slimy now, wouldn't it, to back up and say, Well, I really believed in you all the time, gimme your cross, take care of me.

And as for the stake through the heart — why, most of the time the vampire's body wasn't even there. And his body had no heart; it was the collected shadows of the dead, wrapped in his evil cloak.

"Trey?"

"Yeah?"

"Remember you mentioned a creepy girl used to live in my house?"

Trey and William both shuddered. "Whew, was she ever weird," said Trey.

No wonder she was weird, thought Devnee. I'm feeling pretty weird myself. "What happened to her?"

The boys shrugged. "She just disappeared one day. She used to date a guy in this school. He graduated. Her parties were legend. Everybody wanted to go up into that tower, and she would never let them." Trey laughed. "She told her boyfriend that the shutters were haunted."

William laughed, too. "I remember that now. If she'd said her house was haunted, or her tower — you could believe that. It's such a spooky house. But shutters? Did ghosts live in the slats?"

There was space between the two sets of shutters. Was that the vampire's tomb? A tomb of darkness on the inside and light on the outside? A tomb with access to towers and skies? A tomb from which shadows cast long black paths?

"What was her name?" said Devnee.

Nobody could remember the creepy girl's name.

"Do you guys ever go up into the tower?" William wanted to know.

"It's my bedroom."

"No kidding! *You sleep there?*" William put a middle finger into his mouth for gagging on.

Devnee managed a laugh. "My bed is up there. But no, nobody could sleep there. Too much going on, what with the ghosts and the haunts and the banging shutters and the vampires. I get very little rest."

The boys smiled, and Mrs. Cort dragged out another set of quiz questions. French history. Talleyrand and Mitterand, Charlemagne and Charles de Gaulle. Devnee, of course, knew them all. "What famous building did the people of Paris destroy at the beginning of the French Revolution?" said Mrs. Cort.

"The Bastille," said Devnee. This is what it would be like, she thought, if they substituted computers for brains. You would know how to pronounce it and spell it, what it looks like, the date it came down. You would spew out the answer like a laser printer. But it wouldn't be yours. It would be the computer's. I want to put the facts inside my brain by myself. I want to give Victoria back her mind.

Devnee faced the fact that she did not want to give Aryssa back her beauty.

Either I take the vampire's evil gifts or I don't, she thought. I can't decide that half of it's evil and the other half is nice and I'm hanging on to it.

She wondered what the poor creepy girl had given to, or taken from, the vampire. And where was she now? Safe and well? Or one of the shadows beneath his cloak? Was the cloak filled by the shadows of girls like Devnee, who once had taken the bus, done homework, gone to basketball games . . . and made a fatal wish?

There would be no more wishes for Devnee Fountain.

She would never use the word again.

"What famous edifice in Paris was erected for a World's Fair?" said Mrs. Cort.

"The Eiffel Tower," said William.

The three team members smiled at one another. They were good.

"I hope we win over Durham High," said Trey. "They whipped us last time. I can't stand being whipped."

"I think we will," said William. "Devnee was fabulous against Roosevelt High."

"I know we will," said Mrs. Cort. "Between the three of you, you seem to have everything covered."

In another life, at another time, Devnee would have spoken out loud, adding her own thought. Devnee's sentence would have begun with two words she was determined never to touch again: *I wish* we would win.

What a contrast to the others. They hoped, or thought, or knew. They didn't wish.

Be careful of wishes, thought Devnee.

They might come true.

Chapter 17

Devnee entered the house with a spring in her step.

She felt not just beautiful and not just brilliant, but also strong and clever and tough.

She bounded into the big front hall.

"Mom?" she called.

There was no answer.

The house seemed much darker inside than usual.

Devnee stood very still.

"Mom?"

The house filled with faint sound. Fluttering here, rasping there, creaking above, and hissing below.

"Mom!" shouted Devnee.

Her mother's voice was soft as a flute. "I'm in the tower, darling."

Devnee took the stairs two at a time.

Halfway up, she smothered in a tapestry of black. Choking, pushing it away from her face, she kicked at it. It swirled around her legs, caught her hair, tilted her head back as if to strangle her. "Trying to back out?" said the vampire.

His cloak was ice water, lowering her temperature, lowering her resistance.

"Trying to retreat?" said the vampire.

His glass eyeballs were not in their sockets. His fingernails were not on his hands. His parts shifted and slithered and stank.

"Mom!" screamed Devnee.

"I'm up here, darling. I made the loveliest wish. And it came true."

The vampire's giggle was like bubbles underwater. She had the sense that she could bottle him, like seltzer, swamp-flavored. I'm going to be hysterical, thought Devnee. I can't fall apart. Not now.

"Mom. Come downstairs. Now."

Her mother did not answer.

Devnee's own shadow melded with the shadows in the vampire's cloak. She could not tell where hers left off and his began. "Give me back my shadow," she cried.

"There is no giving or taking with a shadow," said the vampire. "There is merely light and dark. Your shadow seems to be part of the dark, my dear. You have lost it. And shortly, very shortly, your mother will lose hers."

"No, she won't! You can't! Stop this! She's my mother!"

"Victoria has a mother. Aryssa has a mother. You didn't seem to worry about them. I don't quite see the difference."

"I was wrong," whispered Devnee. "I'm sorry. Please undo it. Take back the beauty. Take back the brains. Let me have my mother, please."

"You'll have your mother, my dear. She'll just be . . . a little different."

"What did she wish for?" screamed Devnee, hand over her mouth. I don't want my mother any different, she thought. I love my mother the way she is.

"That's not what you said before," the vampire told her. "I distinctly recall how fervently you wished for a better family. More interesting. Slender. Attractive. Socially acceptable."

"I was wrong. I didn't mean it."

"You did mean it," said the vampire, and he was right. Devnee knew he was right. She had meant it; she had made the wish; the wish had been strong.

"I learned a lesson," said Devnee desperately.

"Human beings always do," agreed the vampire. "Just a little late, that's all." He smiled, and the smile grew from a tiny piece of pleasure to a great gaping cave of fangs and dripping eagerness.

"Not my mother," pleaded Devnee.

The vampire did not speak again. His cloak swirled, closing in on him like a container. If only she could rope him, handcuff him, smash him! But the wind tunnel of his leaving sent her staggering backward down the stairs, struggling just to breathe, let alone fight.

He faded before her eyes, and when the door to the tower stairs opened, there was no hand on the knob, no steps on the treads, no cloak wafting in the air.

She backed up because she had to.

She ran into the kitchen. Of course there was no garlic — her parents did not like garlic. There were no stakes — why would you have a stake in the kitchen?

But there was a door, a door with a cross: the powder room door.

It was on two hinges: pins stuck down shafts. She tried to remove the pins but they did not budge. She tried to jerk the door off anyway but accomplished nothing. She ran back into the kitchen. Found the tool boxes. People who were remodeling had tools everywhere. Grabbed a screwdriver and a hammer. Raced back to the door, sticking the pointed end of the screwdriver on the bottom of the pin and hammering upside down to get the pin out. It was awkward, it was difficult, it took so long! How long would the vampire take to . . .

She could not bear to think of it.

Not her mother!

At last, the pin came out. The door hung stupidly on one hinge.

She got the other pin out. The door fell on her, and it was solid wood, and heavy. So heavy.

How can I ever carry this? thought Devnee. Up two flights of stairs?

Sobbing, she staggered through the kitchen and into the hall, dragging the door after her.

It has to go ahead of me, she thought. The cross has to break through.

But it was too much for her to lift.

What am I doing? she thought, tears spattering her cheeks.

"Mom!" she screamed. "Are you all right?"

There was no answer. There was nothing at all. The silence of the house was as complete as death.

I wish — thought Devnee, and made a dying whimpering sound. I *don't* wish. I — I —

She clung to the edges of the door.

No wishes. *I am.* I do not *wish* to be strong. I *am* strong.

She lifted the door. She balanced it, tilted it, and somehow, pointing it like a ship's prow, got it up the first set of stairs. No velvet cloak blocked the way, no smothering swamp air suffocated her. She stood the door up on its end and opened the tower door. She was panting and sweating. The door weighed as much as an SUV.

One more flight, she said to herself. Then I'll be there.

She went up, pressing her body against the right wall and sliding the door along the left.

She came out into the tower.

Sunlight streamed in every window.

Shutters, yellow with fresh paint, gleamed like love.

Carpet cut into a circle lay like a fluffy lemon on the floor.

"Mom?" whispered Devnee. "Mom, where are you?"

"Right behind you," said her mother. "My goodness, darling, what are you doing with a door?"

Devnee whirled, almost dropping the door. Her mother was standing by the back wall, in white work pants and sweatshirt. She was holding a big can of plaster and with a flat trowel was filling in the cracks on the inner walls.

"I wished," said her mother, before Devnee could stop her, "for good weather."

"That's it?" said Devnee. "That's your wish?"

Her mother smiled. Same old smile. Same old face. Same old pudgy huggy body. "What else is there?" said her mother. "I have the best family and the most interesting house in the world."

Devnee sighed very very deeply. Then she sighed again.

"Why the door?" said her mother again.

"I wanted the door with the cross on it," said Devnee.

Her mother nodded. "Keeps vampires out. Good idea."

Devnee stared. *Keeps vampires out?*

Her mother giggled. "You can never be too careful, Devvy. Listen. I just heard Luke come in. Let's all have hot chocolate and brownies." Her mother set down the plaster and the trowel and wiped her hands on her pants. "I'll go heat up the milk," she said, "while you hang your door."

Her mother clattered down the stairs.

Devnee looked around the tower.

It was all light, all sun, all diamonds and freshness.

There was no trace of things dark and cruel.

She did not exchange doors. She leaned the cross door up against the shutters. Even though it blocked some of the sun, the tower stayed cheery and warm.

I'm not sure I needed the cross, she thought. I just needed character. I was weak. I thought somebody had to give me things, or I had to take them away from the people who owned them. Now I'm strong. I know I have to get things myself. Not wish.

He cannot come where wishes do not whisper.

No more whispering for me.

"I am Devnee Fountain," said Devnee out loud. "I am strong. And I am also sorry. I am going to try to give back what I stole."

She looked at her feet. Yes. The sun that came in the window cast a shadow behind her, where it belonged; the outlines of the shadow were firm and clear. But there was no substance to the shadow; it was nothing a vampire could collect; it was just part of her. Mom's right, thought Devnee. The only thing to wish for is lovely weather.

She opened one of the windows and leaned out. It was cold, but crisp and healthy. "Aryssa!" she yelled. "Victoria!"

She filled her lungs with good clean air. "ARYSSA! VICTORIA!"

The vampire had said that human beings learned their lessons — but too late.

Was it too late to return what she had stolen from Aryssa and Victoria?

"It's here!" shouted Devnee. "It's yours! Ask for it! Hope for it! Demand it! Take it!" Just don't wish for it, she thought, and she was laughing, and the laugh was sweet and generous, and if there was any dark path in the yard around the mansion, it was dissolved by Devnee's laugh.

"Dev!" yelled her brother. "Come on. Chocolate's hot!"

She did not look in the mirror as she left the room.

Being beautiful or being ordinary no longer mattered the way it had. What mattered was that she was Devnee Fountain, and her family was wonderful, and her house was interesting.

Down the stairs she clattered.

How ordinary were the sounds of her house! Her mother's voice, her brother's chair scraping, a spoon banging on a pot.

That's what's beautiful, thought Devnee. Ordinary things.

She danced into the kitchen. Her mother had put Marshmallow Fluff on the hot chocolate. Devnee loved Fluff. Life with Fluff was good. Fluff stuck to her lips and she licked at it.

"You look like a dork," said her brother affectionately.

Devnee laughed.

"She does look different," agreed her mother. Mother and brother studied Devnee, heads tilted, struggling to analyze.

"You look happy," said her mother.

I don't have beauty, thought Devnee, feeling it leave, feeling it returning to Aryssa, who needed it so much more. I don't have brains, thought Devnee, feeling that leave, returning to Victoria, who had been kind even without it.

But I have love, and I have happiness.

In school tomorrow I'll find out if that's enough.

I'm strong now.

And I think — yes — that's enough.

FATAL BARGAIN

Chapter 1

Lacey was the first to realize that a vampire shared the dark with them.

"What's that smell?" she said. She already knew. The knowledge seemed to have been born in her centuries ago, waiting for this single moment, this particular evening, this very darkness, to emerge. Somewhere, in another life, in another country, she had smelled this before.

A low-growing mold, like an ancient cellar with a dirt floor.

The smell began beneath Lacey's feet and rose up around her like swamp gas.

She already knew it was too late to run, and that even if she could run, she could not escape.

Her sneakers were flimsy and light, pretty little summer canvas shoes, bought to last a few weeks and then be discarded. She tried to take a step, but the rubber soles stayed where they were, as if she were caught up to the ankles in sucking mud.

In the queasy darkness of the old building, the sneakers no longer seemed bright pink with white laces. They had taken on a dank and soiled look, as if something had been drained over them.

"Do you smell that?" whispered Lacey.

But nobody else did, because Roxanne, dressing for the evening, had splashed her new perfume on her throat and wrists, and because Zach, always on the verge of starvation, had opened the popcorn. Popcorn and perfume lay on separate levels in the room, and beneath them, the smell of the vampire rose in dirty tendrils.

It was early fall. Still warm out. Lacey was wearing a slip dress silk-screened with golden wildflowers. Lacey felt on display. As if she really were a golden wildflower, and the vampire a honey-bee. He would see her colors. And then, a moment later, he would be aware of her scent, as she was aware of his.

The silly teenage laughter and the popcorn munching of the others in the room bounced on the surface of the terrible smell.

Lacey breathed deeply to calm herself, to slow her pounding heart and ease her cramped lungs, but the smell overwhelmed her. She could hardly bear to breathe at all. She could feel the soft pink of the insides of her lungs being contaminated by the vampire's smell, like miners breathing in coal dust.

Perhaps that's how it works, she thought. Perhaps you suffocate yourself. You pass out. You don't feel anything when he stoops over you. You don't even know what's happening until it's too late.

Lacey trembled in the middle of the dark room.

He is here for me, she thought.

How could she have been so foolish as to wear cotton summer clothing? Every inch of her flesh was vulnerable. She needed more. She needed to be wrapped in something. A long leather coat. High boots. Certainly a thick collar or a tightly wound scarf on her neck.

The electricity had been cut off months ago.

The old mansion had no power. No lights.

Of course, that had been the point: to party in the dark. To frighten themselves. Make the night long and panicky.

It was a time-honored tradition among teenagers.

Randy had almost been embarrassed to suggest it because it was trite. Overdone. The old party-in-the-abandoned-house trick.

But everyone he had invited had come.

And to his shame, they were not the ones who were afraid.

Randy was.

Although the house was darker than anyplace Randy had ever been — no moon, no stars, no streetlights, no headlights, no house lights — Randy saw something even darker.

A piece of the dark darkened more, like gauze becoming velvet, and then it moved toward him.

It was like seeing wind.

Seeing that wind swirl, and turn on itself, and suck up the dust.

It was a cape without a person inside.

Randy's short hair stood up vertically, like a cat on a fence. He sat on the floor, cross-legged, a handful of popcorn in one hand and a can of Pepsi in the other, while the vampire slowly filled out his cape.

A hand that was more bone than flesh came first. It flexed itself, and fingernails grew from the tips, crinkled and split like torn foil. Its skin was the color of mushrooms. The hand caught the edge of the darkness and tucked it in tighter: It could make a cape out of the very air in the room.

And finally, the teeth were visible. Teeth that hung over thin lips like stakes on a picket fence. The teeth even peeled like fence posts in need of paint.

But it was not paint these teeth needed.

Randy had wanted an adventure.

He had not thought of this one.

Lacey backed away, trying to find the door.

She had been very silly to agree to this dumb adventure. Very, very silly to lie to her parents about where she would be, when she would get home, whom she would be with.

Time to go. Yes, definitely, time to end this party.

"I possess the door," said the vampire. His voice

spread through the room like a groping, rising tide and then just lay there, quivering.

He was correct. Though the door was open, and the stairway to freedom beckoned below it, the air was solid. Lacey was not going anywhere.

The backs of her eyes and her neck grew cold, as if she were being anesthetized.

Perhaps she was.

Perhaps she was to be the first.

She was the only one standing. The rest at least were sitting near one another, could hold hands, could have the strength that only a group can give.

Lacey whimpered and the vampire smiled, courteously covering his teeth.

Roxanne had been thinking that it was time to dump Bobby. It had been fun, running around with a younger boy, but senior year was moving right along, and Roxanne had to think in terms of the prom. She certainly wasn't going with Bobby. So far, her friends thought it cute and funny that she would dabble in tenth-graders, so to speak. But if it lasted much longer, she would just seem weird, and Roxanne did not wish to cross that line.

Roxanne had been sitting on the floor playing with her hair. She had been growing it out forever and ever, and it was finally below her shoulders, but now that she had it, she couldn't stand it. Long hair was such a pain. She was ready to cut it short again. Maybe even a crew cut. She wanted a new persona: sharp, bright, vivid, demanding. No more of this sweet romantic stuff.

Roxanne wanted to make waves. Astonish people. Set trends.

She flipped up her hair, making a pretend ponytail, and then twisting the handful of hair tightly on top of her head.

On her bare neck, a queer cold finger pressed down.

But whose finger? She could see all the others. Old ditzy Lacey, standing alone. Silly cheerleader Sherree, doing what she did best, giggling between Randy and Bobby. Zachary, lip curled in an above-it-all sneer, attracting Roxanne so much she could hardly stand it.

There was nobody whose hand could touch her neck.

But the hand remained.

And a terrible voice, slimy with mud or entrails, said, "I possess the door."

Randy had promised everybody that this would be a night to end all nights. The six teenagers were motionless, unbreathing, unwilling to show fear. They were waiting for Randy to show them this was a trick, an event staged for their amusement.

The pressure on Roxanne's neck ceased.

The cape, empty, circled the six.

Within it, the hands, the feet, and the face came and went.

When the vampire spoke again, they knew it was not a staged event. "I was asleep," said the vampire reproachfully.

"I'm sorry we came," said Randy. He found that he had crushed some popcorn in his fist. Salty, buttered crumbs covered his palm. "It's my fault," he said quickly, hoping to make peace. "We'll leave."

The vampire shook his head. "Now that I'm up," said the vampire, "I am quite hungry, you see."

They could see. It was very dark in the tower of the old house, and yet the vampire reflected his own light, just as he swirled in his own wind and stank with his own odor.

"We're trespassing," said Bobby, as if acknowledging the crime made it okay. His was the bright confident voice of the jock, the emerging and coddled school star, the one who could get away with anything. "We'll leave you in peace."

The vampire smiled and this time did not bother to cover his teeth. "I've had enough peace for this decade," said the vampire. "I don't believe I am interested in peace tonight."

Lacey wondered how long her knees would continue to hold her up.

The teeth seemed to grow even as she watched, white fangs over which a sort of moss hung.

The six teenagers looked down at their own skin, largely bare in their skimpy summer clothing. How precious their skin seemed. Luminous. Phosphorescent, almost, as if they had dunked themselves in some neon mixture prior to the party.

"You were showing off," the vampire said to Randy, shaking his head regretfully.

"I'm sorry," whispered Randy. "I won't do it again."

The cloak rasped like dried leaves, and it shed, like a scattering of evil herbs. "That is true," agreed the vampire. He smiled immensely, a politician, perhaps, who knew nobody could vote against him.

"Boys," said the vampire meditatively. "Boys have to press the accelerator to the floor. They have to drink harder and kick footballs farther. It is never enough for a boy to *know* that he is quicker than the rest. A boy has to prove it, and he has to prove it over and over and over again."

The cloak fell back, and they could see more of him now, musty and unused. Undercooked.

"Nothing is more dangerous than a boy aged sixteen," said the vampire. It seemed to be a favorite subject of his. "Their parents know it. The insurance companies know it. A sixteen-year-old boy is a pulsating envelope of the desire to show off. The only ones who don't know it are the boys. They think what they're doing is perfectly reasonable."

Good, thought Roxanne, the rest of us are all right. It's Randy he wants. Randy brought us here, and the vampire is going to make him pay for that. Relief flooded Roxanne.

"You were showing off," said the vampire to Randy. He shook a long, thin index finger at Randy. The fingernail glittered like crushed aluminum.

Randy said he was sorry. Randy said he would never show off again. Randy said they would clean up and get out.

Parents were always on your case to clean up. It was a plan with which they were all well acquainted: cleaning up their act. The six began reaching around, grabbing soda cans and popcorn bags and the portable radio, trying to leave the house with no trace of themselves.

"I'm awake now," said the vampire. "And I'm not sorry at all, Randy. I believe I'm quite happy about it."

He did not look happy. He was smiling, of course, but with those teeth, it was not a pleasant smile.

"Suppose," said the vampire, "that I leave you for a while." He looked deep into the eyes of each of them.

Roxanne let go of her ponytail and massaged the back of her neck.

Sherree and Zachary flinched.

Even Bobby shivered.

Tears crawled down Lacey's cheeks.

Randy found that he had bent the antenna of his boom box into a U.

"While I am gone," said the vampire, "you will have an important discussion."

We will run, thought Bobby, who was in splendid physical condition. No zombie fresh out of the grave was a match for him. Bobby eyeballed the distance to the stairs. He'd make it. He didn't know about the others. He didn't care about the others.

Only Lacey, still standing, knew that they could not go anywhere. The open door was solid with the vampire's atmosphere.

"I will let five of you go in safety," said the vampire. He was beginning to laugh. He was not simply hungry for blood. He was hungry for entertainment.

"You will choose who among you is to satisfy my hunger," said the vampire. "That person will stay with me. Here. In the dark. In the quiet of this tower."

Sherree began to sob.

The vampire smiled appreciatively. His eyes assessed their necks. "The person you choose . . ." he said, lisping through his teeth, "and I . . ." he said, lingering on every syllable, ". . . will have much to occupy us."

He withdrew his teeth, tucking them slowly behind his lips. They hardly fit. He dried his mouth with the edge of his dark cloak.

The vampire said, "I will still be here, of course. The door will remain mine. But I won't listen in on your little talk. That wouldn't be fair."

He disappeared quite slowly, folding himself up in his cloak.

His smell stayed after him.

Chapter 2

When Randy had suggested breaking into the Mall House with the girls and spending the night there, he thought he was being clever. Randy needed to show off more than most boys because he hated his name. Randy was such a weak-kneed name. He wanted to be named Bobby, which sounded relaxed and strong, or Zach, which sounded successful and quick, but those were the names of his two best friends. Bobby and Zach were somehow always ahead of Randy. Not by much, but by enough.

And whenever Randy was the first to think of something, Bobby and Zach were the first to tell him how dumb his idea was.

"The Mall House?" said Bobby. "That pathetic old mansion with the broken shutters?" Bobby was a sophomore, Randy and Zach juniors. But Bobby had always seemed older than Randy because he was always in a position of honor, winning games and trophies for every team.

"The Mall House?" said Zach, laughing. Nobody could laugh with such scorn as Zach. "Come on, Randy. They stripped the place of anything valuable years ago."

Actually it had been only a year ago that the last occupants had moved out. A weird family. Not that anybody normal had ever lived in the mansion. There were stories about a girl named Althea who'd moved away before Randy was in high school. The mansion had been vacant for a while. And then Devnee's family had moved in. Randy remembered her clearly. A girl he had found plain at the beginning of the school year, captivatingly beautiful during the middle, and ordinary again toward the end. He had never figured out what she had done to herself to metamorphose like that. But Devnee's family, too, had left town. Vanished.

Nobody seemed to enjoy living in the mansion.

"It's just waiting for the wrecking ball," said Zach in his most put-down voice. "I heard they're finally pulling it down next week." Zach always had facts nobody else had.

"Right," said Randy. "If we're gonna do it, we've gotta do it now."

"Why," asked Zach, "would we want to do it at all?" Zach was thin and languid and took his time at everything, from schoolwork to sports, and yet still he managed to ace and to win. Sometimes Randy worshiped Zach and sometimes he hated him. This was a hating time.

"Because the girls would be scared," said Randy.

Bobby yawned, affecting mild amusement that his friend was so immature he'd rather scare a girl than kiss her. "Come on, Randy," said Bobby. "We stopped scaring girls when we were twelve."

In Bobby's case this was actually true. There was nobody in the entire school system as socially advanced as Bobby. In sixth grade he had had ninth-grade girls flirting with him and now that he was in tenth, seniors were falling at his feet.

Bobby just jogged off the playing field and made a choice among the eager females waiting on the sidelines. This year, incredibly, Bobby made not one choice but two. He was not only dating Roxanne, a beautiful and brilliant senior, but also Sherree, a bubble-bath-cute tenth-grader. Bobby would alternate between Sherree and Roxanne, and either Sherree and Roxanne didn't notice, or they adored Bobby so much they didn't mind. Randy kept expecting a nursery rhyme situation in which the calico cat and the gingham dog would eat each other up, but no. Each girl linked arms with Bobby when it was her turn and stayed friends.

As for Zachary, he did not date. He said this was because he had high standards, and local girls simply did not meet them. Bobby said Zach did not date because Zach would not participate in anything where he could not get an A-plus, and you were never entirely sure whether you'd be an A-plus with any girl. It's okay to get a C in class, Bobby told Randy confidentially, but it's really lame to have a C average in girls.

Both Bobby and Zach felt that going around with Lacey was a C average in girls.

Randy tried to defend his suggestion about partying at the old mansion. "Lacey loves to be scared. We go to amusement parks, and she screams on the scary rides, and we go to movies, and she screams at the scary parts, and we —"

"Lacey is an airhead," said Zach. "I can't believe you go out with her."

Part of Randy wanted to tell Zach where to go, or beat Zach up and settle it with broken bones. But a larger part of Randy hated himself for dating a girl that Zach considered an airhead. Zach, of course, would never be seen near an airhead.

Randy addressed Bobby instead. "Bring Sherree or Roxanne," said Randy. "Or both. We'll sneak into the house around eleven o'clock, and —"

Bobby laughed out loud. "Randy, get a grip on yourself. Bring Sherree or Roxanne to the Mall House? They'd die first. Those are girls I have to spend money on, huh? Get it? They don't sleep on floors, Randy. And they don't lean back against splintered walls, eating in the dark from a bag of potato chips, and pretending it's fun."

Bobby and Zachary lost interest in Randy. They picked up the slick advertising circular from the biggest video rental place in town and discussed what DVDs to rent. Did they want chases and archaeology? Or should they concentrate on war and technology? Horror and axes?

Randy's insides knotted with rage. Nothing could be worse than being dismissed. If Bobby and Zach had not turned their backs . . .

But they had.

And so Randy turned his back as well, and left the room — although it was his house; he had the best home theater of any teenager in town. In his heart he knew that was why Bobby and Zach hung out with him — for the electronics he provided. Randy went to the telephone.

The rage percolated into courage, and he made three phone calls.

Phone calls he would never have made under normal circumstances.

But he was showing off.

And it seemed reasonable at the time. . . .

. . . Randy stared at the vampire. It was becoming clear why this mansion had been sold so often.

Lacey did not know that anybody was referring to her as an airhead. She happened to despise Bobby and Zachary, the most conceited idiots in the entire high school, but although Lacey had a strong personality, she would not have been able to laugh it off. Being called an airhead by two such popular boys would hurt.

Lacey had never had a boyfriend before Randy.

Randy made her nervous and unsure, and dating made her very nervous and very unsure. But she wanted to participate; she wanted to be doing what all the songs on all the radio stations said you should be doing — falling in love.

She didn't really love Randy, but she was trying.

She stuffed her head full of love-thoughts, and sat in love-postures, and listened to love-music.

It didn't take.

Randy was just a nice ordinary kid, half twerp and half jock. He was growing in all directions at once, both mentally and physically, and it was hard to keep track of Randy, or know if she even wanted to. She was fond of him, but mostly she was fond of going out.

Lacey felt very guilty about this.

Should you go out with a boy just in order to leave the house and be seen in other places? This seemed mean and low-minded. Lacey was a nice girl and didn't want to be mean or low-minded.

And yet, Randy kept calling her. He must be happy.

On that crucial night a week ago, Lacey had been half hoping he would call. Strange the way a telephone could rule your existence. It had become her center of gravity; she rotated around it like a moon around a planet.

And I don't even love Randy, she thought. I wonder what it's like when you really do love the boy.

She dreamed of love, of the boy she would meet one day, when stars and rockets and fireworks would fill her mind and soul and body.

And when the phone finally did ring, and it was Randy, she felt so guilty for dreaming about somebody better that she was ready to do anything Randy asked.

It took some serious planning to be able to arrange for a Saturday night without parental knowledge of her whereabouts. Lacey was always hearing about unsupervised teens whose parents hadn't seen them in days and didn't care where they were or what they were doing, but she, personally, had never encountered such a parent. All the parents she knew foamed at the mouth and confiscated car keys if anybody vanished for even an hour.

It was agreed that Lacey would say she was at Roxanne's and Roxanne would say she was at Sherree's. If there were phone calls from parents, they all had their cell phones and could fake it, nobody would get in trouble.

Lacey had never been in trouble, or even close to trouble, and found herself strangely attracted to the idea. But if they checked on her, she would be in the Mall House and they would never know.

Lacey's family lived on the far side of town and usually didn't have occasion to drive on this road. Her mother was not of the shop-till-you-drop persuasion and would not have kept up to date on the possibility of a new mall going up where once a decrepit house had stood.

Nobody had called it the Mall House when it still had a family living there.

It got the name Mall House when the zoning committee decreed that nobody could rip the place down because it was a "Historic Building" and the would-be builders said, "No, it's a piece of junk." For months people argued the pros and cons of this situation, and the old boarded-up mansion had gotten its nickname.

Wrong nickname, thought Lacey. It's the Vampire House.

The vampire sifted slowly out of sight. Not because he left, but because he ceased to be. She felt his molecules still drifting around the room, like an evaporating perfume. She did not even want to breathe, for fear that vampire threads would clog her lungs.

Sherree had never had a phone call from Randy before. She had to stop and think who on earth this could be. Randy, she had pondered. Do I know a Randy?

Luckily Randy expected her to be confused and he added, "You know. Bobby's friend. You came to my house to see a movie last month."

"Ooooh, yes! You have that fabulous media room, with the carpeted levels and the big soft floor pillows and the little kitchenette full of snacks and sodas right downstairs. I never saw a

TV that big in somebody's house! Sure, I remember your house, Randy."

Sherree did not hear her own sentence. (She never did quite hear what she was saying out loud.) She did not realize how hurtful it was to be told your TV room was easier to remember than you were.

"A sleepover?" said Sherree dubiously. "I don't know, Randy. My parents are pretty strict."

She paid attention to his offer because she paid close attention to anything a boy said. Sherree did not believe there was much worth thinking about except boys. Luckily there were so many of them. Sherree knew perfectly well that Bobby was dating Roxanne at the same time, but Sherree had learned that what boys wanted most was what other boys already had. Going with Bobby was increasing Sherree's desirability, and pretty soon Sherree would extricate herself from Bobby and take advantage of the boys who envied him. She had pretty well decided to wait until after Christmas because a girl who dated Bobby last year said that Bobby was really a big spender in December.

Sherree could not bring Randy's face to mind. Normally her brain was like a huge yearbook of available boys. Why hadn't she registered Randy? Was there something wrong with him or had the rented movies been especially good?

Randy wanted Sherree to pretend that she was really spending the night at a girlfriend's house, but he would pick her up and they were going to stay in a haunted house. Bobby and Zach would be there, too.

"A haunted house?" said Sherree. "Give me a break, Randy."

Randy plowed on. The house, he insisted, really was haunted. That was why they were ripping it down. Not because they were going to build a mall there but because of the terrible things that had happened to the human beings who had lived in that house, listened to those banging shutters, climbed those creaking stairs.

"Well . . ." said Sherree.

"We'll have fun," said Randy. "I'll bring the food."

"And movies?" said Sherree. "I love movies."

(Randy had just told Sherree that the house didn't have electricity anymore, but apparently Sherree had drawn no conclusion from this. Perhaps she thought Randy traveled with his own generator.) He said they would have so much fun that they wouldn't need movies. "In fact," Randy said, "I'll bring along a video camera and film us! *We'll* be the movie!"

"Well . . ." said Sherree. "Are there going to be other girls?"

"Of course. Lacey's coming, for one."

Sherree couldn't remember Lacey, either. Randy patiently described Lacey and after she had heard the description three times, Sherree felt as if she knew Lacey after all. "Oh, right," said Sherree. "Sure. Lacey. Great."

"Now we don't want lots of people there," warned Randy. "Spoil the fun, you know. So don't tell anybody."

"I won't tell anybody," promised Sherree. She hung up feeling confused. She did not know why they were going to the haunted house, nor quite what they would do once they sneaked in, but Randy seemed very sure of himself.

Sherree wondered what to wear to an event like this. She stood quite happily in front of her closets and bureau drawers, matching and re-matching, thinking maybe she would call this Lacey to see what she was wearing.

The only kind of movie for which Sherree did not have a taste was horror. She never watched those. They were too scary. She could not sleep at night after a horror movie, and if she ever managed to get to bed she had to sleep in a fetal position because she was afraid of what would happen to her toes if they stuck out.

Sherree was wearing sandals and her toes stuck out.

But even without the information she might have gotten from late-night movies, Sheree knew that she did not have to worry about her toes.

The vampire's attention was elsewhere.

And his teeth — his teeth seemed to be everywhere.

They slid in and out of focus, as if lenses on cameras had fogged up.

Sherree tightened herself into a ball, thinking: Lacey's standing up. He'll take her first. I'll run. He can't do two at once.

When the phone rang that night, and it was Randy, Roxanne bit back a laugh. If there was anybody who did not make waves, who did not set trends, and who was not interesting, it was poor Randy. He was the classic case of the kid with the terrific car, the terrific media room, and unlimited use of credit cards. People hung out with him to use him, and Randy had no idea.

Roxanne could not imagine what Randy was talking about, wanting to have a party in a deserted house. Roxanne being Roxanne, she pointed out the flaws in his planning: how they would have to break in, which was illegal; how the police might be called by neighbors; how very possibly the house was structurally unsound and they might fall through a stair tread or otherwise hurt themselves. How, assuming they did get in, a dark house might be interesting for a minute or two, but then what were they going to do?

"Lighten up, Roxanne," said Randy. "There are no neighbors, and back when they built that house, they built 'em to last for centuries. Nothing's broken in there."

"The shutters are," Roxanne pointed out. "It gives me the creeps just to drive by. Especially now, with everything around the place leveled."

The house stuck out of the ground as if it were

a growth or a mold. Strange twisted lightning rods stabbed the sky from the peaks of the porch roof and the ugly tower. Bulldozers had razed everything around it, even pulling down the immense dark hedge of towering hemlocks, but the downed trees had never been hauled off. They lay on the ground, dead and brown, a barricade of scaly bark and rotting limbs.

"But what's the point?" said Roxanne. Roxanne's life was filled with master plans. She did not like to undertake anything unless there was a good result from it.

"Something to do," said Randy.

Roxanne's calendar was very full. She did not need "something to do." She was willing to rearrange her schedule only if it were something *worthwhile* to do. "But what will we do once we're there?" said Roxanne.

"I'm not telling yet," said Randy.

Roxanne wondered if this was because he had no idea yet.

"I'm just promising," said Randy, "that it'll be a night to end all nights."

And that was a tempting phrase. Roxanne even agreed to help Lacey lie to her parents, although Lacey was about as interesting to Roxanne as dust under the bed. Even after she found out Sherree was going, too, Roxanne stuck with it. It would be an amusing test of Bobby's social abilities: Could he juggle two girls at once? In front of his two skeptical male friends? If the other guests had been people who mattered deeply to Roxanne, perhaps she would not have risked it. But even Bobby had ceased to be at the top of her list. It was her senior year and she was ready to shrug off these younger kids and get back to what counted.

Roxanne looked around the tower.

She looked at the swirling cloak as it waited to learn which human body would be encapsulated within it.

She looked at the five teenagers trapped with her.

One of us must be sacrificed, she thought. One of us has to spend the night with a vampire.

Well, it won't be me.

Chapter 3

Zach was having difficulty pushing the little black lever on his flashlight. He could not seem to make it go forward. His hands were trembling. He, who was always in control of a situation (Zach picked his situations, so he would never be in one he could not control in the first place), could not even control his own fingers.

Zach had to go back quite a few years to remember being afraid. He was often nervous. Zach had high standards. When he entered a class he did it with style. When he made an introduction, he was amusing. When he told a joke, he timed the punch line just right. When he took an exam, he got 95. When he went to a party, he was the life of it. He rehearsed all these events; he actually practiced room-entering, sauntering offstage, tie tying, laughing cruelly versus laughing gently. And because it mattered so much to him that he got these details right, Zach was accustomed to being nervous.

But afraid?

Zach frowned, remembering. He had probably been five, because he easily pictured his Halloween costume: He was Superman in a big red cape his older sisters had worn before him, but he had gotten separated from the group and found himself in a black yard with evilly grinning pumpkins, and a skeleton swinging from a tree, and spiders cascading off a gutter.

With abject terror he had fallen to the ground. He had not even been brave enough to run. He had not even screamed. He had just collapsed, a little puddle of panic.

He had refused ever again to be a little puddle of panic.

Zach controlled his fingers. He got the flashlight on. He moved its rays in a circle around the tower. The light revealed five terrified faces. Nobody was screaming, nobody was even running. They were little puddles of panic.

The vampire was not visible. Either the vampire had told the truth when he said he was not going to stay while they made the decision, or he was composed of a material that did not shine in the dark.

We shouldn't have come up here, Zach thought, furious with himself for making this error. If we'd stayed downstairs . . .

Well, they hadn't.

Zach was having some difficulty planning a strategy. It seemed to take so much more of his energy to hold the flashlight still than this minor physical action should require. His heart was pounding so hard that he did not seem to have much left over for running and escaping.

For the first time, Zach wished he were a jock like Bobby.

Bobby trained for this kind of stuff. All that bench-pressing and lap-running — now it would pay off. Whereas studying for British literature exams — that would get Zach precious little distance from a vampire.

Zach focused the shaft of light on the single, open door. Stairs led down to a broad landing on the bedroom floor below the tower, twisted once, and then led down to the old front hall. The teenagers had not, of course, come in the front door. Standing on the old creaking porch, they had peeled back a large slab of plywood that had been nailed over a broken window in the old dining room. Randy had brought along a clawed hammer to pry up the nails.

Zach disliked taking risks without rehearsing them first.

There was quite a bit that could go wrong if he tried to run ahead of the others. Zach flashed the light temptingly out the door and down the tower stairs, hoping one of the others would bolt, and Zach could follow in the wake, let someone else take the risks for him.

*   *   *

Ever since the vampire had appeared, the tower had been filled with a weird combination of light and dark. There were no lights, and yet Bobby could see himself and the others. The vampire had no color, and no form, and yet Bobby had been able to see him perfectly.

I possess the door, the vampire had said.

Bobby had believed it. The mushroom skin, the dripping fangs, the oozing cloak — it could possess anything it wanted.

But it had evaporated, leaving behind its strange illumination of the tower. And now he believed it less. Even a vampire could not possess air, and air was all that could fill the door opening.

Zach leveled the beam of his flashlight on the doorway and Bobby was relieved: The beam passed through the door. If light rays could travel in that space, so could Bobby.

Bobby planned his route.

He was a little worried about stumbling on the stairs. He'd been teasing Roxanne and Sherree so much about things that go bump in the night he had paid no attention to the layout of the house. Once he left here, he'd have to move it; there could be no fumbling on this pass.

Bobby was a player of team sports, but it did not occur to him that perhaps this was a sport and perhaps he had a team with him. He thought only of saving himself as quickly and efficiently as possible.

Bobby took a running start from the back of the tower room and hurled himself forward.

Sherree had never been afraid of anything, either. There was no need. The people around Sherree did everything for her.

Sherree fulfilled the Barbie-doll premise: She was incredibly thin and yet voluptuous. She had masses of fluffy hair and yet none of it ever fell into her oval face. Her blue eyes were immense, and she wore tinted contact lenses to make them bluer. She even dressed like a Barbie doll. No skirt was too short, no top was too glitzy, no tan was too dark.

Just two weeks ago, her car had stopped working while she was driving along some unknown road. She didn't wonder what had gone wrong, and she didn't worry about what to do next. She didn't even bother to get her cell phone out of her purse. Not too far down the road, she could see an immense sign from some gas station poking up above the tallest trees.

Sherree strolled up to the garage. Sure enough, the men who worked there came trotting out, eager to rescue her. All she had to do was twinkle at them.

Twinkling worked.

Sherree had planned to twinkle through all her problems. But she did not want to twinkle at a vampire. The vampire would want her most, because everybody always did. And she was dressed the skimpiest because Sherree always was.

She knew instinctively that the vampire wouldn't want a boy. That left Roxanne, who was a tough sarcastic type, and Lacey, who was a ditz. They were pretty enough, in their own boring ways, but that was all. I mean really, thought Sherree, what other choices does this vampire have but me?

Sherree assumed that Zach or Bobby would save her.

She did not assume that Randy would. Randy was a little too meager in personality and body to save anybody.

Sherree studied Zach and knew that he was analyzing the situation. She had faith in his brain. He would find a good strategy. She watched Bobby. The athlete drew himself together. He had a fine body, more heavily muscled than most boys his age. No doubt he could rip a T-shirt's sleeves by clenching his biceps. Bobby took a few steps backward, away from the door, gathering himself.

Sherree unwound from her terrified crouch. This was not completely different from cheerleading. You had to bounce off a gym floor from the most ridiculous positions and leap up. She would spring up and follow Bobby down the stairs.

Bobby turned himself into a battering ram.

Sherree lifted like a sprinter at the starting line.

Bobby flung himself across the tower and plunged through the door.

Except that he did not go through.

He remained in midair. Pinned to the atmosphere like a Velcro wall-jumper. Sherree stared. The door was open, and Bobby was hanging there. Not as if there were a noose around his neck, but as if he were an insect in the vampire's collection, pinned at the joints on the bulletin board.

The vampire indeed possessed the door. And now, clearly, he also possessed Bobby.

Roxanne had the hammer.

Her parents were neatness fanatics: everything in its place. If you left your shampoo bottle on the tub rim, they freaked. If you left a CD out of its plastic holder, they freaked. If you allowed a used glass to rest on the counter instead of popping it instantly inside the dishwasher, they freaked.

So, of course, when the teenagers had gotten into the deserted mansion, and Randy yanked the plywood back to hide the opening he had made, and then absently set the hammer down on the same windowsill they had crawled over, Roxanne picked it up.

They might accidentally leave the hammer behind.

Or not be able to find it again in the dark.

Especially if their flashlight batteries ran down.

It was an ordinary enough hammer, slim handle, hard metal head and claws. She was not wearing a belt in her jeans, so she shoved the handle through a belt loop. It hung satisfyingly against her thigh, making her feel like a tough workman.

When Bobby flew against the vampire's space, and stuck there, Roxanne found herself wondering if she would have to pry him off with the claws of the hammer.

"Bobby?" said Roxanne stupidly. "Are you okay?"

Bobby said nothing.

"Well," said Zach, in his most maddening, above-it-all preppy voice, "I guess that lets out the door as an escape route." Zach actually laughed. "You look a lit – tle strange up there, Bobby, my man."

Bobby said nothing.

In spite of his teasing, Zach had not been amused. In fact, he had been unable to maintain his grip on the flashlight, which he dropped when Bobby smashed into the vampire's space.

The pounding of his heart had increased. He felt like the bass drum in a marching band — he was nothing but a huge reverberating gong. His heart was thrashing around his chest just as Bobby had thrashed against thin air.

I'm afraid, thought Zach. He hated himself for it, hated the vampire for causing it, hated the others because they would surely see, and know.

* * *

Lacey retrieved the flashlight.

She examined Bobby's predicament. Then she examined Bobby.

Bobby said nothing.

He was stuck there, and yet when she put her own hand into the air around him, she could not feel anything. She had expected to meet resistance. An invisible balloon skin. She groped around Bobby, but could feel no substance from which to peel him away. He was breathing, his lungs swelled beneath her touch, but still he said nothing.

"Eeeuuuhh!" shrieked Sherree. "How can you put your bare hand out there? What if the vampire touches you?"

Lacey shuddered. The vampire was there, of course. No doubt he was taking pleasure in this; it was, after all, the first entertainment he had had in a long time. But somehow she did not think that her hand was going to encounter his slime.

Her hand encountered nothing at all.

Lacey latched her hands around Bobby's waist and pulled, but he did not come free. And he still said nothing. Nothing at all.

The weird thing was how normal it seemed, as if she had often met boys hanging in doorways and knew just what to do next. If you can't pull, try pushing, she reasoned.

So she stepped through the very doorway the vampire supposedly possessed — the doorway Bobby's body had not penetrated — and then turned around to push Bobby back into the tower room.

"You got through!" cried Roxanne, getting up. Roxanne hefted the hammer, ready to split the skull of any vampire that got close to her.

"Run, Lacey!" shouted Randy. He was so proud of her! She was not an airhead after all; he could brag about her now; *now* Bobby and Zach couldn't say anything about Lacey.

But Lacey did not run.

For beyond the door, at the top of the tower stairs, was the vampire's miasma of swamp gas. Wet slime coated her face and tried to get in her eyes. Horrible smells and even more horrible sounds filled her nose and ears.

The sounds were shrieks from another world: a dead world, a world of bodies the vampire had already used.

He had been here forever, thought Lacey. He was here before the house, and he will be here after the house. He is evil now, he was evil then, he will be evil after I am gone.

And now, Lacey knew why Bobby was not saying anything. He could not. He was deafened by the screams and the cries and the sobbing of the vampire's past. He was looking right into it.

Bobby *knew*.

The rest of them were just guessing.

But Bobby *knew* what was going to happen to one of them.

Lacey screwed her eyes tightly shut, to keep

from seeing the future and the past, and to keep the horrible swamp gas out of her eyes.

Nothing would have made Lacey run down the stairs into that oozing, sucking mud.

She pushed harder and harder on Bobby, but nothing happened.

Or at least, nothing happened to Bobby. Lacey herself stumbled back through the door, back into the tower.

Oh! The unbelievable relief of breathing real air again! No smog of corpses, no relics of pain.

On this side of Bobby's pinned figure were four other normal human beings, with their normal bodies, circulating blood, expanding lungs, functioning brains.

"I know what it is," said Lacey abruptly. She switched off the flashlight.

Sherree screamed. She had a powerful scream, and one that the mansion seemed to appreciate; the scream was welcomed into the terrible dark beyond the door.

Randy whimpered. Zach trembled convulsively. Roxanne's eyes filled with tears.

Lacey said, "I think the dark is better. I think this tower was meant to be dark. I think the flashlight is an invader. We can't use it again."

She was right.

For now that dark had returned, Bobby sank.

Slowly. As if he were at the top of an old playground slide, rusty, no speed to it. A slide for tiny nervous children.

Bobby puddled to the floor of the tower, like Zach in his Halloween memory. Zach and Randy rolled their friend safely back to the center of the room.

In the middle of the tower the six of them huddled.

When Sherree reached out to hold hands, everybody responded.

Then Sherree said, "I can't sit like this. My back is showing. Let's turn around and have all our backs touching, and we'll face out."

"That's worse," said Bobby. His voice had changed. It was dull and leaden. It was not Bobby at all; it was somebody who had known suffering and pain, someone acquainted with fear, someone with no hope.

"Why is it worse?" whispered Sherree. Sherree tried to make herself smaller and smaller, but it was no good; she had spent a lifetime trying to show herself off, and she did not know how to go into reverse.

"I've seen what's out there," said Bobby.

Lacey had not seen.

Only heard.

That was enough.

Bobby's voice was like cement. "Don't go out the door," he said. "Nobody go out the door."

Roxanne felt as if the cement were around her feet and some gangster were going to throw her into the reservoir and drown her.

Bobby read her thoughts. "No," he said, his

voice as drowned as the vampire's previous victims. "It's worse than that, Roxanne. Don't go out the door."

Sherree grabbed her boyfriend's shoulders. *"Then how will we get out of here?"* she screamed.

She could just see his eyes in spite of the dark but she wished that she couldn't.

"We won't," said Bobby.

Chapter 4

Lacey's younger brother, Kevin, who was in eighth grade, could not believe how long it had taken Lacey to get out of the house. Kevin dimly remembered Lacey telling Mom and Dad she was going to stay at Roxanne's, but apparently she was going to Sherree's instead. Kevin had never heard of either girl and his only interest was being alone in the house at last. Once the house was empty, Kevin had a telephone call to make.

The telephone call.

Kevin was deep in his first real crush.

He had told nobody about the crush, since he had nobody to tell.

His best friend, Will, had made such a complete idiot of himself last spring when Will got a crush on Lauren that Kevin trembled at the mere thought of following in Will's footsteps. Kevin was not going to start by buying a huge silver bracelet for a girl who did not even like to sit near him. He was going to start with a simple telephone call.

He was doing his homework, Kevin would say casually, and he remembered that Mardee . . .

Kevin rehearsed the call over and over. Sometimes his voice sounded triumphantly interesting, and sometimes it sounded as if Kevin were the flake of the century.

"We're going, dear," said his mother. "Here's the phone number if you have to reach us. We'll be home around one A.M. Be sure to keep the doors locked and don't watch anything disgusting on television."

"Okay, Mom," said Kevin, who always watched disgusting things on television the instant his parents were out the door. The thud of the closing front door and the clack of the closing lock were music to his heart.

He kept the TV on very low volume, for company, and looked up Mardee's number again, although he knew it by heart.

It took him a full hour to manage the actual call. The sixty minutes were filled with half-dialed numbers, self-scolding and swearing, hysterical laughter and deep despair. Kevin knew that if anybody could see him they'd figure he was a maniac. I am a maniac, he thought, I am insane about Mardee. His fingers completed all ten digits this time and to his horror the phone at the other end was actually lifted. "Hello?"

Kevin's tongue felt like a lost mitten. "Hi — Mardee?"

"Yeah?"

"This is Kevin."

"Kevin?"

"From school. Kevin James?"

"Oh, yeah. Hi, Kevin, how are you?"

"Fine." His voice was not fine. His hands were sweating so badly they had soaked right through his jeans where they pressed down. Disgusting. What girl wanted to hold hands with a water faucet?

"It's funny you should call," said Mardee. "I was just thinking about you."

"You were?" Kevin was absolutely thrilled.

"My older brother, Bobby, is at a party with your sister, Lacey, tonight."

Kevin was puzzled. "Can't be. Lacey's over at Sherree's."

"That's the story," said Mardee. "But you didn't believe it, did you?"

Kevin had always believed every single thing his big sister said. Lacey was the most straightforward and uninteresting person in America.

"Weren't you suspicious when it was Sherree's house they were supposed to be going to?" Mardee was laughing.

Kevin did not know Sherree. How was he supposed to be suspicious?

"Sherree is all body and no mind," said Mardee.

Kevin was pretty sure he would remember meeting somebody like that.

"They're actually going to party all night in the dark in a deserted house," said Mardee.

Kevin was overwhelmed. His sister? Party? "No," said Kevin. "I don't think Lacey parties. She's kind of a—" But Kevin loved Lacey, so he did not say that she was kind of an airhead. But it was true.

"It's a party, all right," said Mardee cheerfully. "Bobby doesn't do anything on Saturday nights but party."

Kevin was rather proud of his sister. It was time she broke out and did something other than study, practice, work out, and be kind to the elderly. Lacey at a party. Kevin could not quite picture this. He wondered if the others would give her partying lessons.

He wondered what Mardee would be like at a party. Kevin had not done a whole lot of partying in his life, either. Starting with Mardee would be a pleasant introduction. He said, "Mardee."

"Yup. That's my name, don't wear it out."

Kevin had thought they stopped saying that in third grade, but evidently not. He went on manfully, "Mardee, what do you say we — um —" but unfortunately, he was too rattled to remember what he had planned to suggest. The only activity that sprang to mind, he could not suggest aloud on a telephone.

"Yes!" said Mardee.

Kevin was awestruck. Would it be as easy as this?

"I know the address," said Mardee. "Of course, neither one of us has a car, but that could be the fun part."

Kevin was eager to have the fun part.

"It's probably a mile if you walk over to my house," said Mardee, "and probably another mile to the Mall House."

The Mall House? That horrible termite-infested porch-rotting monstrosity waiting to be ripped down? Kevin was horrified. Of all the places he did not want to go on a first date —

"What we could do is," said Mardee, giggling wildly, "we could scare them. That's why they went there, you know. To be scared. We could add the extras. The special touches. The really good noises. Tapping on windowpanes. Howling like the wind."

"Let me get this straight. You want me to walk over to your house, get you, we'd walk to that abandoned mansion, creep up in the dark, throw pebbles at the window, hide behind those old fallen trees, and listen to my sister and your brother scream in the dark."

"Right!" cried Mardee. "Won't it be fun?"

Kevin ceased to be an eighth-grade boy striving for adulthood and sex. He became a fifth-grader, dying for Halloween and fake blood, free candy, and screaming girls. "I'm on my way," said Kevin. "Find a flashlight."

"A flashlight!" said Mardee, disgusted. "And let them see us? Nosirree. We're going in the pitch dark, buddy."

"Pitch dark," repeated Kevin reverently. All sorts of possibilities sprouted in his beginner mind.

*   *   *

Roxanne held on to the hammer.

If the vampire came near her, she would let him have it. Roxanne was good at sports, although she had not gone out for any since middle school. The coaches were always after her to be on a team, but Roxanne disliked losing anything publicly. It wasn't so bad to goof up in gym class, and it wasn't so bad to screw up on an exam in an academic class. But in a gymnasium when the bleachers were filled? On a playing field when parents and friends lined the grass?

No, Roxanne liked to stack things in her favor. And in sports, the odds of being an idiot or doing poorly were too uncomfortable.

She hefted the hammer. It felt good and strong in her hand.

"Okay, I'm sorry," said Randy from his corner. He sounded belligerent, the way people do when the whole thing is their own fault, when there's absolutely no way to pin it on anybody else.

Nobody responded.

"I mean, how was I supposed to know?" said Randy.

Whiner, thought Roxanne. Who needs him? She concentrated on the shape of the house. So they could not exit by the door. There had to be another way out then. She and her hammer would get out.

Years and years ago, the house must have been handsome. Big and square, wrapped with an immense porch, its wood trim was curlicued, its many roofs covered with slate, and its beautiful tower had once risen above the gleaming house like a ship sailing at sea.

The hedge must once have been delicately green, enclosing flowers of great beauty and intoxicating scent.

But the hedge had grown to gargantuan proportions, threatening neighbors and roads. As the ground around the mansion had been flattened to get ready for building the mall, chain saws had taken those frightening black-and-green trees down, and bulldozers had heaped them like dead bodies awaiting burial.

The six teenagers had skulked around the downstairs with the flashlight. Anything nice had been pried away and carried off: The mantels over the fireplaces were gone, leaving horrible gaping holes around the brickwork. The beautiful woodwork in the study had been taken, exposing both the framework of the house and the mouse nests. In a butler's pantry, there had once been fine cabinets with beveled glass doors. Long gone. Nothing left but the holes where the screws had attached the cabinets to the studs.

The house was pathetic.

They had gone quickly to the second floor, a dangerous expedition, because the beautiful, carved banisters had been removed. There was nothing to hold on to.

"At least they left the treads," Bobby had said.

"Unless those are just shadows," Roxanne had added.

Sherree had screamed happily. Sherree was a good screamer, which would be a useful asset as the night continued.

But on the second floor a strange thing had happened.

Nobody could be bothered looking into the empty bedrooms or trying out the damaged window seat.

Another, steeper set of stairs coaxed them up again.

Roxanne had actually felt drawn, in a sort of reverse gravity.

The railing was still on this stair, and when her hand touched the surface, it felt warm to her. It quivered slightly, as if wired. They had found themselves getting in line to go up, waiting impatiently, staring with fascination at the lifting feet of the kids ahead of them, and then setting their own feet neatly in the spaces just vacated.

It had been a strange, breathless parade.

Randy had gone first. It was his hand that closed on the knob of the single door at the top of the stairs. His hand that swung the door out. His foot that crossed the threshold into the tower.

The tower was very high, Roxanne knew.

Although the house was in a valley, the tower was visible from far away. During Roxanne's lifetime, various owners had either kept the shutters tightly closed over the tower's many windows, or entirely opened. With shutters closed, the tower looked angry, like a weapon poised. With shutters open, the tower seemed hungry, its flaps checking the air for food.

Once up in the tower, the six made a strange discovery. Not only did the tower have shutters on the outside, it had them on the inside. The inner shutters were tightly closed, giving the room a strange inside-out look.

Roxanne's hands memorized the hammer. Three textures: handle, slipcovered in corrugated rubber for a better grip; shaft, smooth cold metal; head, strong with sweeping claws.

This tower — how many feet above the ground was it? Too many to jump, that was for sure.

Randy was still busy apologizing. He sounded worried that he might get a demerit.

"Somebody has to rescue us!" said Sherree hysterically.

Lacey considered the possibility of rescue.

She thought of the Land Rover, parked so invisibly in the sheltering maze of fallen hemlocks.

Nobody would see it.

She thought of the careful excuses made to trusting parents.

Nobody would worry.

She thought of the little pile of cell phones inside the Land Rover. Randy had insisted that things would be scarier without the comfort of instant communication. Everybody had regarded him with suspicion. She herself had stuck up for Randy, being the first to set a cell phone on the floor of the vehicle. Everyone had followed her example.

Nobody would be telephoning in or out.

"Call somebody, Randy!" cried Sherree.

Why, Roxanne asked herself, if you had to be imprisoned with somebody must it be a brainless goop like Sherree? "Every single phone," Roxanne pointed out, "is sitting uselessly in the car." She glared at Randy.

"I'm sorry, okay?" said Randy. "I mean, I didn't know this was going to happen, did I? You can't get mad at *me* over this. How was I supposed to know?"

"Keep whining," said Zach. "Because you're right. Tonight you won't win any points in your popularity collection game, Randy. The minute we get out of this, we're never looking at you again."

"We're not getting out of it," said Bobby.

Zach glared at him. "You sure gave up easily. Get a grip on yourself, Bobby. We need to talk about what we know about vampires. What exactly do they do? What exactly will happen to us if he gets us?"

"I don't want to talk about that!" wailed Sherree.

"If we gather enough knowledge," said Zachary, "we'll know the vampire's weaknesses."

Sherree burst into tears. "I don't want to know anything about vampires! I want to go home!"

Nobody said anything to that. They all wanted to go home.

"I like my life," added Sherree.

They all liked their lives.

"We're wasting time," said Zach. "List the vampire's weaknesses."

Bobby laughed.

Lacey said softly, "The vampire's weaknesses don't count. Our own weaknesses are the ones that matter."

Chapter 5

It was a new sound.

A completely different sound. Almost gentle. A tribal sound, like something from a film on ancient Africa, of hollow logs or old drums.

Lacey had heard the sound before, just as she had smelled the smell before and seen the cloak before.

I have had other lives, thought Lacey. Were they terrible? Was I as afraid during those lives as I am now? Was I glad to pass into other worlds? Did I go with as much pain and fear as I will this time?

The gentle thrumming continued.

It was precise and rhythmic. It reminded Lacey of somebody absently plucking the bass string on a guitar.

It was a waiting sound: background music, rhythm before the action begins.

Sherree laughed hysterically. "It's the vampire!" she said. "He's knocking." Sherree turned to open the door. "Come in, come in," she sang, like a lost opera soprano. Or a young girl losing her mind.

Only some of the vampire came in. Cloak, rather than teeth. Stench, rather than hands.

Lacey bit her lip, which made her think of teeth, and other, future bites, and she put both hands over her mouth and shuddered behind the wall of her locked fingers.

"Have you made any progress?" said the vampire courteously.

Lacey hated him for being gentlemanly. This was not a mannerly occasion. She found her voice. "We'll let you know," she said icily, in the rudest voice she could manage.

"You must feel free to take your time," said the vampire. "I have all night, of course."

The cloak evaporated more quickly than before, but his smell was greater and stayed longer. Roxanne had a coughing fit.

"That's it!" whispered Zach, wildly excited. "We'll stall. We'll bluff. We'll waste time!" Zach choked in his eagerness to explain the strategy to the rest. "When the sun comes up, he's out of the picture! I saw that in a movie! Vampires can't live in the sun!"

But the vampire's voice was still among them. He straightened Zach out. "I can make the night last as long as I wish, you see. You chose a sealed house, my friends. Plywood . . . nailed over broken panes. Light sockets . . . without bulbs. Wiring . . .

in which no electricity flows. It is always night in this house."

His voice went on shivering for some time.

Always night.

Always night.

Always night.

A shutter caught Zach's attention. It rattled its louvers as if it were talking to him. Zach nearly answered. Then he stopped himself. Those were strips of wood. Nothing else.

I've got to get out of here, he thought. Before I lose my mind.

It seemed to grow darker in the tower. The room added shadows and layers. The walls became farther away, the ceiling more distant.

I have to do something, thought Zach, before we are in total darkness and total silence.

Somehow he knew that once the horror became complete, nobody would be able to think, nobody would be able to act, nobody would be able to escape.

His mind tumbled like clothes in a dryer, falling, mindless, knowing nothing but heat and gravity. He could not grip any of his thoughts; he could come to no conclusions; he could plan no strategy.

All night. Their lives would last all night. Their lives would be nothing but night. Endless night.

Unless Zach could find a way out.

*   *   *

"We have to get out of here!" cried Roxanne. "Now! We can't just stand here and pretend somebody is going to rescue us. Nobody is going to rescue us! Somebody do something!"

Roxanne clung to the hammer.

What would happen to the vampire if she swung the hammer at it? Was there anything to bruise or break? Did it have substance or was it some sort of reflection of itself? Did it need — Roxanne could not bear imagining this part — did it need a meal in order to have flesh and skin?

In her panic, Roxanne pressed down with the hammer. It caught in the crack of the floorboards. Her body was so clenched with fear that she was gripped by an involuntary spasm, and she wrenched the hammer upward. The floorboard under which the claws were hooked came upward a half inch.

What's under there? she thought. Roxanne did not know what houses were made of. Beneath this floor would be the ceiling of the room below. What was the room below? What were ceilings made of? What would be in the sandwich of top floor and bottom ceiling? For a moment, she worried about live wires that could electrocute her should she stab a hammer claw through one. Then she remembered the electricity was off. She actually blushed in the dark, grateful that people like Zach, who were intelligent, did not know what a stupid worry she had just entertained.

Roxanne looked down. It was much too dark to see anything. She held tightly to the hammer handle. She pulled harder. The strip of flooring came up another inch. Nothing, absolutely nothing, would have made Roxanne stick bare fingers under the floor. With everything else there was to be afraid of, how did she have energy left to be afraid of touching the open edge of a piece of wood? You would think I'd have reached a fear saturation point, she thought.

But no.

Perhaps you could always become more afraid.

After several moments of gathering courage, Roxanne worked the claws of the hammer a few inches down the flooring strip, and pried again.

Zach touched the shutter. It felt punky. Rotted. Like a piece of tree fallen years ago in a storm, full of insects and becoming mulch on the forest floor. It contained its own damp. It felt as if he could roll it up in his hand.

Instead, he opened the shutter.

At first, although he knew he was looking at sky now instead of tower wall, he could see no difference. It was nighttime. There was no moon. There were no stars. No plane sparkled red and white in the sky. No immense beam from a car dealership or a carnival circled in the sky.

Zach touched the glass window.

Slowly, he lifted it. It held, staying up.

He put his hand outside into the night air. The

vampire might possess the door, but he did not possess this window! Zach said nothing to the others. Who knew what the vampire could feel happening in his own house? Who knew what the vampire saw? Best not to start loud frantic conversations on the subject of getting out via the window.

Zach thrust his head and shoulders through the opening.

The air was fresh and clear.

He had not realized the extent of the vampire's pollution until his face was breathing in clean air. The vampire had so completely contaminated the tower they might have been breathing the exhaust of decrepit trucks.

Over and over again, Zach filled his lungs with the wonderful clean oxygen of the night sky.

There was no longer a yard around the old mansion. There were ditches and troughs where bulldozers had gouged away shrubs and stone garden paths. The bulldozers had not followed up on their task. Heaped around the ground were dirt and debris mountains. If Kevin had been a little boy, and had had his toy trucks along, he would have had a wonderful time road building.

"There's the car," whispered Mardee. "They're here, all right."

Randy's Land Rover was a dark color and blended into the fallen hemlocks like a jungle animal into dense leaves. Kevin had not even seen it. There was something terrifying about the way it was parked. Randy must have driven into the Mall House yard, circled, and backed carefully into the immense black branches with their evil stubs of broken limbs stabbing the air all around them. Somebody had had to get out of the Land Rover first and direct him, or they would have been stabbed onto the prongs of the dead trees like meat on a fork.

The house was sordid and ruined.

There was nothing romantic about it.

It had a caved-in look, a place so completely gone, so completely lost, that even homeless drug addicts and mentally ill street people would not come here. The building itself looked mentally ill, its shutters crooked, its shingles curled upward, its roofing sagged.

The silence around the mansion was complete.

Life had stopped here. No birds, no small animals, perhaps not even any insects. No heart beat here. No lungs filled.

Life had stopped here. No flowers, no shrubs, no trees, perhaps not even weeds or grass. No roots dug into the fruitful earth. No leaves drew sustenance from the heavy air.

The air was truly heavy, as if the weather were about to change. Or as if something evil and unthinkable were passing through.

Kevin and Mardee found that they were holding not hands, but bodies. As if, should they stand apart, something else would fill that little space between them, and separate them forever.

On the lower floor, sheets of plywood had been nailed over the windows. The pale plywood made blind eyes against the dark house walls.

"They can't be in there," whispered Kevin. "There's no way in."

"They got in somehow; their car's here," breathed Mardee. "Let's go around the house and see how they broke in."

Kevin did not want to circle that house. He did not want to be near that house, or see that house, or even smell that house. Kevin was not actually gagging, but the smell of the house filled him and became part of him, and he felt weirdly older. As if that smell were carrying his body through its life span, and by dawn he would be ancient, used up, ready for burial.

Kevin wet his lips and regretted it. The smell gathered substance and landed on his damp lips, coating them. He tried to rub it off on his sleeve. It didn't come off.

Mardee was hanging on to him with both hands now. Kevin tried to enjoy this, but enjoying anything was impossible under the circumstances. Kevin could not imagine his fastidious, careful sister actually going inside.

Lacey wants to be popular, thought Kevin. I guess we all do. Her new friends were going in this horrible place, so she took a deep breath and went along.

Though how anybody could take a deep breath around this house, Kevin could not imagine. Earth and air percolated a vile stench. It was too dark to see the ground.

The source of the smell must be lying open — a septic pit — a sewer tank — a poison-disposal field. Kevin put one foot ahead of the other knowing he had never done anything so stupid, but doing it anyway. They circled the house and found nothing to show where the others had gotten in.

"Maybe they didn't get in," muttered Kevin. "Maybe they fell into whatever pit it is we keep smelling."

Mardee shook her head. Her hair brushed his cheek and he briefly forgot the house and turned his face down into her hair, intoxicated by it. It was satin compared to his own. His was like the tips of old paintbrushes; hers was like ribbons. In the deep darkness he could see into her eyes, the only bright spots on the earth. Kevin forgot the cesspits he had worried about and fell into Mardee's eyes instead.

Mardee whispered, "Let's go up on the porch and see if we can peel back any of the plywood."

Girls were supposed to be so romantic. How come he had chosen one who concentrated on things like this?

*   *   *

I'm wasting time, Zachary thought.

Zach came from a family in which time was never wasted. It was important to make the best possible use of all time. Zach's mother had had an extensive program of cultural activities for Zach when he was young; they had always been going to the Egyptian wing of the museum, or the children's concert and lecture at the symphony. Zach's father set an example of always having a book on tape should they be caught in traffic or a book to read should they have to sit an extra half hour in a doctor's waiting room. Zach's parents saw to it that all summer vacations were Important Experiences and all evening events were Meaningful and Packed with Knowledge.

Zach counted his breaths, and when he had taken ten lung-restoring heaves, he knew that was sufficient and he had no right to waste time tasting air, when he could be planning an escape.

By now his eyes were used to the dark and that made Zach feel better; time had not been wasted; he had just been acclimating himself to the dark.

He was three very high stories up in the air. If he were to jump, he would certainly break a leg. If not a spine. Zach had no desire to be a paraplegic. On the other hand, he had no desire to be a vampire's long-awaited dinner.

"Actually," Lacey was saying, in her methodical way, "we wouldn't be his dinner. The correct meaning of breakfast is to break the fast, and the vampire has been fasting for a long time now. So we'd be breakfast."

"Thank you for clearing that up," said Roxanne sarcastically.

Zach actually grinned. Then he studied the roof. There was a sort of gutter around the base of the tower. If he could wriggle out, he could perhaps use that as a crawl space, and inch his way to the roof beam of the rest of the house, which was, of course, lower than the tower. Perhaps he could slither along the roof beam and find his way down to the roof over the big porch. Then when he dropped to the ground he'd have a much better chance of living through it.

But what if the gutter were as rotten as the shutters? He'd still fall.

Zach was not a physical daredevil.

That was Bobby's style.

Zach preferred to let others take the risks, while he got the excellent grades, made the brilliant jokes, and led the pack.

But he did not see any way out of this except physical daring.

The thought was exhilarating. Zach had been brought up to conquer the world. This was his moment. Yes. It was time. Now he had to take the world by the shoulders and show it what he could do.

Once I'm down, thought Zach, I'll get my cell phone out of the car and call the fire department.

They have the high ladders. They'll get the rest out.

Zach knew that he would not call the fire department. He could not dial 911 and tell them to rescue his friends from a vampire. It was too ridiculous. Nobody would believe him. He would be laughed at. Zach could take anything except being laughed at. People would point at him, and chuckle, and call him names. *That's the kid who thought there was a vampire in that old shack they're tearing down to build a mall, isn't that hysterical?*

The tower's exterior shutters banged eagerly, a drumroll for whatever happened next.

His right leg felt the air. His hands gripped the sill tightly. He tried not to think of the great distance to the hard, hard earth. He managed to press his knee against the steeply sloping slates and drag the other leg out.

Good thing I'm not a big guy, thought Zach, who had always before wanted to be a big guy.

His shoes tried to find the gutter he had seen from the window.

But all they found was slick roof, and more slick roof.

His fingers began to ache. He could not grip the sill much longer. He had to put some of his weight on his feet instead of his hands. He kicked, trying to find a footrest.

Something touched his right hand.

Something foul and wet, like a moldy leftover in

the refrigerator. He hung on only because his life was in the balance. He could not see what touched his hands. After a few seconds, it did not simply touch his fingers. It applied pressure.

Something was peeling his fingers off the sill.

Somebody had decided to help him fall.

Zach began to scream. He tried to shift his finger grip, but the sill was slick.

He began to fall.

I'm going to die, thought Zach, quite clearly.

He tried to dig his fingernails into the punky wood. He tried to haul himself back into the tower. He screamed for the others to grab him, but nobody came.

With a satisfied little chuckle, the creature peeling him away finished its task, and it leaned forward to watch Zach's fall.

The last thing he saw was a face neither white nor black, skin neither tanned nor pale — but absolutely clear. A face that went right through to the other side, all its interior on display, like some horrible living laboratory model.

And then he was airborne, and screaming his last scream.

Chapter 6

Mardee's scream could have pulled the rest of the nails out of the plywood.

Kevin could not let go of the wood he had hauled back, or it would snap against her and stab her to the window frame. Mardee was still standing next to him and yet she seemed to be pulled forward, into the house.

Something was pulling her by the hair.

Like taffy, Mardee stretched. Her scream went on and on, as if it, too, were being pulled out of her throat, taut like a rubber band.

Kevin put all his strength into the plywood and actually tore it the rest of the way off the house. He flung it down onto the porch floor. He grabbed Mardee and yanked her back against himself. She did not come easily. It felt as if she had been stuck with adhesive. He whipped her around to face him.

The scream stopped. Mardee's face, whiter than any moon or star, was twisted in such horror that

Kevin could only imagine she had looked into the scene of a mass murder.

"What happened?" he whispered. His heart was racing double-time, working so hard he felt crazed with its speed.

Mardee was as close to him as another skin. "Didn't you feel it, Kevin?" she whispered. She wet her lips, gasping for breath. "Didn't you see it?"

"See what?" He had been busy prying the plywood back from the window. He had not seen much except wood. Why were they whispering? What was happening? What had —

"A vampire," said Mardee.

He was technically rather young, the car thief.

He had dropped out of school before he was sixteen and spent time in prison before he was twenty, and that had aged him. He was older and more cruel than his actual years.

There was nothing nice about him. He did not have a heart of gold, he did not feel neighborly love. He did not mind injuring people who got in his way. People often got in his way, and he often injured them. He never thought about them when he hurt them, and he never thought about them afterward. He did not have a conscience.

What he mostly had was a great need for money.

It had been a difficult summer. Things kept going wrong. In spite of the people he had hurt, the car thief had not acquired any cash.

He had no particular destination in mind as he roamed the streets. He had no particular plan in mind. All he had in mind was greed.

He was panting with it.

He could think only of money and what he would do with it; what he would buy with it; how much better life would be once he had some.

He did not normally walk down the valley road. Of course, he did not normally walk anywhere, but he had lost his various forms of transportation, and so he was reduced to this pathetic, loser-style of going someplace.

He had to walk.

It outraged him that he was on foot. People like him did not deserve this humiliation. Somebody would pay for this, he would see to that.

The car thief walked onto the site where the shopping mall would soon begin to rise. In the dark, it was a shambles. Piles of dirt and trash. Ruts from immense tires. Metal barrels, old railroad ties, and discarded junk. A few scattered, white-painted barriers making a feeble attempt to close off a huge area.

He crossed the acreage hoping to find something — anything — that he could steal and sell. Perhaps a backhoe worth tens of thousands of dollars that he could somehow start up, drive off in the night.

There was nothing.

He walked toward a huge shapeless stack. It had no shadows because there was no light to cast them. It was not until he was very, very close that he realized the stack had no theft potential; it was a bunch of huge old dead trees bulldozed down and left to rot.

He was furious.

He kicked a tree.

But it was not satisfying to kick a tree. It didn't whimper, or cry out, try to run, or hand over its wallet. He wanted a human to kick. Something where you could laugh when it cried out.

He kicked the tree again, and felt no better that time, either.

But he saw something.

Something . . . something large and glossy glittered faintly within the trees.

He began to work his way around the branches to get at the thing within them.

It was, thought Roxanne, a vampire without its cloak.

A vampire without its skin.

Nothing but the interior: the silhouette of its bones and its organs.

It seemed to come out from between the shutters, first as flat as a pane of glass, and then thickening, and becoming more visible. It was grinning, its teeth exposed like a dentist's drawing. It peeled Zach off the windowsill and grinned even more widely as Zach screamed and fell.

Zach's screams came from everywhere.

Then they ceased.

He could not have lived.

Well, thought Roxanne, that's one way to escape being the vampire's victim. Die first. Poor Zach. Poor, poor Zach! He had so many plans.

Roxanne found that she was weeping. Her face was covered with tears for Zach. Or was it for herself?

How selfish am I? thought Roxanne. I will know tonight. We will all know tonight.

She thought of the vampire's requirement. Oh, it was truly evil! Not only did they have to witness the "event" — they would have to participate in it; they would have to choose and live with that choice.

She found that while Zach was falling and her eyes were weeping, her hand and her hammer had continued prying up floorboards.

"What are you doing?" hissed Randy, hearing the creaks and snaps.

Roxanne shook her head, but, of course, he couldn't see her. She had managed to lift a whole length of board and now she shifted her hammer to start on the adjacent strip of wood.

She had no idea what she was doing, or why. Perhaps since they could not go out the windows, and they could not go out the door, they could just descend right through the floor.

"What are you doing?" hissed Randy again. Louder.

Randy's such a stupid person, thought Roxanne. The vampire hadn't noticed yet. Roxanne certainly didn't want him to notice *her* now — let alone the possible escape route she was uncovering.

Ten miles away, in an isolated subdivision of only nine houses, a mother and father were furious because their sixteen-year-old son had not brought the family car home. "He was told to be here now, or else!" said the father.

"Now, Dad," said their other child. She was eighteen and sympathetic to lateness. "He'll be home in a minute. Don't panic."

"I am not panicking, Ginny. I am furious. Your brother is dead."

"No, he's not," said Ginny reassuringly. "He's fine."

"I don't mean he's lying dead in a road somewhere," shouted the father. "I mean, I'm gonna kill him! I told him to get that car home by nine or die. So he's dead." The father stormed back and forth in the tiny front hall. "I should never have let him get his driver's license. I'm taking it away the minute he walks in the door. He's dead."

"Now, Dad," said Ginny. "You and Mom haven't missed much of the party. The Kramers will party till dawn, you know that. If you don't get there for another few minutes, it won't be the end of the world."

"It'll be the end of your brother's world," said the father. "He was told he could take the car for the first half of the evening but we had to have it for the second half. If he ruins our weekend, I'm ruining his *year.*"

Ginny thought she saw a way to get something good out of this situation. "The moral of the story," she said cheerfully, "is that our family should have a second car." She smiled hopefully.

Her parents gave her a tight-lipped glare.

Oh, well, thought Ginny. Worth a try.

Out in the driveway a car appeared. But it was not her missing brother. It was Ginny's date. "Jordan and I could drop you at your party, if you want, Dad."

Her father refused to be mollified. "Your mother and I will wait, thank you, until your worthless brother gets here."

Her date bounded up to the door. Jordan was one of these courteous-to-adults types, who wanted to hear the whole story. "Are you worried about your son's safety?" asked Jordan, getting deeply concerned and worried himself.

"The time to worry about my brother's safety," said Ginny dryly, "will be when he gets home."

"Yes, of course, we're worried!" said Ginny's mother. "This just is not like him! He's a very responsible boy!"

Ginny rolled her eyes. There was no such thing as a very responsible boy.

Jordan said, "Hey, no problem. Ginny and I will cruise around and find him."

Ginny, who had been looking forward to something else entirely, was quite irritated. "Really," she said, "I'm sure he's fine. He'll be here in a minute."

"I'd like that, Jordan," said Ginny's mother. "I am genuinely worried. He knows what his father would do to him if he's late tonight. He knows how important it is. So why isn't he here? Anything could have happened! He could have had an accident! He could be bleeding somewhere!" Ginny's mother had worked herself up into tears. "He could have been stolen away! We'll never see him again."

Ginny tried to bring a little reality to the situation. "Mom. He's six-two. He lifts weights. He could bench press an SUV. Nobody stole him away. We're going to see him again. Probably in five minutes."

But Ginny's date loved this kind of thing. He loved action and heroism. Jordan would much rather cruise the entire city and all its suburbs tracking down a lost child than go to a party where somebody had rented a movie he had probably already seen, and then order pizza, which, after all, he had just eaten for lunch. The fact that the lost child was bigger and stronger than Jordan was did not matter.

"We'll find him," Jordan promised. "Don't worry! We'll look everywhere!" He took Ginny's hand and bounded with her back to the car. Full of enthusiasm, he switched on the engine, revved the motor, crammed the gearshift into first, and left a patch on the street. "Where do we start?" he said happily. He was already looking left and right, peering behind shrubs and picket fences.

Ginny regarded him stonily. Then she turned on the radio, put the volume where she liked it, and said, "Somebody's having a party at that horrible old mansion. The Mall House. Maybe he decided to crash that."

Her date sighed with pleasure.

He did not come to a full stop at the end of the little housing division road. He looked swiftly both ways and, instead, accelerated through the stop sign and let his tires scream as he turned left.

Ginny sighed. It was going to be a long night.

And all for a brother.

When you got right down to it — who needed him?

Lacey could not stop hearing the scream.

Even though she knew that Zach must have hit the ground by now, must be crushed flat against it, she could still hear the scream.

Zach! she thought numbly.

Bobby and Zach were the kind of boys to whom nothing bad ever happened; they were inoculated against trouble from birth. Their lives went smoothly, their complexions went smoothly, their relationships went smoothly.

And now look. Zach was dead or broken. Bobby was catatonic.

In the silence of the tower room, into the muffled panting and weeping of the five left standing there, came a new sound.

A rhythmic series of thuds.

Steps coming up the stairs.

Lacey's heart roared like a locomotive.

The vampire had not made noise before. Whose step was so heavy? Perhaps a real person was walking up those stairs.

Could it be the police, coming to see what was going on? To find out who had screamed? Were they about to be rescued?

Was it some horrible, drug-crazed murderer escaped from an insane asylum?

Lacey could not bear to look at the door, but neither could she look away. It was as though her eyes no longer belonged to her, but were ruled by some other force.

Be the police! she thought, and prayed, and begged. Please be the police. Please save us! Please end this! We don't deserve this! We want to go home! We want our mothers! We —

Through the door came the vampire.

His cloak swirled and his stench rose up.

Under his arm was the burden that gave him weight.

Zach's body.

Chapter 7

"A vampire?" repeated Kevin James. He actually began to laugh.

"Don't you laugh at me," snapped Mardee.

"I can't help it. A *vampire*?"

Mardee pulled back from him. The creep. To think that she was alone with this idiot. Nothing, nothing in the entire world, was more maddening than somebody who laughed at you. Mardee pulled her lips together in a furious pout. She folded her arms over her chest. "Yes," she said. "A vampire."

Kevin laughed again, and louder.

It was a Land Rover.

The car thief grinned widely. Some of his teeth had rotted, and some were missing.

Somebody had already stolen the Land Rover once, obviously, or it wouldn't be here. Some fool who had not had the foresight to drive it out of state or provide a closed garage. Some beginner who had tucked it here until morning.

Well, come morning, it would not be here.

Land Rovers. That whole class of vehicles made the car thief laugh. Big, high, tough SUVs, bought exclusively by weak and wimpy suburbanites. Big strong SUVs for difficult terrain and steep grades, which would never go anywhere except a parking lot.

And loaded. These babies always had a great sound system. Air-conditioning. Telephones. Last summer he even got one that had a fax machine in it.

The car thief felt around the cracks of the doors. In the complete dark it would not be easy to break in.

He did not think he had ever been anywhere as dark as this.

Although he was rarely afraid — he preferred to scare others than to be scared — the car thief felt a prickle on the back of his neck.

It was not fear. It was not some sixth sense.

It was an actual touch.

Fingers brushed his neck.

The car thief bit back a scream and whirled, ready to strike back.

Nothing was there.

He was left trembling, his knees jellied.

He hated that. It made him deeply angry that anything could frighten him.

Nothing was there, he told himself. And yet that outraged him. He did not make things up! He did not get scared of the dark!

His hands went back to feeling around the door. His hands were trembling and sweaty. He ground his teeth together, to get rid of the debilitating fear.

And again, gently, exploring, lifting the long hair that lay against the neck of his T-shirt, came the touch. Something was actually feeling the back of his neck, imitating exactly the way he was feeling the car.

He whipped around for a second time, and this time he struck blindly into the air, making fists, fighting it.

But nothing was there.

It must have been the tip of a branch. A wavering end of one of these dead trees. It had, actually, felt dead. Even though it had moved, touching him.

The car thief ran his bare hands through the air, as one feeling for a spiderweb. But he encountered no branch, no web that could have touched the back of his neck.

Instead there came a new sensation. A smell. A smell like raw sewage. It rose up around his ankles as if he were sinking into some terrible hole.

He grabbed at the only thing available. The door handle of the Land Rover. He gripped that faint silvery shine.

And the door opened.

The Land Rover was not locked.

The car thief grinned.

*   *   *

"Let's go get some ice cream," said Kevin. The entire evening was so weird. He kept laughing. Who would ever have thought you could have a first date like this? Who could he even tell about this?

"Your sister is in there with a vampire, and you want to have ice cream?" said Mardee. She was outraged.

"If my sister were in there," Kevin pointed out, "she would have said something by now. She had to have heard your scream."

Mardee looked at him in astonishment. "I didn't scream," she said.

The vampire carried Zach like a grocery bag. Set him on the floor like a loaf of bread.

Mildly he said to the others, "This is wasting time, you know. Not that I didn't appreciate the effort, dear boy," he added. "It was most interesting. And the scream — quite well done. I like a good scream." The vampire reflected on this. "In fact," he said, "I am a connoisseur of screams."

"In that case," said Lacey, "you will get absolutely nothing from us but silence, you dirtbag."

"Lacey!" hissed Randy. "Don't call him names. It'll make him angry."

Lacey stared at Randy incredulously. What possible difference could it make if the vampire was angry? His teeth were just as sharp.

In the mournful voice of a school principal yearning to retire, the vampire explained that they had disregarded his directions. It really was time for them to begin their important decision.

"Buzz off," said Lacey. "Are you all right, Zach?"

Zach sat up and brushed himself off. The tower room was quite light. The vampire was giving off the phosphorescence again. Zach looked around in a daze. He looked down at his fingers, which had been peeled away from the sill, and his legs, which had not been broken against the ground below.

"You caught me," he said to the vampire. "You saved my life."

The vampire said sympathetically, "You had an assignment to complete, as you recall. This is not homework. You may not skip it and average your grade. Tonight you will choose."

Zach closed his eyes. He had not closed his eyes when he was falling. But the knowledge that he had accomplished nothing, that he was still here, that he still faced one chance in six — it was too much to look at. So he closed his eyes. With his eyes still closed he said, "If you were going to save me, why did you peel my fingers away from the sill to start with?"

The vampire was insulted. "I would never do a thing like that," he said.

"Then who did?" said Zach.

"I don't suppose anybody did," said the vampire. "How would it have benefited your companions to do that? The sill was slick and you had a poor grip, that's all. It was a poor plan to start with."

Roxanne stared at the vampire. She had seen

him. With her very own eyes. She had watched him send Zach plunging to the ground.

"Let us return to the primary consideration," said the vampire.

"No," said Lacey. "Dry up and blow away." She glared fiercely, as if she actually expected this third-grade curse to accomplish something. The vampire merely looked at her with more interest than he looked at the others, so Lacey quickly looked away again. She happened to look toward Randy.

Poor Randy was losing his grip. Perhaps it was because he was the only boy who had not yet attempted escape. Perhaps he felt a manly duty to hurl himself in some outward direction, but there were none left.

Randy was pulling things out of his pockets and fondling them like lucky charms. He had his keys in one hand; he had a Bic pen, which he continuously capped and uncapped; he had a disposable lighter, whose slick plastic side he stroked with his thumb; he had several quarters, which he tumbled from one palm to another.

Bobby seemed marginally more aware than he had been, but he still wore a fogged and stunned look.

Sherree was sitting in a little ball, hugging her knees to her chest, rocking back and forth.

Roxanne appeared to be trying to scrape through the floor with her fingernails.

Lacey was furious with the vampire. Who was

he to do this to them? She whirled back to face him. When Lacey was angry, she screwed up her face so that all her features met in the center, wrinkled and sharp. "We do have things to discuss, actually," said Lacey, glaring. "We will begin with your character. Or lack of character. I demand to know why you do terrible things like this to innocent people."

"I don't do anything terrible." He was affronted by the accusation.

"It isn't nice to kill people."

"This is nature," explained the vampire. "Nature is built on the laws of birth and death. Predator and victim. Hawk and mouse."

The six were not happy with that metaphor. Even Bobby in his daze flinched. No one ever wants to be the victim or the mouse.

"But I don't kill anyone, if you need details," said the vampire. "No, you see, after the . . . event . . . we will call it an *event* . . . you will be very tired. There will not be much left of you. Not much personality. Not much energy. Not much for people to bother with. You will become a shadow of your former self."

They cherished their characters. They were proud of their personalities. They liked who they were.

A shadow of that? Not much left? Nothing for other people to bother with?

"Perhaps," said the vampire, his voice like chocolate, dark and slippery, "to hasten the final ending, each of you should present a defense to the others. Each of you should explain to the other five why he or she should — or should not — be the choice."

"That is sick," said Lacey sharply. "We are not going to lower ourselves to your level."

Randy said nervously, "I'm not so sure you're right, Lacey." It seemed to Randy if the vampire had all the facts, he might make the choice himself. That would be so much easier. Randy felt he was carrying enough guilt. It was his fault they were here at all. He did not want to carry more. On the other hand, he did not want to be the choice.

"We are not going to let you have anybody," Lacey informed the vampire. "You may as well face that, you hairball. We didn't come here to be your choice."

The vampire definitely did not like being called names. His snarl seemed to cross the room, independently of his cloak and form. His teeth overlapped, as if he were biting his own chin, and his upper lip twitched like a dog guarding a back door.

Sherree began to make dog noises herself, whimpering and moaning.

"You came here for adventure," the vampire pointed out to Lacey. "I am giving it to you." His snarl turned into a caricature of a smile. "Never wish for anything," he whispered joyfully. "You just might get it!"

"You may leave now," said Lacey imperiously. "And don't come back."

The vampire ignored her. He met the eyes of each of the other five. "One of you will be given to me by the others," he said gently. "And that is that. However long the night, however difficult the choice, you will complete the assignment."

Roxanne had completed every assignment of her life.

Roxanne had been well organized since first grade, and always knew what chapter they were on, and which outline was due on Friday, and which quiz would be given on Monday.

And Roxanne intended to complete the rest of her life as well. This was her senior year! She had college out there, and a yearbook. A prom, and a future. She couldn't be letting some vampire suck her life away.

The vampire disappeared. He did not seem to go out the door, but simply faded slowly. You could not tell whether he was still in the room or not. Roxanne counted to one hundred before she began prying at the floor again.

Roxanne saw her dreams turn into reflections in a cracked mirror. Roxanne moved on to the third floorboard and yanked.

The house was full of its own noises. Its shutters banged, and its roof clattered. Its porches creaked, and its shingles curled. Roxanne's noise blended into the fabric of the night. And whatever was below her made no noise of its own. Instead it made a smell. As if the vampire were not enough of a stink, a new one rose from between the floors.

"Shut up!" said Mardee fiercely. She hated Kevin now. She could not believe she had thought spending an evening with a boy would be fun. Boys. Ugh. They were disgusting. They laughed at you. Lives were in danger and what did they do? They suggested ice cream.

Kevin put his hand tightly over his own mouth, making a gag from his palm, pantomiming absolute silence. Behind his palm he grinned insanely. He was really having an excellent time. Weird. But excellent.

The laugh that had so angered Mardee, however, continued.

From out in the yard, and from up in the tower, separate laughs spun through the fetid air.

One laugh was as high-pitched as a broken piccolo.

The other laugh was deep and mucky as oil wells.

Both were evil.

On both their heads, the hair shivered. Kevin's hair shifted position as if fingers were going through it, as if the laugh possessed hands to examine his scalp. Mardee's hair blew around as if some tiny private tornado had settled in it.

Kevin was terrified.

It made him furious. Terror was for girls. What was with this panic seizing him?

He wanted to wet his lips but could not bring himself to open his mouth. Something would fly into his mouth if he parted his lips. From behind the protection of his own palm he whispered to Mardee, "Let's go sit in the Land Rover."

Roxanne had six floorboards lifted.

It was like war, fighting the nails, but the way Lacey was riling up the vampire, he was going to quit the original option of choice and just hurl himself on somebody's throat. Roxanne wanted to be gone.

Needing more leverage, Roxanne stood up.

Ignoring the stares of the others, she yanked on the boards, taking immense pride in her strength.

The nails screamed as they were ripped out. Or was it the vampire screaming?

Roxanne could not spare the time to look up.

She had the misfortune to be looking down, therefore, when she finished opening up the floor. She had found the vampire's sleeping place.

His coffin.

She fainted, falling directly into the rotting nest she had exposed.

Chapter 8

The vampire was gone.

It was so strange. The fetid atmosphere of the tower was simply air. The overwhelming slimy horror of the place had vanished. The murmuring of the past, those victims whose souls lay under the mansion, ceased.

Lacey walked in a slow circle around the tower room. She touched the walls.

It was just a house.

Plaster.

Glass.

Wood.

Nothing more.

"He left," whispered Sherree. She stood up from her crouch and dusted herself off, as if she had been sitting on the sand at the beach and was ready to go in the water now. Immediately Sherree began worrying again what she looked like, and whether her hair still looked good, and if she needed to reapply her lipstick, and if she'd

wrecked her clothes from the dust and ickies that floated around this horrible place. She wanted a mirror so she could do a proper inspection of her face. Sherree dug deep into her pocketbook, searching for her mirror.

Bobby came out of his trance. When he was still pinned in the air, he had been forced to stare into the ruined lives of the humans the vampire had taken over the decades. The horror of their destruction had turned his mind to ice. His screams had tightened in his throat and turned solid, and his heart seemed to thud in a vacuum, keeping him alive, but giving him no warmth, no pulse.

When he had come down, he was a blank.

It was truly like being half dead. Bobby had been able to investigate himself: He had seen that his flesh continued to function in its earthly way, taking in the air it needed, circulating the blood it required. And yet he was not all there. His mind — his soul — his very self — whatever those things were composed of: They hung suspended.

He had thoughts, but they were distant. His thoughts seemed to have traveled out of state. Or out of body. His thoughts floated around him without meaning anything to him.

Bobby, the consummate athlete, had never before had no grip on himself. No possession of his abilities.

But now the vampire was gone. Bobby looked around, confused and disoriented, but was himself again. He felt his personality come back, as if it lay in puddles around the room, and was now tilting, sliding, coming back into the jar of his mind. I'm me again, he thought. The vampire didn't take me after all. He just showed me what he can do.

Zachary's body had not slowed like Bobby's. While Bobby had seemed to enter a mental hibernation, Zach had entered a horrible trembling, a constant vibration. Even when he could not see his muscles quiver, even when he could not observe his joints shivering, he could feel his corpuscles and cells shuddering. His complete interior, everything under his skin, was shaken by the fall. Shaken by being caught. Shaken by the taste and flavor and stench and feel of the vampire's cloak.

That cloak that had draped itself over his body. Truly it had been the lining from thousands of coffins. It was not moss, yet it was wet and green and growing. Every centimeter of his skin had recoiled in horror at its touch.

The vampire himself had never touched Zach.

He had been caught and picked up and removed to the tower by the cloak. Zach had not even been able to feel the vampire's arms supporting him, although they must have. What strength could a cloak have?

But now the vampire was gone.

The vampire's departure was so complete that Zach's body knew it right down into the depths of his gut, and he ceased to shake from his fall.

The vampire was gone.

Zach was afraid to look around. In his shuddering self-oriented existence, had he missed the "event"? Had the vampire taken a victim while Zach was busy trembling? Was Zach going to count heads and find there were now only five teenagers in the tower? Who would the sixth be? Which of this group was missing now? Missing forever? Missing into that unspeakable horror that had scraped Zach's skin? Peeled Zach's fingers from the window and yet caught him at the bottom?

And where? Where would that sixth one be right now? Swallowed in that cloak? Feeling the jaws of —

Zach wrenched his mind away, and counted.

He saw Bobby. He saw Lacey. He saw Randy. He saw Sherree. For one long, hideous, ghastly moment, he could not see Roxanne. And then his eyes lit on her: half fallen right through the floor.

Zach's body heaved itself in one last final shudder, more of a convulsion, really, and he stumbled forward to try to get Roxanne out of whatever pit she had slid into.

Their fingers met, and Roxanne's were surprisingly warm and calm.

Roxanne was rather proud of herself. She was actually lying in the dreadful cavity of the vampire's hibernation, and yet she was no longer afraid. For several fine moments she congratulated herself on her courage; awarded herself prizes for being the bravest on earth. Then she realized that the vampire had disappeared. Her own bravery — or lack of it — had nothing to do with the situation. There was no longer anything to be afraid of. The vampire had left.

But where? thought Roxanne. Where does he go when he's not here? He can't get into this nest. I'm in it. And if he were here, visible or invisible, I would know.

So where is he?

"He's gone!" repeated Sherree cheerfully. Sherree did a little dance. She tapped both toes and heels in a happy pattern on the wooden floor of the tower. She rocked a little, swayed a little, giggled a little. "Let's get a move on, guys! Time to roll. Time to close the curtain on this little show." Sherree headed for the door.

But Lacey frowned. She preferred to have an understanding of events. "What could have made him leave?" said Lacey. She was suspicious. What was going on here?

"Roxanne invaded his nest," said Zach. "I think he had to flee."

Zach, Bobby, Randy, and Lacey stared down into the ghastly little coffinlike space between the floors.

Sherree stomped her feet. "What is with you idiots?" she shouted. "Stop worrying about the vampire's housing situation!"

Lacey and Roxanne giggled in spite of themselves.

Sherree said, "Come on, you guys. The night is still young. We can party some place intelligent instead of this dump."

Roxanne said, "You know, Sherree, I'm starting to like you." Lacey, Roxanne, and Sherree giggled together, not quite sure what was funny, but finding themselves together in some girlish emotion.

Roxanne started to get out.

"Stop!" shouted Randy. He actually pushed her back in.

"What am I supposed to do?" Roxanne shouted right back. "Set up housekeeping? Of course I'm getting out of here. Help me." She stuck out one hand to Randy and Zach took the other.

"Listen to me!" said Randy fiercely. "Zach is right. The vampire left because you invaded his nest. And that means," said Randy, "he'll come back the minute you're out of it."

Roxanne shook Randy's hand free. Then feeling stronger still, she shook Zach's off, also. She was very pleased with herself, getting out of the opening with help from nobody. I'm tough, she thought. I'm strong. I'm proud. "You are such a loser, Randy," she said.

Lacey tested the open doorway.

There was nothing in the door space but air.

The vampire no longer possessed the door. Nothing at all possessed the door. It was just a door.

"We can leave," she said briefly. "Come on, everybody. There's no time to waste."

Sherree giggled again, and danced her way over the floor. "Wow, Randy, I mean — like — you told us this would be a night to remember. How did you do it? Did you hire an actor or something?" The vampire had been gone only minutes, and yet he was sliding from Sherree's mind. Already she wondered if this was some weird combination of hologram and costume. Sherree caught Randy's rejected hand and swung it happily. Randy had indeed given them a night to remember. In Sherree's mind, Randy had gained points.

Roxanne discovered that she had physical proof of the vampire's existence. The vampire's leavings clung to her skin. It was as if she'd coated herself with suntan lotion: Vampire oil was all over her flesh.

While Lacey, ever cautious, crept toward the tower opening, and Sherree danced, and Randy worried, and Zach and Bobby gathered momentum and courage, Roxanne was forced to look down at her very own body, which had lain in a vampire's nest.

Roxanne came very close to throwing up.

When she got home, Roxanne thought, she would take a shower several hours long. She would use Clorox and Ajax instead of Ivory soap. By the time she was done, it would be daylight and she would dry herself in the yellow sun, soaking up safety and light. She would revel in those precious hours in which vampires could not function.

And if they ever did build that new mall here,

on this very site, she, Roxanne, would never shop in it. Because who knew? Who knew where else a vampire could dig in? Who knew what cracks in new buildings his stinking spirit might find?

"Hurry up," said Lacey. Her voice was taut with urgency.

Roxanne moved to the center of the group. Let Sherree and Randy go first. Let the vampire grab their ankles and yank on their hair. Roxanne hung on to Lacey's waist.

The group was going too slowly for Roxanne. She began herding her friends along, as if she were a sheepdog. "Go on, go on," she said, practically nipping them. "We don't have all night!"

Randy and Sherree reached the small landing at the top of the stairs.

Sherree took the first step down.

Nothing happened.

She took a second step.

Roxanne could almost hear six separate hearts whacking chest walls, pumping furiously. Her own heart was going insane with the need to move, to run, to race, to get out of here while there was time! "What are you waiting for?" shouted Roxanne. "Get going!"

Nobody was in the tower now. Three of them were on the stairs, three were crowded onto the little landing.

Don't look back! thought Bobby. Whatever I saw when I was pinned in the air, it's back there! I must not look back. I must not look down. I just have to get out! Out! Out!

Bobby caught the nearest hand. It was Lacey's. He had never held anything so gratefully.

Bobby would have shoved the rest forward, used all his athlete's strength and just pushed them all down the stairs, except what if somebody fell and broke a leg? They had enough problems as it was. "Hurry up," Bobby whispered. "Get going. What is taking so long?"

He could not tell whether he was talking out loud or not.

Outside, he thought, all I want is to be outside.

Sherree, incredibly, began taunting the vanished vampire. "You did-n't get us," she called, singsong. "We're go-ing ho-ome. Nan-ny nan-ny boo-boo."

Why, Roxanne asked herself, were people like Sherree allowed on the planet? Enough of this, thought Roxanne. I have to get home and scrub off an entire layer of skin.

Roxanne shoved through the silly delaying pack and plunged forward.

Her brain turned into a mental map of the mansion. Nothing mattered but exits and speed.

First set of stairs, she thought. Turn right in upper hall. Go down second set of stairs. Turn at bottom. Enter abandoned dining room. Go through window. Reach porch. Run like the very —

But she could no longer run.

She could no longer move at all.

She had collided with the vampire.

Or his cloak.

It was not like running into a wet sheet hanging out to dry on a clothesline. It was more like sinking into the mud of low tide. The stench and vapor of the vampire hit Roxanne's face, filling her open mouth and her nostrils as if she had fallen into pudding.

I refuse to let this happen! thought Roxanne. She shoved both hands forward, with all her might, to push him out of her escape route.

Her hands went right through his body.

"I'm not entirely here yet," the vampire explained. "It's because I need a meal. I'm becoming extremely hungry, you know. It's all this time you are wasting. All this running around you're forcing me to do."

The vampire had begun walking up the stairs.

Bobby, Zach, Sherree, Randy, and Roxanne were forced to back up, also.

Roxanne, coughing and spitting, tried to wipe the vampire off her face.

Sherree was sobbing and beating on Randy with her fists. "Tell him to stop this!" she said. "He's earned his money. Fire him, Randy!"

The vampire continued to sweep them up the stairs.

Sherree thinks it's an act, thought Lacey. How astonishing. All this evidence and she still does not believe in vampires.

Lacey stood her ground. She hung on to the

railing and dug her sneakers into the stair treads. "We are not going back in your tower," she said. "It does not matter how hard you shove. We are not moving back up those stairs."

But the five other teenagers moved around Lacey the way water moves around a rock in the stream. Backward, up the narrow tower stairs they moved.

"Don't cooperate with him!" cried Lacey. "Don't go back in that tower. That's where his power is! Out here on this staircase, he can't do much."

"You are incorrect," said the vampire. He remained courteous.

Lacey did not. She aimed a savage kick at his shins.

But of course, he had not fully materialized, and like Roxanne, she found her foot entering a sort of gel that sucked and clung.

Lacey lost her balance, and fell back.

It was Randy who caught her, grabbing her under the arms, hauling her back against him, dragging her up the stairs.

"All right!" shouted Sherree. "All right! I believe in you! It's okay. Don't get mad! We'll talk. We'll do anything you want!"

The vampire's chuckle was like broken glass, crunching under their shoes.

"No!" screamed Lacey, fighting Randy. "Don't go back in there! Stay out of that tower! We can hold him off! There's strength in numbers!" Lacey hung on to the banisters.

"You have a discussion to complete, as I recall," said the vampire. "The rules were made quite clear to you."

"We are not going to have a discussion on any subject whatsoever!" screamed Lacey. "We are going home!" Lacey grabbed at the retreating bodies of the others, trying to force them to stand next to her. What is the matter with them? she thought. Don't they understand?

"Regrettably," said the vampire, sounding rather like a guidance counselor, "due to Lacey's interfering and unpleasant manner, I am not going to be able to facilitate your discussion after all."

"Push your way through!" shrieked Lacey. "Don't —"

But the vampire rose up the stairs like fog rolling in from the sea.

His misty blanket enveloped them in his gelatinous pollution and they could not breathe under it or near it, and they staggered back into the tower.

The weird sick light of the vampire illuminated the circular space.

Roxanne thought she would drown in the vampire's smell. When will I ever be able to wash this off? she thought. She began to sob.

Zach's trembling began again, even deeper and more complete than it had been before. Bobby felt his mind leaving his skull, felt himself dividing, floating, coming apart. Randy felt terror filling his body; it was inside him, slithering around.

The tower seemed smaller than before.

Or else the vampire was taking up more space than he had.

"You made it worse, Lacey," Sherree said furiously.

"I did not make it worse!" cried Lacey. "It can't get any worse!"

"If I had just moved faster," sobbed Sherree, "I'd be out of here by now."

"There is," said the vampire, "only one way to get out of here."

His voice silenced them. They looked up. They saw. The vampire's face was present now, his skin the color of mushrooms. His teeth were as green as seaweed. He wiped them against his sleeve until they were white once more.

Sherree whimpered like a kicked puppy.

"The way out," said the vampire, "is not through a door."

The vampire's teeth filled more and more of his mouth. "The way out," said the vampire, "is not through a window."

"What way, then?" cried Sherree. "I'll do anything. Just tell me how to get out."

"You must choose my victim," repeated the vampire. He smiled. The teeth slid over his lips and touched his chin. "Although you have not discussed the issue as I requested, I think you all know, if you consider it for a moment, who has caused the most trouble here."

Sherree nodded. Without the slightest hesitation, she said, "I nominate Lacey."

"She's not running for office!" shouted Roxanne. "You don't nominate her."

"Yes, I do. The vampire wants a name, and that's what 'nominate' means. I name Lacey." Sherree was calm. Relaxed. She was comfortable with her decision.

Sherree's calm spread through the tower just as the vampire's stench had. Bobby's mind seemed to return. Zach's trembling lessened. Randy's terror dwindled. Roxanne's anger quieted.

They looked at Lacey.

And the vampire, too. The vampire looked at Lacey.

"Lacey," repeated the vampire, as if tasting the syllables before he tasted the victim. "*Lacey.*"

Sherree is giving me to him, thought Lacey.

She was unable to believe it. She had been sure they would stick together as a group. But no. Darwin was correct. Survival of the fittest. What it meant was — throw out one member to save the rest.

How primitive humankind is, thought Lacey.

How sophisticated the vampire is compared to our species. We cannot last a night without caving in. He can last for years, without food, without light, without anything.

The vampire's eyes were soft and yearning. They fixed on Lacey but did not meet her stare. The vampire was studying her throat.

Lacey waited for sturdier minds to kick in. Roxanne. Zachary. Bobby. She doubted if anybody could count on Randy in a crisis. Clearly not Sherree. But the rest . . . they would come through for her. They would not abandon her. Not to this. They would save her! She knew they would!

"Probably not, my dear," said the vampire gently, reading her thoughts. "It is always a shock to learn how cruel one's supposed friends can be."

Lacey wrenched her eyes off the vampire.

She turned to witness the actions of her supposed friends.

Sherree was already out the tower door.

Bobby's head was tilted slightly. He drew his glance away from Lacey, and then he drew himself to the tower door.

Roxanne massaged her wrists, as if she had sprained them. She was pouring her attention into her own body — carefully, calculatedly, forgetting Lacey's body.

Zach smiled at her nervously. He seemed embarrassed. And ready to go.

They had accepted Sherree's nomination.

Without speaking, they had voted.

Lacey's mind was flat and without words or thoughts. Perhaps this was how newborn babies were, before words and knowledge and experience were acquired to fill the void. Lacey so completely could not believe the other five were abandoning her that her mind abandoned itself rather than accept the truth.

The vampire drifted slightly closer. His fangs seemed to lengthen, like fence posts coming out of the ground.

The five safe teenagers moved through the door.

"Don't start till I'm gone," said Sherree to the vampire.

The vampire laughed. It sounded like glass breaking on stone. Little glittery sharp pieces of death, falling out of the vampire's mouth, landing in a pile of used laughter at Lacey's feet.

But my life, thought Lacey. My plans. My family. My hopes.

She was unable to back away from the vampire. Unable to try to join the others. Was terror rooting her to the spot, or had the vampire already reached her, so that she, too, was simply waiting for Sherree to be gone, so the real evening could begin?

Nobody said good-bye.

Perhaps it was too normal a word.

Perhaps you did not say good-bye when you were consigning a friend to hell. Perhaps you just slithered away, like the snake you were.

Lacey could no longer watch them go.

She could only watch the vampire approach.

Chapter 9

The cloak of the vampire moved by itself.

It swirled toward Lacey.

Perhaps it had muscles and a will of its own. Perhaps it was the real vampire. Perhaps the thing inside the cloak was just a mirage.

Lacey's eyes opened wider and wider. And yet she could see less and less, for the cloak of the vampire filled the entire room, its hem sweeping the ceiling and the floor together.

Her muscles yanked together, demanding action, but instead of running or fighting, Lacey stiffened and could not move.

Mom! she thought. Dad! Kevin!

The cloak rippled in symmetrical folds. It was a wet dripping thing to be used to line caves. And in another moment, it would encircle her; she would be nothing but "an event" to this cape.

I won't cry, thought Lacey. I won't whimper or moan. I certainly will not scream, because he said he liked that best.

But she knew that she would scream. The scream was building up in the bottom of her lungs, and demanding release; the scream was a living creature all by itself, and it, too, was climbing. She could feel the scream erupting like a volcano.

Would they hear? The five who had left her here? Would they hear her scream? Would it chill their hearts?

But they don't have hearts, thought Lacey. If they had hearts, they would not have left me here.

The corners of the vampire's cloak curled up, like fingers.

Dripping, the fingers crept toward her.

Sherree was the first one out the door. The first to put a foot on the top step of the stairs. The first to grab the banister and taste the wonderful freedom that waited outside the mansion.

Sherree envisioned the great outdoors. The real world. The acceptable, ordinary world of normal people doing normal things.

A world in which you could worry about what to wear, and how to accessorize, and with whom to flirt. A world in which you could do homework, or watch television, or drive a car.

A safe world.

Sherree put her mind into that safe world, that world without slime and without terror.

But her mind would not go.

Her mind stayed with Lacey.

Lacey. Alone with that *thing*? What would it be

like for Lacey? Alone? No human beside her? Just Lacey and Evil?

For Sherree, to whom the parties and friends and shopping and ringing telephones were life, to be alone was the greatest curse of all.

Lacey is alone, thought Sherree.

I nominated her to be alone.

Forever and ever.

This is like the sinking of the *Titanic*, thought Roxanne. Survivors didn't even wait for enough passengers to fill the lifeboat; they just rowed away, listening to the screams of the drowning — who could easily have fit into their half-empty boat.

I'm leaving Lacey, thought Roxanne. This girl with whom I was supposed to be at a party. Laughing. Dancing. Joking. The party went sour, but I went more sour. I left her there. Alone.

I'll be free. I'll be safe. But not unless I row away from a drowning friend.

Roxanne thought of the high school yearbook. What would they write about Roxanne, after twelve years of school in the same town?

A flamboyant personality! A girl of vast talent and a brilliant future! But of course . . . in the end . . . Roxanne was the first to abandon ship. Let somebody else drown! said Roxanne. I'll take the lifeboat, thank you. (That was Roxanne's motto. Who needs Lacey, anyway? Show me the door. That was our friend Roxanne.)

Roxanne took another step down. And then another. At the same time, the vampire must be taking another step toward Lacey. And then another.

Would Lacey scream?

Would Roxanne hear that scream all the nights of her life?

Bobby had not really been thinking. Being pinned in midair had left him with the strength of a laboratory specimen. He had just sort of been lying on a table, ready for dissection. He was there, and his shape was no different, but his mind had been dulled.

The only thing that had penetrated the curtain of fear was his athletic training. Team sports. Through the gluey thickness of his mind, Bobby had a sense that he had let his team down. But what was the team? What was the sport? Who was the player?

Bobby had a sense that he was moving the wrong way down the court. He was going to make a basket for the opposite team. Wait, he thought. Wait. Look around. What is the strategy here? Whose team am I on?

Zach's mind, however, was sharpened by fear. He could readily imagine the vampire wanting to renegotiate that contract of his. Would Lacey be enough for the vampire? What if the vampire was not satisfied by Lacey alone?

Sherree plowed to a stop. For one horrible moment Zach thought the vampire had changed his mind, and had once again taken possession of the stairs. That "escape" had all been a cruel joke. *Nobody would escape.* Not now. Not ever.

"Hurry up, Sherree!" Zach didn't want the vampire to realize how slowly they were leaving. Who knew how quickly the vampire's "event" with Lacey could take place? What if it happened in the few seconds they wasted getting downstairs? What if Lacey merely whetted the vampire's appetite and the vampire followed them down?

Zach did not want to be last in line.

The thing was to get down the stairs, get out that dining room window, get off the sagging porch, and get off this property. As far as Zach was concerned, Randy's Land Rover could be abandoned until daylight. Or forever. Zach was going to hit the grass running.

And yet his feet hardly moved.

At the back of his mind, at the heels of his escape, he saw Lacey.

Alone.

A sick taste rose up in his throat. He told himself it was the atmosphere in the mansion. Horror had a flavor and an aroma all its own.

But he knew in his heart that the truly horrible event of the night was not what the vampire intended to do.

The horror was himself.

Leaving Lacey.

*　　*　　*

Randy saw an opening between Zach and Roxanne and slipped through, moving to the head of
the pack, catching up with Sherree. The house was
a pit of blackness below the tower, but Randy
could see perfectly. He could see freedom and
safety and his life reemerging. He could see clean
air and hear the quick start of his car's engine. In
one minute, he would be driving away and never
thinking about this again.

That would be the key, of course. Never to think
about this again.

Because if you thought about it . . .

Randy thought about it.

With all his inner strength, he tried not to, but
Randy did not have great inner strength. In fact,
here on the stairs, he knew that he possessed
nothing but weakness.

Randy had invited to this party nothing but a
collection of egos. Selfish, selfish people.

Roxanne: the selfish achiever.

Sherree: the selfish beauty.

Bobby: the selfish jock.

Zachary: the selfish classy act.

Randy himself: the selfish hanger-on.

And Lacey.

Randy could not believe he had ever let anybody call her an airhead What was an airhead,
anyway? He was. They all were.

I invited Lacey here, thought Randy. She's here
because I asked her to come.

How to treat your date, he thought hysterically. Give her the night of her life.

I offered her, thought Sherree. Those were my words. *I nominate Lacey.* I cannot live with that.

I didn't even argue, thought Roxanne. I would have seconded the motion if the vampire had asked me to.

I can't do this, thought Zach. If there's any test in life, this is it. I can't fail it. I can't fail Lacey.

I'm half the vampire's anyway, thought Bobby. I should be the one he takes. He's got some of me anyhow.

Sherree turned. Bobby turned. Roxanne turned. Zach turned. But they were not the first. Randy had already raced back into the tower. "Stop!" he shouted. "Don't touch her!"

Randy flung his arms around Lacey.

Lacey was untouched. The vampire, after all, had not moved quickly. Why let pleasure evaporate before he had had time to enjoy it fully? Only the cloak had changed position. Only the fangs had lengthened.

"Take me instead," said Randy.

The vampire's fangs vanished behind his lips. The lips drew into a thin bloodless line and tucked themselves into his face and disappeared.

Randy was filled with glory and pride. "Take me," he repeated, and his voice sounded rich and splendid in his own ears. "I dare you."

Lacey could have wept.

Randy. Volunteering to sacrifice himself. Randy, whom she had found the most useless in the group. She did not love him. Perhaps nothing could command the emotion of love. Perhaps love had to arrive on its own. But he had redeemed himself.

I am all right, she thought. *Randy came back.*

The cloak jerked away as if it had been attacked and wrapped itself tightly around the vampire.

Randy's forearm was in front of Lacey. She looked down at its classic pose: man slaying dragon for fair maiden. Oh, Randy! she thought. You are so far away from being a dragon-slayer. But you slew him anyway.

The room filled with humans instead of sick evil cloaks. "We came back!" shouted Roxanne.

"We're not cowards after all!" cried Sherree.

The girls pushed Randy away and hugged Lacey themselves, laughing and proud. "We were decent in the end," said Roxanne.

Lacey did not tell them how terrible it had been for her, how their desertion had hurt her more than any vampire's fang ever could. Lacey did not tell them how it felt to be utterly alone. Alone forever. She looked at Roxanne and Sherree and she let them be proud. She said softly, "Yes. You were decent in the end."

She wondered if that was enough. Did it erase doing something very bad, if you rushed back and undid it as quickly as you could? Or were you stained by that bad thing? Was it part of you now, like a scar on your heart?

The vampire, flushed like a bird from a thicket, fluttered around the room. He did not leave, although he became more shadow than substance.

Randy, standing taller, feeling broader, feeling better than ever before in his life, shouted, "What are you — a coward? You can't take me on after all? I volunteer. Understand that, vampire?"

The vampire's voice creaked like an old floor under their feet. It scratched their souls like chalk on a blackboard. "You won't be a hero," said the vampire. "You do realize that, don't you, Randy?"

"I'm not trying to be one," said Randy, who of course was trying very hard. Who had already decided he was a hero. Who had already reworked his entire life plan, so that he would be a hero in everything now, always. What would he do next? He had saved Lacey, perhaps next he would save the world. It was simply a matter of choosing which enemy to whip. Would it be global politics or virus research or —

"Ah, sixteen," said the vampire, returning to his original subject. "A dangerous age. This is, I suppose, a moral equivalent of pushing the accelerator to the floor. You, little Randy, will run the farthest, you will scurry the fastest, to save your little friend."

His voice was condescending: the adult who understood reality in a roomful of children who did not. His smile reemerged. This time, all the teeth were pointed, and neatly aligned, as if something had redrawn them — as if a new and more calculating vampire was going to fill the room.

Randy felt a puncture wound in his side: not from the vampire, but from some new horror yet to be explained.

He stared as one, and only one, of the fangs lengthened.

It seemed to pierce his strength, his determination, his resolve.

The old selfish Randy — who had vanished only moments ago — began to grow back. No! thought Randy. No! Please — let me be a hero!

"You see," said the vampire comfortably, like an old armchair, "you will not be a hero because your friends will forget the events of the night as they pass out of the building. They will retain no memory of you, Randy. No memory of me, either. No memory at all."

It's true, thought Roxanne. I had already forgotten that I am covered with vampire slime. I had already forgotten that I have to scour myself clean and bake in the sun to get rid of his leavings. I had already forgotten that I lay in his nest. I, Roxanne, was contaminated by his actual lair. And I forgot that in those few steps down the stairs. If we had gone just a few more steps, *we would have forgotten Lacey*. Out of sight, out of mind. We would not have felt guilty because we would not have remembered there was an "event" to worry about.

"Otherwise, of course," added the vampire, "your friends would get fire trucks and police and who knows what? Obviously that cannot be allowed. So they will not remember. And a person who is forgotten, my dear Randy, cannot be a hero. A hero, by definition, is one whom his friends adore."

"He is a hero," said Lacey steadily. "They are all heroes. They came back. They did not run. And that is the definition of a hero."

The vampire's eyes grew larger and clearer. He studied Lacey with as much interest as he had before. "There is another interesting reality," he said. A second fang grew down to meet the first. How could he talk with his teeth shifting like that? And yet, the voice hardly seemed to come from the mouth at all. It came from the entire room.

"Nobody's interested in your dumb old realities," said Randy. He flung his head back. He spread his legs. He jammed his hands into his pockets, as if he had guns in holsters and would beat the vampire to the draw. "I don't even think you can really do this, anyway," sneered Randy. "I don't think there's any such thing as an 'event.' You're nothing but a slimeball. Maybe I'm not a hero. But you're not a vampire, either. You're just a thing without power."

The darkness in the room became entire.

The vampire gave off no phosphorescence.

The room was utterly silent.

They could hear no breathing. They could see

no cloak. They dared not move, because they could not see their feet, nor the gaping hole in the floor that Roxanne had created.

Roxanne could not help it. She wrapped one arm around the back of her neck.

Sherree, tightly clinging to somebody's hand, suddenly wondered just whose hand it was she held. Was it a human hand?

Randy called the vampire's bluff. "I'm waiting," he said.

Chapter 10

"Aw, come on, Ginny, lighten up," said Jordan.

Ginny was at a crossroads with Jordan, literally and figuratively. They could turn onto the valley road and head for the Mall House, or they could go on to their friends' house where they were expected.

It was, thought Ginny, so annoying that you could not just go out for the evening. Everything always had to involve some sort of choice. Some sort of principle.

All Ginny wanted was friends and pizza. A little company, a few laughs.

Instead, she had a boyfriend problem.

If she said, "No, Jordan, we're going to the party, forget this driving-around-and-hunting-for-my-brother nonsense," was she simply asserting her rights in this relationship, or was she bossing Jordan around?

If she said, "Okay, Jordan, whatever you want, Jordan," was she being good company and lightening up, or was she being a doormat on whom Jordan would scrape his shoes forevermore?

Ginny was aware that one of her biggest personality problems was a tendency to analyze too often.

Of course, one of Jordan's biggest personality problems was that he never analyzed anything at all.

What we need here, thought Ginny, is a compromise.

Ginny frowned, climbing into her brain cells, hunting for a satisfactory compromise.

The problem was, Ginny didn't like compromising. Ginny liked having her own way.

"I can't idle at this intersection for our whole lives, you know," remarked Jordan.

"Why not?" said Ginny. "There's no traffic tonight."

Jordan nodded in a slow, thoughtful way. "I don't understand that, either," he said. "Saturday night at this hour? There should be all kinds of cars going by, especially right here, and right now." Jordan fluttered his hands like a passing ghost. "Perhaps," he said, in a deep ghoulish voice, "there are other forces at work tonight."

"Perhaps," said Ginny, letting herself get drawn in, "my little brother has been absorbed by an evil being."

"No doubt," said Jordan. He rolled down the window of his car. "In fact," he whispered, "the very air is redolent of evil."

Ginny rolled down her window.

A strange thick smell sifted into their car.

It was not car exhaust.

Ginny did not know what it was. She only knew she was beginning to prickle all over with fear. "Jordan?" she whispered.

Jordan was staring out the window he had just opened.

His eyes were open far too wide. His hands had fallen off the steering wheel. His breath was coming in strange little spurts.

Ginny looked where he was looking.

Down the valley road. Down where once the hemlocks had towered around the old house with the twisted tower. Down where someday a parking lot would lie flat and black against the ground.

The tower was visible against the sooty sky.

And from the tower came curving, slinking squares of blackness like immense pieces of paper, curving and reshaping themselves.

The smell grew worse.

Ginny felt her lungs tiring, her heart slowing.

Jordan's hands went back on the wheel. Jordan's foot lifted from the brake. The automatic transmission moved the car forward, slowly at first, and then gathering momentum. Jordan was not quite steering and not quite touching the gas pedal. The car was going down the valley road, going all by itself toward the black shape that lowered gently, as if to meet them.

Ginny thought: Nobody will come to look for *us*.

Because we're supposed to be the ones doing the looking.

"As I say," repeated the vampire, "there is another interesting reality."

Randy tried to glare at the vampire, but it was difficult. The vampire did not stay in one place, and the parts of him that materialized changed each time.

"You see," said the vampire, "being a hero is a human reality. It is not part of my world. And it is within my world that we operate tonight."

"What are you talking about?" said Lacey. Could it really be correct that the six teenagers would retain no memory of the night's events? How terrible that would be! Randy's wonderful courage — lost like a fog burning off in the morning sun. Her own shattering fear — vanished like pain from a paper cut. This new deep knowledge of one another; this new view into the depths and the shallowness of five others — evaporated.

Would Lacey really not know Sherree, or Zach, or Roxanne, or Bobby when school opened on Monday? Would they really be strangers to her as they had been strangers before? And Randy . . .

What would Randy be?

There would be less of him, the vampire had said. Not dead, and yet gone. Still breathing, and yet lacking personality.

And would she, Lacey, for whom he had sacri-

472

ficed, even know about it? Would she ignore him in the halls? Not see him in the cafeteria? Not care about him on the bus? Would Randy be faceless? Even though he had endured this horrible fate by choice, for their sake?

Lacey did weep, after all.

At least Randy saw that. At least Randy had a moment of tears.

And then she wondered — would *Randy* remember?

Would Randy be a zombie, staggering dimly through the remaining years of his life, lacking even the comfort of his own courage? Or would terrible knowledge lie within him — useless, unspoken?

"My world," said the vampire, very softly and very low. "In my world, you will recall, you had to choose my victim from among you. Randy has volunteered instead. And this, of course, saves him. Randy can no longer be my victim." The vampire smiled. In his voice as rich as dark chocolate, he murmured, "I neglected to explain to you that a person who volunteers to sacrifice himself for others . . ." and here, the vampire smiled a smile so full of teeth it seemed that there were several vampires living in his mouth ". . . is always safe. You may leave if you wish, Randy."

Randy stared at the vampire. What was going on? What had happened to his great bravery, his sacrifice, his splendor?

With a swirl of his cloak, the vampire discarded Randy. "You are out of the running, Randy. Very clever of you. Very self-serving."

Randy felt the world being yanked out from under his feet. "I didn't volunteer to be clever," he protested. He wanted to be a hero. He wanted to be applauded and lauded like athletes after great victories: like Bobby, for example.

"No," said the vampire gently, knowing Randy's mind, "those are the daydreams of humans. They are not the realities of vampires."

Lacey was glad that Randy was safe. She had seen the best in Randy, and she wanted Randy to continue on that road — to be good and worthy and generous of heart. She smiled, looked down for privacy in her thoughts, and smiled again. At least something good would come from this.

"Randy is safe?" repeated Zach.

"He is safe," agreed the vampire.

Zach, Sherree, Bobby, and Roxanne studied Randy in his new role as the safe one, the one who would go free, the one who would definitely get home tonight. They felt a strange rage at Randy, because he was no longer part of the group; he had been removed to another zone.

"The field," said the vampire, "is narrowed. There are now five remaining choices for me. Five," he repeated greedily. "Five. Five. Five. Five."

Lacey's shudder was deep in her gut, but she knew that the vampire was aware of it, and enjoying it, and hoping there would be more.

Only Sherree moved logically to the next point. "Heck," said Sherree, "then I volunteer, too."

"Thank you, my dear," said the vampire. His eyes softened with dreamy pleasure and his largest teeth slid over his damp lips and hooked at the bottom of his chin. "You may all go now. Except Sherree, of course. Most thoughtful of you to resolve the situation, Sherree." The tongue that licked his lips was pointed like a red ribbon. He moved far more swiftly to Sherree than he had toward Lacey.

"Wait!" screamed Lacey, grabbing Sherree's arm and yanking her back. "This isn't fair! You keep changing the rules."

"I am not changing the rules at all," said the vampire. His breath came in spurts, like whiffs of swamp gas. "You just don't know them. I can't help it that you are not acquainted with the workings of my world. I have certainly taken the time to become acquainted with *your* world."

The vampire's cloak encircled Sherree's arm. It began to haul her in, as if she were clothes on an old-fashioned clothesline, being reeled onto the back porch. From beneath the folds of his horrible wrappings came his fingernails, like crushed foil, and then his hands, longer than human hands, bonier than human hands, stronger than human hands.

Sherree screamed in horror. The vampire was ecstatic. Screams were his appetizers.

"Wait!" said Lacey. She had one of Sherree's

arms and the cloak had the other. "Wait. I have to think."

"You may think outdoors," said the vampire. "It's time for the five of you to go."

"No!" shouted Lacey. "You said to start with that *we* had to choose your victim. Well, we didn't! You broke the rules. This does not count."

"Sherree volunteered for selfish purposes. I accepted. It's not frequent for a victim to request being taken, but it is not unknown in history," said the vampire, "and I am content with it."

Sherree broke free both from the vampire's cloak and from Lacey. She ran in circles around the diminishing tower. There were no exits. Once again, the vampire possessed the door. Ripping mindlessly at the remaining shutters blocking the tower windows, Sherree tried to find a way out of her fate. Her strength far surpassed even Bobby's, fueled by adrenaline from her deathly fear.

Gradually, her frenzy diminished.

Gradually, her crazed attempts ceased.

And yet the vampire did not approach her. His head was cocked as if he had ears hidden beneath his horrid oily hair, as if he were listening to something.

They all listened.

Somewhere in the house, somebody was laughing.

The policewoman was bored.

Night duty was often boring.

She did not actually want anything to happen, and yet if she were to stay awake, something had to happen. She drank from the take-out paper cup of coffee. It was chilly now. Pretty awful stuff. But she had nothing else to do, so she sipped again.

The policewoman was quite young. She had graduated from the local high school not so long ago herself.

One-handed, she drove through the dark and quiet town. There used to be a lot more action on this side of the city, but since so many acres had been cleared for the future shopping mall, there was not much here. She paused at an intersection and considered driving past the old boarded-up mansion.

When the policewoman had been in high school, she had been a cheerleader, and had briefly known the girl who lived in that mansion. There had been parties there. Parties at which everybody seemed to know more than they let on. Parties from which people seemed to come and go as if they could move through walls. And then the girl herself had gone, as quickly and quietly as if she, too, had been walled up.

When the house was abandoned, nobody had ever gone there.

It was odd.

You would think — certainly the police force expected — that the teenagers of the town would see this as an ideal hangout.

But nobody had tried spending the night in its

abandoned rooms. Nobody had spun doughnuts in its pathetic old gardens, and nobody had spray-painted initials in red paint on its sagging roof.

The policewoman had had a tumultuous high school career herself. There was not much she had not done, or tried, or at least watched. It was one reason she went into law enforcement: She was pretty familiar with the mood or the need that made a person break the law. She was stern now, but she understood.

There was no traffic. Really, it was remarkable. And on a weekend! Where were all the partying teenagers? The drunks who should be plastered by this time? The moviegoers who should be headed home after the late show?

The police car edged forward, as only police cars can, taking its eternal time, because nobody can argue.

But there were no other cars in sight that would mind the delay.

Setting the awful coffee in the cup holder, she approached the intersection of the valley road and the main downtown avenue.

The bright red taillights of a single car crept down the valley road and vanished.

The policewoman wondered whose driveway could possibly be down there. For a moment she waited to see if the taillights would reappear, as a very lost driver backed out of a very unpromising drive.

But none appeared.

Truly, the night was dead.

In lieu of any other action, the policewoman decided to go to the drive-in window of Dunkin' Donuts. A jelly doughnut, she pondered, or a glazed cruller?

The police car turned the opposite direction from the twisted tower. The policewoman was not looking in her rearview mirror to see what was happening there.

But it would not have mattered if she had looked.

For vampires do not have reflections.

Sherree was swinging on one of the shutters, as if to hurl herself through the window, through the night, and come to a safe landing miles away.

The laugh shivered through the cracks in the plaster and came up through the cracks in the floorboards. It lay in the attic and it slid off the roof and it collapsed in the basement.

The laugh wrapped them like a gift box.

Except that the laugh was evil.

"Do vampires laugh?" said Zach. Zach did not sound as if he would ever laugh again.

"Vampires laugh," said the vampire, "when they have a victim in sight. Other than that, it is quite rare."

The shutters clattered.

All their little wooden slats clapped.

Sherree slid down from the shutter to which she had clung and fell in a heap on the floor.

A second vampire entered the tower.

Chapter 11

Two vampires, thought Lacey.

It was beyond thinking about. She seemed to have no mind left. She could draw no conclusions and take no action. She could only stare.

The first vampire — Lacey could not stop herself from thinking of him as *their* vampire — was so much more cloak than this new one. This new one was gelatinous, sticky and dark like molasses dripping on a floor.

Once when Lacey was quite small, she and her father had been working in the garden, only to push the sharp edge of a shovel right down into a ground wasps' nest. There had been a very brief moment in which wasps had zoomed out of their hole, circled once, and then attacked Lacey and her father. Lacey had not even known what a wasp was, but she knew enough to run.

Her father scooped her up as he fled, and they flew like rockets to the back door, slamming it against the buzzing horrors that followed them.

Between them, Lacey and her father got eleven wasp stings.

We've found a vampires' nest, thought Lacey. We pushed the sharp edge of the shovel down into the ground where vampires live.

What had really happened to the families who had lived in this house? Had they actually moved away? Or had something truly terrible happened to them? Had they hung wallpaper on a wall, only to learn who lived behind it? Had they dusted a shutter only to find the dark ooze of evil coming off on their innocent hands?

Tear it down! thought Lacey. Tear this house down! This house must be ended. Once the house is gone, these vampires must surely also be gone.

Facing two vampires was infinitely more terrifying than facing one.

Their vampire stood by the door he possessed. The new vampire blocked the shutters. Beyond him, since Sherree had yanked open all the shutters, the night sky was exposed. It was black. Nothing hung there, not a star, not a distant plane. Only blackness.

The vampire had told the truth. Inside this house, night would last as long as he needed it to.

Perhaps the house would never be torn down; perhaps the vampire could even control time, and the time to build the shopping mall would never come, and the time for rescue, and the time to go home — these would never come, either.

Zach and Roxanne kept swiveling their heads.

They seemed to think as long as they kept an eye on each vampire, nothing could happen.

The vampire who had emerged from the shutters eventually stopped laughing. The laughter had poured out of him like water from a faucet, and Lacey had wanted just to turn him off, like a faucet, and be done listening to his noise.

Sherree, whose flesh the new vampire had brushed, kept making faces and gagging and crying, "*Eeeeeuuuuuuhhhh!*"

Bobby stared out the window, as if expecting somebody else to come in, some shape or horror not yet envisioned.

Only Randy seemed untouched by the new circumstance. He, after all, could not be prey. The rest were now, as the vampire had said early in the evening, simply small animals about to be taken by larger ones. But Randy was out of the running.

The vampires did not seem to be friends. Perhaps vampires did not have friends. And although they had long resided in the same house, one living between the floors, and the other living between the shutters, it seemed that they had not met in many years. Their schedules, it seemed, and their need for nourishment, did not coincide.

For the second vampire was starving. He had been closed up, he said, for a long, long time.

Zach said, "You're the one who peeled my fingers off the sill, aren't you?"

The vampire was pleased to be recognized.

"Eeeeuuuhh, he touched you, too?" said Sherree. "Eeeeuuuhh, this is so sick."

Roxanne suddenly giggled. Sherree kept adding touches of human reality. It gave Roxanne a divided sensation, as if she had been split down the middle like a piece of pie: She was half in the vampire's world and half in Sherree's.

This is not real, thought Roxanne. This is either a really weird party or a really weird nightmare, but this is not real. It relaxed her greatly to reassure herself that this was not real.

"Why did you do that?" said Zach.

"I didn't expect to be awakened," said the new vampire. "Naturally I was annoyed to find human fingers all over my shutters. But now that I am up, I recall that it was time anyhow. Our building will be removed from this world in only a week. I have things to do. A new home to find. A nest to build."

The old vampire nodded glumly. "They are wiping out our habitats."

Zach burst out laughing, a response that obviously pleased him, because it sounded normal and in control. "You sound like environmentalists," said Zach. "As if we should preserve a forest for you. Or at least a cemetery."

The new vampire looked with distaste at Zach. (Zach felt this was probably the best way to be looked at by a vampire.) "You allow them to speak like this in your presence?" the new vampire said to theirs. "This generation is most unpleasant. They have no reverence for the old ways."

Their own vampire smiled. "They will," he said. His soft eyes landed especially on Roxanne, who had been pretending this was a bad dream.

"By dawn," whispered the vampire, looking so deeply into her eyes it felt as if he could see down into her throat, "they will have respect for us again."

Both vampires were lost in thought over this probability.

"No, we won't," said Lacey. "I don't know where on earth you could get the idea that anybody would respect you. We all despise you. So there."

The vampires regarded Lacey steadily.

Then they faced each other. "I would like to finish up in here all by myself, if you don't mind," said their vampire. "But there is no need for you to go hungry. You need only slip outdoors. There are more humans waiting in the yard."

"Just standing there?" said the shutter vampire. "Waiting to be taken?" He rubbed his bones together. They clacked. They sounded just like the shutter slats.

Lacey thought perhaps they *were* the shutter slats. No wonder the previous occupants of this house had been so weird. Shutters made of vampire bones.

"Why is the house suddenly so popular?" mused the shutter vampire. His eyebrows were hairy and pointed, like fur-trimmed church windows.

"My understanding," said their vampire, "is

that younger humans enjoy being frightened. It's the age, you know. Sixteen. Dangerous. To them, of course. Not us."

The second vampire smiled so broadly that his teeth seemed to circle his skull. "How touching," he said.

"Precisely."

"I shall be off, then," said the second vampire. "I must plunge in," he added. He liked this turn of phrase, and he watched the teenagers as each one slowly understood the pun — what the plungers were, and into what they plunged.

But the vampire of the shutters did not go out of the window yet. Instead, he studied the six with a sort of melancholy, a kind of deep longing. "You aren't really going to let five of them go, are you?"

The first vampire nodded.

"I suppose that was a promise?" the vampire of the shutters said sadly.

"It was merely *my* promise," said the first vampire. "*You* didn't make it."

Mardee had had it.

First of all, even though they could see the Land Rover right there, they could not reach the vehicle. It was surrounded by these stupid fallen trees. And they weren't little piddly Christmas trees you could just drag off. They were immense, as big as ranch houses. How on earth had the others gotten that vehicle in there, anyway?

Mardee snagged her legs and her ankles and her hair in every single hemlock branch there was.

Kevin, of course, was unscathed.

I will never associate with a boy again, Mardee told herself.

Mardee's brother, Bobby, was a total annoyance in her life. His friends and teammates were even more annoying. Given this depressing exposure to the opposite sex, Mardee had never been willing to give boys much of a chance. People said things looked up after eighth grade, and boys became human, but Mardee had seen no signs of this in her brother.

So here she had taken a chance on Kevin, because he had such a sensible sister — Lacey — and all Kevin would do was laugh at her, accuse her of screaming, and lead her into thickets of scraping, vicious, dead trees.

"You said on the phone," Kevin reminded her, "that we would come over here and make noise and frighten the kids inside."

"The *noise*," said Mardee frigidly, "*came* from inside. It was probably your very own sister, whom you are *deserting*."

"Deserting," said Kevin, delighted with the pun he was about to utter, "in order to have dessert. Come on. Let's go get ice cream. Nobody's here."

"Have you forgotten what just happened?" shouted Mardee.

Kevin stared at her, genuinely surprised to be yelled at.

And Mardee saw that, truly, Kevin had forgotten what had just happened. He did not remember the wet slimy mass that had slid past them, holding some terrible sobbing burden in its grasp. He did not remember the terrible force of its wake, the sucking wind that had yanked Mardee in through the window. He could no longer hear the moaning and the weeping that Mardee had heard coming all the way out of the earth, out of the soil, out of the cellar, out of the ages. He did not remember the cruel horrid laughter that sprang like opposite choruses of evil from the sky and the ground.

He had forgotten.

He was just a teenage boy, equally inspired by food or girls.

"Let's sit in the backseat of the Land Rover," said Kevin, leering.

Mardee favored him with a look of absolute loathing, but Kevin, being as stupid a boy as her brother, Bobby, misinterpreted Mardee's look as one of agreement: that backseats and kisses were tops on her list, too.

Boys, thought Mardee.

She was getting in the Land Rover, all right, and then she was slamming the door and staying nice and safe in there until everybody came out from whatever ghastly party they were having inside and she didn't care what dumb old Kevin did. He could have all the ice cream on earth for all she cared.

Mardee climbed over the last interfering branch and grabbed the handle of the Land Rover.

Teeth glittered through the window.

Roxanne was the first to understand this new piece of information. "You mean, even if we get out," shrieked Roxanne, "even if you take only one of us, this other vampire can have more?" She could not believe this. A deal was a deal. What kind of game were these vampires playing?

"Perhaps if you make your choice more speedily," said the vampire, "my guest will still be busy with the humans in the yard. Perhaps in that case, you will indeed escape notice by my guest."

Who on earth could be in the yard? thought Lacey. Who else was dumb enough to be here at this hour? In this terrible dark? With the horrible smells and atmosphere?

Lacey took swift steps to the open shutters. Grabbing the window rims, and leaning into the fresh air, she screamed out the window. "Run!" she shrieked, calling on every molecule of lung power. "Get out of here!"

There was no sound anywhere.

Not in the tower, not in the yard.

"Go away!" screamed Lacey. "Quick! Run!"

The vampire of the shutters said gently, "You are clearly not, although a human yourself, a student of human nature, my dear. When told to run, human beings inevitably stand still. When told to be afraid, human beings inevitably become curious instead. What you have done, of course, is merely to whet the appetites of those below." The vampire smiled, this time courteously covering his mouth. "And my appetite, too, of course."

He sifted between her and the windows. Lacey did not flinch. She would not give him the satisfaction.

The vampire evaporated, slowly, his eyes going first, then his flesh, then his teeth, and at last his wrappings.

He drifted out the window rather like smoke from a fireplace, slow and thick and gray.

"And now," said their vampire, "let us finish up."

Chapter 12

The voice that screamed from the tower was his sister's.

It was Lacey.

Airhead Lacey was, after all, partying in the mansion.

Kevin had never heard her scream like that. He had never heard anybody scream like that. The ferocity in her voice — *Run! Get out of here! Quick!* — stunned Kevin.

He could not worry about the person sitting in the Land Rover, whoever he was. He could not even worry about Mardee.

Mardee had actually fainted. Kevin had been thrilled. He had not known this happened in real life, either — girls passing out lightly in their boyfriends' arms. Of course, Mardee despised him, but on the other hand, he had caught her before she fell all the way, so perhaps that would count for something.

But he forgot Mardee. His hands didn't forget;

they yanked her vertically to her feet, although this was not the proper reaction for dealing with faints. She became a simple burden to him, a thing to haul along, like schoolbooks down a hallway.

"Lace!" he shouted. "Lace!"

Nobody answered.

The house was silent.

Mardee had not actually fainted, just dropped down so that the vampire in the Land Rover would not see her so clearly. Now, clearly, she could see it was not a vampire at all, but some boy with bad teeth. Randy must have loaned his car to the guy.

This was definitely not the place for a girl with an overactive imagination. Mardee shook her head to clear it of idiocy. Perhaps it was Kevin's influence, seeing all this nonsense.

"We'll be out of your way in a moment," she said to the driver of the Land Rover. The guy gave her the creeps.

"She's in there," whispered Kevin, staring up at the tower.

Shutters banged. Down here among the dead trees there was no wind, but the wind at the rooftop must have been strong, for blackness seemed to dip and sway along the windows, as if the sky itself were casting a shadow on the mansion, and then taking it away.

"I heard her!" whispered Kevin.

"Told you so," said Mardee.

Boys drive me crazy, thought Mardee. I said to

Kevin, I said, Lacey's in there. Your sister. And he said, Nah, let's go get ice cream. I said, Kevin, there's a vampire in there. And he laughed at me. Now he's acting as if *he's* the only one who noticed that something is wrong!

Kevin tried to find his way out of the fallen trees. "I'm coming, Lacey!" he yelled.

"Alternatively," said the vampire, "you may all stay."

The room was absolutely quiet.

"After all," said the vampire, "if you each wish to experience this event, who am I to deny you?"

The thickness of his atmosphere was so great that they had difficulty breathing.

"I would think it more logical to choose one for me and save the rest, but if you feel you should all stay," said the vampire, and here his teeth seemed to point individually at each of them, "I am willing to work harder tonight. I am willing to work all night."

The vampire laughed.

Jordan's car steered into the driveway and stopped.

Jordan opened his door.

Ginny opened hers.

They got out.

The shadow in the sky drifted slowly down across the roofs, like a sleepwalker, and descended gently to the ground.

Yes, thought Ginny, not knowing what she was saying yes to, or why she felt that yes was the right syllable. Only knowing that something — some strange gravity — was pulling her toward that shadow. It was pulling Jordan, too, they were going in a pair.

Ginny wanted to call out, "Over here!" but she could not seem to move her lips.

She was not afraid, and yet she was terrorized. Her body was doing things without her, as if this had been rehearsed for all her life.

Jordan felt like paper. He was blank. Nothing was written on him. Nothing was on his last page and nothing would be on his next page.

He did not feel like a man or a boy or a human being.

He did not even feel.

He was hardly even there.

His feet continued to move, and yet he did not feel as if he were walking. He felt as if he had become sort of amoeba with jellied expansions instead of legs. He was floating in a new kind of water.

Whatever the shadow was, whatever the shadow meant, Jordan would be absorbed into it.

Yes, thought Jordan.

Lacey could hardly absorb the vampire's words, let alone the diluted oxygen left in the tower. That was my brother down there, thought Lacey. My brother, Kevin. What is he doing there? My brother,

Kevin, who is going to be the other vampire's victim!

Lacey and Kevin had led remarkably separate lives for a brother and sister whose bedroom doors were separated by only thirty-six inches. They shared no hobbies, they had no common friends, they participated in none of the same activities. Since Lacey had become a teenager they had hardly even had dinner together, because her schedule was not similar to her brother's.

At family gatherings, like Thanksgiving, Lacey and Kevin sometimes discovered that they, too, were having a reunion. That they would actually have conversations in which Lacey would think — so this is the kind of guy that Kevin is! They would actually catch up with each other when the room was full of relatives, as if they, too, were distant cousins who saw each other only on holidays.

"Lace!" came her brother's voice from outside, from the safety zone, from the ground beneath the tower. "I'm coming, Lace!"

He did not call her Lace instead of Lacey because he was fond of her and this was a favorite nickname. He called her Lace because he was cutting down on the time he spent thinking of her — one less syllable spent on a dumb old sister.

For the same reason, she usually called him Kev.

We will each die, she thought. Well, no, not die. The vampire explained that death is not part of this. But we will be finished as human beings.

Our poor parents. Tomorrow they will have half-children. Half-personalities. Half-energies.

We will live together in some sort of mental and physical fog, drained by the vampire, and we will not know. We will not remember.

Lacey stared at the vampire, imagining the "event." The vampire stared back, also imagining it. Although with more enthusiasm.

It was evident that, this time, the vampire was not going to leave.

There would be no escape.

There would be no exit unless granted by the vampire.

And her brother was in the yard. Coming up into the house.

I must get my brother out of here, thought Lacey. And while I'm at it, I must save the rest.

Lacey examined the others. She was no longer in human time, but vampire time: time that continued for aeons in a single black night. She did not have to rush. The vampire that had slid from the shutters was not rushing toward her brother, but savoring the moment.

Lacey looked at Sherree. Selfish. Silly. But Lacey felt a strange deep love for her. The kind of love, perhaps, that parents have: an unconditional love, for whoever and whatever their child turns out to be. Lacey liked it that Sherree had come back, had danced a little jig of joy because she had been a good person after all. Lacey liked the strength with which Sherree had tried to escape, even though that had let the vampire out of the shutters.

What strange lives these vampires led: half frozen by their own hibernation, half frozen by the lack of available victims.

Perhaps all evil was like that.

Perhaps it lay in wait for you, lying behind the door, in back of the shutters, hidden by walls and strangers and habits . . . but it was there.

Perhaps you had only to say the words, and evil could begin growing, filling every room and mind with its sick odor and its disgusting cloak.

I know the truth, thought Lacey. I understand the world. And what difference does it make? I will never get out there to tell anybody.

Lacey studied Bobby, whose magnificent muscular body had engineered many an athletic victory. Had Bobby learned anything from the night? It was hard to tell. With a person like Bobby, you tended not to look past the physical person to locate the emotional person. Bobby would always be able to hide behind his body, so to speak. He could put his muscles and his masculine beauty out front and nobody would know who was in back.

Zach, to whom appearances meant so much: Zach, expending so much energy trying not to be embarrassed or nervous or uncool. In a way she loved Zach most, because he was the most desperate to pull it all off. She wanted him to pull it all off. She wanted Zach to have it all, and not know how frail he really was.

Roxanne, who was not frail, and who did have it all, and who knew it. Lacey decided that after all, she liked Roxanne best, because Roxanne was toughest. Strong enough to rip nails out of floors, strong enough to herd scared kids down dark stairs.

Lacey admired strength. I won't have any ever again, thought Lacey. Once the vampire takes me, strength will be gone forever.

She studied Randy, although he was safe without her.

Randy, who was everything the vampire had accused him of: dumb as ever, a sixteen-year-old show-off who didn't know when to stop. But Lacey loved him for wanting to be a hero. She loved him for being crushed when it turned out his bravery saved only himself. If all the world wanted to be a hero, perhaps evil would never come out from behind the shutters.

I just hope he doesn't drive too fast when they speed away from the mansion, thought Lacey. I just hope they catch Kevin and take him with them. They have to do that. My parents have to have one whole child.

"Take me," she said to the vampire.

In a businesslike way she said to the rest, "Hurry on. There's no time to waste. My brother is down there. Take him home with you. Get going."

Chapter 13

This time it was for real.

They would go.

She would stay.

The others touched Lacey. Stared. Rested a hand briefly on her shoulder. But they did not hug or kiss. They were too stunned. Too fearful.

"But we won't remember you!" cried Sherree. "I have to remember you! I want to be a better person. I want to have you to go by."

Her gift to me, thought Lacey. I accept. If she were permitted to remember, she would remember me, and be a better person for it.

But they won't remember. They will walk out that door and not remember. All their lives, as they go on in safety and joy, it will be because of me. And they won't remember.

Lacey thought of herself as dead, lying in a cemetery, but with a blank stone because nobody remembered. She was just a granite slab to mow around.

She did not cry. She had made her decision. It felt firm and right to her, though sad.

She thought of the days in which we honor the vanished: Martin Luther King Day, Memorial Day, Veterans Day, Presidents' Day. I never honored anybody, thought Lacey. I just went to the sales at the department stores.

I forgot them. I live because they died. *And I forgot them.* As I will be forgotten. As I will forget myself.

Lacey felt that being forgotten was worse than anything.

To be good, and do right, and yet disappear with the rising sun.

Bobby cleared his throat. "Lacey?" he said.

She managed a smile.

"I wish we could go out. I always wanted to go out with you."

Lacey was amused. Bobby actually believed that it would make her feel better to know that he, Bobby, had considered her as a date. Not asked, of course. Not actually phoned. But taken it into his mind.

"Thanks, Bobby," she said, being just a fraction sarcastic.

Athletic swing intact, Bobby turned to leave.

Roxanne whispered, "Oh, Lacey! I guess I should have volunteered. It's all on you. It's so unfair." She tried not to cry.

Lacey could have been mean. She could have said, Yes, you should have, you rotten person!

Lacey wanted to say it. But even though nobody would remember, and the words would be erased as if they had never been spoken, she did not say anything mean.

"It's okay, Roxanne," said Lacey kindly. "Just be sure you get Kevin."

Roxanne had a task to do now, and it strengthened her; Roxanne was a girl who needed a purpose. She moved quickly toward the door.

Zach did not get close to Lacey. He gave her a sort of salute. She understood that he was eager to forget, that Zach, too, knew he should have volunteered, should have fought, should have remained steadfast against this vampire. Zach was practically leaning down the stairs, getting himself out the dining room window, so ready to forget that it might not work for him; he might be the only one to remember.

What will be worse? thought Lacey. It will be terrible to forget . . . but to remember. To remember all that you could have done and didn't . . . perhaps that will be worst of all.

Randy gave her an awkward pat with his bunched fist, the way boys greet each other. It was hardly the motion for a date to give the girl he was leaving behind. He knew it after he'd done it, and was upset, and did not know what to do next.

He'll never know what to do next, thought Lacey. He'll be one of those people that's always a social nuisance. But he tried. He'll always try.

She hugged Randy, and only Randy.

Randy was deeply moved, even thrilled.

She was a human sacrifice who accepted him, Randy, for her last human touch in the world.

Zach was not leaning toward the door in order to forget. He was leaning in order to remember. Zach's well-ordered family used many Post-it notes on refrigerator doors and medicine cabinet mirrors and car dashboards so that they would forget nothing in their busy lives. He had, of course, a thin pad of adhesive note squares in his pocket and a tiny pencil, so he could jot down important thoughts and destinations.

To be sure he did not abandon Lacey here, Zach had written instructions to himself.

Call Police.

Call Fire Department.

Call Mr. and Mrs. James.

Lacey is in the Mall House alone. Get her out.

Zach would have been crushed to find how low an opinion of him Lacey had formed.

Sherree liked simple solutions.

When Sherree was depressed, she made no attempt to solve her problems. She just went shopping.

When Sherree felt less successful and less interesting than other girls in her class, she made no attempt to study harder or develop hobbies. She just slid her favorite CD into her sound system and danced.

She was not in a position to go shopping tonight.

Nor did dancing seem like a solution to Lacey's internment with the vampire.

There were only two other things on earth that interested Sherree: boys and cars.

The boys had been spectacularly unsuccessful at rescuing anybody.

So Sherree thought *car*.

She would drive the Land Rover right up the porch and into the house. A Land Rover was the kind of vehicle that could knock down walls, weak ones, at least, and this house was destined for that anyway. It would surely distract the vampire to have a car driving into his home. Sherree would lean on the horn and attract lots of attention and people would come and finish the rescue for her.

It would be very exciting.

Sherree had always wanted to drive in a demolition derby, and, of course, she belonged to a family where the slightest scratch on a car sent them into frenzied phone calls to the body shop, so this was a childhood dream come true.

Randy had a different view of the situation. He had brought a camcorder and, stupidly, left it in the Land Rover. But the point was, the camera was there and waiting for them. He was sure that vampires were afraid of having their pictures taken.

He would advance on them, holding his camcorder like a shield before him, and film them and they would flee.

Lacey would be his forever.

Lacey.

How brave she was.

She could have been one of those pioneers who, deciding to cross the Rocky Mountains come hell or high water, had pushed the family's belongings in a handcart, and carried the babies on her back, and brought with her the seeds to plant the first garden.

No wonder the vampire was pleased that Lacey had accepted the offer.

She was the only one in the room worth having, even by a vampire's standards.

Randy thought about his and Lacey's future together. He didn't care what the vampire said; Randy would forget nothing. And Lacey would not forget, either; Randy would be her hero, and she would adore him.

Randy thought of the dates they would have, and the way she would look up to him.

Roxanne held the hammer back in her hand. Her mother was Irish and paid close attention to any troubles in Northern Ireland. When those guys attacked one another, they liked to smash kneecaps. From what she had heard, this was a painful and lasting way to cripple somebody. The vampire was now fully fleshed out. Roxanne would kneecap him.

Roxanne pretended to walk toward the door.

She shifted over a little, though, getting closer to the vampire even as Randy was hugging Lacey good-bye.

Her hand tightened on the hammer.

She was wildly proud of herself. Violence! That was what would work. Lacey was being kind, but kindness, in the end, would only lead to her destruction. Roxanne would use what television had taught her to use: a weapon.

Bobby swaggered.

He tried to take up a lot of space. He flexed his arms and fingers as often as he could to warm up. He didn't like the fact that this heavy action he had in mind had been preceded by such weakness on his part, but there was nothing he could do about that now.

He had Lacey to save and he had revenge to take.

And he was, Bobby knew for sure, the only one with a workable plan.

He would rip the cloak off the vampire.

The cloak was obviously part of the creature, and in some way his powerful, protective part. And yet it was separate. The vampire liked to uncover only his teeth and his hands and parts of his face. Bobby would shred the thing.

Even if it did not destroy the vampire, which Bobby was sure it would, it would give everybody lots of time to run out while the vampire tried to save himself and wrap himself back up.

Strength and determination flew down Bobby's veins and arteries and coursed through his muscles. Bobby felt like a giant, a linebacker, a soldier for hire. There was nothing he could not do.

Lacey ran a hand down Randy's chest.

Randy's chest swelled with pride. He had never felt so strong and so needed. I'll save you, he thought, careful to give no hints. He must not let the vampire know what he was up to. The vampire might try to foil him. The vampire might even rush the "event" along, giving Randy little time to save Lacey.

Lacey put her head against Randy's chest, and Randy nearly melted. He was so distracted, he nearly forgot his master plan.

"Don't worry, Lacey," he whispered. "Everything will be all right. I promise."

Lacey looked up, gave him a gentle close-lipped smile, and stepped away from him.

The vampire's fingernails were weightless.

They scraped over Zach's clothing, dipped into his pocket, and removed his notes.

"You won't need these outside," said the vampire softly.

He chuckled. He was enjoying himself.

Oh, it had been a night to remember, all right.

But the one who would remember, the one who was having the most fun, the one who was playing the longest game, was the vampire.

Zach could not believe he had been noticed.

Had been stopped.

"Go," said the vampire to Zach, and the word was so intense, so meaningful, that Zach could do nothing else.

He went.

The doorway was open. It was possessed by nothing. Zach did not stumble. Zach did not falter, and his feet found the way in spite of the darkness.

Then the vampire caught Sherree's hand. Her clenched fist fell open at his touch and she whimpered when he took the car keys. "No," she blubbered. "See, I need the car keys. I took them from Randy because I need them."

"Don't worry," said the vampire. "Once you are out of the mansion, you will forget why you needed them. You'll hunt for a while, all of you feeling in your pockets to see who has them."

The vampire, still holding Sherree's hand, tossed the car keys out the open tower window.

"Eventually," said the vampire, "you'll see them in the grass. You'll wonder why Randy dropped them there, and what took the five of you so long to see them."

Randy thought: How will I even be able to open the Land Rover? I have to have the keys!

He willed himself to remember that the keys had been thrown into the grass, so that he could find them quickly, open the car, grab the camera, race back inside, scare off the vampire before the vampire could . . .

"It would be a waste of your energy," explained the vampire. "Although you are welcome to try. We aren't afraid of having our picture taken, it's just that we don't show up on film, Randy. So it's an ineffective threat." The vampire smiled widely. His teeth hung cruelly and he scraped them along his chin, as if sharpening them. His eyes left Randy and traveled eagerly over Lacey.

"Time for you to go," said the vampire softly to Sherree and to Randy, and Sherree and Randy found themselves going, obeying, as if they were possessions of the vampire in the same manner that the door had been a possession of the vampire.

The door was open.

They went through it.

Only Roxanne and Bobby stood between Lacey and the vampire now.

The vampire is horrible, thought Roxanne. He's horrible. He has no right to stage things like this, so we can't beat him back. But I have a hammer, and steel isn't stopped by vampires, steel isn't camera film or car keys, steel will break his bones.

Roxanne swung the hammer back, savoring the heft of it, looking forward to the crunch of bone when she hit the hideous creature. She threw herself forward. The hammer swung through the air and made contact with absolutely nothing.

There was nothing there.

She fell forward, her own velocity carrying her right into the vampire, and still there was nothing there but stinking evil. She fell onto the floor of the tower and the vampire gently retrieved the hammer from her hand.

How can he react so gently to us, thought Roxanne, when in a moment he will show total violence?

"It is my way," said the vampire to Roxanne, "to damage human bodies, but fortunately, humans cannot damage my body. It's time for you to go, Roxanne. There is the door."

She was on the floor.

His eyes fixed on her and his teeth leaned toward her and she scrabbled toward the door, not quite crawling, not quite getting up.

The vampire watched with satisfaction.

Bobby took advantage of the vampire's distraction and hurled himself at the vampire. His fingers wrapped solidly on the cloak and he ripped and tore with all his football player's strength.

And nothing happened.

He swung there, as he had swung in the doorway.

And through the hideous fibers of the rotting cloak he saw what would happen to Lacey.

"The cloak doesn't come off," explained the vampire. "You could rip for eternity, and you would just hang in the wind." The vampire walked toward the door and deposited Bobby on the other side. Bobby's fingers unwrapped. His feet found the first step. A queer wind blew him forward, escorting him down the steep stairs after the others.

Already his mind was vague, his thoughts muddy, his words slurred. "Hey, you guys," he said. Nobody turned to answer him. All five simply staggered down and across, and found the window, and struggled to get out.

For them, the evening was over.

Chapter 14

When she was with Jordan, Ginny was usually acutely aware of her looks. In some ways, in fact, it was more relaxing not to be with Jordan. A boyfriend's presence demanded so much. Ginny had to worry about lipstick and hair and perfume and clothing and being funny and being sweet and being interesting and being . . .

Oh, it was exhausting.

She liked being in love, but she was also sort of looking forward to the time when she would not be in love, when it would be rather dull and ordinary and she would not have to pour so much energy into it.

It was most odd to have been in a car together, in the dark, unaware of Jordan. She knew he was there, of course. And yet she did not look at him. Not when they drove up to the horrible old house. Not when they got out of the car. Not when they moved over the ground toward the shadowed building.

Her eyes seemed caught inside the cylinder of a kaleidoscope. She could look nowhere except down into the pattern, into the tumbling, falling, changing colors.

Ginny felt herself and her life tumble, fall, and change, and yet there were no colors.

There was only texture, and all of it black. First it was a square of velvet, and then it was the bottom of a cave. It whirled and turned and became moss and then silk, caked with mud.

Its curving approach was the most exciting thing Ginny had ever seen, and the most frightening.

She wanted to run and yet the only direction her feet took was directly into it.

A smell like a cesspool filled her head.

She looked up and saw the kaleidoscope of meshing white teeth.

Usually Jordan could think of nothing but Ginny. Her shape, her scent, her laugh, her teasing, her hair . . . but he had lost that. Ginny receded from his mind, as if she had set off on some long unknown journey, and they would meet again years from now.

Jordan knew that his girlfriend was right there, only a few feet from him, and yet he did not think about her.

He saw nothing but that building: that sagging porch, those boarded-up windows, that tilted tower, those shining slates.

But there was no moon. There were no stars.

There were no streetlights. What could shine on the roof? What was he seeing?

It was entirely dark, and yet it gleamed.

Jordan shuddered, suddenly afraid, and that outraged him, because Jordan did not believe in fear. If you had the proper attitude, you controlled any foolish emotion like that.

Fear possessed him.

Fear had actually become Jordan, like eye color or height.

He wanted to hang on to something, to steady himself. He wanted to go back to the car, but the only direction his body seemed to know was forward.

The porch, he thought, I'll hang on to the porch.

He tried to steer his feet to the porch, as if beneath that underhang of roof and gutter he would be safe from the descending blackness.

The dark was incredibly thick, as if it knew more than Jordan ever would. The darkness took on life and smothered Ginny.

There was no time for thought, which was lucky, because Jordan could formulate no thoughts about what was happening. He tackled Ginny, as if they were football players. The two of them smacked the ground, and the blackness curled away from them, because they were two, and the vampire could take only one at a time.

The vampire simply smiled. There were plenty more. No need to fret over a lost victim.

* * *

It was Zach who came first through the window. Zach whose shivering hands pushed at the plywood one more time, and pried open a slot through which he could crawl.

He was outside.

He felt that his whole life had been a preparation for this moment: that this was the first time in his sixteen years he had truly breathed. How wonderful the oxygen was. How clear the night. How good he felt. How strong and intelligent. Zach smiled, and he could even feel his teeth: how straight and white and —

Teeth.

The word gave him a shudder, but he did not know why.

He stood on the porch trying to think, but thoughts did not fill his brain the way they normally did. He felt empty. As if something had siphoned him off.

Notes, thought Zach. I took notes. He found the little pad of Post-its he always carried, and the stub of a pencil. He held the tiny pages up to read, but the top one was blank.

Blank, thought Zach. I need oxygen, he thought next.

Get off the porch, he told himself. Get out of this place. Breathe deep. Relax. Calm. Then figure out the next step.

The vampire of the shutters decided next on the little girl racing away from the car tucked among the dead trees. The vampire loved dead trees. Yes, this really was a wonderful location. He greatly regretted that his home was vanishing under the bulldozers. He swooped upward for a moment, and smiled, preparing for the final, the precious, the wonderful descent.

Sherree staggered right into Zach as she climbed out the dining room window. "Zach!" she said, as if he were the last person on earth she would have expected to run into.

They stared at each other. "Hi, Sherree," said Zach.

"I'm here with Bobby," she said.

"I remember," he said, and they beamed at each other. They were delighted to possess a fact. A tiny piece of memory.

"We're in a hurry," said Sherree. "I have to get the car. I have to drive somewhere. I'm sure that — I think that — I know that —"

But she was not sure. She could not think. She did not know.

She and Zach frowned at each other and examined each other's frowns, as if peeling away the wrinkles might lead to explanations.

The policewoman went inside Dunkin' Donuts.

She sipped her coffee slowly.

She nibbled at her jelly doughnut, making it last.

No static came from the radio clipped to her

waist. No stations were busy. No action was occurring anywhere: not in the police department, not in the fire department, not in the ambulance department.

The evening was dead.

Darkness swarmed like a million wasps wanting to nest in her hair.

Mardee screamed.

Fingers touched her skin.

Damp stinking air, as if it had life and swamp breath, crawled down her neck.

Mardee leaped forward with more strength than she had known she possessed and grabbed hold of Kevin's belt. Kevin, yelling, "Lace! Lace!" reached back without slowing down and yanked Mardee along with him.

There was a weird, sick moment in which they seemed suspended, as if something had caught them.

And then Kevin broke free and took Mardee forward with him.

Zach reached the railing of the wide steps that led off the porch. Another hand was there before him. It was a young man, but nobody Zach knew.

Police? thought Zach. He didn't want to get in any trouble. Whose idea had it been to party at the Mall House anyway? Stupid idea. Zach could not imagine why they had come. He could not imagine why they were leaving, either.

His hand gripped the banister only inches away from that other hand. The fingers faced opposite directions. The other hand was coming in, as Zach was going out.

The young man said, "I'm looking for Ginny's little brother."

Zach and Sherree stared at him. Do we know somebody named Ginny? thought Zach. I know I don't know anybody named Ginny. Who's here, anyway? Zach turned around to look. Randy, he thought. Bobby, he thought. Who else?

"Ginny's little brother?" repeated the man. "Did he crash the party? Is he in there with you?"

Sherree said slowly, "Somebody crashed the party. I remember that . . . somebody . . . but . . . I don't think it was Ginny's little brother."

It was Lacey's little brother who raced up on the porch. Zach couldn't think of the kid's name. He wasn't as much of an airhead as his sister, but still Zach had never had much use for him.

"My sister!" shouted the kid.

Right behind him came Bobby's little sister, Mardee. Zach didn't have a whole lot of use for Mardee, either. In fact, Zach was beginning to feel quite annoyed that he was spending a perfectly good weekend in the company of so many airheads.

The porch filled up.

The party had come outside.

Roxanne was there, and Randy and Bobby.

An older teenage girl Zach didn't know joined the guy looking for a kid brother.

The place looked like an airport. Everybody racing around trying to find the right gate. They raced around the porch instead. They had the same mental franticness of lost passengers. Where's my plane, where's my luggage, who's meeting me, where did we leave the car, didn't I have my coat with me?

Zach had never been to a farm and never seen live farm animals, but he had once read the phrase "running around like a chicken with its head cut off." That sentence was enough to keep Zach from ever going near a farm, let alone having chickens. What kind of animal ran around after its head had been cut off? And why would you want to cut off its head anyway?

But that's what they behaved like.

Chickens with their heads cut off.

Nine people, darting left, darting right, running down the porch stairs, running back up, clutching one another, barging into one another.

You'd think our heads were cut off, thought Zach.

It was not their heads that had been cut off, of course. Just their memories. To have no memory was deeply confusing. They did not know where they were going or where they had come from. They did not know what to do next or with whom to do it.

And they did not, this confused, blank-minded crowd of nine, look up at the sky.

Even Ginny had lost sight of the sky, caught up with Jordan and these people circling the porch steps like birds at a feeder.

It is true that there is safety in numbers.

The vampire of the shutters could not penetrate so sturdy a crowd.

He had taken time with his descent, reveling in the silly human mob behavior. Humans were so predictable. They lost their heads and what did they do? They ran back and forth, as if they thought they would find their thoughts lying on one side of the lawn or the other.

The vampire slid like a migrating bird from one side of the sky to another. Each human attracted him in its own way. Each had a certain something that made the human appealing.

Which would he take?

How would the "event" progress?

It was wonderful to be awake. To have his mind active, to feel his teeth growing, preparing themselves. To have his cloak sift through the night air, instead of being trapped indoors as he had been for so very, very long. The vampire felt strong and able, and he felt eager and excited.

For several minutes he simply watched. If they had looked up they would have seen his smile. It was quite distinctive.

But the humans were concerned only with each other. They knew so pathetically little of the night. They knew nothing of stars, or darkness, or shadows. In fact, they tried to pretend the night was not there. They turned on lights the instant there was the slightest suggestion of night in the sky. As if night were the enemy.

Night was a friend.

To me, at least, thought the vampire.

He waited patiently for one of the pack to wander from the rest, to be sufficiently in shadow that nobody would see the vampire's descent.

"I was supposed to be doing something," said Randy nervously. He was twitching, patting himself, as if a clue would stick out from his shirt pocket.

"Going home, probably," said Ginny sharply. "We were out hunting for my brother. My parents are crazy with worry."

"We'll give you a ride," said Jordan. "Everybody pile in."

Sherree loved a crowded car. "We can't possibly all fit," she said, giggling. Her parents were very stern on seat belt use. There would be twice as many people as there were belts. "I'll sit on someone's lap," said Sherree eagerly and, just as eagerly, both Bobby and Zach volunteered their laps.

Randy stood on the bottom porch step, looking around. "I forgot something," he said, feeling thick and stupid.

"Your car," said Jordan, pointing. "You guys are pathetic. I mean, what did you think was going to happen here anyway?"

"We were going to make it happen," said Randy. He remembered what he had forgotten. His car keys. He patted his pockets again.

"I took them," said Sherree, patting herself. But she had no pockets, and she was holding no keys.

The night seemed curiously romantic to Mardee. Kevin seemed unexpectedly strong and attractive. She had a sense of being interrupted, as if they had been doing something fascinating and worth repeating. She touched Kevin's shoulder as if she were afraid of it, and he caught his breath as if he were afraid of her touch, too — as if it would lead to something.

"Let's not go with them," whispered Mardee.

Kevin nodded. "We walked over, we'll walk back."

They clasped each other's waists.

A molecule of memory hit Kevin. "Wait," he said to the others. "My sister. Lacey. Wasn't she with you?"

"That airhead," muttered Zach. But he did not say it loud enough for the airhead's brother to hear. And the moment he called her that, he felt guilty. And wrong.

As if he knew better than to say a thing like that.

He caught Sherree glaring at him. "She is not," said Sherree sharply.

"I know," said Zach guiltily. But he did not know why he felt guilty or why he knew that Lacey was not an airhead. He looked up at the mansion.

It stood dark and formless in the night.

He knew its roof was a sharp pattern of angles and dips, of slate and tower. He knew because —

I fell off that tower! thought Zach. I — I — I —

But how could he have fallen off that tower? He'd have been killed if he'd fallen from that height.

Weird, thought Zach. We must really have partied. Zach shook his head to clear it, but it did not clear. Something in his thoughts remained murky and dulled.

Lacey's brother said, "Are you sure Lacey isn't with you?"

Everybody looked around. Lacey did not seem to be there.

"She must have left early," said Ginny. "Making her the only smart one in the group." Ginny pointed to the backseat and began herding passengers into Jordan's car. They got in slowly.

Lacey? thought Roxanne.

Lacey? wondered Bobby.

Lacey?

But their thoughts did not come clear.

They took no action.

They formed no response.

One by one, they got in Jordan's car, giggling, because they were as crowded as clowns, and it was fun.

One by one the victims that had escaped the first vampire also moved out of reach of the second vampire.

The vampire of the shutters was furious.

Fury made his teeth sharper and his hunger more urgent.

He retreated. Height helped him stay calm. Height gave him the velocity he would need for a surprise attack.

The car was just too crowded, and Mardee was feeling too young and too romantic to wedge herself into that group. "Let's walk," she reminded Kevin, and they wrapped arms around each other's waists and moved past the station wagon and out toward the road.

"We had a good time, didn't we?" said Kevin. He felt confused saying that because he could no longer remember what kind of time they had had. But Mardee squeezed him tighter and he no longer cared, either. He was happy. He didn't look back. He didn't remember the building only yards behind him, he didn't remember the screams only moments earlier, and he didn't remember the threat that had nearly peeled Mardee from his side.

He didn't remember his sister, Lacey, at all.

The vampire saw movement deep in the dead trees. A car door opening, and a head peering out. Another human. A human who had previously been hidden in the shadows. Another human caught in curiosity, that strange human weakness.

The vampire knew immediately that this human was different. This was a human who used the dark. This was a human within whom there was also an element of darkness. The vampire enjoyed the innocence of some of his victims, but there was a certain pleasure, also, in a victim who had had victims of his own.

This was not a clean nor an attractive human.

But the vampire of the shutters had no standards in that regard.

Slowly his black folds enveloped the car thief.

In the starless, moonless night there was no sound, no sight.

Only a slow suffocation.

Chapter 15

Lacey had not been thinking of Randy when she put her arms around him. She had been interested exclusively in the contents of Randy's shirt pocket. The little toys with which Randy had played all evening. The objects he had caressed, like worry beads, to pull himself together. In the end, all six teenagers had pulled together, but memory would defeat them.

Loss of memory, that is.

Lacey, however, would suffer no such loss. Not until afterward.

Right now, in this tower, facing this vampire, the situation was all too clear.

One by one, the vampire dismissed her five companions. Soul by soul, the room contained less humankind, and more evil. How reluctant the vampire was to let them go. After all, when would he again have such a lovely situation? The rules by which he lived were not simple.

But the rules by which I live, thought Lacey, are not simple either.

I refuse to be his next "event." And that's it. I will direct my life and it will go on the way I choose. Not the way he chooses. So there!

The vampire was too busy playing games with the other five to pick up on her thoughts. Lacey took a small slow step to the center of the room while the vampire was busy collecting Zach's notes. She took a second, slow step while the vampire was tossing the car keys out the window.

Her hand was tight on the tiny object she had taken from Randy's pocket.

The timing had to be exact.

Her feet were at the edge of the nest that Roxanne had exposed. She did not change position again. Instead she inched her foot forward, until she could tell that half her foot was in the air, poised over the vampire's lair.

The vampire took his time. His eyes glittered as each potential victim passed, untouched, through the door.

Lacey never took her eyes off the vampire.

There was no point in watching the others. There was no point in anything now, except her plan.

For Zach had been right, after all, when hours ago he had called for an analysis of the vampire's weaknesses. Lacey knew one. Roxanne had exposed it.

Whatever this opening was in the floor . . . this

cell . . . this tomb . . . this grave . . . he had to have it. When Roxanne had invaded the nest, the vampire's power had vanished. He had disappeared from the room and from their hearts and souls as if he had never been.

Zach was correct. There was weakness. The vampire had to have his nest. If Lacey destroyed it, he would have to waft away, or dematerialize, or whatever it is that vampires do.

The other five teenagers were gone. The sound of their footsteps dwindled away. The sound of their guilty voices disappeared.

The vampire turned with a sweet smile. His teeth were not showing. He said, "Do not be afraid, my dear."

"I'm not," said Lacey loftily. But she was.

"And do not waste time tipping yourself over into my home. I will merely join you." His cloak came first and she shuddered. That made him smile. Now his teeth sprouted.

How pathetic and unlikely her plan seemed in sight of those teeth.

"You could scream," said the vampire.

She remembered that he liked screams. Perhaps if she screamed, the others, who must by now be climbing out the dining room window, would remember her long enough to do something.

"No," said the vampire courteously. "That is not a possibility. The human brain is shallow. It retains nothing for long. No lesson, no experience leaves a human with lasting knowledge. Sad," whispered the vampire, coming closer, "but true." His breath encircled her and she could not breathe.

"However," said the vampire, "it works to my advantage."

Lacey fell into his nest.

The stench of it, the oily horror of it, nearly ate through her mind. I won't be able to finish! thought Lacey. I won't have enough oxygen to finish.

Was there even enough oxygen to do what she needed to do?

Lacey stared up into the descending folds of the vampire's cloak and, with her hidden hand, flicked the lighter. There was enough oxygen.

The vampire could control many of the laws of nature.

Gravity could be his, if he chose.

But not fire.

The house was old. Very old. And very dry.

The wood was tinder, waiting for fire. The splinters Roxanne had torn up turned into leaping, screaming golden flames. The vampire retreated. He screamed, "You'll burn yourself up!"

Lacey got out, fanning the fire with the edge of the vampire's own cloak. "Burn!" she shouted at the fire. "Burn!"

The flame ate the nest and moved forward, as if to begin to burn the hem of the vampire's cloak.

The vampire put out his crinkled hand, like used aluminum foil, and retreated to the corner of the tower. "You can't do this!" he screamed.

"I already have," she pointed out. "Go ahead and scream. I don't mind. I like the sound of a vampire screaming."

The vampire's mouth was wide open, wide, wide, wide. And yet its teeth were of no consequence. It could only scream. "My home!" it screamed. "You can't destroy my home. I will have nowhere to go when dawn arrives."

"*Your* weakness," said Lacey. She bared her own teeth: her small, square, even, white teeth. Her human teeth. She turned them into a smile of triumph.

"You'll suffocate!" he warned.

"I'd rather take my chances with smoke than teeth."

Whatever nesting material lay in the hollow between the floor joists had turned to ash. The room filled with smoke. Lacey could not go out the windows, because the flames, desperate for oxygen to eat, the way the vampire had been desperate for blood, were reaching through the windows.

In school, home of the frequent fire drill, they told you to get down on the floor in case of fire: There you would find better air.

How laughable.

Down on the floor was the swamp gas of the vampires.

But she obeyed the school directive she had heard three or four times a year since kindergarten.

Stop, drop, and roll!

How many times had they made posters for Fire Prevention Week?

Stop, drop, and roll!

Lacey heard the vampire screaming. Her own lungs were starved for air, her eyes burning with heat. She crawled to the door. Would it be blocked? Would the vampire have taken possession of it again, once the other five were safely out.

Stop, drop, and roll.

Lacey rolled to the door. The flames engulfed the floor as if the fire were chasing her feet.

The doorway was open.

The vampire had not taken possession of it.

He had trusted her.

Lacey actually smiled.

A creature that dealt in evil trusted a human who dealt in good. The vampire had believed in Lacey's volunteering. The vampire had assumed along with volunteering would come cooperation and an assortment of screams.

He had not expected any double-dealing from Lacey James, who was good.

But sometimes, in tight corners, when your back is against the wall and the world is against you, you have to fight back in unexpected ways.

Lacey rolled down the stairs to get away from the smoke and the flames and felt nothing on the way down: no pain, no bruises, no fear. And most of all, no pursuit. For the vampire could not get through the sheet of flames that rose up between his victim and himself. She got up and ran down the lower flight, found the abandoned dining room, felt along the walls until she found the window.

Coughing, lungs hurting, she climbed out onto the porch and staggered onto the lawn.

There was nobody there. No Bobby, no Zach. No Sherree, no Roxanne. No Randy. No friends at all.

A car was driving away. In the fading darkness she saw its red taillights.

Ashes from the burning tower flew into the air and spun in circles, like tiny tornadoes. The wind carried them, and dropped them into the huge pile of dead trees. The dry hemlocks caught fire and became a ball of flame as big as the Mall House itself. So much for the Land Rover, thought Lacey.

She ran across the yard. Out what had once been a gate, what had once been a driveway.

She raced across what was still a road.

The house screamed. Or was it the house? Could a house scream?

Lacey turned to stare. The Mall House was caving in.

For one moment the tower was a complete circle of fire, and then it fell, tumbling over the rest of the roof and falling to the ground. Lacey put her hands over her hair, as if it could shield her from catching fire, and ran farther, putting the firebreak of pavement between herself and the inferno.

On the other side of the street stood her brother. Her little brother, Kevin! "Kevin?" said Lacey, astonished. "What are you doing here?"

"What are *you* doing here?" said Kevin, of course.

Lacey did not know the girl with him. What an odd world it was. She had never dreamed her brother liked girls. But then, she had never dreamed that vampires really existed, either. Let alone in her town. In her life. Among the houses and streets of her world.

From far away she heard a siren.

Somebody had alerted the fire department.

Lacey looked back at the flames and the collapsing walls. Sirens screamed louder than victims. Sparks shot into the sky, and fell back, and the rest of the house turned into one vast bonfire.

The only smell in the night was the rich smoky burning of wood.

"Keep walking," said Lacey, and the three kept walking. Whatever mechanism had taken memory from the others had not worked on Lacey. Not yet, at least. In her mind, she turned over what had happened.

The road was full of shadows, but none of them descended. They were shadows of other trees, other buildings. But not shadows of other worlds. The vampires had lost their nests: lost their floors and ceilings, shutters and towers and mansion.

Had they lost their power, too?

Or could they drift, unseen, through the sky before the coming of dawn?

Could they find another hole? An open coffin? A mausoleum with a broken door?

Or had they been destroyed?

They were evil, thought Lacey. I don't think evil can be destroyed. Only subdued for a time.

"Hi," said the girl with Kevin. "I'm Mardee. Bobby's sister. I'm glad to meet you."

Lacey said hi.

A squad car driven by a policewoman took the corner at top speed. The tires screamed. The night, in fact, was full of screams.

But not mine, thought Lacey. I did not scream. I won.

And instead of screaming, Lacey James laughed.

For she had looked at her watch. It was not even midnight. All this had happened in so few hours it was not even a new day.

"Thought you were spending the night with somebody," said Kevin.

"Changed my mind," said Lacey.

Memory faded. Lacey and Kevin and Mardee walked along the road, and turned up the hill, and forgot the mansion behind them, the shadows, and the screams.

The hard-learned lessons, the heroism, and the sacrifices were gone as if they had never been.

And the shadows that were the vampires hung in the sky, and departed, desperate, for they had only a few hours until dawn, only a few hours in which to find another nest.

But usually, for a vampire, a few hours is enough.

About the Author

CAROLINE B. COONEY has written nearly seventy books for young people, including *Freeze Tag, Fatality,* and The Losing Christina trilogy: *Fog, Snow,* and *Fire*. Her books have sold more than ten million copies and have been printed in many languages. She lives in Connecticut with three pianos, two computers, and lots and lots of books.